Other Books You May Enjoy

A wolf in princess's clothing

The princess appeared in the window with an even wider smile. "What a valiant display of courage! You really must be a Pennyroyal girl!" She laughed with such malice that it reminded Evie of a witch's cackle.

"How's old Beatrice doing these days?" said a second princess, appearing at the front door.

Evie's fingers were shivering so violently that she was having trouble unlashing Boy's reins. She pulled them loose and swung atop him, jerking his head toward the lane. The princess was running at her, only a few feet behind.

"No need to leave on our account, Cadet!"

Boy whinnied in protest, but obeyed. Evie glanced behind her. One princess's silver blade glinted in the light of the torch at the entrance to the inn. The other two joined her, each with a sword in hand.

"Go! Go!" screamed Evie. Boy's hooves found purchase, and they bounded off into the darkness. She turned back to see three dark figures standing in the lane. Their swords shone through the dark of night.

And each of them wore a razor-sharp wolf's fang around her neck.

Jousting Lists

Abandoned Barracks

Richard's Keep

Knights' Barracks

Joringel's Stem

Armory

Piper of Hamelin Ballroom

Wolfseye Keep

Pennyroyal Castle

THE SHADOW CADETS OF PENNYROYAL ACADEMY

M. A. LARSON

PUFFIN BOOKS

PUFFIN BOOKS
An imprint of Penguin Random House LLC
375 Hudson Street
New York, New York 10014

First published in the United States of America by G. P. Putnam's Sons,
an imprint of Penguin Random House LLC, 2016
Published by Puffin Books, an imprint of Penguin Random House LLC, 2017

Library of Congress Cataloging-in-Publication data is available.

ISBN 9780399163258 (hardcover)

Puffin Books ISBN 9780142427132

Printed in the United States of America
Design by Annie Ericsson

1 3 5 7 9 10 8 6 4 2

For Delilah

THE SHADOW CADETS OF PENNYROYAL ACADEMY

"COME ON, GIRL, just build it up in your gut and let it loose!"

Evie scowled. Her sister had been calling her "girl" ever since she'd returned from Pennyroyal Academy at the start of summer. She supposed it was meant as a term of endearment, or perhaps a not-so-subtle joke that she was the only human in a family of dragons, or...

No, she didn't know why her sister called her that, but there was no doubt it had become *annoying*.

"My name is Evie."

The great dragon smirked and turned her head toward the marsh. From where they stood at the edge of the forest, the bulrushes glowed gold in the late-afternoon sun. Across the marsh, in the distance, mountains cut high into the sky, each bigger and greener than the next. Lazy clouds drifted past, headed east. Soon the stifling heat would end, giving way to another cool night, another black sky scattered with stars, and more memories of the Academy and the friends Evie had made there.

But first, she had something to do. She picked out a bunch of grass that was swaying gently in the breeze and stared at it, narrowing her eyes. She was trying to focus, but in truth she wasn't really that bothered. She was doing it only to please her sister.

Besides, it was impossible to concentrate with those huge, black swatches her sister had already burned into the bulrushes on her right.

"Come on," said her sister, in the charred grumble common to all dragons. "Once you've done this, you won't be able to stop, believe me. Then we're on to flying!"

Evie sighed and turned to her sister, exasperated.

"Oh, go on, don't give me that look."

"Well, maybe if you'd stop talking . . ."

"All right, all right," the dragon said, chuckling.

Evie turned back to the marsh while the birds sang merrily in the forest behind her. A drop of sweat ran down the back of her neck. It felt like the crawling legs of a fly . . .

Focus, Evie, focus. Engage the heart—that's what Father always said.

Father, that's who she needed. She tried to picture him. His eyes appeared first, soft and tender, then the scar-crossed slope of his snout and the massive spikes of his teeth. His scales were white and gray, his right horn sheared off at the top from a battle that had happened before she'd even known him. He smiled, and her stomach roared to life.

It's working, she thought. *I'm actually going to do it.* A charge of excitement shot through her. Excitement and hope. Maybe this time would be different.

She inhaled so deeply that her throat and lungs began to tingle like they did in the dead of winter, when the air was so bitterly cold it hurt to breathe.

It's really working!

This had never happened, not in all the times she'd tried to breathe fire before. The details of the marsh faded away until all she could see was the paintbrush outline of the grass. She burped, grimacing from the acid taste creeping into the back of her throat. A cauldron was bubbling in her stomach.

Now.

She sucked as much air into her lungs as she could. The pain was so intense that tears began to fall from her eyes. *Do it!*

She opened her mouth. Searing heat lanced up from her stomach and . . .

"Ack!" she cried, clutching her chest. "Ahh! Ugh!"

She could hear her sister roaring with laughter. Evie spat out saliva and disgusting greenish bile as she choked for air.

"You're thinking too much, that's all," rumbled her sister. "You'll get it. Look, you did manage a nice bit of smoke. That's a first."

Evie rolled onto her side and forced one eye open. She was still hacking and coughing herself red in the face. Her insides were on fire, from the pit of her stomach up through her nostrils and mouth.

But there it was. A cloud of black smoke wafting up to the sky. A second later it was gone, but it had been there.

Splash! Frigid water hit Evie like a fist. She clenched into a ball from the shock of it, still unable to breathe. A moment later, she reached out to her sister.

"Give it," she said, though her throat was as scorched as the grasses her sister had used for demonstration. The dragon reached over, a wooden bucket speared between claws as long as broomsticks. Evie slurped down the water left inside. The relief was overwhelming.

"You've nearly got it," said the dragon. "You just need to develop a bit of scar tissue in your throat."

Evie planted her hands in the soggy earth and leaned back, letting the water soothe her insides. "Stop talking." Her voice had almost completely burned away.

Her sister shrugged, then stood and stretched her hind legs. She'd grown immense since Evie had last seen her. That had been halfway through Evie's first year at Pennyroyal Academy, when she'd run away and come back home. Her sister had persuaded her to return to her training, but when she'd tried to help Evie sneak back in, a dragonslayer's lance had complicated matters. And now, midway between the dragon's shoulder and hip, a small patch of scarred flesh peeked out from behind the scales. Evie winced. She hated looking at it, but couldn't stop herself. Only a foot or so difference and the lance might have pierced her sister's heart.

"Right, shall we go find some fireflowers, then?" said her

sister, rolling her serpentine neck from side to side like she'd been sitting still too long.

"Let's," croaked Evie, and she collapsed in another coughing fit.

"Oh, it's not as bad as all that. A dragon can't have fire without a bit of heat, now, can she?"

Evie lapped up water that had pooled on the ground. "I'm not a dragon!"

"That's right. You're a *princess*. Well, come on, then, Princess, let's go take care of that throat you just scorched by nearly breathing fire. As princesses do."

The dragon loped away with a chuckle, her feet crunching through the forest undergrowth. Evie stood and brushed dirt and grass off the backside of her sodden dress. It had been like this ever since she'd returned from the Academy. Strained. Of course they were all thrilled to see one another at first, Evie and her sister and mother, but then a strange tension had settled in, and had only gotten worse as the weeks dragged past.

Evie hiked after her sister while birds called to one another from the treetops, warning of the dragon in their midst. She ran her hands down her pale pink tunic dress, bordered in gray with matching sleeves. It was smudged and stained from months in the forest, and it didn't fit her properly, but the feel of it still made Evie smile. She let her mind wander back to the Kingdom of Waldeck, where she'd been given the dress, and to the incredible thing that had happened there . . .

· · ·

Evie and Maggie had been two of the last to depart Pennyroyal Academy at the end of term. They'd just been made second-class princess cadets, and they wanted to linger in the joy of that as long as they could. Finally they'd found a spot on a half-empty coach bound for the Kingdom of Waldeck, somewhere along the northern border of the Dortchen Wild, one of the most dangerous enchanted forests in all the land. After many hours rumbling through the forest, they'd arrived atop a mountain range and entered the Kingdom of Waldeck. It stood at the cliff's edge, hundreds of feet above a sprawling lake that reached into the forest with curling inlets all along its shores. Waldeck's outer walls were relatively low, at least in comparison to Marburg, the kingdom where Evie had first enlisted to become a princess cadet. Marburg had been a stunner, a powerful limestone fortress overlooking vast pine valleys. After a life spent in the forest with dragons, it was the place where she'd first seen and fallen in love with humanity. But partway through the year, Marburg had been taken by witches.

Waldeck, however, was still free. From inside the walls, she could see millions of miles in every direction as the red sun slowly sank to the horizon. Tiny specks of torchlight flickered from another kingdom on a distant mountaintop. The coach deposited them in a courtyard, and they walked together to the high street, lined on all sides with merchants' stalls. People milled about, inspecting the ironwork, the produce, the fine linens. Millers and coopers, bakers and barbers. Tradespeople haggled and bartered. Children tugged on their mothers' skirts in boredom. Ordinary life was being lived. And right there in the middle of it stood Evie and Maggie.

"I'm so sorry, Evie, but I've really got to go. If I miss the coach to Darmancourt, it'll be a month before I can make it home."

"Don't worry, I'll be fine."

"Are you sure you won't come with me? You can spend the whole summer if you like. It's just going to be me and Dad." She let out a long, rueful sigh. "Me and Dad . . ."

Evie knew how thrilled Maggie would be to host her for the coming months. Maggie's mother had died not long before she'd come to the Academy, and she hadn't had much of a relationship with her father even before that. In addition, her desire to be a princess and constant studying had left her with virtually no friends back home in Sevigny, a remote kingdom so far removed from the rest of the realm that no one there much cared about the comings and goings of royalty.

"I'd love to, Maggie, but I've got to get back and see my own family."

Maggie smiled sadly. "All right, but send me a note if you change your mind. Or don't. Just come. I won't be doing anything except waiting for next year. With Dad."

Evie laughed and hugged her friend. "Next year! Can you believe it?"

"I know!" said Maggie with wide eyes. Her curly hair was illuminated a brilliant red from the setting sun behind her. "How are you getting home, anyway?"

"I'll manage," said Evie, though in truth, she had absolutely no idea how she'd make it back to the Dragonlands. "Go find your coach."

"Bye, Evie." Maggie took off her knapsack and ran off down the high street.

Evie stood alone in an unfamiliar kingdom with no idea what to do next. But not for long.

"Pardon me, miss," said a man behind her. "Did that girl just call you Evie? Cadet Evie?" He was short and stout, his spine curved dramatically to the left. A woman with wild, frizzy hair stood next to him. "You're that one they've been talking about, ain't ya?"

"Sorry?"

"It's her, Liesa, what'd I say? She's the one what found that witch!"

"It ain't!" squawked the curly-haired woman, her face screwed up questioningly. "You ain't really her, are you?"

"Look here, everyone!" called the old man. "It's that girl from Pennyroyal Academy! The one who found the witch! It's her!" He turned back to Evie with a nervous smile. Several of his teeth were missing, and those that remained were various shades of brown. "I can't believe you're here! We've been hearing about you all day long, we have. Every coach to come through, 'the girl who saved ol' Pennyroyal,' they all say. And now here you are!" He clapped his hands. "Blimey, I never—on my life, I never!—thought I'd be standin' here with someone as famous as you."

"That ain't her," said the woman.

"Listen, now, what you done," said the man, his face suddenly solemn. "It's a hero's work. If anything happened to that Academy, why . . ." He trailed off, shaking his head.

He was referring, of course, to what had happened during the Helpless Maiden, the final test for the third-class cadets. After a full year of princess training, the girls had been dropped deep in the enchanted forest with only their wits and their training to help them make it back to the Academy. Evie's stepmother, Countess Hardcastle, was supposed to be assisting the staff in protecting the cadets. But Evie had discovered that she was a witch in disguise. Even more insidiously, her daughter Malora, a fellow third-class princess cadet and Evie's stepsister, was also a witch. Had Evie not uncovered Hardcastle's plot to create a witch with the powers of a princess, the fate of the Academy, and indeed the rest of humanity, might have been very dire indeed.

A small crowd began to gather. One woman leaned down and whispered to the little boy holding her hand. "She's the one who . . ." was all Evie could make out before the boy's face bloomed with excitement.

"You sure that's 'er?" said Liesa, the skeptical woman, looking Evie over like she was some sort of strange insect.

"Of course it's her!" snapped her husband. "Go on, fetch the blade! The ironmelt one I made yesterday!"

"You're not giving it to her."

"Certainly I am! Go!"

The woman walked away toward one of the stalls, peering back over her shoulder at Evie. More voices in the crowd, more smiles and expressions of shock.

"It's her! Only the Warrior Princess could have turned away those witches!"

"She's the one they've all been talking about!"

"She's finally come to save us all!"

Evie's cheeks went pink. Early in the year, a witch had prophesied that the fabled Warrior Princess, a leader who would rise and rid the world of witches once and for all, was in the current third class. Evie's class.

Now, because of what she'd done during the Helpless Maiden, these people believed *she* was the Warrior Princess. "I'm sorry, but I really must be on my way—"

"My daughter would've been older than you by now if the witches hadn't got her," said the old man. "One morning the cock crowed, and when I went to fetch her for chores, she was just . . . gone." He snapped his soot-stained fingers. "Like that. Snatched right out of her bed."

Evie glanced around the crowd, unsure what to say or do.

"I don't really know why I'm tellin' you that. I just want you to know that Pennyroyal Academy is one of the most special places in all the land. And you're a hero for stoppin' them witches. A true hero." He nearly choked on the words, wiping his eyes with trembling fingers.

"Hear, hear!" called a thick man with a shiny head and bushy beard.

The old man's wife shoved through the crowd, carrying a glinting sword. The blade was as red and shiny as copper. She handed it to her husband, who took it by the hilt and offered it across his other forearm.

"For you, Princess."

"For me? But I don't know the first thing about swords."

"Please. Take it. I'm only an armorer, but this is the best I've ever made. And you should have it."

Evie reached out and cradled the blade in her hands. It was cold to the touch, lighter than she'd expected, and the shiniest thing she'd ever seen. "Thank you. Thank you very much indeed."

"'Tis my sincerest pleasure."

"Are you sure that's her?" squawked the man's wife.

As Evie studied the sword, she was beset by other townspeople offering gifts.

"Do you need a room?" shouted a woman.

"How are you getting home?" called a man. "My cart's got only one wheel, but you're welcome to it."

Within minutes, she'd been handed several new dresses, two leather saddlebags stuffed with dried meats and fruit, and a beautiful brown horse to put them on. One man had even given her a map of the world inked across a delicate parchment and shown her how to get home, though none of them could quite believe she was really going to the Dragonlands.

With the crowd growing ever bigger, she had mounted the horse and offered an overwhelmed thank-you to the villagers.

She rode through the kingdom and out of the gatehouse, where the rest of the world was growing dark. Once she was alone beneath the stars and the moon, she could no longer contain her emotions. It had been kindness unlike any she'd experienced before. She rode all the way home atop one villager's gift, filling her belly with another villager's gift, entertaining herself with the swoosh of the blade of a third villager's gift ...

And now a fourth villager's gift had a stain on the bum that she just couldn't get out.

"I don't know why you insist on wearing those scraps," said her mother. Evie had changed into another of the dresses she'd been given as she scrubbed the dirty one against a coarse stone. "There are plenty of options right here that don't look nearly so foolish. Spiderwebs, tree bark, lashed ferns ..."

"I happen to like it," said Evie.

"Leave her alone, Mother, she's a pretty princess, remember?"

They were in the main chamber of the family cave, an enormous cathedral of dripping stone set into the side of a mountain. Moss covered the walls. Trickles of water ran down from the mouth and disappeared deeper into the cave. A fire blazed in a natural hearth cut into the wall by years of erosion. Evie's mother pulled the charred carcass of a goblin off the flames and dropped it to the floor. She nudged a claw into a huge pile of rotting bileberries, pushing dozens of the fruits closer to the main course. Supper.

Evie's sister tore into the blackened meat and flipped the berries into her mouth. "Come on, girl, or I'll have it all."

"Go ahead," said Evie, eyeing the meal with distaste. Roasted goblin used to be one of her favorites, but she'd lost interest in dragon fare since tasting the delights that came out of the Academy's kitchens.

"Too sophisticated for a bit of goblin, are we?" growled her sister.

"No!" snapped Evie. "I'm just not hungry." She tried to ignore the sounds of gnashing teeth and slurping as she scrubbed the stains from her beautiful dress—

"Here, you've got to eat something." *Thwap!* A bileberry exploded against the fabric, leaving a splash of deep blue juice.

"Why would you do that?" shouted Evie.

"I'm sorry," her sister said, chuckling. "I just don't want you going hungry."

Evie snatched her dress off the stone and stormed through the chamber toward the cave mouth.

"Sister, please! I didn't mean to hit your dress. Don't get upset!"

Evie ignored her and stormed out into the night. Above the mountains the sky was clear and awash with stars. Crickets chirped and a cold wind blew. She held up the dress. Even in the dim moonlight she could see the bileberry stain.

"She shouldn't have done that," came the gravelly voice of her mother. "It wasn't kind."

"No. It wasn't."

The dragon stepped forward and lowered her head. "I'm sorry this hasn't been the easiest summer. I think we've all found it to be a bit of a struggle without Father."

"It's not Father," said Evie, a bit too sharply. "I just don't belong here. I'm not a dragon and I never will be." She regretted saying it instantly. The words seemed to hang there amidst the sounds of the night.

"I'm sorry to hear you say that. I believe you *are* a dragon, daughter, even in moments when you don't wish to be. I believe that it doesn't matter what you look like, or whether you can breathe fire, or if you'd rather eat ridiculous human food instead of goblin." She snaked her head forward so that she was in Evie's peripheral vision. "I believe there's only one place any of us can truly be a dragon. And that's here." A claw settled against Evie's chest.

Evie fought to hold back her tears. She refused to look at her mother.

"Time is like the sea, daughter. Right now, you and your sister are swimming as hard as you possibly can, but the water is always moving. The tides are always shifting. The water doesn't care what you want. It moves you both about despite your best efforts. Sometimes it may feel like you'll never reach each other again, but if you don't keep swimming, one day you'll find that the waves have moved you too far apart. And the next thing you know, there'll be a whole ocean between you. It would break my heart to see that happen. Perhaps even more than losing your father."

The dragon turned and disappeared back into the cave. Evie wasn't interested in "swimming toward her sister." All she wanted was to be back at the Academy with her friends, training for her future.

She heard her horse whicker from the nearby cave where she kept him. It was much smaller than the family cave, but plenty big for the horse. A good shelter from the rain and summer sun. She walked over and stepped inside, running a hand down his shoulder.

"Hi, Boy," she said. As a lifelong dragon, she wasn't particularly adept at the concept of naming things. She herself hadn't even had a name until her human friends gave her one. "Up for a little ride?" She stroked his golden mane, fitting him with the saddle and tack she'd been given by the good people of Waldeck. Then she swung herself up—she'd become quite good at that—and gave his sides a sharp kick. He bobbed his head and snorted, then stepped out into the night. She led him with the reins, though she didn't really need to. He knew where to go.

They rode straight into the forest for the better part of an hour. Finally, Boy turned down a path worn through the ferns and into a small clearing. A pond sat stagnant in the center, surrounded by boulders and rushes. She dismounted and went to sit on a smooth patch of ground. The crickets were extraordinary here, one steady chirp coming from everywhere at once.

The lily pads covering the water's surface reminded her of the night she'd spent in the campus bog with Remington, the first human she'd ever met. She'd kissed him the last day of term, not long before departing for Waldeck. That memory had never really left her thoughts since she'd been back at the cave. She wondered what he was doing now. Was he looking up at the same stars? Was he thinking about that moment, too?

She stood and walked to a granite boulder just off the water's edge. She rolled another stone away to reveal a small hollow filled with her things.

She pulled out the sword first and felt the weight in her hands. She had no idea how to use it properly, but still spent hours swinging it around. The black bark of the surrounding trees was striped with white slashes from where she'd practiced her attacks. She whirled the sword around her body with a whistle, then planted it in the ground. She loved how it made her feel. Strong. Powerful. *Dangerous.*

As a breeze rustled the leaves, she crouched down and reached deeper into the hole. She pulled out a small stack of parchments, brushing dirt and spiderwebs from the ones on the bottom. On top of the letters was her Pennyroyal Academy compact. She ran a thumb across the metal shell, wiping dirt from the etching of the Academy's coat of arms. Inside, she had removed the pressed powder. Instead, opposite the mirror that had helped save her life the previous year by revealing a witch's deception, was a smattering of small coins. She poured some of them into her palm. They were silver and gold, with dragons' and kings' heads stamped into them. She didn't know exactly what they were or how to use them, but they were beautiful nonetheless. Just another gift from the grateful citizens of Waldeck.

She clinked them back into the compact and set it aside. Next in the stack was the only book she'd brought back from the Academy. It was the most recent in a thirty-seven-volume series by Lieutenant Volf, Evie's instructor in Witch Tactics and the world's foremost authority on princess history. She'd read the stories inside many times over the past few months, stories of Princess Hannelore and Cinderella and Middlemiss, as well as those of lesser-known women who had contributed to the war against the witches in their own ways. The section on Princess Middlemiss was Evie's favorite, in part because Middlemiss hadn't been a particularly good student at the Academy, which gave Evie hope, and in part because she was stationed in a region that wasn't far from the Dragonlands. Volf wrote that she lived at the One-Shore Sea, where the world ended, swallowed up by an eternity of water. According to the map Evie had been given, it was only a few days' ride east. That, too, made Middlemiss feel more like a real person and less like a story.

She set the book aside and unfolded the first parchment on the stack. It was a letter from Demetra, one of the first friends she'd made at enlistment. Demetra was a highborn girl from the Blackmarsh, arguably the most prestigious kingdom in the east.

Dearest Evie, read the letter, *I hope everything is going well with you and your family. Now learn to fly so you can visit! Anisette and I talk about you all the time! She says she'll have to find a way to sneak back into the Academy if she can't see you this summer. And then the Fairy Drillsergeant will have to throw her out again and it will be a whole to-do, and frankly, it would be much easier if you'd just come here.*

Evie smiled. Every letter in her stack had come from Demetra, nearly one a day. It had confused her at first. She'd been practicing with her sword when a hawk had come screaming down from the sky. She'd covered her face, ready to be slashed by claw and beak, but instead felt a soft tap as a parchment landed on her. Having never received or sent a letter, Evie hadn't seen a parchment hawk up close before. But now they came regularly, bombing from the sky like predators, then turning into letters and landing as softly as autumn leaves.

Demetra told Evie all about her summer and the trips her family was taking to nearby kingdoms and the things she planned to do when the Academy reopened. Evie wanted to write back, but had no idea how to turn the parchments back into hawks.

She hadn't heard from Remington, but that wasn't terribly surprising. His parents were probably using every minute of his summer to prepare him to be king. Her other friend Basil was too busy dealing with his enormous family to write, she supposed. But she was genuinely dismayed to have not received even a single letter from Maggie. She hoped everything was all right in Sevigny.

She let out a deep sigh and looked up at the stars. The

summer was only half over. How could she possibly last another two months with her mother and sister? She'd end up getting into a horrible row with one or both of them, and then things would be worse than they already were. Why was time passing so slowly?

I just want to be out there living, she thought. *Not stuck here with* them.

Boy stepped to the water's edge and began to drink. And then, like a frog's tongue catching a fly, Evie's mind found an idea.

She flipped through her stack of parchments until she found one of a slightly lighter color. It was the map she'd been given back in Waldeck. She pointed to the Dragonlands, there in the top left corner. Then she ran her finger all the way across the map to the Eastern Kingdoms, a grouping of prosperous territories lining the Bay of Bones. There, right along the northern edge of a jagged peninsula, was the Blackmarsh. Demetra's home. It was a long way, nearly the entire map . . . but why not? What else did she have to do with her time?

"What do you think, Boy?" she said to the horse. "It's a long journey, but it's got to be better than sitting round here."

It didn't take long for the crazy idea to become a sane reality. She filled Boy's saddlebags with the letters and the book and the map, finding a secure place for her compact and money as well. Then she sheathed the sword in its scabbard and tied it tight.

Before she left, she reached all the way to the back of the

hollow and took out one last thing. It was the dragon scale necklace she'd worn throughout her first year at the Academy. The scale had come from her father, stained with his blood from when he'd saved her life after she'd attempted to fly. Pressed into the inside was a small piece of canvas with the only existing likeness of her human father. He was a stout and red-faced man with a thick beard and laugh lines around his eyes. These were the only vestiges of either of her fathers, and it comforted her to keep them together like this. She hadn't wanted to wear the bloodstained scale around her mother and sister, so she kept it near the pond with the rest of her things. But with heavy rains and exposure to the elements, the blood had faded and flaked to the point where it was nearly gone. She slipped the scale over her head and tucked it inside her dress, then mounted her horse and rode for home.

As she neared the cave, Evie considered heading south to visit Maggie instead. Knowing their home lives as she did, Evie thought that Maggie could almost certainly use a visit from a friend more than Demetra. But it was something in one of the letters, an offhand comment Demetra had made, that had decided it. She had mentioned that her father, the King of the Blackmarsh, had once known Evie's human father, King Callahan. The possibility of meeting someone who had known her father proved too much to resist. She would ride east.

When she finally got back to the cave, her mother and sister were gone, most likely off on a hunt. She scratched out a note on a piece of birch bark saying that she wanted to get an early start on her second year, that they shouldn't worry, and that she loved them and would see them again at the end of term. Then she giddily jumped on Boy's back and rode down the mountain. Though part of her felt guilty for leaving without saying goodbye, mostly she was just thrilled to be going.

It's better this way, she told herself as she rode off into the newborn morning. And with that, she headed eastward through the forest to go and find her friends.

IT WAS A RAMSHACKLE PLACE, this inn. The shingled roof didn't seem to have a single straight line in it. The support beams must have been made from wet noodles to create the sagging curves of those walls. Vines grew across its face, some even covering the windows, where orange firelight gave off a homey glow. There was moss in every crack and crevice, and the stone pathway leading from the road to the door looked like it was made of ancient tortoises. Then there was the painted sign above the window: Riquet with the Tuft. It was a strange name, and it didn't tell her much about the business, but she'd been watching from the bushes down the lane for nearly an hour, and it was plain that this was a place for travelers. Woodsmen, riders, even the odd family came and went. Every time the door opened, the smell of hot food floated out into the night. Her stomach growled incessantly.

Evie had largely avoided human contact in the three or so weeks she'd been traveling, but couldn't say why she was being so cautious. Perhaps it was because she knew she'd finally need to use the gold and silver coins in her compact, and had no idea how to go about it. Whatever the reason, it was clear her horse was growing impatient. He whinnied from the tree behind her.

"Quiet, Boy," she said. "We'll go. Soon."

She turned back to the Riquet with the Tuft and heard a peal of laughter from inside, hearty and wheezy. Her stomach fluttered as she tried to persuade herself to step out of the brush.

You've just got to go, Evie. It will be less embarrassing to ask for help with the money than to explain why you're hiding in the bushes.

It had been a long, exhausting journey, but she'd just passed through a range of mountains that made her think she was nearly all the way across her map and to the edge of the Eastern Kingdoms. Boy had performed admirably along the way. He seemed to like putting in long days, even as they kept to the more difficult forest routes to avoid unnecessary encounters with people. He was probably thrilled to be on the move after all those quiet weeks at the cave, and she couldn't help but feel the same. She was headed back to her friends. Back to the new world she'd found at Pennyroyal Academy, and away from . . .

That was the one exhausting bit. For all the traveling she'd done, for as excited as she was to see her friends, she hadn't been able to shake the guilt of leaving without a proper goodbye.

She sighed deeply, then took the compact from the pocket of her dress. She bounced it in her hand, heard the coins inside clank against each other.

"Well, I suppose if I'm going to be a human, I'd better get busy being a human." She returned the compact to her pocket, kissed the dragon scale necklace for luck, and went to untie Boy.

Leading him by his reins, she stepped out onto the grassy lane. The sun was near to setting, and the ferns shimmered green. The air was thick but cool, the first herald of the end of summer. Crickets thrummed from both sides of the road. Everything was descending to darkness, which only made the light from inside the inn seem even more cozy and warm. She walked toward the stone path that led to the front door. Wrapping the reins around a small post, she took Boy's muzzle in her hands.

"I don't suppose you've any advice on using money, have you?" She gave his nose a stroke, then turned to the door. "I didn't think so."

She pulled on the handle and was met with a blast of warm air and the scent of cooking meat. Inside, she found a large common room with a low ceiling and several wobbly tables. Doors branched off to the kitchen, the privy, and other rooms. A staircase in the back led up to the guests' quarters. Animal heads were mounted around the room, with fur pelts scattered about the floor. Fixtures made of all variety of horns hung from the ceiling, flickering with the stubs of candles.

There were several other people in the room, though they sat alone in the darker corners eating supper or drinking from cups made of elk's antler. None of them paid Evie much notice, aside from a glance or two.

"Welcome, lass, welcome to the Riquet!" came a booming

voice. It had to have been the old man she'd heard laughing. He stepped forward, arms in the air, a wide smile wrinkling his face. "Come! Sit! Your mum and da will be outside, then? Marie, horses!"

"Oh, um, I'm alone. That is, my horse is there, but I'm traveling alone."

His smile turned to surprise, his creased eyes popping wide. "Alone! Well, by guppers, we'll have a chat about that, we will! Come, sit. Marie! Food!" The old man was almost perfectly round, with two long, thin arms waving around in front of him, gesturing to an open table. "Over here, lass, over here. Marie! Bring some food! Any bags, my dear?"

"It's all right, I can manage."

"If you can manage alone in these woods, I've no doubt you can manage some luggage!" he said with a hearty laugh. "Terryn! Can you picture this one in the forest by herself?"

The man he was addressing was slumped over, head resting on his arm. His table was covered in so many empty antlers that it looked like a herd of bucks had molted there.

"That's Terryn, one of me best customers. A quality, quality man, that one. Now, what'll it be, lass? Mutton? Rabbit? Ah, you look like a dragon girl to me."

"Dragon?"

"I've only a spot of it left, and it's dried and cured, not fresh. But it's yours if you want it. Dragon meat is a rare treat, it is."

The hunger pains in her stomach turned to nausea. "That's all right."

An old woman emerged from the back. She looked like a pink version of the man, with a pale dress and apron, her cheeks flushed and ginger hair poofing out from beneath her bonnet. She came straight across to Evie and took her hand.

"Now now, don't give a moment's thought to this one," she said, rolling her eyes at the old man. "No doubt you'd like a room. Come with me." She pulled Evie back toward the staircase. "Two silvers for the night, includes a meal and as much mead as you like. Horse eats free."

Two silvers, thought Evie. *Well, that's easier than I expected.* She took the compact out of her pocket, but the woman, Marie, suddenly stopped and faced her. She wore thin-rimmed glasses, and her face puffed out like dough that had risen beyond the edges of its tin.

"Now, my dear, I'll give you our finest accommodation. It's at the front, so you'll have an excellent view of the lane. Supper is whenever you like, though the earlier is probably the better."

"I'll just get settled and—"

"Of course. Come." She tromped up the stairs, the wood groaning and creaking beneath her. "Have you been to this part of the world before?"

"No."

"Well, there's much to see, much to do. Cinderella's Castle is just below the Neck, only a day's ride south. The sea is easterly—most folks enjoy spendin' a bit of time there."

"It's tempting," she said, "but I'm only passing through. I'm on my way to Witch Head Bay." She hadn't planned to lie, but was happy she did.

"Witch Head Bay?" said the old woman with a grimace. "Dire place, that is." Evie had to stifle a laugh. Witch Head Bay was Basil's home.

Finally they reached the landing at the top of the stairs. A thin hallway ran front to back, with several doors along it. The old woman curved around and tottered toward the front of the inn, then opened the lone door at the end of the hall.

"I'd think a girl like you would quite fancy a look at Cinderella's Castle." She turned back to Evie with a wink. "Pennyroyal girl and all." Her eyes flicked down to Evie's hand, to the compact. Evie quickly put it back in her pocket.

"Does she really live there?" said Evie, trying to change the subject.

"No, no, it's only her family home," said Marie as she continued into the bedchamber. She crossed to the window and propped it open with a small stick, letting in the rapidly cooling night air. "Cinderella hasn't been down that way in years. Still a popular destination for families on holiday, though." She turned a knob on an oil lamp and filled the room with warm light. There was a small straw bed and a table, and nothing more, though the walls were covered in paintings of ships at sea. "Here y'are, our finest room. Only the best for a Pennyroyal girl." Then, with another wink, she was gone and the door clicked closed.

Evie took a deep breath. She'd meant to keep her status as a cadet secret, but there was no sense in worrying about it now. The elderly innkeepers seemed happy to have her, and happier still that she was a Pennyroyal girl. She went to the window and looked out at the view. She could see Boy down below, and Marie waddling out with a bucket of oats to feed him. Beyond that, she could make out a bit of the lane to the left in the torchlight, but the inn's sign blocked everything to the right. And straight ahead, there was nothing but the blackness of the forest.

Lovely view, she thought with a smile. She turned back to her room, but there was nothing much to do there. Plus, the aromas wafting up from the kitchen had restored her appetite and made her stomach growl even louder than before. She tried to ignore that some of those smells could be cooked dragon and headed back out of the room. The stairs announced her as she came back down into the common room.

"Over here, lassie, near the fire," said the innkeeper. His arms waved wildly, ushering her to an empty table near the hearth. He waddled into the kitchen and returned with an antler of some bubbling drink and the roasted leg of some unknown fowl that must have been as big as an ox. He plopped down on the bench opposite her. "There y'are, tuck in, tuck in. We don't stand on ceremony here. Ye've got your drink, your supper. Napkin's here." He lifted the heavily stained tablecloth with a smile.

"Thank you for your hospitality, sir. Two silvers, I believe, was the price." Beneath the table, she clicked open the compact and fished out two coins.

"Marie says we've got us a Pennyroyal girl. Isn't that something? Don't get many of them round here."

Evie opened her mouth to lie, but then decided there really was no point. "Yes, but I'm only second class."

"Tell me," he said, leaning forward and fixing her with a serious stare. "What went on there last year? We get news round here, but you can't always trust that, can ye? Give it to me from the horse's mouth."

"You mean . . . ?"

"With the witch! Is it true there was a witch inside the Academy?" His blue eyes bulged intently beneath massive white eyebrows.

"Well . . . I . . . I mean, I *heard* that one of the girls discovered a witch trying to pass herself off as a princess cadet."

"Ah! Terryn, d'you hear? That bloke from Aberdown was right!" He turned back to Evie with excitement. "Go on, go on!"

"I don't know the details, really, just that the witch was uncovered—"

"Aye, and with her, one of Calivigne's wicked plots!" he said with excitement. Calivigne was the leader of the wicked witches, and the most feared witch in all the land. "I said to Marie, I told her, 'If any of them Pennyroyal girls comes round here, we've got to give her the royal treatment. No questions asked.'"

Evie smiled and picked a piece of meat off the leg. It was all she could do to keep from shoving the whole thing into her mouth. Marie came back in through the front door, wiping her hands on her apron.

"Marie! Get over here!" called the innkeeper. "She's tellin' the story!"

Marie hurried over to join them. She scowled when she saw the food in front of Evie. "Is that what you've given her? You old black rat! Where's the cream and cakes?" She smacked the innkeeper up the back of his head, then retreated to the kitchen. His face wrinkled into a smile, and he released one of his bellowing laughs.

"Old Marie, eh? Go on, I gave you the best bit of meat in the county." A moment later, Marie returned with a plate loaded down with cakes.

"Oh, now put that away, dearie," said Marie, taking the compact from Evie's hands and setting it on the table. She clicked the lid closed and the coins rattled inside. "We'll take no money from a Pennyroyal girl."

"That's what I was just sayin' to her!" said the innkeeper. "You've always a room at the Riquet, Princess, at no charge. I don't know what you lot did to that witch, but it seems you've put a right fear into all of them. They're gone, the witches! The whole bloody crew! We haven't seen one slinkin' round here in, how long, Marie?"

"Last witch I recall seeing was months ago, right when business started to pick up. Lots more travelers these days. It's like old times."

"Some girl with a funny name, Ten or Eleven or something of that sort. That's what people who come to stay were saying. They'd bring the whole family to see Cinderella's or spend a day at the sea. All talking about the girl with the funny name."

Evie's heart skipped a beat. Eleven was what she had been called when she'd first arrived at the Academy, before her friends had changed it to Evie instead.

"Well, anyway, eat up, eat up. I'll see if I can rouse old Terryn there to give us a song, shall I?" The innkeeper shouted across the room. "Aha! A song, there, lad! A song!"

Marie patted Evie's hand maternally. "You enjoy your supper, dearie. Whatever you need, you've got a home here."

"Thank you." As Marie got up to go, Evie glanced around the room. A husband and wife sat across from each other at a table in back. Terryn was still slumped across his table, only now an instrument sat next to him, a small, curved piece of wood with strings. Another man nibbled at a heel of bread and stared into the fire. Behind her, the door was shut tight and the windows were painted with reflections of the fire. It was full night now, and the warmth and glow of the inn made her content and happy. She felt more human than she had in a long while. She picked up the leg with both hands and took a bite. Then another. And another . . .

The music thundered up from below. Feet were stomping as fingers worked strings. The chorus of voices alternated between raucous singing and raucous laughter.

Evie had eaten so much that she felt uncomfortable. She was lying on her bed, flipping the dragon scale between her fingers. Not only had the blood faded and cracked away, but the scale itself felt lighter, like an empty cobnut shell. She brought the scale down to her eye, just as she had before, but nothing happened. Dragon's blood had the magical property of being able to predict the possible. Anything that appeared in a dragon's blood vision could come to pass given the right circumstances. But since the blood had faded, all she could see was a smudge of black. She slipped it over her neck with a sigh and tucked it inside her dress as another roar of laughter bellowed up from below. Her stomach felt so stretched that she didn't think she'd be able to sleep, so she decided to go downstairs and join them.

They all had antlers in their hands, frothing down the sides, and pitchers of more on the tables next to them. They'd formed a circle with the tables and benches around Terryn, whose fingers worked the strings of his instrument like spider legs on silk.

"Ah, here she is!" he cried, his fingers never stopping.

"Come, come, lass!" cried the innkeeper, raising an antler in her direction. She walked over and took it, but remained standing.

"Go on, then," said the man who had been absently staring into the fire earlier. He was wiry, with a perfect ring of hair surrounding a shining bald spot. And his expectant smile was aimed squarely at the innkeeper.

"All right, all right," chuckled the innkeeper, stomping his foot on the bench. Evie watched with a smile as he began to sing so quickly that his mouth could barely keep pace:

"Ooooh, there once was an innkeeper in a forest so dark / When along came a dog with a bone and a bark / He shouted, 'Me Master, do ye know where I've been?' / 'Me Master, Me Master, do ye know what I've seen?'"

Now everyone slapped their hands on their legs as fast as they could, all eyes on the innkeeper.

"Bloody hell," he said, rolling his eyes with a cheeky grin, then, *"'I've seeeeeeeen . . . a magic bean, a murder scene, a grimy sheen, a flying queen, a dragon green—'"*

"Aha!" shouted Marie. "Aha! Ye forgot the tambourine!"

The small crowd roared as the innkeeper shook his head with a smile. "So I did, so I did. Right! Round the robin!" He began to drink as everyone continued slapping their thighs and Terryn kept strumming. Then, around the circle, they all threw out a rhyme:

"A raw sardine!"

"Me mum Kathleen!"

"A dank latrine!"

Gales of laughter.

"A dry canteen!"

"A man obscene!" sang Marie, elbowing the innkeeper in the side as he drank. Then everyone turned to Evie.

"Uh, um, a pig who's lean?"

"Hey!" they all shouted with approval.

"A . . . a . . ." stammered the husband.

"Ooooh!" shouted the rest.

"*The bloody number thirteen*, I don't know!" shouted the husband, and they all laughed.

"Thank the Fates!" called the innkeeper, wiping foam from his mouth. He slammed his antler on the table. "Your turn, mate!"

The music and laughter started up again, and that's how Evie's first night as an ordinary member of humanity, not as a cadet trying to remain in the Academy, went on. She learned several new games and an array of songs, until Terryn had finally had enough and staggered up to his room. After that, the rest of the group began to dissipate. The bald man went back to his table and nursed a drink as he stared into the dying fire, hiccupping. The innkeeper and his wife began to tidy up, wiping down tables and collecting cups and plates.

"Can I help?" asked Evie.

"Oh no, lass, you're a guest here and not to be doing any work," said Marie, whose face had gone an even rosier shade of pink. "Up to bed with you. It'll be best if you can fall asleep before this one." She jerked her head toward her husband. "Snores like the devil's band saw, he does."

Evie smiled and moved toward the stairs.

"You'll have no nightmares tonight, I'll wager," continued Marie. "My mother always said that nightmares come when a witch is killed. All them demons hiding inside the witch's skin get out when she dies and travel through the world giving children nightmares. Well, there's no witches round here, and no nightmares neither. Sleep easy, my dear!"

"Good night." Evie went up the stairs and stepped into the dim hallway. Could that be true or was it only a folktale? Was the wickedness inside a witch released into people's dreams when she died? If that were the case, Evie would welcome her nightmares—

Suddenly, her heart leapt like a buck at the snap of a branch. She patted her hips and found her pockets empty. She'd left the compact, and all her money, on the table downstairs. She had just turned to go back down when . . .

Boom! The front door of the inn exploded open, followed quickly by the screams of the innkeeper's wife. Evie froze, holding her breath, her hand perched on the banister. It had gone silent downstairs. Even the bald man's hiccups had stopped. Then she heard the squeak of hinges as the front door gently closed.

"Ladies," said the innkeeper, a tremble in his voice, "welcome to the Riquet with the Tuft."

There was no response. Only slow-moving footsteps across the wooden floor.

"I'm afraid our kitchen's shut for the night, but—"

"Bring us drinks, then," came a woman's voice.

"Yes, Princess," said the innkeeper.

"Princess?" whispered Evie to herself. She heard Marie's feet shuffle into the back to retrieve the drinks. Wooden stools scraped across the floor. The only other sound was the rapid wheezing of the innkeeper and the pop of the dying fire.

"Charming establishment," said another woman's voice.

"Thank ye, Princess. She's a nice old place."

There were *two* princesses downstairs? And if they were princesses, why did she suddenly feel so frightened? Ever so slowly, she began to tiptoe along the banister toward the head of the stairs. The boards creaked softly beneath her. She gritted her teeth, trying to tread as lightly as she could. She clutched the end of the banister and leaned over the staircase . . .

Suddenly, a woman appeared at the bottom of the stairs. She was wearing a black dress, waves of golden hair pouring out from beneath a shining tiara.

Evie froze, her eyes wide. The woman hadn't seen her. She was inspecting one of the oil paintings scattered across the walls. But all the woman would need to do was turn her head to catch Evie peering down.

"Here we are," said Marie, though the joy was gone from her voice. The woman in black stepped away from the staircase, and Evie could breathe again. She heard the *thunk* of cups being set down.

"So what brings ye by at such a late hour, Princesses?" said the innkeeper, trying desperately to sound cheerful and doing a miserable job.

"We're looking for Javotte."

Marie gasped. Then Evie heard a loud thump as someone collapsed onto a bench.

"J . . . Javotte?" said the innkeeper.

"We heard she was somewhere round here. So if you'll kindly point us in the right direction, we'll just be on our way."

Evie stepped down onto the landing, carefully lowering herself to keep the creaking stairs from giving her away. She grabbed the banister and leaned forward as far as she could. Now she could see a bit more of the room. There were three princesses, each of them dressed in black, with corpse-gray trim and sleeves. The two she could see had tiaras in their hair. Marie sat slumped against a table, and the innkeeper's arms hung limply at his sides. One of the princesses sat alone at a table, sipping from her cup. Another roamed the room. She could see only the back of the third.

"I've no idea where to find Javotte, Princess," said the innkeeper. His voice was frantic now, a jarring contrast to the joy and laughter it had held all night. "She hasn't lived round here in years."

"Surely you must have heard something," said the princess seated at the table. "Go on, have a think."

"I'm sorry, but I haven't the first clue where she is," said the innkeeper. "Last I recall hearing, she might've been off in the Snow Spindles—"

"She's not in the bloody Snow Spindles," said the princess, shooting to her feet and knocking the antler to the floor with a sweep of her arm. Evie jumped as foam spiked into the air, then splatted on the ground.

"I-I don't know where she is, Princess, I swear it!"

"What's the fastest way to the castle?"

"Which castle, Princess?"

She lunged at him, grabbing him by the shirt. Then she slapped him across the face, causing a moan from Marie. "You know which castle I mean!"

"Cinderella's Castle is just to the south, Princess, not a day's ride—"

"What's this?" said the other princess, the one who had been prowling the room. Evie couldn't quite make out what she was looking at. Suddenly, there was a thud so loud it made Evie jump, and the horrific meeting of metal. The princess slowly turned back around. As she stepped toward the innkeeper, sword raised in front of her, Evie saw something stuck to the blade. It was her Pennyroyal Academy compact, and it was nearly sliced in two. "Has a Pennyroyal girl been here?"

Evie ducked back into the shadows. She held her breath.

"I-I, well—" stammered the innkeeper.

"Is she *still* here?"

Two more swords *shinged* free of their scabbards.

"No! Stop!" shouted Marie. There was a thunder of feet on the wood floor and then the deafening scream of the innkeeper's wife.

"Marie!" he shouted. "No!"

Evie leaped back around the banister and raced down the hall to her room, slamming the door shut behind her. She needed some sort of weapon . . . anything. But her sword was down with Boy, and even if she'd had it, she wouldn't have had the first idea how to defend herself against three enemy blades.

"Upstairs! Move, girls!"

"Oh, Marie, no!" wailed the innkeeper. "You've killed her! Why? Why?"

Footsteps thundered up the stairs. Evie grabbed her knapsack and threw her shoulder into the opened window, shattering the glass and the wood frame. She climbed out just as the door to her room boomed open. A princess stood in the doorway, her eyes wide, a cruel smile on her lips. "Hang on, Cadet, we only want a little chat."

Evie grabbed the wooden sign and swung out the window. She dropped to the ground with a thud, then sprang to her feet and raced to Boy.

The princess appeared in the window with an even wider smile. "What a valiant display of courage! You really must be a Pennyroyal girl!" She laughed with such malice that it reminded Evie of a witch's cackle.

"How's old Beatrice doing these days?" said a second princess, appearing at the front door.

Evie's fingers were shivering so violently that she was having trouble unlashing Boy's reins. She pulled them loose and swung atop him, jerking his head toward the lane. The princess was running at her, only a few feet behind.

"No need to leave on our account, Cadet!"

Boy whinnied in protest, but obeyed. Evie glanced behind

her. One princess's silver blade glinted in the light of the torch at the entrance to the inn. The other two joined her, each with a sword in hand.

"Go! Go!" screamed Evie. Boy's hooves found purchase, and they bounded off into the darkness. She turned back to see three dark figures standing in the lane. Their swords shone through the dark of night.

And each of them wore a razor-sharp wolf's fang around her neck.

Evie rode hard through the night. Finally, as the sky began to gray, she gave Boy a break. As soon as he'd had some water and a bit to eat, they were off again. She didn't intend to stop until she was safely inside the walls of the Blackmarsh. To Boy's credit, he seemed to be conditioned for long distances. Once she'd slowed from a gallop, he was perfectly happy to continue east, no matter the terrain. And to the Fates' credit, the weather held and the ground stayed dry.

They'd killed that lady. Marie, the innkeeper's wife. Three princesses had entered the inn and murdered an innocent woman. And then tried to kill Evie as well. *Princesses?* But how could that be? None of it made any sense. The whole encounter filled her with a sense of dread she hadn't felt since discovering that her stepmother was a witch.

Halfway through her third day on the run, she arrived. At first, she was confused and frightened by the powerful crashing sounds thundering in the distance. She'd never been near enough to the sea to hear waves breaking over rock before. When Boy finished a steep climb and stepped onto a grassy ridge, Evie was stunned by what lay before her. Even Boy paused to appreciate the view.

They were on the summit of a sloping half bowl of cliffs. A hundred yards below, the purple heather gave way to great spikes of stone, as jagged and unforgiving as any she'd ever seen. Black seawater surged toward the cliffs, breaking against the rock with huge sprays of foam, the crash reaching her a moment later. The water seemed to go on forever, fading into the distant clouds until there was no horizon at all, just varying degrees of gray. Something opened inside of her at the sight of the sea, so large and deep and unknowable.

To her right lay the Blackmarsh. There, the cliffs evened out into gentle hills, forming a horseshoe that butted up against even more imposing cliffs. The kingdom was nestled into the bottom. The curtain walls came up from the water itself, a line of dark green algae marking the spot where waves had been breaking for centuries. The main castle sat near the back of the walled city. It was narrow and tall, rising far above the rest of the buildings that made up the kingdom. Spires jutted from the various towers nearly as high as the cliffs behind. Flags crackled in the sea wind. The rest of the Blackmarsh grew out from the castle in concentric circles, and all throughout there were great patches of green. The terrain around the kingdom was rocky and desolate, but behind the walls it appeared to be a garden oasis. Beams of sunlight broke through the gray, shining down like beacons from above.

Evie's heart soared. Demetra was there. And Anisette. Her friends.

"Come, Boy."

They made their way along the ridge and followed a horse trail down the hill toward the gatehouse. It consisted of two square towers of limestone brick with lookout posts at the top. Between them, wooden doors that must have been as tall as Evie's sister were closed tight. Standing beneath the giant doors, the sea suddenly didn't feel quite so big after all.

"Hello?" she called. There was no reply. "Is anyone there?" She looked past the towers, scanning the wall walk for a guardsman. There, atop a lookout tower directly above the sea, she saw a man in a helmet. A thin trail of stones followed the bottom of the curtain wall, with the roiling sea splashing over it. Evie gulped, then led Boy along the path. "Hello?" she called, but the guardsman never heard her.

Waves exploded on the rocks, sending heavy sheets of water splashing against the wall. Evie screamed as salt water doused her. Boy pulled against the reins to get back to solid ground. And still the guardsman hadn't seen her. She kept along the path, the stones slipping away beneath her feet. *Both of us will end up drowned in the Bay of Bones*, she thought. Still, the jets and splashes of the waves in the bay did little more than frighten and soak her. She managed to follow the curve of the wall all the way to the end until she was directly beneath the tower. A small wooden door was wedged shut at its base. She peered up and saw the man's hands far above. He must have been leaning against the battlement.

"Hello!" she shouted as loudly as she could. "Hello, can you hear me?"

The man's head popped out, looking down at her with wide eyes. He shouted, gesturing something she couldn't understand, but a wave slammed a rock at the same time, the roaring water drowning his voice. He disappeared inside the tower and Evie's heart sank.

"Back, Boy, before we're both killed."

The guardsman's face appeared again, in a lower window of the tower. He shouted something just as a wall of water splashed over Evie and Boy. She screamed, but managed to keep her balance on the precarious stones. When she looked up again, he was gone. Moments later, he reappeared even farther down the tower.

"Use the—"

The loudest crash yet thundered behind Evie, swallowing up the guardsman's words yet again. He was just above her now, but still she couldn't hear him.

She wiped salt water from her face with a soaked hand as Boy shook his entire body, sending sprays everywhere. A moment later, the door popped open and Evie saw the smiling face of the guardsman.

"I said it's open!" He laughed. "Come in, come in."

Evie stepped through the door and onto a mercifully solid floor. She had to coax Boy inside, but managed it just as another eruption of water splashed against the wall overhead.

"Now, how can I help you, miss?" said the guardsman, closing the door. The wind had blown out several of the candles lining the walls, but enough of them remained lit. They were inside a claustrophobic tunnel cut through the wall. It must have been thirty feet thick or more.

"I'm here to see De— er, Princess Demetra?"

"Ah, indeed, indeed. And who might you be, then?"

"My name is Evie. I'm a friend from the Academy."

The guardsman's eyes went wide. "By thunder, she'll be wanting to see you. That's all Her Serene and Exalted Highness can talk about these days." Evie stifled a laugh, remembering how much Demetra despised her official title. He took Boy's reins from her. "Come along. Afternoon guard's just turned up, so I can take you to the castle myself."

Evie followed him through the tunnel and emerged into the Blackmarsh. She had only Marburg and Waldeck to compare it with, the two kingdoms that served as drop-off points for the Academy, but she could tell immediately that the Blackmarsh was in an entirely different class. Blooming up from between the four circular towers of the main castle were a series of thin, ever-taller towers, some with bartizans sprouting off of them, like an exotic plant that bloomed towers rather than flowers. With the light beaming down from the clouds, it all felt entirely magical.

"First time at the Blackmarsh, miss?" He handed her a linen handkerchief. She wiped the seawater from her eyes.

"Yes." Despite being utterly sodden, Evie couldn't keep the smile from her face. *This is what it means to be highborn,* she thought. That castle, so majestic and noble and dreamlike, was Demetra's *home.* Her heart soared at the sight of it, making her all the more certain she had never been meant to live in a dragon cave.

"Well, it's our little piece of heaven, it is. Lived here my whole life. Jensen," he said, reaching out a hand. "Sergeant in the Royal Guard."

"Evie."

"Where have you come from, miss? Not from the north, I hope. All sorts of troubles up there these days."

"No, not from the north."

"Fates be praised," he said. "Bloody business in the north. Our King and Queen never get us mixed up in any of that nonsense. Leave war to the warmongers, I say. We've got no time for it here at the Blackmarsh."

They neared a quaint arched bridge over a stream. On the other side, it was a short walk to the castle's front gates, which were opened wide. Evie looked up to some of the highest spires, with puffs of cloud just above. It was impossible. How could anything be so grand, so beautiful?

"We've taken in lots of folks trying to get away from the fighting, though. One bloke from Diebkunst told me the whole kingdom was destroyed, right down to rubble. And all because one king wanted what belonged to another." He clicked his tongue. "Shame, that. Rough world out there."

Evie didn't respond. As excited as she was to see her friends, and as stunned as she was by the beauty of the sea and this magnificent castle, what Jensen had told her was troubling.

"Don't concern yourself with the battles of others, miss. You're safe here in the Blackmarsh," he said with pride. "You! Boy!"

Evie looked at him with confusion, wondering why he was shouting at her horse. Then she realized he was signaling a stable boy at the side of the palace. The stable boy, mop-headed and slim, raced over. "Yes, Sergeant."

"Take special care of this one. Use the King's grain. Double brushings."

"Aye," said the stable boy, and he turned and led Boy away.

"After you, miss," said Sergeant Jensen.

Evie climbed the short marble staircase to the main gates. Two more guardsmen flanked the doors, spears pointing high above their heads.

"We'll just be along, lads," said Jensen. Neither of them reacted as he and Evie walked through the gates and into the castle. "Don't be fooled by them either," he said. "They're mostly for show. All are welcome in the palace. The King and Queen close the gates to no one."

Evie stepped inside and once again found herself staring

in awe. The ceiling was glass ribbed with curved oak beams. Through the ceiling, the castle's towers stretched up so high that she couldn't even see the tops.

"Now, if you'll just wait here, I'll go announce you," said Jensen, and he ran off toward one of the open staircases that spiraled up around the room like curls of smoke from a campfire. Evie counted the staircases and found eight of them, each leading to a different floor that branched off to a different part of the castle. Round and round he went, higher and higher, until finally he disappeared and the echo of his boots began to recede.

She stepped toward the middle of the grand entrance and looked at the walls between the spiral staircases. They were covered in enormous windows, the biggest pieces of glass Evie had ever seen. Between them were scenes done in stained glass, scenes that depicted centuries of life in the Blackmarsh. Ruby-red banners draped the walls with what must have been Demetra's family's coat of arms.

I can't believe this is where Demetra lives. She never said a word about this—

"Aaaah!" A scream echoed down from upstairs, followed by the clack of footsteps. "Evie!" Demetra appeared at the top of the staircase, a huge smile on her face.

"Demetra!"

She looped round and round the stairs, holding the skirts of her pale orange dress off the ground to keep from tripping. She laughed the entire way until finally she reached the bottom and sprinted to Evie, grabbing her tight. "I can't believe you're here!"

"Nor can I!"

"You're absolutely soaked through!" She held Evie by the shoulders to get a better look. "I didn't think I'd see you again until Waldeck!"

"I'm sorry to turn up like this, out of the blue—"

"Are you mad? I've been hoping all summer you'd turn up out of the blue."

Behind them, Jensen cleared his throat. He'd followed Demetra down the stairs. "Will there be anything else, Your Serene and Exalted Highness?"

Evie laughed. Jensen's face fell, as though he'd done something wrong.

"No, sir," said Demetra, "and thank you for taking such good care of my friend."

"Of course, Highness," he said with a bow. "I'll just be off to the stables to see that your guest's horse is well attended."

"Thank you, sir," said Evie, and he turned and left. "It's so good to see you, Serene and Exalted One!"

Demetra rolled her eyes. "Stop or I'll have you beheaded." Then she smiled widely, studying her friend's face. "Oh, Evie, it's good to see you, too. So you got my letters?"

"I did. Lots and lots of letters."

"I can't help it. I was so sad when I got home from the Academy. I felt like all of you must be out there having fun together and I was stuck here at the Blackmarsh on my own."

"That's how I felt!" said Evie. "I would've written you back, but I don't know how to use the, er, the birds."

"Don't worry about that. Come, you must meet my family." She took Evie by the arm and led her to the staircase. "It's a good thing you got here when you did. They've already got me packed and one foot out the door. If you'd come tomorrow, I'd have already been gone."

"But I thought we'd have at least a week."

"Ordinarily, yes. But now that the witches have gone into hiding, Father wants to make it a family trip to Waldeck. He says it's to spend more time with me, but I know he's secretly going to negotiate some sort of trade agreement with them. There's nothing he loves more than a good trade agreement."

They reached the top of the staircase and emerged into a wide hallway lit by multiwicked candles as big around as clubs. Two enormous doors at the far end were open wide. Voices came from inside, as well as the sounds of various thuds and slams and scrapes.

"Come on. Don't mind the mess—my parents aren't particularly good at packing for trips. Sometimes I think they'd rather just put the whole castle on wheels."

They went down the hall and into an enormous light-filled antechamber. Tapestries as large as ships' sails covered the far walls. A rug with swirling patterns stretched from one end of the room to the other. There were carved oak tables and chairs padded with velvet cushions, and clothing was draped and piled *everywhere*. Women in simple dresses scurried about amidst open trunks, while the Queen stood in the middle of the room orchestrating it all. She was tall and slender, with a raised chin and nose, and hair as golden as her daughter's.

"No, not that one, the vermillion one. That is clearly not vermillion," she said, waving a servant away.

"Mother, we wear *uniforms*. I don't need any of this," said Demetra.

"Piffle," said the Queen. "That is why I am doing your packing. You don't understand a thing about it."

"This one, Highness?"

"Yes, that's the one. Put it with the traveling clothes. Monique! Monique, what have you done with the shoes?"

Demetra looked at Evie and shrugged. "Come on." They stepped farther into the room, where Evie was nearly run down by a scurrying servant. "Mother, I'd like you to meet one of my friends from the Academy. This is Evie. Evie, this is my mother, the Queen of the Blackmarsh."

"How do you do," said the Queen, with barely a glance. Her mouth was turned up at the corners in the remnants of a smile that hadn't been used in years. There was a hint of Demetra in it, though only a hint.

"A pleasure, Your Serene and Exalted Majesty," said Evie, dipping into a curtsy. This was something her friends had taught her the previous year, after she'd revealed that she had been raised by dragons. The girls in the third class had grown up knowing how to curtsy, even the lowborn. Even *Basil* knew how to curtsy. But not Evie. So they had practiced with her, helping her master the technique until she could do it effortlessly.

"Evie's the one I've been telling you about, Mum—"

"No sign of the embroidered hennin, Majesty, only the plain ones," said another servant, holding two long, pointed hats in her hands. Each had a ribbon of silk dangling from the top.

"Impossible. Look again."

The servant dipped her head and ran off.

"Mother, Evie's the one I told you about. Remember?"

"I'm sorry, Demetra, I simply don't have time to memorize all of your little friends."

Demetra gave Evie an embarrassed look. "Mother, it was Evie who discovered the witch. She saved my life—"

"No! I specifically asked for the thirty-two-inch trunks, not the twenty-eights! Take it all out and start again!"

"Yes, Majesty."

"The one who saved your life . . ." said the Queen, distracted. Then, as though realizing what she'd said, "The one who saved your life? This is . . . Evie, is it?"

"Yes, Your Serene and Exalted Majesty," said Evie, curtsying again.

"The Warrior Princess." Now the Queen looked at Evie for the first time, studying her.

Evie blushed. So the idea that she could be the Warrior Princess had made it as far as the Blackmarsh. It embarrassed her, but she didn't dare contradict the Queen.

"You are quite wet, aren't you? Miriam, dry clothes! I suppose I owe you a debt of gratitude for saving my daughter's life."

"I didn't save her, she saved me, Your Serene and Exalted—"

"Evie, stop," said Demetra.

"Sorry. Just 'Your Majesty,' right? Anyway, if Demetra hadn't pushed me out of the way of the witch's spell, it would have gotten me."

"Oh! That reminds me!" Demetra exclaimed. She untied her belt and unlaced her dress. She lifted it to reveal her under-clothes, then pulled them aside at the hip.

"Demetra! Where is your decorum?" sighed the Queen. "Ugh!" She shook her head with disgust and went off to chastise another of her servants.

Evie's eyes were fixed on Demetra's bare skin, or, rather, the sizable chunk of ice that seemed to be embedded inside it. "Is that . . . ?"

"It's ice," said Demetra happily. "Remember how Maggie guessed that Hardcastle got me with an iceflesh spell? She was right. Go on, touch it."

Evie reached out and placed a finger on the wound. It was as cold as, well, ice. The patch was about the size of an apple, frosty clear fading into Demetra's skin.

"I've got to keep it covered or things end up sticking to it, like when you touch your tongue to an icicle."

"Demetra! Enough!" called her mother.

Demetra rolled her eyes and shook her head, but laced her dress back up anyway. "Want to meet my sister?"

"Camilla isn't here," said the Queen, perking up at the mention of Demetra's older sister. "She's following a lead on a witch up the coast. That girl doesn't know what to do with herself now that the witches have gone. She says she'll be home before we leave tomorrow morning."

"She'd better. Father hates nothing more than lateness—"

"Aldegaard? Aldegaard!" bellowed a voice from the doorway at the far end of the antechamber.

"Speak of the devil," said Demetra.

"Aldegaard, where in blazes is my gold shield?" Demetra's father charged into the room wearing only his breeches. He was a thick man, bulging in the middle like a water pitcher. "I sent it to be polished weeks ago! I'll not turn up to Waldeck with a silver shield like some sort of common vagabond!"

"Yes, Majesty," said one of the servants before ducking out of the room.

"Father!" called Demetra.

"Quiet, girl! I've got a shield emergency!"

"Father, this is my friend Evie."

The King looked over with a scowl. He had the face of a young boy inflated into a man. "Who?"

"Evie. She saved me from the witch."

He turned up his hands in annoyance.

"Her father was King Callahan?"

"Callahan! Well, strike me down." He charged toward Evie like a bull, the servants diving out of his path. He loomed over her, taking her hand in his with a hard squeeze and shake. Evie cringed in pain. "Callahan was as fine a king as ever ruled in this land. It's an honor to meet his daughter."

"So it's true. You knew my father."

"Knew him! My dear, he and I used to hunt together! Put a bow in your hands and I could see a bit of him in you, though I daresay it seems you were fortunate to be blessed with your mother's looks." He barked out a laugh.

"No! Bring me a thirty-two instead! Don't force it!" shrieked the Queen from across the room.

"Father, Evie's come all the way from—"

"Quiet, girl! Young lady, King Callahan was a delight and a pleasure every time I saw him. I'm very pleased to meet you. Won't you join us to Waldeck?"

"I'd be honored, Your Majesty."

There was a crash, and a scream from the Queen. "Fool! Can't anyone manage a simple trunk?"

"Aldegaard?" bellowed the King, storming away in his underclothes.

"I'm going to show Evie the gardens," said Demetra. In the chaos of the room, no one seemed to particularly care. She shrugged and turned to Evie. "Let's go."

Once they'd made it back down the staircase, Demetra led Evie out a rear entrance and into the fresh air. They passed beneath a delicate gate of wrought iron and into yet another scene that left Evie stunned.

"Welcome to the Garden of the Dancing Princess. It's my favorite place in all of the Blackmarsh."

They were in a grove of trees unlike any Evie had ever seen. Rows upon rows of them, punctuated by iron benches, packed dirt footpaths, and intricately sculpted shrubbery. The trees, fluttering gently in the breeze, had leaves of silver, gold, and diamond.

"Are those . . . real?" said Evie with wonder.

"Mm-hmm. Come on!" She took Evie's hand and led her down a footpath flanked by glimmering golden leaves. "My father paid a fortune to have them brought here."

"I've never seen anything like it." Evie caressed one of the leaves with her fingertips. It had the same coarseness of any leaf, the same pliability, but it was made entirely of gold.

"I spend quite a lot of time out here. The kingdom where they're from was just going to destroy them. Can you imagine?"

"That would be a crime."

"Camilla and I pestered Father for weeks to bring them here until he finally agreed." They passed other villagers, from members of court in finely detailed doublets and dresses to peasants and workmen in mud-stained frocks. All bowed their heads respectfully to Demetra as they passed, and all had an extra twinkle in their eye to see her. They turned at a fork in the path and entered a row of diamond trees. The leaves tinkled like music as Demetra ran her hand along a lower bough.

"Listen, Demetra, it's really nice to see you and I hate to spoil this lovely day, but there's something I've got to tell you. I'm afraid it isn't very nice."

"What is it? What's happened?"

"It's a bit difficult to explain. On my way here I stopped at an inn—"

"You were robbed, weren't you? I've heard people always get robbed at inns."

"No, I'm afraid it's much worse than that. I was upstairs in my room when these three women burst into the place. They were dressed all in black, and they had these . . . *fangs* hanging from their necks."

"What?"

"It was all very confusing, but they . . ." Evie sighed. She couldn't think of a way to soften what had happened. "They killed the innkeeper's wife. With swords."

"Oh, Evie!" She took Evie's hand. "Are you all right?"

"I'm fine, though they did come after me as well."

"Who were they? Bandits?"

"No," said Evie. "They were princesses."

Demetra blinked several times, as though she couldn't quite comprehend what Evie had said. "Princesses?"

"Yes. That's what the innkeeper called them. And they knew Beatrice as well."

"That can't be right," said Demetra, shaking her head. "Real princesses would never do something like that."

"I don't know how to explain it. But that's what I saw."

"Well, it's over now," said Demetra, putting a comforting hand on Evie's shoulder. "You're safe here. We'll talk to Camilla about it tomorrow when she gets back, all right?"

"All right."

"Oh, Evie, I'm so sorry. That's really horrible. But don't worry, Camilla knows everything about everything. She'll be able to explain it."

Evie nodded and took a deep breath. "You're right. It is over." She glanced around the shimmering garden, then gave Demetra a smile. "Come on, show me the silver ones."

"They're right over here. They're my favorite in the wintertime." The girls walked along the path and turned at the bend. There, rows of silver leaves twinkled in the sunlight as the wind shivered through them.

"So how is your sister, anyway?" said Evie as they walked on. "I'm quite eager to meet her."

"How's my sister? Well, she's Camilla, isn't she."

Evie laughed. "What does that mean?"

"It means I'm ready to be back at the Academy." Now Demetra laughed as well. "I do love my sister, but she sort of sucks up all the air in the room until there's not much left for anyone else. D'you know what I mean?"

"I think so."

"Everyone's so concerned with Camilla, Camilla, Camilla. It's fine, I understand. She's a great princess. I really do mean it when I say she knows everything about everything. But sometimes I'd like . . . well, I'd just like to get back to the Academy, really. And none of this takes my brother into account."

"You have a brother? Where is he?"

"Who knows? Probably up a tower somewhere chucking stones at chickens. He's only four, and an unholy terror. But he's the future king, so everyone delights over every little thing he does." She sat down on a bench and Evie sat next to her. "Enough about my family. I've spent the entire summer with them, but I haven't seen you at all. What have you been up to?"

"Well," said Evie, "I did a bit of fishing with my sister. Practiced with a sword I got in Waldeck. I don't know, that's about it, really."

"What about Remington, did he write you?" asked Demetra with a smile.

"He didn't, actually. I suppose he was busy at court, or—"

"That lazy git! I told him to write you!"

"You spoke to Remington?"

"He was here last week. His father brought him along to teach him about diplomacy or some such. I told him multiple times to write you, and he assured me he would."

"He was here?"

"It's quite annoying he didn't write," said Demetra. "He asked after you as soon as he'd arrived. He even found Anisette and asked her about you as well."

Evie stared at the ground, where a shimmering diamond leaf sat in the dirt.

"What about Maggie? Have you heard from her?"

Evie shook her head, though her mind was still on Remington. *He asked after me.*

"Am I the only one who writes letters round here?"

Evie laughed. "I reckon you might be. Basil never wrote either."

"Basil is excused," said Demetra. "I saw him about a month ago as well. There's a ball each summer where the kingdoms on the north of the bay get together with those on the south."

"And how is he?"

"He said his brothers have been even more insufferable since he became a second-class princess cadet. He spends a lot of his time in the forest trying to avoid them."

"Poor Basil."

"I know. At least I have only two siblings to worry about. Could you imagine twenty-one?" Basil, the youngest of twenty-two boys, had been the only male princess cadet in Ironbone Company. He was very kindhearted, but also a bit awkward, and he always thought he knew more than he really did. Still, he was one of Evie's very best friends, and she couldn't wait to see him again. "So you didn't write Remington either? What is wrong with you people?"

"I told you, I don't know how to use those birds."

"Parchment hawks couldn't be simpler. I'll teach you. Perhaps we can write Remington a letter tonight. I'll even spray a bit of Camilla's perfume on it."

"I'm sure the hawk will like that."

Demetra laughed as Evie blushed, and the two friends sat together in the Garden of the Dancing Princess until night fell and distant thunder began to roll across the bay, driving them back to the safety of the castle. It had felt so good to laugh and reminisce with her old friend that Evie had almost managed to shake the lingering feeling of dread at the memory of poor Marie and the flashing blades of the princesses in black.

Almost.

THE WIND WHISTLED past her face as she soared toward a cloud. She flapped her arms—no, wings. They were wings. She was a dragon, and she was flying. She pinned her wings back and dove for the top of the massive bloom of white. She closed her eyes as tiny ice crystals bounced off her bright green scales. She twirled through the heart of the cloud, her spirit soaring. Finally, she emerged back into the clear blue sky and her wings were gone.

She plummeted through the air as the ground raced toward her at a terrifying speed. Her arms felt like tiny sticks, powerless against the rush of wind. The ground was getting closer. Closer. Just as it was about to smash her to bits, she realized that there was a ring of people standing there watching. They wore black dresses and sharp wolf's fangs around their necks. And all of them were smiling . . .

Her eyes popped open just as she fell off her perch. She landed on the edge of a polished oak table, upending it onto herself with a crash. A moment later, reality caught up with her. It had only been a dream. She was in a lavish bedchamber. There was a four-poster bed with a deep red coverlet. Chairs and tables. Paintings of nobility lining the walls. An iron chandelier hanging from the timber-framed ceiling. A small writing desk in a half-domed alcove with latticed windows that looked out at the thundering sea.

She had been crouched like a dragon atop two chairs with crushed velvet upholstery that had been pushed together, back-to-back, to create a perch. She stood and righted the table. Then, remembering that this magnificent chamber was Demetra's bedroom, she chuckled and shook her head.

If only she could see the chunk of stone where I usually sleep.

She went through the door and into the antechamber, which was only slightly smaller than the dragon cave. "Hello?"

Demetra popped out from a cavernous clothes closet. "Ah, there you are. Here, this'll look lovely on you." She brought Evie a dress the color of a ripe plum with a golden braided belt and matching trim. "Yours is being laundered. It should be ready before we go. Come, put it on! There's someone downstairs who can't wait to see you."

Evie dressed and followed Demetra up and down several spiral staircases until finally they arrived in a wide tunnel leading to the feast hall. It was, as was everything in the Blackmarsh, enormous. Voices and clinking cutlery filled the room. Hundreds of candles lined the walls, illuminating ancient tapestries of knights battling dragons, or battling each other on horseback. The formal table ringed the room like a giant horseshoe, surrounded by high-backed chairs. Everything looked to be made of wood or fur or horn. The smells of steaming food made Evie's stomach grumble.

The King sat at the center of the horseshoe, with the Queen to his right and another woman to his left. Her hair, the same shade of gold as Demetra's and her mother's, was pulled back into a braid with a delicate tiara resting on top. It had to be Princess Camilla.

"Oi, dragonbreath!" came a familiar voice. Evie turned and saw the smiling face of Anisette, one of the first friends she'd made at the Academy. Anisette had been discharged halfway through the first year after a fight with Malora, Evie's stepsister, and had returned to the Blackmarsh to assist Princess Camilla.

"Anisette!" She ran to the small table set back against the wall where Anisette and some others were eating their breakfasts. They hugged. "Oh, I'm so happy to see you!"

"Me as well. How have you been?"

"So much better for being here. And you?"

"Oh, I'm having the bloody time of my life! After watching Camilla in action, I know I was never meant to be a princess. I seen her kill four witches with my own eyes. Four!"

"Incredible," said Evie.

"Come, Demetra! We depart in fifteen minutes!" shouted the Queen.

"It's all right, go on," said Anisette. "We'll have a proper catch-up next time."

Evie turned to Demetra. "Can't we eat here?"

"No, ma'am. You're one of the highborn now," said Anisette with a wink. "Degenerates and basebloods here, I'm afraid."

"That's right!" said an old man, raising his cup.

"I'll see you next time, Eves."

"Come on," said Demetra, leading Evie up to the main table. They took the two open chairs facing the royal family.

"Cutting it a bit close, aren't we?" said the Queen.

"Sorry, Mother."

"Camilla, this is Demetra's friend. The one who—"

"Evie. Of course," said Camilla, tipping her head in greeting. "I heard all about what you did last year. Quite a feat for a third-class girl. And do you believe you're the fabled Warrior Princess, as everyone else seems to?"

"No," said Evie, blushing. "No, of course not." She quickly grabbed a platter of grapes and busied herself with the food.

"Well, that certainly puts you in the minority," said Camilla.

Evie glanced across the table at the King, who scowled as he ate his food. All along the table, other nobles ate their breakfasts in polite conversation.

"Mum," said Demetra, "I've given Evie that dress, if it's all right—"

"Fifteen bloody minutes," said the King darkly. "Why do we always have to leave so bloody early? I'm the king of this land, I should decide when we leave!"

"Yes, yes, you're the king of the whole world," said the Queen. "But that doesn't mean you can alter time, now, does it."

The King hunched over and continued shoveling food into his furious face.

"Your heroics with that witch have helped us immensely," said Camilla. Evie was starting to notice that Demetra's sister never smiled. She had intense eyes, intensely focused. "It's allowed us to determine their power structure much more accurately—"

"More of this nonsense!" bellowed the King. "Can't a man eat in peace?"

"Father doesn't like mornings," Demetra whispered to Evie. "Or afternoons or evenings."

"It isn't nonsense, Father," said Camilla, completely unintimidated. "Thanks to Evie, we've been able to piece together the witches' hierarchy—"

"Hierarchy?" he roared. "They're bloody witches, girl, they live in mud huts in the woods! You've all gone fat-witted on your own self-importance!"

Camilla just shook her head and rolled her eyes. "You've no idea what's happening out there, Father. These modern witches appear to be far more organized than you think, not like the solitary hags you're used to. And Evie here has helped us map out their leadership. That's why we've taken to calling them the Seven Sisters now. The six we already knew of plus Evie's mother—"

"She's not my mother," said Evie, a bit more forcefully than she'd intended.

"Right, of course. Sorry."

"Yes, well done. You've managed to rename a bunch of witches," grumbled the King.

Camilla rolled her eyes, then addressed Evie. "I've been working with other Pennyroyal graduates from across the land to gather information about the Seven Sisters' movements. We've been compiling a dossier that we hope will one day allow us to—"

"A dossier!" shouted the King, spitting a piece of sausage across the table. It landed in Evie's hair, and she quickly wiped it away. "A dossier? And what do you call these?" He pounded his fist on a stack of parchments in front of him.

"Father, the witch charts don't show—"

"The witch charts show everything! Clear straight through to Waldeck!"

Camilla shook her head and turned back to Evie. "The witches are in retreat, he's right about that. When you disrupted their plans last year, it left them in complete disarray. And it isn't just here. We've been getting reports from across the land that they've gone deeper into the enchanted forests. The people have more hope now than they have in ages."

"Yes, precisely," said the King, jamming a knuckle down on the witch charts. "They've gone. Nothing more needs to be said, does it?"

"Just because *you* don't understand witches doesn't mean they shouldn't be understood. And just because they've gone a bit quiet doesn't mean they've gone."

"Bah!"

"Oh, Mum, that reminds me," said Camilla. "You've got to close the upper gates. Princess Quicksilver said in the latest newsletter that witches have started studying a kingdom's weaknesses before they attack—"

"Bwa! Bwa-ha-ha!" bellowed the King. "Witches attacking the Blackmarsh, have you gone batty?"

"It's true, Your Majesty," called Anisette from the lowborn table. "We captured one in the forest and she knew all about the upper gates, didn't she, Princess?"

"Malarky!" he shouted with a laugh. "Malarky and cheese soup, that's what I say! Enough of the upper gates, and enough of your bloody newsletters!"

"Father, there is far more value in princesses communicating with one another than in any of your old-fashioned ideas about instinct."

"Instinct, girl," he said, aiming a chicken bone at Evie's face. "That's all a good princess needs, and don't you forget it. Newsletters and princess meetings and Seven Sisters and all that rubbish, it's all there to get your head going round and round 'til you can't see straight!" Now he wheeled on Camilla. "All you need to do your job is your own instincts. There could be Seven Thousand bloody Sisters and they still couldn't attack the Blackmarsh!"

"Estella!" shouted the Queen to one of the servants. "Why aren't you upstairs filling the last of the trunks?"

"I'm sorry, Majesty," said the servant as she bowed out of the room.

When the Queen stood, the breakfast quickly began to dissolve. Evie and Demetra devoured as much as they could as the rest of the slow-moving royal family began to head toward the door. Finally, with their cheeks still bulging, they followed.

The castle bustled with footmen and handmaids, with trunks and heavy cloaks. Demetra whisked Evie through the chaos and outside to the courtyard, where the traveling party was organized and waiting, including Boy. He looked better than he had since she'd gotten him, brushed and washed and well fed. The King and Queen worried their way down the stairs, shouting orders to anyone within earshot. Demetra swung atop a white horse, lightly caparisoned in silks of Blackmarsh red, while Evie climbed onto Boy.

"Look at that!" said Anisette, coming down the staircase with a smile. "Demetra's been riding every day this summer. She's completely over that fear of horses."

"That's right," said Demetra proudly. "It was the one thing I wanted to work on this summer. The first few weeks were agony, but after a while I really started to enjoy it. They're not so bad once you get comfortable." She patted her horse affectionately.

"Listen, Evie," said Anisette, checking Boy's straps. "The witch charts are quite good, but keep an eye out. There's a lot of nasty stuff out there. If there's one thing I've learned working with Camilla, it's that a whole pile of treaties won't stop a gang of bandits—"

"Wait," said Evie, remembering. "Camilla! We can't leave until we've spoken to Camilla, remember?"

"Of course," said Demetra. "Where's she gone?"

"Camilla?" said Anisette. "D'you want me to find her?"

"I'm right here," said Camilla, emerging from the castle. She handed some documents to one of the guardsmen in the traveling party, then came over to join them. "All ready for year two, then?"

"Listen, Camilla," said Demetra, "Evie's got something to ask you about. Go on, Evie."

"You'd better make it quick," said Camilla. "We're hosting some of the local princesses from the south bay, and they should be arriving any minute. Are we ready for them, Anisette?"

"I'll make sure of it, Princess. Good luck, ladies!" she said with a nod to Evie and Demetra.

"Bye, Anisette."

She ran up the stairs and disappeared into the castle. Camilla looked up at Evie without a smile.

"Oh, uh . . . well, I saw something on my way here, and I wasn't quite sure what to make of it—"

"She saw three princesses kill an old lady," said Demetra. "Sorry, Evie, you're too slow."

"Three princesses?" said Camilla. And for the first time, she seemed genuinely confused. "Are you quite sure? Why should princesses want to hurt anyone?"

"They burst into the inn where I was staying and started harassing the innkeeper. Asking if he'd seen someone called Javotte. Then they—"

"Javotte?" said Camilla.

"Yes. He said he didn't know where she was and they just started attacking. It was horrendous."

"Javotte," said Camilla with a frown. "That's very odd."

"See? I told you she knew everything about everything," said Demetra. "So who is she?"

"Javotte is a princess of the blood who went mad many years ago. She was discharged from Pennyroyal Academy after her first year and just sort of lost her mind. She vanished some time ago, and no one has heard from her since. I've no idea why anyone would be looking for her, much less three princesses."

A trumpeter blasted a short fanfare. The King and Queen climbed into their carriage, and a whole fleet of horsemen started down the hill toward the gatehouse. "Come, Demetra!" bellowed the King.

"You'd better go," said Camilla. "Don't let it worry you, all right? I'll mention it to the princesses when they arrive and we'll keep an eye out."

"Thanks very much," said Evie.

"Demetra, move that horse or we're leaving you behind!"

"Come on, Evie. Father doesn't make idle threats."

"Be safe," said Camilla. "Mind the witch charts and mind your instincts. And most importantly, don't forget to enjoy your second year!"

Evie and Demetra waved goodbye, then rode after the traveling party. They made their way to the gatehouse just as the enormous slabs of wood inside creaked open to reveal the heather-covered cliffs arcing around the bay. Evie glanced up at one of the towers and saw Jensen there, waving. She gave him a smile and followed the rest of the party out into the wide world.

As the group climbed the hill to the tops of the cliffs, Evie's eyes remained to her right, to the roiling sea below. Huge slaps of water rose high into the air, dissolving into sprays of foam. She thought of her stepsister, Malora. She hadn't in quite some time, but Camilla's mention of Countess Hardcastle over breakfast brought that day on the tower rushing back into Evie's memory. After spending the previous year learning how horrible, how truly evil, witches were, it was quite a shock to feel such compassion for one. As the water rolled toward the shore, a wall of black covered in feathery white waves, she wondered if Malora had managed to keep any of her humanity, or if she was a witch completely, right down to her heart and soul, or whatever a witch had in place of a heart and soul. And on top of all that, where was she now? Had she joined the Seven Sisters, or was she all alone out there in the great big world?

As the days passed, the royals and their entourage lumbered along through the mountain passes, the King and Queen forever arguing about what seemed to be trivial things. Which route should they take home? Who would greet the Queen of Waldeck first? Was Demetra's little brother warm enough or was he, as the King said, roasting alive like a pigeon on the sun? There was no sign of trouble, witch or otherwise. They kept to the main roads, and each kingdom they encountered welcomed them like the royalty that they were. It was a much easier journey than the one Evie had taken alone with Boy. She hadn't eaten a single slug since they'd left the Blackmarsh.

One day, as they passed through a gentle valley between two spectacular, snow-topped mountains, Evie and Demetra were playing a game to pass the time, envisioning what sorts of curses they would put on people if they were witches. Demetra nearly fell off her horse with laughter at Evie's suggestion. The previous year she'd cured the curse of an unlikable grump of a cadet named Prince Forbes, turning him from a pig back into a human. If she were a witch, she said, she'd turn him into a plate of bacon.

"There you are!" came the gruff voice of the King, interrupting the game. He rode back to join them, his wolf furs fluttering in the chilly autumnal wind, and jerked his chin at Demetra. "Go handle your mother, will you? She's convinced we've left a trunk back in Woodgate and I'm afraid I'll throw her in the lake if I have to listen to any more of it."

"Yes, Father," said Demetra. She rode ahead to find the Queen's carriage.

Evie was suddenly quite uncomfortable. The King wasn't leaving. He rode next to her, an awkward silence in the air.

"What was your name again?" His voice was brusque, though he was clearly trying to sound less so.

"Evie, Your Serene and Exalted—"

"Oh, stop it. I can't stand that bloody title. So you're Callahan's little girl."

"Yes."

"Well, I must tell you, I hadn't thought about that old bear in years. But hearing his name has made me realize how much I miss him."

"Did you know him well, Your Majesty?"

"Well enough, I should think. He was quite the hunter, or so he believed."

"Did you know my mother as well?"

"No, I only saw Callahan on hunts. No queens, or talk of queens, allowed." The King chuckled to himself. "Exceptional man, he was. Though he did have his quirks, didn't he?"

"I'm afraid I don't remember much about him. He died when I was only five."

"Ah, I see." His tone softened a bit when he heard that. "Well, he could be a bit of an odd duck, your father. One thing I remember quite well about old Callahan, he never needed much in the way of sleep. There was a group of us, kings mostly from the east, but a few others as well. We'd all go out for a fortnight each spring looking for bears, stoats, whatever crossed our paths. Callahan even shot an arrow at a dragonfly once." He roared with laughter, which made Evie smile. "Truth be told, those hunts were mostly an excuse to get away from our children." His laughter rumbled again. "Well, old Callahan, he had his own ways about him. The rest of us would make camp for the night, roasting whatever we'd caught that day, then trading stories until we fell asleep round the fire, drowning in mead or whatever disgusting concoction King Hubert had made that day. And every night round that time, old Callahan would ride off from camp. I'd wake to relieve myself or have another bite of venison, and he'd be gone. Always made it back for morning, though, and never the worse for wear, even without sleep."

Evie was riveted. She'd never heard anything about her human father except what Countess Hardcastle had told her, and she didn't know if she could trust any of what the witch had said. "Where would he go?"

"Ah, so you're as curious as I was! I'd had enough of the old man's sneaking about, so I followed him one night. After watching him do it for years, I had to know what he was up to. Now that I think of it, that might have been our last hunt before he was killed. In any event, who can say why I picked that night to follow him—too much wine is the likely answer— but follow him I did. He rode due north until he reached the coast. I settled in at the edge of the forest where I could still see him but he couldn't see me. And do you know what he did? He stood there, knee-deep in the sea, just staring. He looked up at the stars from time to time, took a little stroll down the beach to feel the sand in his toes. But mostly he just stood and stared out to sea. For hours. I kept waiting for the old loon to do something!" The King laughed. "Then, just before dawn, he mounted up and rode back to camp for another day of hunting, just as chirpy as could be. An odd one, that father of yours. Though as good a shot with an insult as a bow."

The King's laughter faded to silence as Evie let his story linger.

"Father!" cried Demetra. "Father, hurry! Mother's trying to turn the carriage back!"

"Blast!" he yelled, then spurred his horse ahead.

Evie imagined her father, the man whose portrait was pressed inside the dragon scale dangling around her neck, standing at water's edge in the dead of night. What was he thinking about? Why was it so important for him to come to the sea? It made her heart ache to think she'd never know the answer.

They made camp that night beneath the stars. The fight between Demetra's mother and father had cost them the opportunity to reach the next kingdom. But even sleeping in the wild was an elaborate production with Demetra's family. Giant pavilions striped red and white were erected, with goose-down pillows to sleep on. The Queen insisted they move back from the road, with the royal pavilion positioned in the middle in case anyone came along. The King argued that he'd rather sleep beneath the big oak tree, but his wife insisted that decorum be observed. Finally, once everything had been settled (leaving the King in his customary bad mood), Evie was able to lie down on her back and stare up at the stars, the only sound Demetra's heavy snoring. She held her father's picture above her so the stars were behind him. She stared at his laughing face until her arms finally gave out, then she went into the tent and fell asleep with his picture resting over her heart.

. . .

The King and Queen once again dominated breakfast the next morning. As easily as Demetra seemed to ignore it, Evie had to admit she found it somewhat entertaining. The guards stood by, expressionless, as the royals bickered and made up, then bickered again. And the more she saw them behave like just another ordinary family, the more comfortable she felt around them. Perhaps even more comfortable than she was around her own family.

They packed up camp and continued west. Aside from the steady tromping of hooves and the creaking of axles, only the wind through the leaves made any sort of noise. The world was still and quiet, tucked beneath a puffy white blanket of clouds. Evie rode along in silence for more than an hour, the King's story about her father drifting in and out of her thoughts. Then, quite suddenly, the quiet of the day was disrupted by distant shouts from the royal guardsmen at the front of the party.

"Smoke! Smoke!"

Everyone urged their horses forward, and as they followed the road over the crest of a hill, they saw what the guards were shouting about. White smoke rose from the smoldering remains of an outpost at the bottom of the valley.

"Looks like someone wasn't too keen on there being a village here, Majesty."

"Indeed." The King's face darkened. "Come."

He rode down the hill, his guardsmen following behind. Demetra and Evie rode after them, leaving the rest of the party to follow. A small castle, crumbled and covered with black plumes of scorch, was being picked over by peasants. Other buildings, apparently made of wood, had not survived. Casks of grain spilled across the ground. Chickens and goats milled about, free from their damaged pens. Two knights, their embroidered doublets clearly distinguishing them from the villagers, helped to haul giant bricks of mortared sandstone out of the rubble. Sweat dripped from their faces despite the bite in the air.

"What happened here?" bellowed the King.

"Good day, Your Majesty," said one of the villagers. The knights noticed the King and fell to their knees.

"Stand, lads, stand and tell me what's happened."

"Well, Your Majesty, my friend and I were just over those hills at Pardoogan's Castle when we saw the smoke. We came as quickly as we could, but this is all that was left." He looked around at the devastation. "The villagers swear it wasn't a dragon attack, Majesty. Nor witches either."

"It's true, Majesty, it's true!" said an old man, limping toward the horses. His face was filthy, and a streak of blood ran down the side of his face. "It was a whole group of them come through! Destroyed it all!"

"A group of what?" said the King.

The old man's face wrinkled in thought, as though he couldn't quite grasp the answer. "Well, Your Majesty . . . they looked a bit like her." He raised a gnarled old finger and pointed straight at Demetra.

There were more shouts from the north, and the thundering of hooves coming down the road. The guardsmen unsheathed their weapons, but when they saw that it was only a single rider, and most likely a knight, based on his garb, they stood down.

He was charging toward them at top speed, shouting something they couldn't understand.

"Now what in blazes is *he* on about?" said the King.

"Dragons," said Evie.

Sure enough, as he drew nearer, his words became clear as ice. "Dragon! Dragon!"

The knights ran to their horses and mounted up as the third knight slowed to a stop. He was terrified, his eyes wide as the moon. "Help me, sirs! Help! A dragon's attacking the village!"

"Go!" shouted one of the knights, and the three of them thundered away over the hill. From somewhere far in the distance, they could hear the echo of roaring and crumbling stone.

"We'd best double our pace if there are dragons about," said the King. "Onward!" He led the party down the road to the west. Evie wiped a tear from her eye and tried to block out the distant screams of the dragon as they resounded across the countryside.

The old man whose home had just been destroyed looked up at her.

"I'm sorry," she said.

"Cost of life." He turned and began to clean up the rubble. "Cost of life."

FINALLY, AFTER NEARLY a fortnight on the road, the flags of Waldeck appeared in the western sky. The rest of the journey had been mercifully uneventful. Now the traveling party needed only to circle around the lake and climb the mountain on the far shore to arrive at the kingdom gates. It sat heavily atop the mountain, thick turret towers peering out from behind granite walls. Compared with the Blackmarsh, Waldeck wasn't a particular beauty, but the sight of it filled Evie with gratitude.

"Look, Boy," she said softly. "It's your home."

He tore off a bouquet of grass and ate, stomping his hoof to chase the flies.

They made their way around the lake, and as they approached the kingdom, the gates opened wide and a welcoming party rode out to meet them. Six guards in deep violet robes with a coat of arms sewn into them approached. They dismounted ten feet in front of the royal carriage and each took a knee.

"Your Serene and Exalted Majesties," one of them said, causing Demetra to roll her eyes. "Welcome to the Kingdom of Waldeck."

"Thank you, sir," said the King.

"If it pleases you, Majesties, the Queen should like to see you immediately."

"Now?" grumbled the King. "Before lunch?"

The guardsmen, still on their knees, exchanged uncertain looks. "Uh . . . that was her request, Your Majesty." The King scowled darkly. "Er, though I'm certain we could find something for you to eat somewhere. Some local fruits, perhaps? Or some bread?"

"I've got bread in my house," said one of the other guards, not noticing the King's ever-darkening scowl. "It's only a week old. Me wife scraped the mold this morning."

"Brilliant. We'll just pop round his and fetch the bread, then—"

"Oh, sod the food, let's go. If she wants us straightaway, then who are we to argue."

"Very good, Your Majesty."

The Waldeckian guard led the traveling party through the gates, where it was met by roads lined with villagers.

"Now, that's a proper welcome," said the King with his first smile in days.

The villagers, cheering and screaming, weren't holding the flag of Waldeck, however, or even the flag of the Blackmarsh. Everywhere waved the four-field flag of Pennyroyal Academy.

As they rode through the crowd, it quickly became apparent that Evie and Demetra were the ones they'd come to see.

"Insolence," muttered the King. "Not a single Blackmarsh red."

"As y-you can see, Your Majesty," stammered one of the guards, "the kingdom is quite excited to host the new recruits. We've all had a bit of princess fever after what happened last year."

"Mmm."

Demetra smiled and waved to the crowd. Boys and girls waved back, some dressed in handmade costumes designed to look like Pennyroyal uniforms. "Come on," she said to Evie. "Let's get down to enlistment and see if we made it before the first years."

"But what about . . . ?"

"Father!" she called, reining her horse to a stop. "We're going now!"

"Eh?"

"Evie and I are going to enlistment. I'll see you at the end of term."

"Off the horse, then," he said. She scowled at him. "Well? Are you planning to just leave him by the side of the road? That's a quality horse."

Demetra dismounted and began untying her small pack. She handed the reins over to one of the guards, who led it away with the rest of the traveling party.

"Goodbye, Mother!"

A hand came out of the carriage window and waved a silk kerchief.

Demetra turned to Evie with a smile. "Shall we?" She began walking down the road, away from Castle Waldeck. Evie glanced back at the royal family, but they seemed far more interested in making themselves presentable to the Queen than in seeing the girls off.

Evie dismounted and led Boy after Demetra.

"What about all those trunks your mother packed?"

"I told her not to bother. All I need is in here." She patted the small knapsack she'd been given as a third-class princess cadet.

The kingdom had a gentle slope that led away from the castle, which they followed at a leisurely pace. It felt good to be walking, escaping the crowds who waited near the gates for more future knights and princesses, and it felt good to be alone with Demetra.

"Let's make one stop before we go down there."

"Of course," said Demetra. "Where to?"

They wandered through the kingdom in search of the marketplace. Everything looked vaguely familiar to Evie, though she'd only been there less than an hour last time. Still, after a short walk, they found it. The stalls weren't nearly as busy as they'd been before. Half of them were closed up, and the other half were minded by bored or, in one case, sleeping, shopkeepers. Evie scanned the high road until she saw a woman in a brown frock with a bonnet on her head.

"Come on!" They approached the woman, who was just starting to shutter her horse tack shop. "Pardon me, ma'am."

"Yes?" said the woman. When she turned around, she looked as though she'd seen a ghost. "It's you!"

"I've brought back your horse. It was terribly kind of you to lend him to me."

"I never lent any horse to you, young lady. That was a gift."

"And I very much appreciate it. I don't know if I would have made it home without him. But I'm headed back to the Academy, and I'm afraid he can't come with me."

"I'll not take back a gift. It's bad luck."

"I see. Well, perhaps you'll look after him for me, then, while I'm away. I could come back for him again at the end of term?" She held out the reins.

The old woman's face broke into a smile as she patted the horse's back. "Very well, my dear, I'll look after your horse. He always was one of my son's favorites."

Evie stroked Boy's head and leaned her face against his. "I'll see you soon, Boy. Thank you for everything."

She transferred her things from the saddlebags to her Pennyroyal Academy knapsack, then untied her sword and held it awkwardly in her hands as the old woman led Boy to a trough. She was speaking to him in a gentle voice as they walked off.

"That was very kind, Evie."

"What they did was kind. I'm just trying to repay it," she

said, awkwardly tying the scabbard to the belt of her dress. It pulled a bit, but held. "Shall we?"

"I'm not sure they'll take too kindly to a girl walking through a kingdom armed. Where did you get that, anyway?"

"Here," said Evie. "It was given to me." She pulled it halfway free.

"Blimey, that's a beautiful sword!"

"I know. It's fun as well. While you were writing letters, I was slashing enemies."

"Just keep it sheathed and we should be all right. It'd be a shame to have it confiscated."

And with that, the girls made their way through the deserted roads of Waldeck in search of the enlistment area. Aside from the large crowds at the entrance, the kingdom felt rather empty. Still, the closer they got to the courtyard where they had been deposited the previous year, the more their excitement grew.

"This is going to be so much better than last year!" said Demetra.

"Well, this bit will be, anyway," said Evie, remembering. "Enlistment was horrendous."

"It wasn't all that bad. I remember there was so much excitement in the air."

"That's because you didn't turn up in spiderwebs."

Demetra laughed. "I'll never forget the look on your face when Beatrice came down and gave you that horrible name. Eleven. At least it wasn't something unruly like Seventy-Eight."

She took a deep breath, smiling up at the wan sunshine. "Ahh, it feels so good to be myself again."

Evie didn't say anything, though she did register the comment. And it was true. She had noticed during her time with the family that they tended to push Demetra to the side a bit.

They turned right at the statue of a woman on horseback, a sword in her hand. Evie wondered if that was what she had looked like riding across the land, sword at her side. *Not when I was climbing out that window at the inn, scared for my life, that's for sure.*

They crossed another wide road of packed dirt. The buildings looming over them had white walls lined with dark wooden beams. There was a tavern and a butcher and a smith, but all were empty.

"Where is everyone?" said Evie.

Her question was soon answered. As they neared the end of the road, they were met with a rumble of voices. They angled left into the courtyard, and both stopped dead in their tracks.

"I reckon we've found them," said Demetra.

It was chaos. There were people everywhere, most of them girls roughly Evie and Demetra's age, but also a large number of parents, staff, and other villagers. Guards in Waldeck violet held back massive crowds at the edge of the courtyard, all cheering for the new recruits. The crowds were so big, Evie couldn't even see to the far side where the enlistment tables were set up.

"What in the world . . ."

"There must be twice as many as last year."

Even as they stood marveling at the massive crowd, more girls raced up from behind to enlist.

"I don't understand," said Demetra. "Surely they can't all be coming. How would they fit? I'll put up with a lot, Evie, but I'm not sharing a bunk."

"Come on. There's Princess Hazelbranch."

They stepped into the crowd, which was positively crackling with excitement. There were smiles as far as the eye could see, girls from all across the land hoping for their chance to become princesses.

"This is madness," said Demetra. "D'you suppose the knights' enlistment is like this?"

As they worked their way toward Princess Hazelbranch, the kindhearted woman who had been their House Princess the previous year, something unusual started to happen. All around them, girls stopped what they were doing and turned to look. And to a person they were looking at Evie.

"It's her!"

"She's here! She's here!"

"Mum, look! It's Eleven! She's the one they were talking about!"

The previous year, when Evie had turned up at enlistment, all eyes had fallen on her because she was so grubby and filthy, and had arrived with Remington, the most famous knight cadet in all the land. This year, she was once again the center of attention, but it was for a very different reason.

"I can't believe it's you!" squealed one girl as she leapt forward and touched Evie's arm.

"You're the one who inspired me to come here!"

"Can I sit with you on the coach?" said another, walking backward in front of Evie and Demetra. "Or perhaps you'll have lunch with me?"

"Sure," said Evie with an uncomfortable smile. Then she stepped behind Demetra and let her cut a path through the crowd. "What is going on?"

"You're famous, Evie."

The roar grew louder as word of the-girl-who-saved-the-Academy's arrival spread to the townspeople at the edge of the courtyard. More and more delirious girls called her name. More and more smiling parents looked down at her. She couldn't make herself small enough behind Demetra's back to stem the flood of attention.

"You're the one who stopped Malora!"

"I love your work!"

"You saved us from the witches!" said one of the fathers, who was as awestruck as all the young girls around him. "You've driven them away!"

The crowd was pushing in on them, making it harder to get to Princess Hazelbranch. One girl was so overwhelmed to be in Evie's presence, she had tears streaming down her cheeks. "I want to be just like you!"

"Let's get out of here!" cried Evie.

"I can't move!"

"Girls! Girls, over here!" called a voice above the din.

"There she is!" yelled Evie, pointing to the smiling face of Princess Hazelbranch. She was slightly taller than the girls enlisting, and was able to force her way through to meet Evie and Demetra. "Step back, please! Everyone make way!" she called, though her voice never lost its soft sweetness. Finally, she took hold of Demetra's hand, pulling them free of the crowd and off to the side of the enlistment tables. Now that Evie was with a member of staff, the crowds gave her some space, though they all kept staring and repeating her name.

"It's so lovely to see you, girls!" said Hazelbranch. "This is quite an event, isn't it?"

"These can't possibly be the new recruits," said Evie.

"Most of them, yes. It seems you've become as famous as Cinderella, young lady," said Hazelbranch with a wink.

"Where are they all going to sleep?" said Demetra. "I can't share a bunk, Princess, *please* don't make me share a bunk!"

"That's what the poor Headmistress General is trying to work out. I'm afraid we weren't at all prepared for these sorts of numbers." Evie glanced down the line of enlistment tables, where one recruit after another was processed and sent to the coaches, to where Beatrice, the Headmistress General of Pennyroyal Academy, was being run ragged with questions. She looked completely overwhelmed as staff and parents alike inundated her and her snarling assistant, Corporal Liverwort. "We've sent for more coaches, but I heard one of the other princesses saying there aren't any available. It could take days with all the back-and-forth just to get everyone there, let alone processed. We've sent an entire forest of hawks asking for help. Poor Rumpledshirtsleeves is already hard at work sewing hundreds of new uniforms." She smiled with such joy that the sight of it calmed Evie's nerves after the crush of the crowd. "It's been quite some time since we've seen the Academy as full as it will be this year. And I, for one, am *thrilled*."

"Where do you want this?" said a surly-looking man in peasant's rags. He was pulling a cart filled with foul-smelling shrubs.

"Ah, good! That coach there, please." As the man hauled the cart away, Evie had to turn her head away to keep from retching.

"What is that?"

"Those are fairyweed bushes. We'll have extra staff this year to accommodate all these cadets, which means we'll need extra provisions for the fairies."

"*That's* what fairies eat?" said Demetra. "No wonder they're so angry."

"Now, ladies," said Hazelbranch, her eyes wide. "You mustn't breathe a word of this to the Headmistress, but I've done a bit of poking around on your behalf. I've been known to be a bit of a sneaker-abouter from time to time," she said with a cheeky grin. "I can't help myself, I'm always so desperate to see where my girls will end up. You and the rest of the Ironbone cadets have been placed in Leatherwolf Company this year!" She did a happy little clap.

"What?" said Evie. "Why have we changed companies?"

"Because you're in the second class! Ironbone Company is only for third-class cadets." She noticed the crestfallen looks on their faces. "This is a good thing, girls. And Princess Copperpot will be a wonderful House Princess for you. She's a bit unusual, but tough as an ogre. I think you're going to like her."

"So we're not with you?" said Evie.

"I'm sorry. I'll have my hands full with all these new girls. But there is one bit of news that should please you. Leatherwolf Company is made up of the girls from Goosegirl and Ironbone, and Goosegirl's commanding officer will be rotated to Schlauraffen Company—I've no idea who they're going to assign to all these new companies. In any event, the Academy has a rather complex formula for issuing assignments that involves alternate-year rotations and the like. It's of no importance except to say that you will get to keep your commanding officer!"

She beamed at them. As it dawned on Evie exactly what Hazelbranch was saying, her heart sank. "You mean . . . ?"

"You'll have another year with your fairy drillsergeant!"

Evie flinched just hearing the words.

"Now, I'd highly recommend you get on this next round of coaches so you don't find yourselves trapped here in Waldeck. I'll see you at the Academy, girls! Off you go!"

They said their goodbyes and tried to navigate through the throngs of recruits. It was difficult to keep hidden with so many girls trying to get Evie's attention. The previous year she hadn't even had a name. Now she couldn't escape it.

"Wait!" she said to Demetra. "Shouldn't we try to tell Princess Beatrice about the attacks?"

"In this?" cried Demetra. "It can wait!"

A girl at the enlistment table screamed so sharply that it cut through the noise of the crowd. She jumped up and down, clutching her hands to her chest. "I'm Cadet Eleven! I'm Cadet Eleven!" Behind her, several other girls looked distraught.

"This is too strange," said Evie with a look of distaste. "Let's get out of here."

"Remington's going to be so jealous. You're more famous than he is!"

Finally they made it out of the crowd and headed for the coaches. Parents and their daughters said goodbye and promised to write, but Evie and Demetra paid them no mind as they searched for the Leatherwolf coach.

"There's no way to tell which is which—"

There was another scream. Evie wheeled just in time to see a spray of red hair, and then she was on her back in the dirt. Her arm was pinned beneath Demetra, who was herself pinned beneath . . .

"Maggie!" shouted Evie. The three of them hugged in a huge pile on the ground.

"You're here!" she shouted. "You finally made it!"

"Yes, well, if you don't mind, I'll just say hello from here," came another voice.

Maggie climbed off, and there stood Basil in the door of the coach, his usual uncomfortable smile on his face.

"Basil!" shouted Evie.

Maggie pulled Evie and Demetra to their feet, then hugged them each properly. "Come on! We've held spots in the back."

Evie gave Basil a hug. He stepped aside to let her in. "After you," he said to Demetra.

Inside, they made their way through a coach that was three-quarters full of the eighty it would eventually hold. Evie recognized many of the faces. Even some of Goosegirl Company looked vaguely familiar from the previous year. But now they were all one. Leatherwolf Company. That would take a bit of getting used to.

"Straight back here," said Maggie. "Basil and I were just catching up on the summer. Didn't you get any of my letters? I was so hoping you'd come to Sevigny." She plopped down on an empty bench, the smile wide across her face. "This is so exciting!"

Evie and Demetra took the bench in front, and Basil sat next to Maggie. "I never got any letters," said Evie. "I mean, I got loads from Demetra, but none from you."

Maggie's smile fell. "Really? That's odd. I sent quite a lot." She shrugged and her smile returned. "Ah, well, I suppose that's what I get for living so ridiculously far away. It'd be a miracle if any of my letters made it past the Glass Mountains."

"Speaking of living far away," said Basil, "I heard you were in the Eastern Kingdoms and didn't even bother to pop by, Evie."

Evie looked at Demetra, who shrugged and said, "I wrote him, too. I write everyone."

"Next time you're off to the Blackmarsh, you've got to come by Witch Head Bay and collect me first. Save me from my brothers for a bit."

"Hang on, you went to the Blackmarsh?" said Maggie.

"I had to get out of the cave. And Demetra invited me, so . . ."

"Nice, isn't it?" said Basil. "Beautiful kingdom."

"It's the most incredible place I've ever seen. You should see the palace, Maggie. Oh, and the garden with all those leaves—"

"The Garden of the Dancing Princess," said Maggie. "I've wanted to see that my whole life."

"And Anisette was there as well!"

Maggie gasped. "Does that mean you got to see Princess Camilla?" Her eyes were as wide as some of the girls outside who had just been goggling at Evie.

"Oh yes. She told us all about how Pennyroyal graduates are compiling information about Calivigne and the Seven Sisters."

"The Seven Sisters?" said Maggie.

"That's what they're calling the witch leadership now."

"Oh. I didn't know that. Must've been fun to be part of the latest excitement. I spent the summer scraping ice off my father's cart." There was a hint of disappointment in Maggie's voice, but none of the others noticed.

"How in the world are they going to fit all these firsties in the barracks?" said Demetra, looking out the window at the roiling crowd.

"I'm jealous you got to meet Camilla," said Maggie, her smile gone. "I'm such a big admirer of hers—"

"Ah, there you are," came a sharp voice. It was Kelbra, one of Malora's best friends. Just behind her was Sage, a girl who had been cursed with no sense of humor. "I was hoping you lot would've just stayed home."

"Come on," said Basil. "Malora's gone. Can't we just move on from this?"

"Move on from what?" spat Kelbra, her lip curled in a snarl. "*Her* thinking she's better than the rest of us?" She flicked her head dismissively at Evie. "I suppose she's got you all convinced that Malora really was a witch, hasn't she?"

"Of course she was, don't be—"

"Right, and did anyone else see it? Anyone? No, they didn't. *Not one person.* So we're all supposed to just take your word that my best friend was a witch who deserved to be tossed out of the Academy."

"What are you talking about? Of course she was a witch!" said Evie. "Have you gone mad?"

"It seems everyone else has. I know what happened out there in the forest. I know that you couldn't bear to be in your sister's shadow. You couldn't bear that she was better than you in every possible way. So you had to make up lies to get her discharged."

"Kelbra, you're wrong about—"

"She was my *friend*," said Kelbra, jutting her finger toward

Evie's face. "And you ruined her life. You'd better hope no one does the same to you."

She glared at Evie for a moment, and then she and Sage turned and found an empty bench near the front of the coach.

"Well," said Demetra with a sigh. "It seems we'll pick up right where we left off."

"Look at the bright side—at least there are only two of them this year," said Basil.

IT WAS NEARLY SUNDOWN when the coach finally emerged from the enchanted forest and into the clearing that held Penny-royal Academy. Evie's heart swelled at the sight of the towers and castles perched atop the hillside. The Queen's Tower, still one of the most remarkable structures she'd ever seen, glowed like a diamond above campus. She couldn't wait to get off the coach and smell the fresh air and the dank corridors and to hear the voices of fairies shouting orders and trumpets sounding across campus at daybreak.

She was home. She was home, and her dragon family was the furthest thing from her mind.

The coach rolled across the stone bridge and into the court-yard arrival area. The old familiar fountain, a princess and a knight standing triumphant, trickled with bubbling water over soft green moss. There were already people everywhere—princesses and knights and woodsmen and scullery maids and trolls and fairies—all scurrying to prepare for the first night with a truly full campus.

"Open the door! All of you off, *now!*" came a familiar voice. The Fairy Drillsergeant had started shouting before the coach had even come to a stop. "Come on, you layabouts, summer's over! Move!"

Evie felt a surge of excitement in her stomach as she followed Demetra down the aisle and off the coach. Even the shouts of the Fairy Drillsergeant couldn't quell the fluttering inside her. It was as though her yearning to be back at the Academy had actually grown stronger now that she was finally there.

"No time for pleasantries, this is an emergency situation!" shouted the tiny fairy, multicolored dust shimmering from her wings. "We've got bargeloads of cadets headed this way and nowhere to house them! The woodsmen are hard at work clearing away the brush, but we've got to get the old barracks sparkling and we have only a few hours to do it!"

A heavy *thunk thunk thunk* echoed across campus, followed by the shouting of men's voices.

"Well? Shall I arrange a gilded carriage to ferry you to the barracks? Or are you going to *move?*"

"What about our things?" asked Kelbra.

"The trolls will see to your things. Now get over there before I solve the barracks problem myself by sending you all home!"

The girls of Leatherwolf Company, with many looks exchanged that said, *Here we go again*, ran off across Hansel's Green, the great, grassy meadow that served as a training field, and headed toward the barracks.

"Not that way, you dunderheads!" shouted the Fairy Drill-sergeant. "Over there!"

Evie looked every which way, but didn't even see the Fairy Drillsergeant, much less which way she was pointing. But then the front of the group began to turn, like a flock of birds in the sky, heading for a small grove of trees and brush about one hundred yards to the left of the main grouping of barracks buildings. Several immense men with hairy backs and massive axes were hacking down trees at a rapid pace. And there, peeking out from the vegetation, were several more long, low barracks buildings. They were overgrown, some so completely covered in bushes and trees that they looked like small hills rather than man-made structures.

The company slowed to a stop at the edge of the grove. Two woodsmen hauled a giant piece of tree trunk away and threw it on top of a stack. Another tree fell, revealing another building buried beneath dirt and moss.

"Welcome to your new home, ladies. We haven't had to use these barracks in years, but now they're all yours."

Small pieces of the barracks' stone walls peeked out from beneath stumps and vines and trees and bracken. Even those were covered in moss and lichens.

"We're going to live in *there*?" said Demetra with distaste. Evie couldn't help but smile. After the cave, these old barracks were positively luxurious.

"Well? You can't *look* them into shape! Get moving, unless you plan to sleep out here on the grass!"

"At the moment that sounds rather appealing," said Basil under his breath.

"Cadet Basil!" said the Fairy Drillsergeant with a smile in her voice. "Oh, how I've missed you."

Basil's face fell. "Er, hello, Fairy Drillsergeant."

"I'd no idea you were such an admirer of our grass here at the Academy. Why don't you and I get to know it a bit better while the rest of the company prepares the barracks?"

"I didn't mean anything by it, Fairy—"

"Cadet Basil has just volunteered to demonstrate a new exercise I've prepared for you second classers! I call them Frog's Legs. And now he's going to show you why. Run in place, Cadet! Move those froggy legs!"

"But—"

"*Run in place!* The rest of you, get to work unless you'd like to join him!"

The girls began to climb through the undergrowth to get to the buried buildings. Evie glanced back at Basil. He was running in place, and every time the Fairy Drillsergeant shouted, "Croak!" he had to drop to his stomach and then jump back to his feet. After only five of them, he already looked as though he might be sick.

"You know who we've got to thank for this, don't you?" said Kelbra loudly. "The famous Cadet Evie!"

"Kelbra, please," said Demetra. "Are we really going to have to listen to this all year?"

"Croak!"

The girls fanned out around the barracks and got to work. Evie could feel the eyes of her new company-mates, the girls who had been in Goosegirl Company the previous year, on her. But all *she* wanted was to be a normal second-class princess cadet like everyone else.

In short order, the cadets were covered in dirt and grime, their faces and arms scratched bloody from branches and thorns. The woodsmen continued to knock down the larger trees, opening up more of the sky to the fading blue of dusk. Basil had rejoined the company after a half hour of Frog's Legs, and his thighs were so wobbly, he could barely stand. The barracks were now mostly uncovered. Some of the girls had gone inside and begun opening windows, chasing away rats and spiders, and scrubbing bunks. About an hour into the work, the other second-class company had arrived from Waldeck. Bramblestick Company was made up of the other two third-class companies from the previous year, Schlauraffen and Stonewitch. They got straight to work on the barracks buildings still hiding beneath the growth, though one of them didn't seem to be at all usable. A corner of its arched rooftop had collapsed, and vines had begun growing inside.

Evie was busy scrubbing windows, which were black with mold. The steady chopping echoed around her. She glanced over at the entrance area, hoping, in truth, for a glimpse of the knight cadets, and among them, Remington. Instead, she saw coach after coach arriving, dumping cadets into the area in front of Pennyroyal Castle. There were people everywhere, with staff shouting to organize them all. Torches had been lit across campus. Evie recognized straightaway which ones belonged to the Dining Hall. Her mouth watered at the thought.

"This is incredible," said Maggie, passing by with an armload of sticks. "How are they possibly going to handle all these people?"

"When do we get to eat, that's the real question," said Basil, scrubbing another window near Evie's.

"Could someone help me here?" said Demetra, struggling under the weight of a fallen branch that was leaning against the roof.

"Hang on!" said Evie, setting her bucket down.

"We've got it!" called two of their new company-mates who had been in Goosegirl Company the previous year. One was tall and lithe with smooth dark skin, and the other was shorter and had tight ringlets of brown hair swept back from her face. Both of them seemed effortlessly regal, even as they strained to help Demetra work the heavy branch to the edge of the roof, where gravity brought it thumping to the ground.

"Thanks!" said Demetra.

"No problem. I'm Nessa and that's Liv," said the taller of the two.

"Demetra."

"Yeah, we know," said Nessa. "She's from Oxie and I'm from Arrie."

"Oxenholtz and Arrenholtz? Really?"

"Yeah," said Liv. "My family holidays at the Blackmarsh every summer."

"What a small world!" said Demetra. "Oh, uh, these are my friends Evie and Basil, and that's Maggie."

"Hiya," they all said.

"They're from Oxie and Arrie, the two kingdoms just below the Blackmarsh. So you must know Prince Düvier, then."

"Of course!" said Nessa, laughing. "He's married to my cousin Marlow—"

"Attention, second-class cadets!" sang Princess Hazelbranch, making her way through the gathering darkness with another woman at her side. Bramblestick and Leatherwolf, the two second-class princess companies, assembled on the grass in front of the most habitable of the barracks. Hazelbranch handed her torch to one of the woodsmen, who used it to light the hearths inside the newly excavated structures. Smoke rose from the chimneys. The whole area began to glow orange as the sky faded to black.

"Isn't this exciting?" said Hazelbranch, her eyes wide. "Nearly full capacity! This is what it used to be like round here!"

"Yes, Princess," said several of the girls lethargically.

"My name is Princess Hazelbranch, House Princess for Ironbone Company, over there." She pointed into the darkness, toward the barracks where Evie had lived all of the previous year. "Now, before you're excused for supper, I'd like to introduce you to your House Princesses. Bramblestick Company, may I present Princess Helgadoon."

Helgadoon stepped forward and curtsied. Her black hair was braided across her shoulders, her eyes as kind as Hazelbranch's. "I'm very pleased to meet you, cadets," she said. "We're going to have a lot of fun this year. And I want you to know that if there's anything you need, any concerns you might have about anything at all, my door is always open. I am here for you."

"Yes, Princess," said the Bramblestick cadets.

"Right, well, let's go have our supper, shall we? Come along." She led her cadets across Hansel's Green toward the torchlight of the Dining Hall. Those who remained looked at Princess Hazelbranch with confusion. She appeared to be alone.

"Fear not, Leatherwolf Company, I haven't forgotten you. Your House Princess should be along any moment . . ." She peered over her shoulder into the darkness, but there was no one there. When she turned back, her voice had gone quiet. "Now, ladies, I must warn you about Princess Copperpot. She's had a very bad time of it with witches over the years, but don't let her appearance fool you. She's one of the most experienced princesses the Academy has got, and you're very lucky to have her." She glanced back again, then said loudly, "Ah, and here she comes now! Cadets, let me introduce your new House Princess, Princess Copperpot."

A malformed figure lurched out of the darkness. It was a

princess, that much was clear, but she seemed to have been cobbled together in a workshop. She wore an ash-gray tunic dress with emerald trim that bent around the strange S shape of her body. Both of her arms were left arms, as evidenced by one of her hands facing outward. One of her legs was made of wood and had no knee or ankle joints built into it. An eye patch covered her right eye, and long scars peeked out on either side. Wispy white hair sprouted from the left side of her otherwise bald head, and an elegant tiara was perched on top.

Evie could feel the entire company recoil at the sight of her. To make things worse, Princess Copperpot seemed to arrive furious. She cast her eye over them, her mouth pursed into a smile that threatened to break into a shout. "Good day," she said in a voice that sounded like a hen's cluck, "Leatherwolf Company."

"Right," said Princess Hazelbranch. "Shall I just leave you to it, then?" She beamed at the girls, then turned and walked off toward the Ironbone barracks. Evie's heart sank as she disappeared into the night.

"Line up, please, cadets," squawked Copperpot. The girls did as they were told, forming a grid on the newly cleared lawn. She ambled slowly between them like a cart with one square wheel, her head bobbing and darting about. "You might have noticed something a bit different about me. My chicken!"

Just then, a rooster *buhgawk*-ed from the edge of the firelight. He had white feathers with black spots, a frizzled white crest atop his head, and a brilliant red wattle dangling below his beak.

"Rooster," said Copperpot. "Same thing."

The rooster *buhgawk*-ed again.

"His name is Lance. He is my most trusted compatriot, and he is fully authorized to assume my command should I become incapacitated." She jerked her face in front of Maggie's, eyes wide. "This has all been cleared with Beatrice, and you can check if you like!"

Maggie said nothing, just held her breath until Copperpot backed away to continue her patrol.

"Now, where was I . . . Leatherwolf Company. A second-class company. You shall undergo the standard course of second-class training, where you will learn courage, compassion, kindness, and discipline, as well as a host of other practical princess skills, all, of course, leading up to Witches' Night, and finally your end-of-year exams . . ."

"Pardon me, Princess. What's Witches' Night exactly?" said Cadet Idonea, a highborn girl who had been in Goosegirl Company the previous year.

"Witches' Night is the greatest obstacle of your second year. It will test all that you have learned thus far at the Academy. You will not know when it is coming until you are in the middle of it, but surviving Witches' Night is the only way to progress to the final year. Do you understand?"

"Yes, Princess."

"Good. Now, as I was saying, you will have the standard second-class curriculum, which Lance and I have prepared in schedule form." It was unsettling listening to Princess Copper-pot. Every other word was either shouted or spoken at a higher pitch. "There are two additional items for which you will be responsible. The first is the completion of the third-class work you missed during the unfortunate events of last year."

Unfortunate, thought Evie. *That's one way of putting it.*

"During the first few weeks of term, you will divide into your former companies after breakfast. Ironbone, you will complete Enchanted Forest Orienteering with Captain Ramsbottom. Goosegirl, you will complete Well and Tower Escape with Haragan the troll. You will then regroup before lunch for your second-class training. Are there any questions?"

"No, Princess," they said as one.

"Good. In addition to all of that, our second- and first-class knight and princess cadets will be required to help the staff with administrative duties. There will be far more cadets this year than planned, and as such you will all need to lend a hand. Crown Company will assist in the laundry. Bramblestick will help with the birds. And you will be working in the kitchens."

There was a flurry of whispers. "I hope you lot like icecakes," said Maggie with a chuckle. "Only thing I know how to cook—"

The rooster began squawking ferociously, flapping his wings and racing back and forth between Copperpot and Maggie.

"What's he doing?" said Maggie, backing away from the crazed rooster.

Copperpot ambled back to where Maggie stood and peered

down at her with a sour look. "I do not enjoy having foul tastes in my mouth, Cadet."

"N-no, Princess," said Maggie, glancing around for help.

"Then why have you just put one there?"

"I'm sorry—?"

"What is your name?"

"Cadet Magdalena, ma'am."

"Make a note, Lance," said Copperpot to the clucking rooster. Then she addressed the company as a whole. "I do not like foul tastes! Any of you who puts a foul taste in my mouth three times this year will be discharged. Lance has an excellent memory and will remind me should the need arise."

"But surely you can't rely on a rooster to decide our futures!" said Maggie. "That isn't fair—"

"Fair? Is life meant to be fair?" shrieked Copperpot, raising her matching left hands. "I'm right-handed! How fair are things for me? Not bloody very! But you don't hear me grousing, do you?"

"N-no, Princess," stammered Maggie, staring at the dual left hands in front of her.

"Two foul tastes on the first day, Lance. The future looks quite dim indeed for this one."

"*Buhgawk!*"

Maggie's skin had gone gray. She was on the verge of being discharged before they'd even broken for supper. Thankfully, Copperpot tottered away from her and continued on.

"Starting tomorrow, you will begin your day in the kitchens, preparing food for the third class."

"The third class?" scoffed Kelbra. "There's bloody millions of them!"

Copperpot sneered. "Lance, make note of this one. She's given me a particularly foul taste."

Kelbra sighed, but kept her mouth shut.

"Now, let's take a look at your work, shall we?"

And with that, Princess Copperpot and Lance began their inspection of the barracks. She ran her one bulging eye over the decrepit structures, clucking out instructions, which the cadets jumped to address. After another half hour of sweat and mold and grime and rot, Copperpot told the girls to wash for supper. She gave them, the entire company, only five minutes to do so. Evie, Maggie, Demetra, and Basil raced for the latrine, but so did every other member of Leatherwolf Company. By the time the five minutes were up, only half the cadets had been able to use the cold, murky water in the washbasins.

Copperpot handed each of them a small parchment with a weekly schedule scrawled across it, and then they trudged across Hansel's Green, exhausted, grimy, and frustrated. Inside the Dining Hall they found a festive atmosphere, and supper already under way. Delicious aromas and excited chatter wafted all around them. The third-class cadets were packed tightly into long tables near the back, admiring their uniforms, meeting new friends, and reveling in their first taste of freedom. Even more tables were being hauled in and set up for those who had yet to arrive from Waldeck.

Everyone turned to gawk at Leatherwolf Company as they

trudged silently through the hall toward the only empty table. Not even a single day of training, and already they looked war-weary. And they hadn't even gotten their uniforms yet.

"Completely bloody humiliating," muttered Basil.

Through the shock of seeing the grimy, exhausted cadets of Leatherwolf Company, the happy atmosphere began to return as the third-class cadets noticed Evie. She tried her best to ignore the sea of eyes staring at her with adoration.

"Company, sit!" bleated Copperpot. The girls obeyed. Then she staggered to the staff table, her wooden leg clunking on the stone. Lance strutted along behind her.

"'Company, sit'?" came a deep, polished voice. "Are you a company of dogs now?" Evie's head whirled to find Remington sitting among them, just on the other side of Demetra. Down at the end of the table, staff princesses began to distribute hastily assembled plates of food for the late arrivals.

"Remington!" said Maggie. "Where did you come from?"

"She said to sit, so I sat." One side of his mouth curled up in a smile. "Hello, everyone. Lovely to see you. What do you think of my new uniform? I'm a Huntsman Company lad now." His doublet was a brilliant scarlet embroidered with black patterns.

"Very nice," said Demetra. "We're called Leatherwolf Company. Apparently they've forgotten our uniforms."

"Ah," he said. "Tragic." His eyes flicked over to Evie, and she felt a surge of heat in her face. All those thoughts she'd had over the summer, all the times she'd imagined him . . . None of that mattered now that he was right here in front of her.

"So, Remington, did you have a nice summer?" asked Maggie.

"I did, thank you. My father thought it best that I start sitting in on some diplomatic meetings, so I learned all about striking deals where no one is happy."

Demetra laughed. "My father certainly wasn't. You should have heard the things he said about your dad after you left."

Maggie signaled to Evie with her eyes, imploring her to speak.

"I must say, that was one of my favorite excursions of the summer. You've got an absolutely lovely home."

"Thank you," said Demetra. "Though you missed seeing Evie by a week."

"Did I?" he said, his eyes twinkling and intense. "What an utter shame."

Evie smiled politely, but couldn't think of anything to say. Maggie slapped her forehead in disbelief.

Remington held her eyes for a moment, then said, "I do hate to dash, ladies, but I'm afraid I must. My new House Knight doesn't seem all that partial to . . . well, to me."

Demetra laughed.

"See you on the field." He gave Evie one last look, then hurried across the hall to join Huntsman Company.

"What was all that?" snapped Maggie, scowling at Demetra.

"All what?"

"He came to talk to Evie, and you completely dominated the conversation."

"I did not! I was just being polite. If I hadn't said anything, no one would have."

"Well, you might try being a bit more sensitive to your friends next time."

"Don't take it out on me because you ran afoul of that rooster..."

As the squabble between Maggie and Demetra continued, Evie absently scooped fish pie into her mouth. The truth of it was, Demetra was right. Why couldn't she think of anything to say? Yes, she hadn't seen him in months, but so what? She glanced over at his table and saw him laughing easily with his friends.

It's only Remington, she tried to tell herself, but no amount of thinking would give her what she really wanted, which was to start the night all over again.

As the Dining Hall emptied out, the four friends made their way through the darkness to their new barracks. The night was cool and crisp, and the air itself seemed charged with excitement and possibility. Oh, how she'd missed this place...

"What is this nonsense? Theory and Practice of Witch Systems with Professor Ziegenbart?" Basil was peering at his schedule by the moonlight. "Advanced Castlery, that one's with the Fairy Drillsergeant. Riddles and Puzzles. Life at Court. Applied Courage. We're meant to do all of this *and* our enchanted forest work *and* cook meals for the whole bloody Academy? I should have stayed home."

"I'll be home before breakfast at this rate," said Maggie.

"You'll be fine," said Demetra, who appeared ready to forget all about their little argument. "Just don't talk when she's around."

"Oh, is that all?" said Maggie with a laugh. "So help me, if I miss out on becoming a princess because of some dumb rooster, I'll . . ." She didn't finish the thought, but the anxiety in her voice was clear.

When they reached the barracks, a familiar face waited in the aisle between the rows of bunks. Rumpledshirtsleeves, the tailor troll, watched as his tiny assistants raced from bunk to bunk, fitting each mattress with fresh bedding and pillows. He slumped over his gnarled cane, bloodshot eyes peering out from beneath a thick, warty brow.

"Welcome, Leatherwolfians!" he said, his voice croaking out from his throat like a bullfrog in desperate need of a drink. "Fabulous work with your barracks!"

"Rumpledshirtsleeves!" said Evie, a smile blooming across her face. She hurried over and gave him a hug. He smelled of jasmine and smoke, and his body squished like sand beneath her arms.

"How are you, Cadet? I see the summer sun hasn't dulled your elegance."

"Thank you, sir." Other cadets approached him with hugs and greetings, then made their way through the barracks to their freshly made bunks. "I missed you while I was home."

"And I you, my dear. I've thought of you quite often these

months. And I hear I have you to thank for returning these barracks from the dead."

"I don't know about that," she said, rubbing away some dried mud on her arm.

"Oh, take the credit, please. It does an old troll's heart good to have these barracks back in operation. I never thought I'd live to see the Academy operating near capacity."

"Evie! Come on, before they're all taken!" called Maggie. Sure enough, the bunks were filling fast.

He tipped his head to her, then greeted Basil and took him outside to show him the storehouse where he would be staying. Evie walked down the row of bunks. She had to admit, it did feel nice to be back in a full barracks again. It had been many months since this had happened. The Ironbone bunks had steadily emptied as the previous year had gone on. The warm light of the torches glowing in the sconces, the buzz of voices as two old companies became one new company, the thrill of an entire year ahead. A smile bloomed across her face as she plopped down on the empty bunk Maggie had reserved for her.

She was home. Now, finally, after so many months, she was home.

As she glanced around the barracks, the warm feeling in her heart began to cool. Although there was much laughter and happiness, she also noticed several girls taking out parchments and quills to write letters. To them, Pennyroyal Academy wasn't home.

"Maggie," she said. "Could I borrow a parchment?"

"Why, are you finally going to write me back?" She noticed the look on Evie's face and dropped the banter, handing over a fresh parchment.

"And a quill?"

"Of course." She took a quill from her knapsack and a small pot of ink. "Let me know when you're finished and I'll show you how to send it."

"Thanks."

Evie took the blank parchment and lay back, propping it against her knees. She carefully dipped the quill in the inkpot and ...

She stared at the blank parchment. She couldn't think of a single thing to write. A drip of ink was about to land on her blanket, but she managed to get the pot beneath it in time.

"Just write what you feel," said Maggie, half watching from her own bunk.

"I know, I know," said Evie. But still her quill didn't move.

As torches began to go dark around the barracks, Evie sat up and put her feet on the cold stone floor. On one side of her, Maggie was asleep. On the other, Demetra was asleep. She set the quill and inkpot on the windowsill, folded the blank parchment, and snuffed her torch.

"I DON'T LIKE IT," said Maggie. "I was really quite fond of the blue."

Evie smoothed the gray material over her body, then looped the rich green belt around her waist. "It does look a bit odd, doesn't it?" Having spent the summer in the various garments she'd been given by the people of Waldeck, Evie found that wearing the gray and green of Leatherwolf Company wasn't as jarring as it could have been. Still, it didn't seem natural to see Maggie in a color other than Ironbone blue. "Well, we'd better get used to it, I suppose. Where's Demetra? It's almost breakfast."

"She's over there with those Goosegirl cadets."

Demetra was on the far side of the barracks helping Nessa and Liv with their new uniforms. She had a mouthful of pins and was busy altering their dresses. Nessa said something and they all laughed.

"Let's just meet her over there," said Maggie. "I can't be late."

When they stepped out into the predawn for their first

morning of kitchen service, they found Basil waiting in his own new custom uniform, a Leatherwolf gray tunic with pale breeches and a green belt, courtesy of Rumpledshirtsleeves.

"Morning, ladies," he said, though the crisp black sky signaled anything but. A trio of former Goosegirl cadets whispered to one another and giggled as they came out of the barracks and walked past him. His smile disappeared.

"Come on, Basil," said Maggie, taking his arm. "I can't wait for you to show me some of your recipes."

"I just hope they have the right grind of flour," he said. As he and Maggie followed the stream of cadets past huge stacks of logs and onto Hansel's Green, his chipper attitude began to return. Evie lingered for a moment, waiting for Demetra. Other Leatherwolf girls came out and headed across the field, but not Demetra and her new friends. Finally, Evie left.

The night's torches and candles were still lit, though the first hint of dawn was starting to lighten the air. They filed into the Dining Hall through a small door in the back. The kitchens were enormous mazes of ovens and tables and food sacks and basins. Candlelight and stove fires provided plenty of light and warmth.

"It's actually quite cozy in here," said Evie.

"Not as cozy as my bed," grumbled Sage as she trudged inside.

A handful of staff princesses and woodsmen were there, cracking eggs, kneading dough, and slicing vegetables. The cadets did as they were told, following the recipes as best they could. Basil even offered suggestions—most of them unwelcome—on how to improve the oatcakes. Eventually Demetra, Nessa, and Liv joined them, but they were so late that they were given serving duty.

As Evie sleepwalked through the rest of the breakfast preparations, she realized how much she'd rather be eating the food than cooking it. Unfortunately, she wasn't allowed to touch anything until the staff released them to their breakfast table.

"Well done, cadets," Princess Copperpot finally squawked. The morning sun had appeared through the windows, and the voices of the rest of the Academy had begun to rumble in from the Dining Hall. "You may go. Those of you who are serving may begin."

The Dining Hall was packed wall to wall with cadets, even more than the previous night, their voices bouncing everywhere.

"Were *we* this loud?" said Basil, holding his temples. "I think I'd prefer the Fairy Drillsergeant's shouting at this point."

As Evie looked toward the first-class girls, her eyes passed the staff table atop its raised platform in the front of the room. It ran the entire length of the hall and was lined with thrones. And there at the end stood the Headmistress General. She was issuing orders to a group of trolls who were carrying more thrones for the extra staff.

"Well, I think it's exciting," said Maggie. "It's just like when we were third class. There are so many dreams over there waiting to come true."

"Loads waiting to be smashed as well," he said.

"You're such a cynic, Bas."

"I'm a realist."

"Save my spot, will you?" said Evie, rising from the bench and walking to the edge of the platform. "Pardon me, Headmistress?"

"Good morning, Cadet," said Beatrice, though her eyes never left the throne-hauling trolls. "No, not that one. Over there! Bloody trolls."

"Could I speak to you a moment?"

"No, you fools! Slide Professor Njord round the side and you can fit at least three more there." She shook her head, annoyed, then came over and stood above Evie. "What is it?"

"Um, well, something's happened that I wanted to speak to you about."

"Speak."

"Well, um, you see," stammered Evie. She'd forgotten just how intimidating Princess Beatrice could be, particularly while standing on a four-foot-high platform. "There were these three women. On the way here. And I . . . well, I . . . I saw a woman killed."

Beatrice's forehead creased with what might have been either confusion or anger, but was probably both. "One of these women was killed?"

"No, no. They killed another woman."

"Will you spit it out, Cadet."

"There were these three women . . . They burst into the inn

where I was staying and killed an old woman. They all had swords, you see, and—"

"Three women murdered an old woman."

"Yes, Headmistress."

"And you saw this happen."

"I did, Headmistress. But the thing is, they were princesses. The three killers, not the woman who was killed."

"Three *princesses* murdered an old woman."

Evie nodded uncertainly. She knew what she had seen, but it all sounded so absurd coming from Beatrice's mouth.

"And where did this happen?"

"I'm not sure. Somewhere near Cinderella's Castle."

Beatrice's expression never changed. Her mouth was tight and angled downward. Her bright blue eyes bored down into Evie's. Each line in her skin made her look several degrees more magnificent and terrifying. Evie thought she must have been the most frightening person who had ever lived.

"Thank you for telling me, Cadet. I'll have Princess Bujanov look into it. She's one of our best, and she lives in that region."

"Oh," said Evie. "Thank you." She didn't know what sort of response she had been expecting, but that was not it.

"Will there be anything else?"

"No, Headmistress. Just . . . well . . . why would princesses want to . . . do that to someone?"

"Those were not princesses, Cadet. They were almost certainly witches."

"Witches? But the innkeeper called them princesses. And they—"

"This is standard witchery, my dear, and quite frankly I'm surprised you didn't learn this in Lieutenant Volf's class last year."

"Well, we did, I suppose. He told us about shape-shifting and witches disguising themselves and . . ." She trailed off when she saw Beatrice's expression ratchet to an even angrier tightness. "Thank you, Headmistress. Thank you." She bowed and backed away from the platform as Beatrice turned to talk to Corporal Liverwort. She breathed a sigh of relief and headed back to the Leatherwolf table. It hadn't gone as smoothly as she would have liked, but she couldn't help but be pleased with Beatrice's response. Of course princesses would never do something like that! She smiled as she rejoined Maggie and Basil. Just in time for the first day of training, a lingering weight had been taken off her shoulders.

"There she is!"

"Hi, Evie!"

"She's so beautiful . . ."

Evie felt her cheeks go pink as the Ironbone half of Leatherwolf Company trotted past a group of third-class girls on its way down the hill. The other half, the Goosegirl half, had split off and run to Hansel's Green, while the rest of them made for the wall.

"Go on, laugh!" shouted Basil from somewhere behind her. "I've made it farther than most of you lot will!" She glanced back and saw that he was shouting at some of the third-class cadets who were pointing and laughing at the boy running with the girls. She slowed to let him catch up.

"Just give them a few days to get used to it. They'll stop."

"It's bloody humiliating. I thought last year would be the worst, but I can't bear the snide smiles on these new girls' faces."

"Forget about them, Bas. Come on, isn't it nice to be back at it again?"

"Mmm."

They ran in silence. Evie looked up at the morning sky and felt the autumn chill in the steel-hued air. *She* was certainly happy to be back at it again. When they reached the bottom of the hill and approached the small stone wall that ringed the campus, she saw a collection of red uniforms waiting on the other side. The boys of Huntsman Company.

Remington.

Leatherwolf poured over the wall and ran to join the knight cadets at the edge of the enchanted forest. The ground there was soft and pillowy, covered in a thick blanket of moss.

"Come along, girls!" came a voice that was surprisingly airy and light, especially coming from the fur-clad beast who'd spoken it. Captain Ramsbottom was as thick and hairy as two bears fighting. He towered above the knight cadets, a ratty brown beard crinkling down almost from his eyebrows. "Gather round, gather round. Make way so all can see."

Evie scanned the knight cadets until she caught Remington's eye across the group. He gave her a smile and a slight nod. She smiled back, then turned her eyes to the instructor. She couldn't stop smiling, though. She could still feel him looking at her.

"Let's get started, shall we? This is called smokewood," said Ramsbottom. "That's naturally growing wood singed by a dragon's breath."

And just like that, Evie's smile fell away. She realized in an instant where she was standing and which dragon's breath had caused the smokewood. The trees behind Captain Ramsbottom were streaked with the scars of intense fire. Their leafless branches jutted into the air like the spiked stalagmites in Evie's cave. She looked away, trying to block the memory of the lance rising toward her sister's side . . .

"All wood is flammable, we know that. But when an enchanted tree meets dragon fire and doesn't burn, it becomes smokewood. This is very important: it must be an enchanted tree. You'll see why in a minute. Now, smokewood is the most flammable substance in all the land. And if you know how to use it properly, it can save your—"

Suddenly a branch swept out and slammed into his back, launching him into the cadets like a large, hairy arrow.

"Are you all right, sir?" asked one of the boys.

Ramsbottom wheeled and looked back at the tree with fear. Then he got to his feet and brushed himself off. "Yes, yes, I'm fine, lad. Thank you." The branches, even those charred into smokewood, swayed victoriously. Both companies took a step back.

"I hope he's not expecting us to go near that stuff," said Basil.

"Isn't this what books are for?" said Maggie, peeking out from behind him. "I'm happy to *read* about smokewood."

Captain Ramsbottom limped forward, being sure to stay well out of the trees' reach. "Well, there you are. An excellent demonstration of the first thing you'll need to remember. Smokewood is, as I said, enchanted. So, er, watch your backs." Several of the cadets giggled nervously. "Now, unless these trees smash me to bits first, I'm going to show you how to use this as a resource if you find yourself lost in the enchanted forest."

And with that, he trotted off, giving a wide berth to the tree that had gotten him, and disappeared into the forest. The cadets exchanged uncertain looks. Evie glanced over at Remington, who was busy talking to one of his company-mates. *Look over here,* she thought.

"He's lost the plot," said Basil. "That thing nearly broke him in half!"

"Where's he gone?" said Maggie.

First they heard footsteps crunching through the leaves and then they saw him. He was running straight for the gap between two charred trees. One of the Leatherwolf girls screamed as two branches crackled to life and swung at him. He leaped into the air, surprisingly nimble for such an abnormally large man, and dove over the branches. They crunched into each other, and an explosion of fire burst from the spot where the smokewood met. He tucked into a roll and ended up on one knee looking back at a shower of sparks. Several small fires burned in the dead leaves carpeting the ground. Eyeing the trees warily, he edged over and scooped up a smoking pile of pine needles and leaves. He blew on it and a flame sparked to life. Holding the small fire in his hands, he smiled proudly.

"There you are. Instant fire. Doesn't matter if it's been raining for days, smokewood still works." He dropped the fire and stomped it out with his boot. "Now, who'd like to give it a go?"

He was met with silence.

"Come on, you've all got to do it." Everyone was looking away, hoping to avoid eye contact. "I can force you if you like, but—"

"I'll try," said Remington. "What's the worst that can happen?"

"The tree could break all your bones and then set you on fire," said one of the knight cadets, and all the boys laughed.

"I've had worse," he said. Evie watched in horror as he disappeared into the woods.

"Right, lad!" shouted Ramsbottom. "Just remember that enchanted trees are quite predictable! Their limbs are heavy, so it's difficult for them to change course once they're in full swing!"

"Cheerio!" called Remington. Moments later he was running straight at them. The trees attacked, one in a swooping arc, the other chopping down with a deafening crackle that sounded like witches' magic. Evie must have closed her eyes, because the next thing she knew, there was a crash and a great cheer. She looked up to find Remington prone on the ground. Behind him, several small fires burned.

"Fantastic, Cadet!" said Captain Ramsbottom, chuckling as he stomped out the flames. "That's how you use smokewood!"

Remington pushed himself up, wiping black sludge from his uniform. He glanced back and admired his work, then rejoined his company. The knight cadets clapped him on the back and congratulated him. He looked over at Evie with a triumphant smile.

A rush of joy washed over her. That look had said it all. He had volunteered to go first because he wanted to impress her.

For the next few hours, the cadets practiced making fire with the smokewood trees. Captain Ramsbottom wouldn't let them return to campus until everyone had done it, even when rain began sheeting down from the clouds. Finally, when they'd all managed to produce at least a minimal flame, the fairies opened the wall and the cadets raced back to their barracks to change into dry uniforms. All except for two.

"Lovely day for a stroll," said Remington as thunder crackled across the countryside. "I don't know why everyone else is in such a blasted hurry."

Evie smiled. They walked slowly up the road toward campus, neither in any particular rush to get out of the rain. "That was quite impressive back there, volunteering to show us all how it's done. You could have been flattened."

"Yes, but these are the things one must do as the most famous cadet at the Academy. People expect you to set an example."

"I'll keep that in mind, since I'm now the most famous cadet at the Academy."

"Are you?" he said with a grin. "I hadn't noticed."

"Perhaps if you'd let those trees flatten you, it might have made you famous again."

He laughed and shook the rainwater from his hair. "Ah, it is nice to see you again, Evie. And I apologize for not writing you over the summer. In a way, you could say it's your fault."

"My fault?" she said with a laugh. "And how is that?"

"I spent quite a lot of time thinking about you and your family on the ride home. Being raised by dragons seems to be the most straightforward part of your history. It all must have been terribly complicated for you."

Though it warmed her heart to hear him say he'd been thinking about her, since virtually all she'd done was think about him, he wasn't wrong about the complexity of Evie's family. She had been raised by dragons, that was true, but even the little she'd discovered about her human family was far from straightforward. Evie's stepmother, Countess Hardcastle, had lied to Evie, saying that King Callahan was actually her stepfather, when in reality he was Evie's father. She still knew nothing about her birth mother, but she had managed to obtain one small image of King Callahan, the one tucked inside her dragon scale necklace.

"It was complicated, yes."

"Thinking about your family made me realize I'd been taking mine for granted. The truth is, my father didn't force me to join him on those diplomatic missions. I volunteered. And I very much enjoyed spending all that time with him, even though it devoured my entire summer. So there you have it. Your fault."

"Well, then, I suppose I'm sorry," she said with a smile.

"Apology accepted."

Small rivulets of rainwater streamed down the hill beneath their feet through carriage wheel ruts. Another dull rumble echoed from the skies. Remington laughed suddenly, as though he'd been trying to stop himself. Evie turned to look at him.

"What?"

"There is one small bit of comedy buried amidst the tragedy of it all. I hope you won't take this the wrong way, but it is simply too funny to ignore."

"What is it?"

"King Callahan was your father. And Countess Hardcastle was Malora's mother."

"Yes?"

"Well, Hardcastle wanted you dead so she could pass Malora off as you, yes? So she could pretend that a witch was actually a princess of the blood?"

"Yes? And?"

He laughed again. "Well? Doesn't that mean your real name is Malora?"

Evie was gobsmacked. She kept putting one foot in front of the other, puzzling through what he'd said.

"I'm sorry," said Remington. "I didn't mean to—"

"My word . . . you're right."

A smile bloomed across his face. "If she was going to be you, then she would need to *be* you! And the records would all have it that *Malora* was King Callahan's daughter!"

"I'm Malora," said Evie, unable to keep from smiling. With all the twists and turns of discovering who she really was during her first year at the Academy, this was the piece that pushed the whole thing into absurdity. She began to laugh. "I'm bloody Malora."

He extended a hand. "Come, Malora, let us get out of this rain."

She slapped it away with a smile. "My name is Evie. And you'd better not tell anyone what you just told me."

"I won't, I won't," he said. "Malora."

She tried to shove him, but he ran up the hill. She chased after as a flash of lightning lit up the midday gray, and her laughter was swallowed up by rolling thunder.

Evie had reached the barracks just as the rest of the company was leaving, so she quickly changed into a dry uniform, then headed off into campus for her first official second-class training of the year.

Leatherwolf Company followed a huge wall lined with

carved rainheads, water pouring from the mouths of the gargoyles and wolves and monsters above, until they found a stone archway to the inside, where the rainfall became little more than a dull whisper. At the center of Richards Keep was a neglected courtyard, overgrown with grass and flowery weeds. The cadets climbed a staircase into a dark, dank corridor with a floor worn so smooth, Basil nearly slipped at the top. It was eerily quiet in the corridor.

"Is this it?" came a voice from up ahead. "I think this is it."

They entered a large chamber strewn with bales of straw. The earthy smell of alfalfa filled the room. Stagnant water pooled in various parts of the uneven floor. Dust swirled through beams of light that came in through holes in the thatched roof. There were candles lit along the walls and strange items strewn randomly about. A hand mirror. A spindle. Several rusted knitting needles. A leather purse. It looked to be more rubbish room than classroom.

"I don't understand," said Basil. "Is this some sort of stable? Why is it inside a keep?"

"Are you sure this is the right place?" said Idonea.

"This is where Copperpot's schedule said to go," said Sage.

"Well," said Demetra, strolling around the room, "we might as well pull up a bale." She plopped down on one, sending a fresh plume of dust into the air.

Evie walked over to join her, but Nessa sat down first. Liv took a spot on the bale next to them.

"Oh, sorry," said Demetra, realizing what had just happened. "Uh, Evie, you've met Nessa and Liv, haven't you?"

"Hi," she said, shaking their hands. "We sort of met on the first day."

"Very nice to meet you," said Nessa with a smile.

"They're from the two kingdoms beneath the Blackmarsh, can you believe it?"

"Yes," said Evie. "So you said."

"We've heard a lot about you," said Liv. "It's a pleasure to be in the same company as the Warrior Princess."

Evie smiled politely. She couldn't help feeling strangely wary of these two.

"There's an open spot right there, Evie," said Demetra, pointing to another bale nearby.

"Thanks." She gave Nessa and Liv a smile, then went and sat on the empty bale. Maggie sat next to her. They didn't say a word, though they did exchange a look. Evie could tell immediately that Maggie was bothered by Demetra's new friends as well.

"Where's the instructor?" said Cadet Rillia. "Princess Whatsit?"

"Ziegenbart," said Kelbra. "And after dodging limbs and rain all morning, I'll be happy if she never turns up."

Basil pulled a bale down from a stack and created a little pillow from some loose straw, then sat back, put his hands behind his head, and closed his eyes.

"Come on," said Cadet Rosamund, formerly of Goosegirl

Company. "If this is meant to be a classroom, then let's make it a classroom." The other Leatherwolf cadets began to rearrange the bales to create more seating.

"I'm giving it five more minutes," said Kelbra loudly. "Then I'm going back to the barracks for a nap." She and Sage hovered near the door.

"Listen!" said Basil, sitting up suddenly. "What's that?"

As the conversation around the room began to fade, the rest of them heard it as well. It sounded like the type of iron bell a farmer would fashion for a cow or a sheep. It even had the loping rhythm of livestock. *Clang-clang . . . clang-clang . . . clang-clang.*

Kelbra peered outside. Then she turned back with a bemused smile. "Wait 'til you see who's come to join us."

The bell clanged closer, and then a grayish-brown goat ambled through the door. She was a doe, with white hair running down from splayed ears all the way to her muzzle. Her legs were short, and her body was thick and square, with a belly that sagged to her knobbly knees. A gray beard poked down beneath her chin. She wore a sparkling silver tiara atop her head.

The cadets stood to look, muffling laughter as the goat traveled through the assembled straw bales toward the far end of the room. Suddenly, it leapt atop a stack of bales and wheeled to face them.

"Thirteen witches," said the goat in the voice of a middle-aged woman. "Thirteen of them slinking through the mist to kill me." The goat turned and jumped atop an old wardrobe with no doors. "I knew I had no chance, yet my courage did not fail me." She skittered along a beam in the ceiling like one of her mountain brethren might, tiny hooves needing only inches of purchase to support her bloated body. "The battle raged. They got me with a curse, as you can see . . ." She landed on the ground with a crack of her hooves, her eyes bulging out from the sides of her head. "But not before I took seven of them from this world."

The goat stood there in front of the shocked cadets. Heavy rain hissed against the stone outside.

"Those vile creatures have millions of ways to attack us. Shape-shifting, levitation, attack spells, even livestock making, apparently. Witches' magic can take many forms, depending on what they stir into their wicked pots." She shook her head, causing a great clanging of her bell. "My name is Princess Ziegenba*aa-a-a-a-a-agh-agh-agh!*" Her tongue thrust out of her mouth as she bleated loudly, then devolved into a coughing fit. "Ahem. Princess Ziegenbart. And this is Theory and Practice of Witch Systems, or as I like to call it, Killing Witches Is Fun." She jumped again, this time landing on what must have been her desk, though it looked more like a rickety pile of wood that had been hastily cobbled together. "I'm going to tell you all about what it's like to go out there and meet the enemy face-to-rotting-face. Now, since you're second-class cadets, the time has come for you to think about what sort of princesses you'd like to become. Will you be one of the Towersitters, protecting a kingdom from those slinking slimies?" With two deft hops, she was once again up in the rafters. "Roughly ninety percent of Pennyroyal graduates are Towersitters. Royal balls, royal weddings, royal everything, but plenty of action as well! Witches lurking outside the walls and only you there to stop them." She puffed out her chest and stared into some imagined distance where true heroism lay. Then, with three more sharp clacks she was back on the floor in the middle of the classroom. "Or will you join the Salty Sovereign? The coastal brigade!"

Evie startled. She'd heard that name before. *The Salty Sovereign*. But where?

"Oh yes, my dears, there are witches at sea as well. Mountain witches, wood witches, water witches. Plenty of hags for us all!" She leaned over and chewed a bunch of straw from a bale. Cadet Rosamund yelped and pulled her dress away to keep it from being eaten. "I spent eighteen months aboard a cog with Princess Middlemiss and Princess Kätharina once. Hoo, did we see some salt witches out there, let me tell you. But I digress."

That's it, thought Evie. *Princess Middlemiss was in the coastal brigade*. She'd read the stories many times over the summer as she'd hidden from her sister near the pond.

"Then there are the Cursebreakers. That's the more scientific branch of the service. Not my cup of meat, but very important nonetheless." Her mouth worked in circles to mash the straw. "Those ladies are on the cutting edge of witch research. The Cursebreakers have chapters in many of the larger kingdoms across the land." She took another bite off of Rosamund's bale.

"They keep us up to date on all the latest witch curses and spells, and are forever looking for new ways to combat them. A fine and noble calling, the Cursebreakers." Then she made a face and pretended to whisper, "If a bit boring."

She continued through the room. As she walked past Basil, Evie could see her hair brushing against his leg. He held his fist tightly over his mouth to keep from laughing.

"Then you've got the reserves, the Sleeping Beauties. You maintain your training with monthly sessions, but are generally free to return to civilian life unless you're called up for battle. Which you will be. I've yet to meet a reserve who hasn't faced off with at least one witch in her life." Ziegenbart walked past Evie, her eyes protruding and her beard fluttering. "Another option is to train for a position here at the Academy. Haven't managed to think of a clever name for that one yet, but it's quite an important job, training the next generation of warriors. Don't discount it."

She reached the back of the classroom. There was a pause. Heads slowly turned to look at her. She was eating again. Then, suddenly, she wheeled and began bounding from bale to bale. Demetra and Nessa screamed as she landed between them. In seconds she was back at the front of the room. "And finally there is the most dangerous, most thrilling, most adventurous branch of the service. The branch in which I proudly served." She reared up and put her front legs on an empty bale so that she looked like she was giving a speech behind a lectern. "The Cauldron Tippers. The witch hunters. The girls with no home, no kingdom to call their own. They spend their days traveling to the darkest parts of the forest in search of witches. The Cauldron Tippers have the highest casualty rate and the highest stone-turn rate in the whole of the princessing service. But curse me if it isn't fun," she said with a smile. "Going into their cottages and hovels, rooting them out where they live . . . There's nothing like it, ladies!"

As the goat started to explain how the knights must also specialize in their final year, Evie's mind began to wander. *A witch hunter. Roaming the land tracking them down, one by one.* Her heart thumped as her imagination took her to the depths of a distant forest. Shadows and mist and ghostly yellow eyes. Could she do it? Could she devote her life to places like that, hunting down and doing battle with wicked witches? Or should she think about joining the Salty Sovereign? When she'd first laid eyes on the sea at the Blackmarsh, something profound had awakened inside her. She'd never seen anything so boundless and deep before. It spoke to her heart. The rhythm of the waves was the rhythm of her blood. Was that where she was meant to be? Or should she just hope for placement in a good kingdom and protect innocent people, which is what a princess is supposed to do? Her head was spinning, and it was only the first day.

"I already know where I'll be," said Demetra, sitting crosslegged on her bunk. "Princess Demetra of the Blackmarsh, understudy to the great Princess Camilla."

"I can't believe you're disparaging the Blackmarsh," said Maggie. "That's one of the most sought-after Towersitter postings in all the land. I'd take it in a heartbeat."

"It's yours. Nessa and Liv both have Pennyroyal graduates for older sisters as well. The three of us can be the understudy brigade."

Once again, Evie and Maggie exchanged a look. Every time Demetra mentioned Nessa and Liv, something bubbled in Evie's stomach. They seemed like perfectly nice girls, but she couldn't help wishing Demetra would just stop talking about them.

"How about you, Evie?" said Basil, sitting on Demetra's footlocker. "Goat patrol?"

"I dunno," she said with a sigh. "We've got all year to figure it out, haven't we?"

"Yes, but it's good to start thinking about it now," said Maggie. "It is the rest of your life, after all."

Evie cringed at that. *The rest of my life. I only started my life last year. How am I meant to decide the rest of it already?*

"They've got testimonials and fact sheets on all the branches in the Hall of Princesses. I'm going tomorrow before lunch to start researching, if any of you would like to join me."

"Don't need to," said Basil. "I already know what I'm doing."

"Oh really?" said Demetra with a sly smile. "Cauldron Tipper, I suppose?"

"Certainly not. My plan is to get discharged long before I have to decide."

"I may be there with you, Bas," said Maggie. "Especially with that bloody rooster clucking about—"

"Attention!" Princess Copperpot's shrill voice echoed through the barracks, and Maggie's skin went gray. Everyone leapt from their bunks and stood tall and straight. Evie could see Maggie swaying out of the corner of her eye. Lance's soft clucking was the only sound as he searched the bearskin rugs for stray crumbs. Copperpot lurched forward and slung a heavy canvas sack to the ground. "It has been a particularly trying day for parchment hawks. I certainly hope the post doesn't continue to be this . . . *voluminous*."

"*Buhgawk!*" squawked Lance.

Maggie collapsed onto her footlocker.

"What was that?" chirped Copperpot. "Who made that noise?"

"I'm sorry, Princess," said Maggie, trying to stand. "I'm suddenly feeling a bit faint."

"By all means, stay seated, then."

"Are you all right?" whispered Evie. Maggie didn't respond. She was doubled over with her forehead in her hands.

Copperpot, meanwhile, leaned down to open the sack. Her two left hands struggled awkwardly with the cinched rope. Finally she worked it free and removed a small bundle of parchments. Evie looked at the bag, marveling that everything inside had once been a bird.

"Cadet Kelbra." Kelbra hurried to the front of the barracks and took her letter with a smile.

"It's from my sister."

"Quiet!" said Copperpot. "No commentary, please."

Maggie audibly held her breath as Lance strutted closer.

"Cadet Wittelsbach. Cadet Pilsen. Cadet Frieda." Those three came forward to claim their letters. Then Princess Copperpot reached down and picked up the heavy sack. "The rest are for you, Cadet Evie."

Evie blinked once, unsure if she had heard correctly. Around the room, other cadets began whispering to one another.

"Well? Would you like them or shall I put them in Lance's cage?"

Evie sidled past Lance to get to the front of the barracks. The walk seemed endless with everyone staring at her. Finally she reached the front, and Copperpot handed her the sack.

"Good night, girls," said the House Princess as Evie returned to her bunk. "And let me remind you, as I will every night, that tomorrow you must be more a princess than today."

"Yes, Princess," they said.

"Come, Lance!" she shouted.

"*Buhgawk!*" He flapped his wings and ran after her to the House Princess's quarters, which were walled off from the rest of the barracks in a private apartment. The door slammed shut. From all around the barracks, girls were watching Evie to see what was in the sack. But she was more concerned with Maggie, who was still hunched over on her footlocker.

"Are you all right?"

Maggie sniffled and wiped tears from her eyes. "I'm fine."

She stood and came over to join Basil. "What have you got in there?"

"You're sure you're all right?" said Basil.

"Yes, of course," said Maggie with an embarrassed smile. "That rooster just gives me such anxiety. Go on, Evie, what's inside?"

Evie pulled open the drawstring and upended the sack onto her bed. Dozens and dozens of parchments spilled out, all covered in ink and colored wax seals. Maggie and Demetra began sifting through them.

"Unbelievable," said Demetra.

"What? What is it?"

"Evie, d'you know what these are? They're letters from your admirers."

"What?"

"Listen to this: 'I heard about you from our town crier,'" read Demetra. "'I never thought about being a princess before, but now I can't want to enlist. Only three more years!'"

"This one's from a father in a village near the sea," said Maggie. "He says he hopes one day his sons can meet you."

Now Basil began riffling through the parchments. "This one's done a picture of you. Look!" He held up a charcoal sketch done in a child's hand. It was a princess standing atop a tower with bright magic pouring from her chest. "'I hope you like this drawing I made of you, Princess Evie. I don't know what you look like, so it's probably wrong. Maybe if I meet you one day I can try again.' Blimey, that's sweet."

Evie was dumbstruck. All she could do was stare at the pile of letters strewn across her bed and try to contain the swirl of emotions inside of her. Confusion. Self-confidence. Gratitude. It was all there.

And amidst all those emotions ran one fleeting thought. *I can't wait to tell my mother.*

Over the next few nights, this strange occurrence repeated itself. Scattered cadets would receive a letter from home, while Evie would trudge back to her bunk hauling a sack full of adulation. By the end of the first week, she had shoved all of the letters beneath her bunk until there was no room for any more. She was starting to worry that she would give Princess Copperpot a bad taste in her mouth for not keeping her area up to regulation.

It was Basil who'd suggested keeping them in one of the trees outside the barracks. "Now, the secret is in the wrist. If you don't snap your wrist correctly, you'll just frighten the parchment and its talons will clench. One of my brothers had them go clean through his arm once." He snapped his wrist and the parchment sprouted legs and wings and a head. It flew up into the tree and perched on a limb. "When you want to send one, you can either scratch out what's there and use the same bird, or you have to wait for them to molt. The only other option is to find a blank one. The tawny ones are blank. The ones with black stripes have writing on them."

Evie tried to do it, but most of hers fluttered back to the ground, still in parchment form. So Basil did them, one after another, until nearly every branch was covered in hawks, the inky words creating black lines in their feathers. An entire tree dedicated to the realm's love for Evie.

Meanwhile, the early mornings in the kitchens had already started to take their toll. "At least last year we woke up with the sun," said Demetra as Leatherwolf Company dragged themselves across the frosty Green. "I can't bear being awake when it's still dark."

"They'll start mucking up soon," said Nessa. "Then there'll be fewer and fewer of them, and we can get our hour of sleep back."

"That's a horrible thing to say!" said Maggie. "You shouldn't wish anyone being sent home!"

"Except for me," said Basil. "I can always dream of that."

Each morning, after eating the food they'd helped prepare, the company would split in two. The former Ironbone girls would join the former Thrushbeard boys to learn some new technique for surviving in the enchanted forest. Increasingly, this was the only time Evie, Maggie, and Basil got to spend with Demetra, at least, without the presence of Nessa and Liv. Then, when Captain Ramsbottom was finished with them, they would rejoin the rest of the Leatherwolf girls for late-morning physical drills with the Fairy Drillsergeant before heading back to the kitchens to prepare lunch. There was a torturously short break after lunch, and then it was off to various parts of campus for more specialized training. Depending on the day, the cadets might join Princess Ziegenbart for Theory and Practice of Witch Systems, which was far more interesting than it sounded. Or Riddles and Puzzles taught by a squirrelly little man called Professor Regensburg, or Life at Court with the elegant and haughty Princess Elmstein. Thursdays, however, were the worst. Those were the days when the cadets were forced to descend into the dungeons below a particularly dire castle known as Finnegan's Grave, where Professor Adelbert, an overblown balloon of a man with sharp, manicured facial hair, would subject them to one horror after another, all courtesy of a magical bag he claimed to have gotten from a dying dwarf in an enchanted forest. That was Applied Courage, and it was Evie's least favorite bit of training.

Still, despite the arduous schedule, Evie seemed to be having the best of it. Since Princess Beatrice had so decisively handled the situation with the three princesses in black, the incident had faded from her memory. And she was very much enjoying seeing Remington during Captain Ramsbottom's drills.

Maggie was not having such a good start to the year. She positively wilted every time Princess Copperpot was near, certain she would make some tiny mistake and be sent home. No amount of reassurance that she was the best cadet in the company could convince her she would survive the day. She spent more and more time in the Academy's various libraries, filling any free moment with studying and reading to compensate for getting in trouble that first day. Demetra, whether she realized it or not, was seeing just as much of Nessa and Liv as she was her old friends. She made some effort to merge the two groups, but whenever they all sat next to one another at meals or stood together while waiting their turn for drills, it always ended up with Evie and Maggie off by themselves as Demetra and Nessa and Liv laughed about some mutual acquaintance from the Eastern Kingdoms. And Basil, poor Basil, might have had it worst of all. The Leatherwolf cadets who had come from Goosegirl Company made no effort to accept him as one of their own. He couldn't pass by a third-class company without laughter and muffled commentary. As the days passed, Evie could see that being an outsider had started to take a toll. His jokes about wanting to be sent home had taken on a worryingly serious tone. It all came to a head at the start of the third week of training, when Basil joined Leatherwolf Company midway through lunch.

"Hiya," he said, plopping down in his usual spot across from Evie. He immediately began tucking into his roasted quail and squash. "Where's Maggie?"

"She ate three bites and ran off to the library. Where were you? You've missed nearly all of lunch."

"In the Crown Castle. I put in a request to transfer to the knights' track."

"What?"

He shrugged. "I asked to become a knight."

"Why in the world would you do that?"

"I dunno," he said, picking meat off a wing bone with his teeth.

"Demetra, did you hear this?"

Though Demetra was sitting just to Evie's right, she was busy talking to Liv. "Hmm?"

"Basil's just asked to transfer to become a knight!"

"You did? But why, Bas?"

"Do you really have to ask?"

"You want to leave us?" said Demetra.

"Maybe it's for the best," said Liv. "He's clearly not happy here."

"Yes, and thank you very much," spat Basil. "No one's asked for your opinion."

"Basil!" said Demetra. Liv's eyes went wide. She turned to talk to Nessa, showing Basil her back.

"I understand she's your friend," said Basil quietly, "but she isn't mine. And I don't particularly care what she thinks."

"Still, there's no call to be rude," said Demetra.

"Can we please get back to this knight business?" said Evie sharply. "What do you mean you want to transfer?" She was surprised at the level of betrayal she was feeling at that moment.

He sighed. "It was all different when we were first years, wasn't it? *We* were different. These new girls look at me like I'm some sort of deviant."

"Who cares what they think?" said Demetra. "I can't believe you did that, Bas."

"Beatrice rejected the request anyway. I'm not going anywhere."

Evie chomped on a piece of granary bread, her face curled up in a scowl. "You could have talked to us first. What if she'd said yes?"

"It doesn't matter, it isn't happening. Though she did say I could observe one of the knights' courses. I was hoping for one on dragon anatomy or chivalry or something, but the only one that works with our off-hours is sword training. I'm not bothered, though. My brothers have already taught me quite a bit about blade work. Bertrand has a beautiful—"

"I'm very cross with you right now, Basil!" said Evie.

"Me? Why?"

She slammed her bread onto her plate with a clatter and marched away from the table. She headed for the door, passing through the third-class tables on the way.

"Hi, Evie."

"Evie!"

"You should come speak to our company, Evie!"

She ignored them all, bursting out into the gray afternoon and filling her lungs with frosty air. They'd been such a tight-knit group of friends back in Ironbone Company, and now Basil was actively trying to leave. She'd been so excited to get back to the Academy to see her friends, and now she had to admit that Basil was probably right about one thing: they *were* different this year.

One particularly misty morning, Evie found herself standing at a large oaken table near the edge of the Dortchen Wild with a jar of bear urine in her hand. The table was covered in all manner of things that could be used to survive in the forest.

Only a few more weeks of this, she thought. *A few more weeks and we'll be finished with third-class training and Captain Ramsbottom and his disgusting bear urine.*

"A trail of bread crumbs?" said the barrel-chested woodsman in his slight voice. "Ha! Ah-ha-ha! Bread crumbs are quite possibly the worst thing you could use to create a trail! You might as well throw down some bloody birdseed! Ha-ha!" He scooped up some of the bread crumbs sitting on the table and tossed them into the forest. They were immediately set upon by birds. "See?"

Evie glanced at the jar in her hand. She wanted to set it down, but he hadn't given her permission yet. It didn't help that Remington was watching her with a smile.

"I can't tell you how many boys and girls have been lost in the forest because they somehow got the idea that *bread crumbs* would help them get back home. You don't leave a delicious trail, it's as simple as that. Dried peas, small stones, things of that nature will provide a much more reliable trail.

"Now, what else have we got here?" Ramsbottom snatched the jar out of Evie's hand, nearly splashing her. "This is bear's urine. If you're concerned about wolves, as all of us should be, there's no better repellant than this." He dumped some onto his enormous hand and splashed it behind his ears. "A touch here and there, and wolves will steer well clear."

"So will everything else," muttered Basil with a grimace.

"Remember," said Ramsbottom, reacting to the disgusted groans from the cadets. "Your goal is to stay alive, not to keep yourself ready for the next formal ball. And staying alive doesn't always smell of roses."

Evie, her hands now empty, stepped away from her urine-soaked instructor.

"Now, on the subject of urine," continued Ramsbottom, "we all know witches have very poor eyesight but an excellent sense of smell. I've never tested bear urine on a witch before, but if you've got a jar of it handy and you see those yellow eyes in the trees, you might think about giving yourself a splash—"

Crack! Crackity! Crack! His words were swallowed up by a flurry of splintering wood and shuddering leaves from deep in the forest. There were huge thumps and more cracking sounds. Something was coming, and the trees weren't happy about it.

"To the wall!" shouted Ramsbottom. "Go!"

The cadets stampeded for the wall as the entire forest crackled to life behind them. The trees attacked whatever was out there, but it just kept coming.

Once they reached the wall, the cadets found that they couldn't get back inside. An invisible blockade of magic rose up in a dome over the entire campus, and only a fairy's wand could open it. There were screams all around. Evie thrust her hand forward, but the air seemed to thicken around it, as though she were reaching through an invisible curtain that became stiffer the harder she pushed.

"Fairies!" bellowed Ramsbottom. "We need fairies!"

Evie looked back. The trees at the edge of the forest were shuddering violently. Whatever was in there was almost upon them . . .

"Help!" shouted Captain Ramsbottom. Realizing they were trapped, he picked up a dead log and wielded it as a club. One by one the cadets turned to face the forest. All they could do was wait and see what was coming out of the depths of the Dortchen Wild.

"Open the gates!" came a voice from the trees. Then, through the crackle of wood and the rustling of leaves, they heard the thunder of hooves. "Open the gates!"

Evie held her breath and braced herself. She reached down and grabbed Maggie's hand. Finally, a figure appeared out of the trees. A horseman, riding full out.

Another galloped along behind him. They were large men in black leather and shining plate. A third rode out next, smaller than the rest. Younger, and wearing a white cloak. The riders began to hoot and shout, circling back to taunt the forest that had just tried to kill them. But the youngest stared straight ahead with eyes the color of a thunderstorm, as though he didn't even see the collection of knight and princess cadets pressed up against the wall.

"You there," shouted one of the horsemen. "Open the gate."

"Do I look like I carry a fairy's wand?" said Ramsbottom. "Who are you lot, anyway?"

"It's Forbes," said Evie. "That's Prince Forbes."

"Forbes?" said Ramsbottom, incredulous. "Blimey, so it is!"

It was him, the boy whose curse Evie had inadvertently cured the previous year. His black hair was a bit longer than it had been, windblown and dangling across his face. He had grown noticeably taller over the summer, though his cheeks were sunken and his fingers were bony. There was blood on his cloak. And his hands. And his horse.

"I hadn't even realized he was gone," said Maggie softly.

"Nor had I," said Evie. "Though I suppose it has been a bit too peaceful round here." She and Forbes had had a contentious relationship the previous year. Most of it stemmed from an argument about the portrait that had cursed Forbes in the first place. He insisted it had been Evie's likeness in the portrait, but she was adamant that that wasn't possible.

"So sorry, Captain!" shouted a fairy from behind the wall. "Trouble with the new fairyweed bushes!"

"You're never to leave the wall untended!" bellowed the Captain.

"You're right, you're right. One of the new bushes died and I . . ." She fumbled with her tiny wand, then gave it a swirl. The air itself seemed to lift off the broken stone and float up into the sky. "Never mind that. It was my shift, and I should have been here. I offer no excuse." The cadets clambered over the wall to safety, still rattled by Forbes's dramatic appearance in the forest.

Evie watched him closely as his horse clopped past her. His eyes were haunted, and his face was somber. He had seen something. Something that had left him shaken to his core.

"I wonder what happened to him," said Demetra.

"I don't know," said Evie. "But it wasn't good."

Behind the barracks, hidden beneath a stand of sprawling oaks, sat a small ravine. Leatherwolf Company had unofficially claimed it, dragging in some of the logs the woodsmen had cut to use as benches. They named it the Pit. Whenever there was a break in the day, if the weather cooperated, they would head down to the Pit and sing songs from home. Two of the former Goosegirl cadets were skilled with stringed instruments. Learning each other's songs had helped bring Ironbone Company and Goosegirl Company together in ways training alone couldn't.

Evie and her friends, however, had never been further apart. She sat alone on a boulder at the fringe of the company, watching the revelry from a distance. Nessa danced down the hill behind her. As she passed, she said, "Come on, Evie, come join us!"

"I'm fine, thanks." She watched Nessa move through the crowd to where Demetra and Liv were clapping along to the music. Maggie had gone to the library the minute the Fairy Drillsergeant had dismissed them, and Basil hadn't come down with everyone else. She was alone.

"I was there when the mountain rose from earth / Poking up to the bright blue skies / I was there when the snow melted down its face / You can bet I'll be there when it dies . . ."

The whole company, eighty strong, clapped along with the Eastern song, even those who weren't familiar. Evie, however, kept looking away from the crowd, back up the hill. Her mind had wandered to Prince Forbes. She had all but forgotten about the cursed portrait the previous year until Forbes's father had made a comment that brought it flaring back into her mind. He had said that the portrait was titled *The Princess of Saudade*, which was exactly what Remington had called her in one of her dragon's blood visions. The coincidence was simply too great to ignore. She was desperate to see the portrait with her own eyes, to see if it really was her in the painting.

At the top of the ravine, Basil stepped out of his storehouse, tightening his scabbard around his waist. He was off to observe the knights' sword training. Evie was suddenly struck by a mad idea. She sprang off of her boulder and bounded up the hill, then ducked into the barracks and ran to her bunk. There, beneath her mattress, was her sword. She raced back out and caught up to Basil as he crossed Hansel's Green toward campus.

"Evie! What are you . . ." He noticed the scabbard in her hand. "Oh."

"You don't mind, do you?"

"No, I don't mind. The better question is, will Beatrice mind? You haven't asked permission, have you?"

All around them, huge flocks of cadets in various colored

uniforms were coming and going, either finishing training or heading out for more. The campus bustled in a way it never had during their first year.

"If Beatrice wants to reprimand me for trying to better myself instead of sitting round clapping with the others, then so be it."

"All right," said Basil. "Let's go."

"And why do we keep our off hands behind our backs, men?" called Captain Lamarche, who had the most spectacular mustache. It looked like the filigree of a wrought-iron gate.

None of the Huntsman cadets answered. They were scattered across a wide expanse of dirt, squared off one against another, each holding an arming sword.

"It's because the empty hand is an easy target," Basil said to Evie. They were sitting atop a small set of risers at the edge of the training area, where they were meant to be observing. Captain Lamarche turned and glared at him. "Oh . . . sorry." He chuckled nervously.

"Yes. The empty hand is an easy target," said the Captain with disdain. "Men, hands behind your backs, please. Positions." The cadets raised their swords and put their free hands behind their backs. "There, you see? One less target for the enemy."

Evie wasn't paying attention. She was looking at Forbes, who was seated at the bottom of the risers in his Huntsman red. He was the only knight cadet not participating.

"Remember, men. When defending, your objective is to be where the strike is not. Group A, I want a simple downward strike. Simple, but deadly. This is combat training. We're not mucking about in the garden. If you get cut, then ideally you will learn to not get cut next time. And if you get killed, well, then you'll have saved me the trouble of sending you home."

There were scattered laughs, though Evie could feel the tension in the air. None of the cadets wore armor. She watched Remington as he raised his sword. He was as tall as anyone else in the company, but with a confidence that made him seem twice as deadly. Still, she had very little interest in seeing his blood on the ground.

"That stance doesn't work if you're using a two-hand sword," said Basil. "You need both hands to trap your opponent's weapon—"

"Will you shut up?" spat Forbes.

"Better yet," said Lamarche, clearly annoyed, "why don't you come down here and join us since you seem to know so much about swordplay?"

"Me?" said Basil. "That's all right, Captain, I'm fine here—"

"Get down here, Cadet."

Basil looked over at Evie and gulped. His hand, already shaking, went to the pommel of his sword.

"It's all right, Bas, it's only training," she said, though her heart was thudding for him.

"Why should some princess cadet get to practice and I can't?" said Forbes.

"We're meant to be easing you back into your training," said Lamarche. "But if you feel you're ready, then by all means, come join him."

Basil stepped out into the training area. Forbes marched to the sword rack and picked up an arming sword.

"Really, I'm only meant to be observing, Captain," said Basil. He was looking quite frail amidst all the burly knight cadets.

"No one has ever learned to use a blade by watching. Now, let's see if your hands are as operational as your mouth. Cadet Forbes, a basic downward strike, if you please."

Basil gulped and raised his sword, which quivered in the air. Evie's eyes met Remington's, and for once he did not look amused.

"Ready, cadets?" shouted Lamarche. "Hup!"

Evie flinched as Forbes lunged forward, his blade slashing through the air. Basil leapt to the side, then grabbed his blade with his off hand and snapped it right to Forbes's neck, where it hovered less than an inch from the skin.

"Well. that's not fair, is it?" said Forbes, who didn't dare move. "He's got a two-hand sword."

Lamarche took an arming sword off the rack and tossed it to Basil, who caught it by the hilt. "Again."

Basil set his own sword aside, then took his position. "See? Hand behind the back to reduce the targets—"

Forbes's blade whistled through the air. He didn't even wait for Lamarche to signal him. Basil's sword shot up and blocked it—*chink!* Forbes looked ready to spit fire. He lunged at Basil, swirling his sword in a series of attacks. Basil hopped away from each, using his blade to deflect them.

"Easy, men! Wait!" called Lamarche, but Forbes continued to rain down strikes. Basil deftly avoided them, then spun around and kicked Forbes's leg out from under him. Several of the Huntsman cadets began to cheer, which seemed to embolden Basil. Forbes hopped up, ignoring Lamarche's warnings, and attacked again. Basil's confidence had grown, however, and he easily batted away Forbes's blade. He moved as fluidly as a squirrel running from a dog.

"Go on, Basil!" shouted Evie with a whoop. His instincts were superb. His blade darted like a falcon as metallic *chinks* rang out beneath the cheers. Forbes could clearly feel himself being bested, and it only made him angrier.

"Agh!" he shouted as he took a mighty overhead swipe. Basil ducked under it and brought his sword up beneath the attack. "Aaaah!" Forbes fell to the dirt, holding his chin.

Basil's triumphant smile began to fade. He'd cut his opponent. The cheering of the others quieted as Forbes writhed in the dirt.

"That's enough!" called Lamarche, racing over to his wounded cadet. But before he could get there, Forbes sat up. There was a slice on his chin. It was bleeding quite badly, but wasn't deep.

"Well done," he said. "Looks like you win."

"I'm sorry!" said Basil, mortified. "Are you all right?"

Lamarche helped Forbes to his feet and inspected the cut.

"It's nothing," said Forbes. "At least I'm wearing red." He dabbed the cut on his sleeve. It made a deep stain on top of the red fabric.

"You're sure you're all right?" asked Lamarche.

"I'm fine. Believe me, I've had worse." He extended a hand to Basil, who hesitated, then shook it.

"I'm sorry, Forbes. It was an accident."

"You shouldn't play with swords if you're afraid of a little blood," said Forbes. Then he turned to Lamarche. "Let's keep going."

Lamarche nodded, his volume returning as he realized Forbes really was all right. "There you are, men. Be where the strike is not. Expertly demonstrated, Cadet . . ."

"Basil."

"Cadet Basil. Now, the rest of you, positions. One single attack. This is a defensive drill, not a sparring session."

Evie's heart was still racing, though now she was exhilarated by seeing Basil's performance. "Captain? Could I try as well?"

Lamarche turned to look at her. Several of the Huntsman cadets laughed. "Come on, then, young lady."

Her legs felt like rubber as she stood and made her way down the risers. Her hand was shaking atop the pommel of her sword. *You shouldn't play with swords if you're afraid of a little blood.* Evie was terrified of blood, particularly her own, but greater than her terror was her desire to swing her sword.

"Captain, if I may," said Remington, stepping forward. "I

taught my cousin to use a sword, and she's one of the best in Brentano. I'd be happy to train this one as well."

"Fine, yes," said Lamarche. "You, over here with me." The boy who had been working with Remington trotted over to join Lamarche. Evie walked over and stood opposite Remington.

"If you cut me, I'm never speaking to you again," she said.

"Don't worry, Malora, I'll go easy."

Evie chuckled and shook her head. "Now it's you who should be afraid of getting cut."

"Blades up!" called Captain Lamarche.

Evie slid her sword from the scabbard. In the dim sunlight, it was nearly as red as a ruby. Remington raised his eyebrows, impressed. "That's an absolutely stunning blade."

"Care for a closer look?" she said with a smirk.

"Ready, cadets? Hup!" shouted Lamarche.

Blades swung all around her. She closed her eyes and tried to block Remington, but her sword just slashed through empty air. When she opened her eyes, she saw him standing there, blade still raised.

"I find it's best to be attacked before you defend," he said.

"Well? Attack, then!" Adrenaline thrummed through her body.

"I just wanted to see how you handle a sword before I strike you. You've got an intuitive sense of balance, it seems."

"And you've got an intuitive tendency to talk too much."

He laughed. "If I may, the very first rule any weapons master will teach you? Keep your eyes open."

"Don't worry about my eyes," she said, bobbing the sword in her hand. "Worry about your own."

He raised his eyebrows, then his sword. All around them, the other cadets did the same.

"Ready, cadets?" shouted Lamarche. "Hup!"

She saw his arm jerk forward and reacted. She threw her blade out, knocking his aside with a *clink!* In the same motion, she brought the pommel around and cracked it into his cheek.

"Gah!" he said, clutching his face.

"Remington!" She dropped her sword and ran to him. "I'm so sorry!"

His cheek had already gone bright red where she'd hit him, though he was still smiling. "Brilliant move, Evie!" He wiped away two small splotches of blood. "I knew you had the instinct for it!"

"Are you all right?"

"Unless my head's rolling round on the ground, I'm fine. Come on, again!"

For the next hour, Evie and Remington traded blows. He offered tips and adjustments to improve her technique, but continued to be impressed with how she handled the blade. She could feel her confidence growing with each jarring clash of steel. Finally, when her arms were shuddering so much she could barely lift the sword, Lamarche called an end to the session. Evie and Remington walked to the risers and sat. He offered her a drink from his waterskin.

"Thanks," she said. As she drank, most of the other Huntsman cadets began to disperse, placing their swords back on the racks and heading to the barracks. Basil and Forbes, however, continued to spar. They seemed to be coaching each other after each clash. "Is it possible we're witnessing the beginnings of a friendship over there?"

Remington looked up just as Forbes took a massive whack at Basil. *Clang!*

"What, Forbes? No, I think he'd be perfectly happy to kill Basil right now."

Evie watched closely as Basil corrected Forbes's stance. The scowl never left his face. "Is he all right? Since he's been back? There's something I'd like to talk to him about, but he's not exactly the most approachable person, is he."

"Forbes? What do you want to talk to him about?"

"You remember that portrait from last year. The one that turned Forbes into a pig?"

"Of course, the portrait of you."

"I'd quite like to see it for myself. Just to satisfy my curiosity."

Forbes took another mighty swing. *Crash!* Basil seemed not to notice his building frustration. "That was good, but you've got to remember your balance. Upper body speed is meaningless if you're on the ground." Forbes gritted his teeth.

"Perhaps you should let me speak to him," said Remington.

"Why shouldn't I?"

"Well, he's having a bit of a rough go of it at the moment.

Rumor round the company is that his kingdom is in the process of being wiped from the map."

"What?"

"His father's made quite a few enemies over the years. It seems one of them has finally decided to do something about it. Forbes fled the city with those two other blokes he turned up with, but his father is apparently still trapped inside." He turned to face her. "Perhaps he might be a bit more open to talking to me than to you."

Clang! Shing! Clack!

"Forbes!" called Basil. "Stop! Forbes!"

Forbes had lost control. His eyes were aflame as he poured attacks on Basil.

"Cadet Forbes, enough!" bellowed Lamarche, but Forbes kept going. Basil retreated, expertly parrying away the attacks. It was only a matter of time, however, before he would trip on the rough ground and Forbes would have the advantage.

Forbes hacked at Basil with everything he had. Basil dipped to the side, then bashed the flat face of his sword into Forbes's back. It knocked him off balance and sent him straight into the dirt. Like a viper, Basil's blade was at Forbes's throat.

"Blimey," said Remington. "That chap certainly knows his way round a blade."

Forbes slapped Basil's sword aside and scrambled to his feet. He tossed his own in the dirt and stomped off toward the barracks. Evie watched him with narrow eyes.

"Perhaps I will let you talk to him after all."

As the cadets of Leatherwolf Company settled in for another foreshortened night of sleep, Evie could still feel every one of Remington's sword strikes in her bones. Her hands were raw and blistered. Still, for all the physical pain, there was a new-found confidence that lingered as well. She liked that bit. Quite a lot.

"All right, Maggie?" she asked.

"Yeah, fine," said Maggie, sitting in bed with a book on her knees. "Just reading the chapter on outsmarting goblins again. Don't want to give Professor Adelbert any excuse to send me home during our Applied Courage exam tomorrow. And I've been trying to prepare for this Witches' Night that Princess Copperpot warned us about, but I can't find anything about it in any of the books. It's all *so* stressful."

"Ah," said Evie. And she didn't know quite what to say after that. Maggie hadn't asked about the sword training, so she didn't volunteer anything about it.

"Don't you ever take a break?" said Demetra, returning to her bed with a breezy smile. She'd come from chatting with Nessa and Liv across the aisle.

"Don't you ever stop taking a break?" said Maggie.

"I'll have you know that we were studying as well."

"Then why don't you find your way back over there again? I already feel dumber since you've started talking."

Demetra's face curled up in confusion. "Why are you having a go at me?"

Maggie sighed in frustration. "Never mind. Just leave me alone. I've got actual studying to do."

Evie and Demetra exchanged a look. Evie shrugged, as if to say, *I don't know either.*

"Attention!" called Princess Copperpot. The girls leapt to their feet and assembled at their footboards as their House Princess lurched inside with another sack full of letters. Lance strutted ahead, searching for things to peck. Maggie held her breath for a full forty seconds as he passed by. "This will be a short announcement, I'm afraid. Only one cadet has received any correspondence this evening."

All around the room, shoulders slumped in disappointment. Evie, her cheeks flushing pink, made her way across the bearskin rugs to retrieve her letters.

"That is all, girls. You may sleep. And remember: tomorrow you must be more a princess than today."

At first, Evie had thought that mantra a threat, as though anyone who *wasn't* more a princess would be discharged. But as one week turned into the next, and as she felt her friends becoming increasingly distant, the words also served as a helpful reminder: *I'm here to become a princess, no matter what else is happening.* If Maggie wanted to snipe at Demetra, if Demetra wanted to ignore Maggie . . . she just had to let all of that go, because tomorrow she would need to be more a princess than today.

She absently pulled open the drawstring and emptied the sack. Demetra climbed into her bed and began writing a letter. Neither she nor Maggie was as enamored with Evie's letters as they'd been that first night. Around the room, torches began to go out. Girls traveled to and from the latrine, toothbrushes in hand. Evie sat on her bunk and absently flipped through the letters as she glanced over at Maggie. *I'm here to become a princess, that's true. But it would certainly be nice if my friends weren't so hostile toward—*

A small package slipped free from her hands and fell to the floor. It was slightly bulkier than the other letters. As she picked it up, she realized that it was made from two parchment hawks that had been stitched together. There were no markings, only a crude wax seal across the back with a string melted into it. She squeezed the package and felt something hard inside. She pulled on the string, which tore a line through the wax. The package opened and something clattered to the floor. She gasped and jumped back as though a snake had slithered out of the package.

"All right, Evie?" said Demetra.

Evie stared at the object on the floor in horror. She slowly reached down to pick it up. She rolled the cold, hard object between her fingers, watching the firelight play off of its smooth surface. It was roughly six inches long, and sharp as a needle at one end.

"It's a wolf's fang," she whispered.

"What?" said Demetra. She climbed out of her bunk and joined Evie, taking the fang from her fingers. "Why would someone send you a wolf's fang?"

Evie opened the letter, her fingers trembling. The message

inside read, *Found this and thought you should see it*, and it was signed, *a friend*.

Something was stuck to the inside of the package with a spot of wax. It was an ordinary parchment, not a bird, and it had been roughly folded. As Evie opened it, she could tell by the coppery tint of the words that it was not written in ink, but rather in blood ...

Vertreiben awakes!
Pennyroyal Akademie burns!

"AND YOU'VE ABSOLUTELY no idea who sent this?" Princess Beatrice stalked around her office, glaring at the blood-streaked parchment in her hands. Princess Hazelbranch, Princess Copper-pot, and Corporal Liverwort were there as well, looking various shades of concerned. There was also a large man with long black hair and silvery stubble whom Evie had seen at meals but never formally met. His name was Sir Schönbecker, and he was the House Knight of Shield Company, the highest company for knights.

"I'm sorry, Headmistress," said Evie, sitting at the edge of one of Beatrice's chairs. "I've gotten quite a few letters this year, and I don't know who sent any of them."

"Are you tellin' me there's more of them things?" snapped Liverwort, one of her eyes closing in a sneer. "And you're only *now* tellin' us?"

"No, not like this one. The others, they're from . . . admirers." She cringed as she said it.

"Admirers? Well, ain't you just the most precious—"

"I believe we're missing the point here, everyone," said Princess Hazelbranch. "Evie's done nothing wrong. She brought me the letter as soon as she got it—"

"And that's another thing," said Princess Copperpot loudly, her one good eye bulging from her head. She awkwardly stroked Lance, who sat nestled in her natural left arm. "Why didn't you come to me? I am your House Princess now, and I am the one to be confided in. This whole affair leaves quite a sour taste . . ."

"I'm sorry, Princess," said Evie. "I suppose I just got in the habit of talking to Princess Hazelbranch last year."

"Bad habits must be broken," she said, glaring down at Evie. "You shall hereafter confide solely in me. That is a direct order, do you understand?"

"Yes, Princess."

"Have you shown this to anyone else, Cadet?" said Beatrice, holding up the letter.

"No, Headmistress. Well, I mean, I may have mentioned it to Maggie and Demetra."

Beatrice flicked her head to Princess Copperpot, who turned and lurched out of the office. "And that's it? No one else?"

"No, Headmistress."

"Good. Thank you for bringing it to my attention. I shall have some of our best princesses out in the field look into this, but I can assure you that it will prove to be the work of witches. We have seen this very thing before, many times."

Evie glanced to Liverwort, then to Hazelbranch.

"You may go, Cadet."

"Yes, Headmistress." She stood and walked to the door.

"Oh, and Cadet, I must insist that you not mention this to anyone else. Let us handle it from here."

Evie nodded, then went out into the candlelit corridor and closed the door behind her. She glanced down the hallway to the staircase that led to the outside, but hesitated. Muffled voices had resumed from behind the door. She took a deep breath, then carefully leaned forward and put her ear to the wood, where a man's deep baritone came through.

"Forgive me, Headmistress, but I'm afraid I've never heard of this . . . Vertreiben."

"And there is absolutely no reason you should have," said Beatrice with disgust. "They are an embarrassment to the princessing service."

"The Vertreiben are an ancient sect," said Princess Hazelbranch. "A sort of secret society made up of women who were discharged for one reason or another."

"Indeed," said Beatrice. "For all those who shine brightly here at the Academy and become Princesses of the Shield, there are a handful of shadow cadets who watch from a distance, growing more bitter and resentful by the day. They are nothing more than sore losers."

"Sore losers with sharp blades," said Hazelbranch. "The Vertreiben were formed not long after Princess Pennyroyal founded the Academy. The girls who started it were, as the Headmistress said, humiliated when they were judged unworthy. Their embarrassment, their lack of opportunity . . . it festered into hatred. As the Academy's graduates began to disperse into the kingdoms and people saw how effective their training had made them in dealing with witches, those other girls felt increasingly hard done by. In their twisted minds, they saw themselves as victims and vowed revenge on Princess Pennyroyal and her staff."

"They are a petulant group of outcasts and nothing more," said Beatrice.

Evie thought back to the girls she'd known the previous year who had been sent home. Anisette would never have joined such a group. She was assisting Princess Camilla and couldn't have been happier with her discharge. Malora was a witch, and had enough of her own reasons to be angry with, well, just about everything. But were there girls Evie had known and trained with who might have turned to this sect to seek revenge? Were any of her old company-mates now members of the Vertreiben?

"The wolf's fang . . . This is their symbol," said Beatrice. "Just as a wolf is immune to a princess's magic, so too are the Vertreiben. And just as the wolf does, they seek to tear the princess to ribbons." Something clinked on the desk. Beatrice must have tossed the fang aside. "I've never heard such rubbish."

"And you're quite certain this threat isn't real?" said Schönbecker.

"This *threat*," spat Beatrice, "could have been sent by some mouth-breathing bridge troll from Viernach for all we know. The fact of the matter is that Cadet Evie's sudden fame has made her something of an easy target for this sort of thing."

"Supposing that—"

"Supposing that the Vertreiben *are* behind this, despite the fact that not once in the history of Pennyroyal Academy have they posed any sort of legitimate threat. I am well aware of our duty, Sir Schönbecker, as leaders of this institution, to be cautious. Overly so."

There was a pause. Evie held her breath and listened as closely as she could, though part of her was afraid her heart was thumping loudly enough that they'd hear it.

"Start your third-class knights on small arms. Swords in particular. Send the older boys to the forges and have them learn to make weapons. Hand-and-a-halfs and back swords, nothing fancy. These are things that need doing anyway, so we might as well do them now."

"Of course, Headmistress," said Sir Schönbecker.

"And do it *quietly*. I'd like to keep this contained to this room, if at all possible."

"Shall we start the girls on small arms as well?" said Hazelbranch.

"No. Our mission is and always will be to defend the realm from witches. We've too great an opportunity with all these new cadets to rebuild our forces, and I won't have that undermined by such a glistening assemblage of fools as the Vertreiben."

"Very well," said Hazelbranch. "But, strictly as a precaution-ary measure, do you suppose it might be wise to send for . . . *her*?"

"Would it help you sleep better, Princess Hazelbranch?"

"Headmistress, if Evie is right, then an innocent woman was killed."

"By witches." There was another pause. Evie pressed her ear even more tightly to the door as Beatrice let out a sigh. "Very well. Corporal Liverwort, send for Princess Lankester."

"Aye, Mum."

"Tell her to report to me as soon as she's arrived. Now, is ev-eryone satisfied?" There was a silent pause. "Then I don't want to hear another word about it. And I don't want any of you discussing this with anyone else. We're quite lucky that Evie's become as famous as she has. People viewed what happened here last year as a triumphant victory over the witches, but they could just as easily have seen it as gross incompetence on our part. The very last thing we need now is a panic, partic-ularly with all these new cadets here. Another instance of in-competence could do irreparable harm to the Academy. Do I make myself clear?"

"Yes, Headmistress," they all replied.

"Good. I shall send word to some of our key princesses that this has happened, and then I shall drop the entire thing in the bin and consider this matter closed."

A bitter wind blew the shimmering dust sideways from the Fairy Drillsergeant's wings. She was floating next to Captain

Ramsbottom. Side by side, they looked like a minnow and a whale.

"Congratulations! You're now second-class cadets," she joked. "Perhaps now you'll start acting like it."

"You've done well, cadets," said Ramsbottom. "Keep practicing the techniques we've taught you and you should be able to survive whatever mischief a witch or a dragon or a giant or a troll sends your way."

The quality of the air had begun to change, becoming thinner and colder and more adept at seeping through the woven linen of the Pennyroyal Academy uniforms. They'd reached the frosted border between autumn and winter in their second year of training, with rain showers that skipped the skin and chilled right to the bone, and the cadets of Leatherwolf Company had finally—finally—finished their first year.

"Gentlemen," said the Fairy Drillsergeant, "thank you for your efforts. Best of luck with the rest of your second year."

"Yes, Fairy Drillsergeant," said the boys.

"Knights of Huntsman Company, move out!" said Ramsbottom.

Remington turned to Evie and winked. "See you at the blades."

She smiled as she watched him march off with the rest of his company. The end of Enchanted Forest Orienteering meant the end of natural meetings between Leatherwolf and Huntsman Companies. Now Evie found a bright side to Basil's transfer request. She would still be able to see Remington during sword training.

The day was a particularly chilly one, with a misty wind coming up from the south. After reuniting with Goosegirl Company, and some good-natured congratulations and cheers about their "graduation" to the second class, the Fairy Drillsergeant moved her princess cadets straight into their Advanced Castlery training. She led them to a dank hallway in the depths of a castle hidden amongst the labyrinthine roads of the western part of campus. The dreary dungeon was lit by a handful of candles. It was little more than a low-ceilinged corridor with iron cages on either side.

"Right, here we are, then. Now that you know your way round the enchanted forest, it's time to learn your way round the inside of a castle. Does anyone know why our campus has been designed in the particular way that it has?"

Maggie's hand shot up. "I just read about this! Though it may seem like a strange hodgepodge of buildings, it is actually a deceptively elegant design. The structures on this side of campus are modeled after the Western Kingdoms, and those on the other side are modeled after the Eastern Kingdoms. The buildings farthest from the Queen's Tower, the third ring, are the simplest to navigate. They're generally replicas of structures from the oldest kingdoms in the land, like the ones you'd find in Gummersbach or Kassel. But the closer you get to the center of campus, the more complex and realistic they become."

The Fairy Drillsergeant stared at Maggie, incredulous.

"If I'm not mistaken, this castle is in the second ring, where the structures are filled with secret passageways, false doors, and intentionally confusing hallways and staircases. Next year, we'll be training in the first ring, which are meant to be some of the most vexing designs in all the land."

The Fairy Drillsergeant's disbelief had become a snarl. "Would you like to teach this course, Cadet?"

Maggie was so deep into reciting the things she'd learned that she didn't even hear the comment. "Supposedly the first-ring castles are so difficult to navigate that two cadets have actually been lost in them forever. Rinkrank's Keep was one and Molehill Castle was the other, I think. Though I couldn't tell if that bit was true or just something the author put in to make them seem scarier—"

"Right, so, you all remember how to pick a lock, yes?" said the Fairy Drillsergeant, cutting Maggie short.

"Yes, Fairy Drillsergeant."

As she continued her lecture on the basics of lock picking, Evie leaned over and whispered to Maggie.

"Have you ever read anything about Princess Lankester?"

"Who?"

"Princess Lankester. Beatrice sent for her last night when I brought her the letter from the Vertreiben—"

"Evie!" gasped Maggie, her eyes bulging. "Princess Copperpot pulled Demetra and me out of bed and threatened to throw us out if we ever mentioned that letter to anyone. Stop talking about it!"

"Fine, I will, but only if you answer my question."

"No," spat Maggie. "I've never heard of Princess Lankester."

"If Maggie doesn't know her, she must be obscure," whispered Basil.

Maggie scowled at them both and moved to the other side of the hall.

"So once you've picked your lock," said the Fairy Drillsergeant, "you're still trapped down here, probably with heavily armed guards. Now you'll need to find a way out of the dungeon itself . . ."

"We've got to find out more about the Vertreiben," whispered Evie. "I don't want to be caught off guard like we were with Hardcastle."

"I find witches to be creepy enough," said Basil. "A secret society of bitter, violent princesses? No thank you."

"Shh!" spat Kelbra. Evie glared at her.

"Many dungeons," continued the Fairy Drillsergeant, "even a lot of them in the Eastern Kingdoms, have secret passageways to the outside. That's in case there's some sort of uprising. The guards can escape and lock down part of the castle until they regain control. Now, the Western Kingdoms favor trick stones and bricks to trip their secret passage entrances. The Eastern Kingdoms favor false furniture. In a dungeon like this, you've got to feel carefully for subtle differences in texture . . ."

"Come on, Evie," said Basil. "You did everything you were supposed to do. Just leave it to them now."

"I hope the lot of you get trapped in a prison someday," snarled Kelbra. "It would serve you right for not paying attention."

Evie scowled and tried to turn her attention back to the Fairy Drillsergeant. Basil mimicked Kelbra's sour face, which made Evie snort with laughter.

"Cadet Evie!" called the Fairy Drillsergeant. "Was that you I just heard volunteering to run the spirals after class?"

"Yes, Fairy Drillsergeant," she muttered. As she stewed in the dungeon and half listened to the rest of the lecture, Evie could already feel her legs starting to burn.

"Let's talk about witches, shall we?" said Princess Ziegenbart. Her bell clanged softly as she walked amongst the straw bales. Outside, rain hissed on the stone. "Now, there are some in the administration who'd rather I didn't share this particular story with you. They're worried it might frighten you off. I say if it does frighten you off, then you were never meant to be here in the first place. Knowledge is far more valuable than magic. If you are going to engage the enemy, then you must know what the enemy is." All was silent in the room except for the rain and occasional rumbling of distant thunder.

"Once upon a time," she began, "there was a lovely little village nestled beneath the mountains on the banks of a mighty river. The townspeople lived simple lives . . . farmers, merchants, mothers and fathers. They worked hard and went about their work with great care and enjoyment, and the sun always seemed to shine down on them in all matters. Except for one.

"The village, you see, had a terrible problem with rats. Because of all the prosperous mills surrounding the town, the storehouses were fat with feed, which, in turn, drew the ra*aa-a-a-a-a-agh-agh-agh*." Her bleating turned to coughing, and then to one final clearing of the throat. "Ahem. Pardon me. Which drew the *rats*.

"Now, the townspeople initially made do by breeding an army of cats, and this worked quite well. The cats ate the rats and the rat population stayed low. But before long, the rats returned, and in ever-greater numbers. They were quicker this time, better able to vex the cats. And soon the village's rat problem had become an emergency. Food stores ran low. Children cried out in their sleep from rats scurrying across their faces and nibbling at their toes. Some of the villagers even began to leave town. Those who remained begged the mayor to do something about the crisis—"

One of the cadets in back screamed as a rat scurried across the floor, causing others to laugh uneasily.

"One day, a man turned up. He was tall and thin, wearing a patchwork suit of colored cloth and a long feather in his cap. None in the village had seen anything like him before. He held a slender golden pipe, and promised the mayor he could rid the town of its rats . . . for a price. The mayor agreed to his terms, eagerly, and watched with bemusement as the man began strolling through town blowing on his pipe. He seemed in no particular hurry to get anywhere; he was simply playing a merry tune and trying not to step on the black sea of rats that began swarming at his feet. Before long, the townspeople's confusion turned to astonishment. The rats followed the piper as he played. They abandoned whole pieces of food in the streets to scurry after him. They came forth from the walls and the gutters and the roofs. He continued his slow procession toward the city walls, the horde of rats following merrily behind. And the townspeople watched in amazement. Eventually the piper led the rats to the river's edge, then played them right over the banks. One by one, thousand by thousand, they were swept down the river, never to be seen again. And before long, the village was as free from rats as the day of its founding."

"Forgive me, Princess," said Nessa. "This is the sort of story we've all heard before as children. Is there some particular—"

"The piper returned," said Ziegenbart, causing Nessa's cheeks to go red, "and was hailed as a hero, quite rightly. However, when he tried to collect his reward, the mayor refused. The greedy old man saw that the rats had perished in the river and thought he could save the village a large sum of money by sending the piper on his way without one gold piece. The villagers, thinking more of their own pockets than the piper's, agreed with the mayor's plan.

"Needless to say, the piper was quite upset. He spent that night in the mountains outside of town, his fury growing. He cursed the people of the village, but it wasn't enough. Nothing he thought or shouted could sate the red desire for revenge that consumed his heart. To everyone's eternal misfortune, he was not alone that night in the mountains." The goat paced before them. She had all of their attention now. "He was soon discovered by a witch. She had heard his cries of abuse at the hands of the villagers and assured him she could help. The piper was terrified of the old hag, to be sure, but his anger at being cheated overcame him, and he listened with great interest to her wicked plan. The next day at dawn, blinded by hatred, he returned down the mountain to the village gates. His black heart was hidden beneath his brightly colored clothes and the jaunty feather in his cap, but it was there all the same. As he made his way through the village streets, playing his happy tune, the enchanted pipe could only be heard by the children of the village, and not by their parents. One after another, they rose from their beds and went out into the streets to join him. Once he'd gathered all the children of the village into his macabre parade, he led them out of the city walls and up into the mountains. With the lilting song of his pipe echoing down the valley, he led those innocent souls straight into a cave where the witch awaited."

Evie glanced over at Maggie, whose face was scrunched in horror.

"The villagers awoke that morning to find all their children missing. In a panic, they scoured every inch of the forest and mountains surrounding their beloved river valley. But even after months of looking, they found not a single trace. Not one piece of clothing. Not one stray hair. Nothing. The witch had already done with them what she'd intended from the start."

Ziegenbart paced back and forth in front of them. The tension in the room was unbearable. *Why has she told us this?* wondered Evie.

"I told you that if you are to engage your enemy in battle, then you must first know her. Well, now we must discuss the greatest enemy of all. The leader of the Seven Sisters. The great witch Calivigne.

"Here are the facts as we know them with regard to Calivigne. It is exceedingly rare for a witch to be named, or, at least, to have a name known outside their own world. Very, very few witches have ever become as infamous as she has. Calivigne is also one of the physically largest witches on record. There are a multitude of theories about why she has grown as large—and notorious—as she has, but I am quite certain I know the truth. When I was in my younger days, and before I was cursed, I was a Cauldron Tipper. And I had it in my head that I would be the one to find Calivigne. This was many years ago, before she was nearly as well known as she is now. I tracked her. Studied her. Learned everything I could about her. And though you won't find it in any of the histories, not even Lieutenant Volf's, this is why, I believe, she has achieved the particular stature that she has . . ."

Evie's heart was racing. She didn't even realize it, but she had slid all the way to the edge of her straw bale.

"The witch who had been in league with the piper was Calivigne's mother."

There were gasps around the classroom. Out of the corner of her eye, Evie saw Demetra's hand go to her mouth.

"It is my belief that Calivigne was made from the hearts of the innocent children lured to their deaths by the Pied Piper of Hamelin. That is why she is so powerful. If I'm correct, never before would a witch have been created out of such hatred and depravity." She stepped forward, and Evie could see how haunted the goat was by the story she had just told. "*That* is your enemy, cadets. Now . . . how do you wish to fight her?"

Evie heaved a vat of broth onto the table and began stirring it with a long wooden spoon. Ziegenbart's story had left a chill inside of her that went all the way to her bones. With everyone telling Evie how wonderful she was, and how the witches had gone into retreat, it was easy to forget the truly wicked things they had done, and continued to do, out there in the real world. "But how could they name anything on campus after a monster like that? The ballroom where Maggie won the Grand Ball last year. It's got his name on it. A murderer!"

"At the time that ballroom was constructed, no one knew the truth about the Piper," said Princess Hazelbranch, chopping celery and onions. "They believed he was a hero who had driven away the rats, rats infested with all manner of disease. No one knew about the children. Or if they did, they didn't believe it could be true."

"Dozens of children gone. How could they not know?"

"Sometimes it can be difficult to discern the truth in a world so filled with magic." She scooped the celery onto her knife and dropped it into Evie's broth. Then she did the same with the onions.

Evie stopped stirring with a frown. "Princess Hazelbranch, could I ask you something?"

"Of course, Evie, anything. But first I'll need you to light the fire."

Evie lit the cookfire, then strained to shift the heavy pot onto it. "If one man could do something as awful as the Pied Piper did, and that led to Calivigne being born, then . . ."

"Yes, Evie, go on."

"Well . . . if all that is true, then how can we ever win this war?"

"Ah," said Hazelbranch, nodding sagely. "That is why kindness is one of the four essential pieces of a true princess. We can battle witches until the end of time, but that is only half of our war. We must also spread kindness to prevent incidents like the one in Hamelin. Had there been a true princess in that village to remind the townspeople of the bargain to which they'd agreed, or to help the Piper see that what he was doing was disproportionately cruel, Calivigne might never have been born."

"I'm sorry, Princess, but are you suggesting that a simple act of kindness might have prevented this entire war?"

"Indeed I am. It all comes back to hope, Evie. A princess represents hope in a world of darkness. And with hope, there is much less darkness."

Evie watched the vegetables swirl in the foaming yellow broth. She imagined those children walking helplessly into the mountain cave . . .

"Now I might ask you something, Cadet."

She looked up. "Hmm?"

"Last year, I almost never saw your face without two other gigglemugs attached. Is everything all right between you and your friends?"

"Oh, yeah, fine . . . fine." Evie glanced across the kitchen at Maggie, who was filling the butter dishes. "Though to be honest, it is a bit different for Maggie this year."

"How so?"

"Well . . ." She looked around to make sure no one was listening. "Forgive me, but it's Princess Copperpot. She sent Cadet Bluebell home this morning for brushing her teeth too loudly."

"I see."

"She came down quite hard on Maggie the first day of the year and it's sucked all the fun right out of her."

"How awful."

"It's a bit different for Demetra as well, I suppose," she continued. "She's got some new friends this year and doesn't seem all that interested in us anymore. We're all still friends, it's just . . . it's not the same."

"One minute to service, everyone!" shouted Princess Rampion. "One minute!"

Hazelbranch began ladling the broth into tureens. "Well, Evie, let me just say this: Friendship is like a carriage. It does not drive itself. Particularly when the road gets rocky."

"Service, please! Everyone else to your seats!"

Hazelbranch wiped her hands on a towel, then gave Evie a

wink and headed for the door. Evie set the tureens on a cart and joined the rest of the serving staff, still thinking about what Princess Hazelbranch had just said.

As they emerged into the Dining Hall, she could see that the enormous numbers in the third class were finally beginning to thin a bit. There were open spots at every table now, and there would likely be more tomorrow.

She walked up and down the aisles, serving broth and bread with a false smile on her face. She'd gotten used to the looks and whispers as she passed, so she had to remind herself that to these girls, she was someone special. The worst thing she could do would be to behave as though she was annoyed with her fame.

"Thank you so much," said one particularly mousy girl with big teeth.

Evie smiled at her and moved along the table.

"Hi, Evie!" said another girl with big brown eyes.

"You should come visit our company sometime!" called another. "We've made up a song about you!"

As Evie ladled broth into a pewter bowl, a cold realization descended over her like a shadow. She spilled the broth onto one girl's lap.

"Ahh!"

"Sorry!" said Evie. "Oh, I'm so sorry!"

"It's all right," said the girl with a laugh. "Now I can say the Warrior Princess spilled soup on me."

Evie was suddenly overcome with claustrophobia. Though

there was plenty of broth left in her tureens, she pushed the cart as quickly as she could back toward the kitchens.

I am the Pied Piper, she thought. *All these girls have followed me here and I'm leading them straight to Calivigne.*

She burst into the kitchens and dropped onto a stool, burying her face in her hands. Her head felt light. *I am the Pied Piper and I've led them right to her—*

"Cadet!" called Princess Copperpot. "You there! Bring this to the staff table!"

Evie looked up, bleary eyed, and saw her House Princess scowling down at her. Lance was on one of the storage shelves eating from a hole in a sack of seeds. "Yes, Princess," she said with a sniffle.

"What's the matter with you?"

"Nothing, Princess, I'm fine." She stood and took the handle of the cart Copperpot had prepared. It held several bowls of roasted vegetables.

"I ordered you to confide in me, so if you've got something to confide, you'd better do it now!"

"No, Princess, I'm fine, really."

"Go on, then! Move!"

Evie took a deep breath and headed for the door. Holding the cart handle steadied her, and she managed to mostly compose herself before emerging back into the cacophony of the Dining Hall. She wheeled the cart up a small ramp onto the raised section of floor that held the staff table. She began scooping parsnips and potatoes onto the plates in front of her, trying her best to avoid drawing attention to herself. She knew there were tears in her eyes and they were on the verge of falling. Still, she somehow managed to fill Rumpledshirtsleeves's plate without him realizing who was doing it. Then she moved slowly down the table toward the center, where Princess Beatrice sat in an ancient oak throne lined in burgundy silk. Next to her was a woman who looked even older than Beatrice's throne. She was slim and shriveled, nearly as short as Rumpledshirtsleeves. White hair fell close to her cheeks, and wrinkles covered every inch of her face. She sat hunched over her plate, barely picking at the beetroots sitting in a pool of juice so deep and red that it reminded Evie of blood. As she drew nearer, she slowed her service and pretended to busy herself with the vegetables.

"You may scoff and snortle all you like, Headmistress, but the signs were there," said the old woman, a trickle of beet juice running down the corner of her mouth. "Someone has been at the Drudenhaus. Many someones, it seems."

Evie scooped her vegetables one by one to the woodsman a few seats down from Beatrice.

"Hunters, bandits, curious children . . . It could be any number of—"

"Curious children? In the middle of the Dortchen Wild?" said the old woman. "No, Princess. No indeed. This was Javotte."

Evie gasped. She began to cough to try to cover it.

"Are you quite all right?" said Sir Schönbecker.

"Yes, of course. Pardon me, sir."

Beatrice and the old woman hadn't seemed to notice Evie's

coughing fit and continued their conversation. She carried on slowly, serving the other staff seated next to them.

"Javotte," scoffed Beatrice. "You have absolutely no evidence of that."

The old woman sneered and wiped away the beet juice with the tablecloth. "I presume you've brought me here to listen to my expertise, and not to mock it. Whether you want to believe it or not, the Vertreiben are real. Perhaps they're in league with the witches, perhaps not. But if they are, it could be catastrophic—"

"Keep your voice down, Lankester. You're only here as a courtesy."

Evie scooped steaming parsnips onto Princess Moonshadow's plate. So this was Princess Lankester, the woman Hazelbranch had wanted Beatrice to summon. She'd almost gotten to where they were sitting, so she began scooping even more slowly.

"A courtesy? You've never had respect for the Vertreiben as an enemy, Headmistress, and now there have been dozens of reports of attacks on Princesses of the Shield—"

"There are attacks on princesses every single day. By witches. Or had you forgotten who it is we're meant to be fighting?" Lankester's eyes flicked over to Evie, which caused Beatrice to turn in her throne. "Will there be anything else, Cadet?"

"No, Headmistress." She quickly pushed her cart along the table, scooping vegetables until her bowls were empty. As she circled back to the kitchens, she glanced at Beatrice and the old woman, her palms sweating. They were huddled closely, both scowling and jutting angry fingers at each other. What in the world was the Drudenhaus, and why was it so important that Javotte might have gone there?

She brought the cart to the kitchens for a troll to clean, then walked back into the Dining Hall and joined her company. She sat next to Maggie and began stirring her peas with her fork, watching Beatrice and Lankester over Basil's shoulder.

"Evie?" he finally said. "Is something the matter? You look as though you're ready to murder the Headmistress."

Evie snapped out of her thoughts. She looked at Basil and blinked. Then she looked over at Maggie. Demetra's usual spot was empty. "Where is she?"

"Where do you think?" said Maggie. "Down there with our replacements."

At the end of the table, Demetra was busy nattering away with Nessa and Liv. "Forget her," said Evie. "We've got trouble."

"Trouble?" said Maggie.

"Do you know who that is up there with Princess Beatrice?"

Basil turned to look. "Never seen her before. She looks a bit grim, though, doesn't she?"

"That must be . . ." said Maggie. She gasped. "Is that Princess Lankester?"

"Yes, and I think she's some sort of expert on the Vertreiben—"

"Stop saying that word!"

"I'm sorry, Maggie, but we've simply got to talk about this."

"Why? If that woman is an expert on the . . . on *them*, then what else is there to talk about?" Her eyes shifted around in search of Princess Copperpot.

"I just heard her mention someone called Javotte. That's who those three princesses were asking after before they killed the innkeeper's wife."

"Blimey," said Basil with a grave face.

"She said Javotte has been in the Drudenhaus. Whatever that is, she didn't seem particularly happy about it."

"This is all making me very nervous," said Maggie, fanning herself. "Do you mind if I change seats?"

"Yes I mind if you change seats! Sit right there and help me figure this out!" She looked around to be sure no one else was listening, then leaned in and spoke softly. "Knowledge is more powerful than magic, right? That's what Princess Ziegenbart said. Well, I think it's time we did a bit of research."

"Oh," said Maggie, brightening. "Is that all? I can help with research. Where do you want to start?"

"By sneaking into the restricted area of the Archives."

Maggie whimpered.

"The restricted area?" said Basil. "But why?"

"According to Demetra's sister, Javotte used to be a cadet here."

"So?"

"So whether she became a Princess of the Shield or not, she's still a princess of the blood."

"Oh, not the Registry of Peerage," moaned Maggie.

"Exactly."

"What's the Registry of Peerage?" said Basil.

"Last year, when Beatrice learned that I was King Callahan's daughter, she put my name in this really old book called the Registry of Peerage. It's got information on royalty from all across the land. If Javotte is a princess of the blood, then she's got to be in there."

"I won't do it, Evie," said Maggie. Her skin had gone ashen, and her eyes were darting around the room.

"I wouldn't ask you to. Not with Princess Copperpot watching you like a . . . well, like a rooster. But I do need one thing from you. I need you to draw me a map. The quickest way from the barracks to the Archives. It'll be dark when we go."

"Evie, this is madness. Sneaking into the restricted area of an official building after lights-out? You can't be serious!"

"It's the only way to find out what's coming for us."

There was a pause. Demetra laughed at the end of the table.

"Good. Well, let us know what you find, then, will you?" said Basil, standing to leave.

"You're coming with me."

He plopped to his seat. "Me? Why?"

Evie glared toward the end of the table. "Bloody Demetra. I'd really like to have a third to help speed things along, but I don't trust her to turn up."

"Basil," said Maggie. "You're not really going to do this, are you?"

"Apparently I am."

Evie thought for a moment, then shot up from the bench and

made her way across the Dining Hall. Eyes and happy whispers followed her as she worked her way through the tables. She ignored them all and went to the Huntsman Company table. "Could I talk to you for a minute?" she asked Remington.

He stood and wiped his mouth on his sleeve, then followed her to one of the hearths. "What is it?" he said, still chewing.

"Would you be willing to sneak out and meet me and Basil tonight? We're going—"

"Of course," he said with a smile. "When and where?"

THAT NIGHT, after the torches had been extinguished and Princess Copperpot had hobbled back to her quarters, Evie rose silently from her bunk. The barracks were almost completely dark on that moonless night, and she had to move slowly to avoid crashing into anything.

"I can't believe you made me do this," whispered Maggie, handing Evie a small piece of parchment.

"Thank you," she replied. Then, armed with the map, she slipped out of the barracks and into the night. A blast of cold air hit her immediately. Snow fell softly from the clouds.

"I'll have you know that my bed was extremely warm," said Basil, standing at the corner of the barracks, his hair already topped with white.

"Right. Let's go," said Evie, and the two of them ran across Hansel's Green, leaving long streaks of black in the pristine field of white. Orange light flickered from the torches lit across campus. They ran without stopping until they reached a small grove of elms near a granary at the westernmost road of campus. Basil slipped in the snow, his arms flailing wildly as he cartwheeled to the ground.

"Shh!"

"It's hardly my fault!" he spat. "No one told me there'd be snow!"

Evie leaned out from behind the granary wall and looked around. "He's supposed to be here by now." She let the ambient torchlight illuminate her map.

Basil breathed into his cupped hands, studying Maggie's map over Evie's shoulder. "There are so many annotations on that thing, it'll take us all night just to read it. 'The Archives are positioned on the south end of campus, with most of the records stored below ground level. The location was chosen specifically for the protection of rare and sensitive manuscripts.' Why would we possibly need to know that?"

"It's just Maggie," said Evie. "That's what she does. Look, none of that matters. We just need to follow this road until we reach . . . whatever this is." She pointed to a spot on the map. "It looks like some sort of monster."

"That's a gargoyle," said Remington, suddenly behind them.

Basil shouted with fright and fell over again. "Where in blazes did you come from?"

Evie scowled at Remington. She looked at the telltale trails in the snow and knew that he'd come as a frog. His great-grandfather had been the original Frog King, and Remington had the ability to become one at will. Of course, Evie was the only one at the Academy who knew his secret. Poor Basil clutched his chest as though his heart was about to explode. Remington grabbed his hand and helped him to his feet.

"So, what mischief are we up to this fine winter's night?"

"Shh!" Evie put her arms out to quiet him. There were voices coming from up the road.

"You should try the tournaments!" said a man. "I've seen you take apart an oak in half the time of some of those champions."

"Kind of you to say, Rodrick," said another voice. Evie locked eyes with Remington as the night guards got closer.

"I mean it. You've a rare gift with an ax."

Basil suddenly began flailing again as his feet slipped out from beneath him. Remington grabbed him and held on until he managed to regain his balance. Evie glared, her eyes spitting fire.

"Leather soles and snow do not mix," he whispered angrily.

"You hear something?" said one of the men.

"Aye," said the other. "My turn, is it? I hope it's not a badger. I hate bloody badgers."

In a panic, Evie shoved Remington and Basil down the hill. The three of them tumbled through the snow, then scrambled up a steep embankment. Their feet slipped out from beneath them with each step, but they somehow managed to get to the top and hide behind a tree.

"Nothing here—"

"*Badger!*"

"AAAAH!"

One of the guards howled with laughter.

"That is not funny! Someday we'll really see one and then you'll know . . ."

The voices began to recede as the men walked down the road. Evie, Remington, and Basil looked around and found themselves at the edge of a flower garden. Evie checked the map, then motioned for them to cut across to the other side. The flower stems were dead and brittle. It felt more like they were in a graveyard than a garden. Finally they reached the far end, where they found the Queen's Tower rising high into the snowy sky.

"Nearly there," said Evie. "This way."

With the exception of a pair of wandering geese, who may or may not have been part of the night guard, the three found themselves at the entrance to the Archives without any further interruptions. It was a grand structure, with square towers at each corner and a gentle arch across its face. A short staircase stretched from tower to tower, leading up to the doors. It was completely dark.

"A library?" said Remington flatly. "I'm risking my neck to break into a library?"

"It's not a library, it's the Archives," said Evie. "And it's important."

"It couldn't possibly be unlocked, could it?" said Basil.

"The front doors are almost certainly locked, but tower doors never are," said Evie. Basil looked at her like she had three heads. "Just be ready when I open the doors." And with that, she raced across the road and disappeared into the shadows at the edge of the Archives. She could feel the blackness around her like a comforting shawl. She ran to the bottom of the tower at the right end of the building's face and looked up. It was around forty feet high. A giant horned beast leered down from the battlements with an open mouth. She put a hand on the wall. It was made up of small bricks composed mostly of mortar, with chunks of various stones mixed in. A rough surface, and good for climbing. She started up the side. Though it was a sheer face and it was snowing, she made it to the top in under a minute. She knew Basil and Remington were almost certainly watching from across the road in amazement, but to her it was nothing. Dragons spent much of their days climbing.

She used the stone beast's neck to swing herself into one of the crenels. There was a small outpost on top with a banner flying above. It had a single door. As she'd predicted, it was not locked.

A hot, musty burst of air hit her. The smell was actually somewhat pleasant. It was leather and vanilla and wood. It was the smell of pages and ink. *I can see why Maggie likes it here,* she thought.

She placed her hands on the wall and entered the stairway. It wound around into total darkness. She stepped carefully, bracing herself against the walls, until finally she emerged into the main chamber of the Archives. A faint light entered through the huge stained-glass windows along the walls. She made her way to the front door and unlocked it. It groaned as she pulled it wide. A moment later, Remington and Basil ran across the road and darted inside. Evie closed the door. The silence was nearly as overpowering as the darkness.

"A bloody library," said Remington, shaking his head.

"Go on, Evie, make some courage or something," said Basil. "Light it up."

"Me? You're as much a princess as I am. You do it."

"I don't know how," he said, almost proudly.

"Well, neither do I . . ."

Flames sparked and they turned to see Remington holding a candle. "Didn't see any courage over here, but perhaps this will do." He lit two more and handed them to Evie and Basil. "Shall we do a bit of reading, then?"

"We're looking for the restricted section," said Evie.

"Well, that sounds promising."

The three of them stepped into a field of wooden tables surrounded by huge shelves that were covered in leather-bound books. They snaked through the tables and entered the stacks. The shelves were at least twenty feet high, with beautiful wooden ladders leaning against each one. The sheer volume of books and scrolls was breathtaking. Shelf after shelf after shelf, and at the end of each, a glimpse of dozens of others branching off in either direction. Finally they reached the stone wall marking the back of the room.

"It's so restricted, it doesn't even exist," said Remington.

"What happened?" said Basil. "Did we pass it?"

"There," said Evie. She pointed to her right, where a diamond-headed archway was carved into the wall. There was a heavy iron chain across the doorway with a sign that read Restricted. "I'd like to get out of here as quickly as possible. Two of us can search in there for the Registry of Peerage while one of us looks around for something about the Drudenhaus." She and Remington both looked at Basil, who rolled his eyes.

"Right. Why don't you two take that tiny little room and I'll search the whole rest of the place by myself." He turned and stalked away, muttering under his breath.

Evie and Remington ducked under the chain, their candles creating shadows everywhere. This room was much smaller, though also filled with tables. The circular walls were ringed with books and scrolls.

"We're not looking for an ordinary book. The cover is as big as a shield."

"Right," said Remington. "I'll take the right."

He walked to the shelf and began his search. Evie went to the left and looked up at the massive bookcases. There were ornate tapestries hanging above, interspersed with balconies from the upper floor. The tapestries depicted kings and queens on horseback, peasants hauling grain, dragons with forked tongues, and wolves doing battle with swordsmen.

"Like this?" said Remington, holding up a rather large book.

"Bigger," said Evie. Her eyes raced across the spines. *A Brief History of Godfather Death. Secrets of the Iron Queen. Identities and Locations of the Twelve Huntsmen.* Maggie would have loved to see these volumes, if she weren't so bloody scared of being caught. She worked as quickly as possible, though her mind kept returning to the barracks, and to the image of Lance strutting in and finding her empty bunk, and of Maggie's eyes wide with fear as Copperpot interrogated her—

"Registry of Peerage, was it?"

"Did you find it?"

"There are loads of them here."

"Where's the most recent one?"

She raced over to join him as he pulled a massive volume down and slammed it onto one of the tables, sending up a cloud of dust. She opened the cover and began flipping through the crackling pages. All were covered in ornate script, and many of them contained ink-rendered portraits of the kings and queens and princes and princesses recorded within. Illustrations adorned the margins, depicting all manner of things: strange beasts and monkeys playing lutes and one-legged birds and snails jousting each other. None of the names of the highborn struck Evie, though, nor any of the images either.

"What exactly are we looking for?"

"Princess Javotte."

"And who is Princess Javotte?"

Evie stopped flipping and let the page fall open. "Her." There, amidst a muddle of words written in a script so ornate it was difficult to read, appeared the name Javotte. Half the page was covered in thick, black ink, blocking out whatever information had been there.

"Indeed," said Remington. "And look at the state of her."

Evie's eyes skipped to the bottom of the page where Javotte's portrait had been painted. The bones of her skull were clearly visible beneath her skin, and her mouth was turned down in a sharp sneer. Her face was riddled with scars, mainly around her right eye, which happened to be the eye most prominent in the portrait. There were deep scratches from her hairline all the way down her face and across her neck. Her eye was closed, and the skin around it was covered in what appeared to be puncture scars.

"What happened to her?" said Remington.

Evie forced herself to look away from the sneering face so she could decipher the words. Princess Javotte, the book said, hailed from a place called Trendelberg, in the vast forests beneath the Eastern Kingdoms. "Some of it's written in an old language, but there's still a lot I can make out," said Evie. "It says she was attacked by a flock of birds at a wedding. That's where she got all those scars."

"*Birds* did that to her?" said Remington. "What in the world did she do to *them?*"

Evie looked back at the picture. Though she didn't want to judge someone because of a portrait, she couldn't help but feel uneasy. Princess Javotte looked angry and cruel, and the scars covering her face did nothing to lessen that impression.

"Listen to this!" said Evie, pointing at the tightly packed scribbles on the page. "It says she was discharged when they caught her torturing another cadet after hours. It was her own sister, Javelle. 'Cadet Javotte was incredibly unhappy about her discharge. Extra security was required to escort her to the wall.'

And there's another note here. In someone else's writing. 'Patrols doubled at the wall for the remainder of the year. No further sightings of Cadet Javotte after the incident.'"

"She's a right ugly bird," said Remington. "But who is she?"

"I think she's the leader of the secret society coming to kill us all."

"Naturally."

"She's one of them, the Vertreiben," said Evie, puzzling through things aloud. "She *must* be their leader. Why else would those others have been looking for her? And why else would Princess Lankester be so worried about her in particular?" She ran a hand over the large patch of black ink. "And why would someone want to cover up half of her story?"

"I've no idea what you're talking about, and frankly, I'm still back on the bit about the secret society coming to kill us."

Evie studied Javotte's snarling, disfigured face. "I've got to talk to someone about this. Princess Beatrice may be warning the kingdoms to prepare for the wrong enemy."

"Evie, I think you'd better tell me what's going on."

"I will. I'll tell you everything. But first there's one more thing I've got to do." She began flipping ahead through the pages, brittle and yellowed, and covered with blue and gold and black and red ink. Finally a face flashed past, and Evie suddenly felt quite dizzy. She turned back to it and there was her father, King Callahan, looking up at her.

"King Callahan," said Remington, reading the name at the top of the page. "So that's your father."

"That's my father." She stared down at him, her eyes full of bittersweet longing.

It was only the second image she'd ever seen of him. In this one, he was dressed in a deep blue robe lined with white fur. A golden crown sat atop his head. Though he looked quite regal, and wasn't smiling, there was an obvious kindness in his eyes.

"Where's my mother? My real mother?" The portrait next to King Callahan's had been torn out. "Who keeps vandalizing this book?"

"Perhaps they should consider better security measures than a chain."

As wonderful as it was to see her father again, it was equally crushing to be kept from seeing her mother. She had once been on that very page, right next to King Callahan where she belonged, but someone had deliberately removed her from the records.

And there, lurking beneath the image of her father, was the face of her stepmother, Countess Hardcastle. Her thin eyes and cold smile sent chills down Evie's arms. The last time she'd seen her, she'd looked nothing like this. She'd looked like a *witch*.

"What's it say about you?" said Remington, his eyes flicking through the darkness to make sure they were alone.

Evie read. Her father had been the King of Väterlich and all its lands, which included Callahan Manor. There was detailed information about his ancestors, kings and queens dating back hundreds of years. Then his family story ended quite abruptly with Countess Hardcastle. And with his daughter.

"I found it!" said Basil, ducking beneath the chain. "I found the Drudenhaus!"

Neither Evie nor Remington reacted. Both were fixated on the book.

"Well done, Bas! Nice work!" he said to himself. "Bah, never mind." He went over to join them, looking at the Registry over Evie's other shoulder.

She, meanwhile, tried to ignore her missing mother, and returned to King Callahan's portrait instead. This was her father. Her blood.

"Hang on," said Basil. He leaned over Evie and peered down at the page. "Hang on, hang on. Am I reading this right? Is . . . is your name actually Malora?"

Remington snorted. Evie turned and glared at Basil. "Yes, but think very carefully about that being your last word, because it will be if you ever call me Malora again."

"Fine," he said, raising his hands in apology. "Evie it is."

"Yes, that's right. Evie it is." She turned back to the book.

"You do realize what all of this means, don't you?" said Remington. "You're Callahan's only living heir. You are the Queen of Väterlich."

"Blimey!" said Basil. "You get fancier every year!"

Evie looked back to the page, her head spinning. She found the long list of family names. Indeed, hers was the last.

"Queen Malora of Väterlich," said Remington with a chortle.

"Shut it," said Evie.

"Oh sure, me you'll kill, but he just gets a 'shut it,'" said Basil.

"Enough of this," said Evie, and she slammed the book closed. Then she went to put it back on the shelf. Remington, still smirking, gave her a wide berth. "Stay out of my way," she said, though she couldn't keep a smile from cracking through. "What did you find out about the Drudenhaus, Bas?"

"Ah, yes. Well, apparently it's an abandoned witch prison somewhere in the Dortchen Wild."

"A witch prison?"

"Yes. Before Princess Pennyroyal, people used to torture and burn anyone they suspected of being a witch. They'd lock them in the Drudenhaus and do awful things to get them to confess. Then once they'd secured a confession, they'd burn them alive."

"And why are we so concerned about this place?" said Remington.

"I'm not entirely sure," said Evie. "Was there anything else?"

"The final days of the prison came when the witches killed sixteen princesses in one go."

"What?"

"They staged an uprising and killed everyone there, but they deliberately let one person go. When a team of princesses came back to try to stop them, the witches were ready with an ambush. Sixteen princesses died that day."

"The Brave Sixteen," said Evie. "I've seen that before in one of Volf's books, but I never knew what it meant."

"Since that day, the Drudenhaus has been abandoned in the forest. The book I was looking at says it's been largely forgotten, though some mothers still use it in fairy stories to keep their children in line."

"Ancient hatred," said Remington with chagrin.

"Ancient indeed," said Basil. "Sounds like it began before Princess Pennyroyal even dreamed up this place. Or maybe it never began at all. Maybe it always just *was*."

Evie paced, puzzling through it all. "Princess Lankester said that Javotte was at the Drudenhaus. Why would the Vertreiben want to go to an abandoned witch prison?"

"According to that book, the Vertreiben used to use it as their headquarters because it was close enough to launch attacks on the Academy. But it also says that the last confirmed sighting of the group at the Drudenhaus was nearly a hundred years ago. Since then, it's just been left to rot."

"Until now," said Evie gravely.

"Until now."

Princess Ziegenbart had just come back from relieving herself outside in the yard. Her bell clanged as she walked back to the front of the class and stood before them. Her hooves left round puddles on the ground. The snow had all melted under a late-winter drizzle, and now the sun was fighting valiantly to break through the clouds.

"Did any of you realize we'd passed half term?" said the goat. She butted a bale of straw aside to give herself more room. "That's right. And do any of you know what that means?" The cadets looked at one another, but no one answered. "You've finished more than half of your total training. You are on the downward slope toward your crowns and castles ..."

Excited chatter crossed the room.

"... though only a third of you will actually make it."

The chatter died like an ember tossed into a lake.

"Half term of my second year is where my life was decided," continued the goat. "That was where I committed myself to the Cauldron Tippers. I consider it the single most important decision of my life. You should all be starting to make some decisions of your own. Come springtime, you'll need to complete an application to whichever branch of service you've chosen." She put a hoof on one of the bales, striking the nearest thing to a heroic pose as she could. "Ah, I miss those heady days in the second class. The whole world stretched out before you, every direction open. You should count yourselves lucky, cadets."

Lucky? thought Evie, her mind still haunted by visions of Javotte's scarred, snarling face. *I certainly don't feel all that lucky.*

"Nice to be together again, the four of us," said Basil with a smile. "Isn't it?"

Demetra twirled her hair and stared straight ahead. Maggie rolled her eyes at him. Evie just shrugged. Several weeks had gone by since their excursion into the Archives, and as urgent as it had felt that night, each passing day made the whole thing seem more and more abstract. Everything at the Academy was carrying on as normal. Evie hadn't heard the word *Vertreiben* since that night, and Lankester seemed to do little more than mope along behind Beatrice like a sad duckling. She felt as though she should be doing *something* with the information she'd gotten in the Archives, but she had no idea what.

"So?" Basil continued gamely. "Any decisions about your branches of service? What about you, Evie?"

"No, not really. Haven't thought about it."

They were each off in their own worlds, despite being packed into a tight hallway with the rest of Leatherwolf Company in a training castle near the Infirmary. Glimmering suits of armor surrounded them as light snow floated through the black sky outside the windows. One by one, cadets were being called into the Great Hall for a live fire exercise.

"That's it, Cadet, well spotted!" The Fairy Drillsergeant's voice echoed out into the hallway. "That's how you stay alive!" Suddenly, she appeared in the doorway. "Next! Next cadet, move!"

Rillia followed her through the door, and small pockets of conversation resumed.

"I've been thinking about becoming a dwarf," said Basil. "Those cozy little beds, strange women coming into your house to tidy everything up. Yes, that's the branch of service for me." Demetra mumbled something, but clearly none of them were listening. Basil sighed and shook his head. "Maggie, surely you must know which branch you'd like to try."

"Well, actually I've been toying with the idea of staying here. Joining the staff."

"So you can carry on seeing Copperpot every day?" said Demetra without looking over.

"As I was going to say, I think I've decided against that. I've always wanted to live the princess dream, so I suspect I'll go for the Towersitters."

"Good. Excellent. And you, Demetra?"

"I dunno. I've been thinking about leaving the kingdoms altogether."

"Have you?" said Evie.

"Nessa and Liv and I have been talking about joining the Cauldron Tippers."

"The Cauldron Tippers? Are you daft?" said Maggie.

"What's wrong with that?"

"Being a Cauldron Tipper is not a summer holiday, Demetra. You'd be out in the forest—*alone*—tracking and killing witches. Without your precious Nessa and Liv."

"What's that supposed to mean?"

"Nothing."

"Next!" shouted the Fairy Drillsergeant.

"I'll go," called Demetra. She pushed through the rest of the company and disappeared into the Great Hall with the Fairy Drillsergeant.

"Well done, Maggie," said Basil.

"What? I'm sick of her rubbing those two in our faces all the time. She'd rather watch them pick their toenails than spend time with us."

"Well, we don't exactly give her much incentive to spend time with us, do we?"

"Stop," said Evie. "Just . . . stop."

Maggie folded her arms and looked away. Basil seemed as though he wanted to say something, but just shook his head instead.

"Good! Good!" shouted the Fairy Drillsergeant. "Someone else! Come on!"

"I'm going," said Evie, making her way to the front. She paused at the door and took a deep breath, then ducked inside. Anything would be better than standing in that hallway.

The Great Hall was a massive chamber lined with fluted columns holding up an arched ceiling. The walls were white plaster crisscrossed with the same dark wood as the ceiling. There were long tables arranged in a horseshoe, all set with dishes and cutlery. On the far wall, above the main table, two rows of ornamental shields hung. Some were red, banded with yellow and blue. Others were white and gold quadrants with black stripes. Still others featured blue lions and green dragons.

She crept farther into the silent chamber. She could hear a soft tinkle to her right, the dust falling from the Fairy Drillsergeant's wings. Other than that, there was only the soft hum of the cadets talking in the hallway. Her eyes darted everywhere. Doorways. Banquets piled high with pewter plates and cups. The stone columns blooming overhead. She could feel something dark in the room. Something evil. It was the same sort of intuitive dread she'd felt when the three witches had ambushed her in the forest the previous year. She looked along each of the tables, but found nothing out of the ordinary—

Suddenly an object popped up behind the table to her right

with a metallic clang. She caught a fleeting glimpse of a wooden dummy witch before she felt the icy blast of a dark spell. She wheeled and dove behind the table next to her.

"NO NO NO!" bellowed the Fairy Drillsergeant, zipping across the room and glaring down at Evie. "On your feet, Cadet!"

Evie stood and looked across at the dummy witch staring back at her. Its arms were raised and a crude, fearsome grin had been painted on its face.

"Analyze your defensive position."

Evie looked around and her heart sank. "There's no angle of attack here. I should have gone for that column instead."

"Exactly right. From behind that column, you'd have a much easier run to those windows over there or even the far door, should you need to escape. And a stone column is always better cover than a flimsy piece of wood!"

"Yes, Fairy Drillsergeant," said Evie.

The Fairy Drillsergeant flew close to Evie's face, so close that she could see the disappointment in her commanding officer's tiny eyes. "Those are not the instincts of a princess, Cadet. A dim squirrel could see you haven't been doing your best lately, and quite frankly, I'm tired of it. If your goal is to be sent home, then by all means, continue doing what you're doing. But if your goal is to become a princess, then you'd better get it together."

"Yes, Fairy Drillsergeant."

"Witches' Night is coming, and if you give this sort of an effort, I can promise it'll be the last we see of each other."

"It won't happen again, Fairy Drillsergeant."

"Good. Then I'll see you in the morning. And I mean the real you, not this version."

"Yes, Fairy Drillsergeant." Evie ran to the exit at the far end of the chamber, where she wended her way through a dark corridor and emerged into the night. She began walking down the hill toward the barracks, but wasn't quite ready to be around other people yet. She stood in the empty road with her face tilted to the heavens, listening to the particular volume of silence that accompanied the falling of nighttime snow. She closed her eyes and let the flakes land on her.

Oh, my friends. How I miss my friends.

Evie's mother had once told her that time was like the sea, forever changing, forever pushing people toward and away from one another. Now, it seemed, she was so far from the bobbing heads of her friends in the waves that she was losing sight of dry land as well. If she didn't swim hard for her goals, she would find herself completely at sea, just another promising cadet discharged from Pennyroyal Academy.

Swim, Evie. It doesn't matter where, just swim.

"You're lucky it was me who came along next and not Kelbra or Sage," said Basil.

Evie yelped and nearly fell to the ground. "Basil! You startled me. I was just . . ."

"You were just enjoying the sensation of being alive. I could do with a bit of that myself. Care to take the long way home?"

He nodded toward a path that wound through a snowy

grove of trees at the edge of campus. They walked in, and the torchlight of the main roads faded away.

"You know, when you're born the youngest of twenty-two boys, you sometimes feel like the Fates are just having a go at you. Then when your mother enlists you as a princess cadet, you feel like a jester in the Fates' court. But for as existentially ridiculous as my life has been the last few years, I was genuinely looking forward to coming back this year. And there were exactly three reasons for that."

Evie said nothing for a moment. The trail arced to the right, descending toward a lower tier of campus. "What's happened to us, Bas?"

"I don't know." He kicked a stone, which skittered down the hill and left a trail in the snow. "I suppose it's just what time does to things every now and then. Shifts them around in ways that you don't always want."

"You sound like my mother."

He laughed. "It's not easy to keep any relationship strong, really. It takes work. Trust me, I've got twenty-one brothers. I've seen every form of broken and mended relationship you can imagine."

A sudden image of Evie's dragon family popped into her mind, and she was filled with sadness. She felt a similar longing for them that she did for her friends. A longing for what her family had once been when she was younger and things were simpler.

"Maggie and Demetra aren't the only ones who have changed this year, you know," he continued. "You have as well."

She gave him an incredulous smile. "I most certainly have not."

"You don't make near the effort you did last year. Except when it comes to sword fighting. But with the princess training . . . I think your heart's still in it, but your mind isn't."

"Lies and slander," she said. They walked on in silence for a moment as the snow continued to fall. "Oh, shut up."

When they'd gotten back, Evie lay awake long after everyone else had fallen asleep. Her hands were folded behind her head and she stared up into the darkened timbers of the ceiling. She was frustrated. About as frustrated as she'd ever been.

She was the one who had seen those three women murder the innkeeper's wife. She was the one who had received the threatening letter and the wolf's fang. She was the most vulnerable cadet there, since, as Beatrice herself had said, her name was known across the land. And yet there she was, stuck inside the Academy while evil forces might or might not have been closing in on her out there in the cold, wintry world. Would it be the Vertreiben who would come for her first? Lankester's version of the Vertreiben, a murderous, angry band of shadow cadets? Or would it be Calivigne and her witches, whose silence felt more ominous by the day? Or, as Lankester had intimated to Beatrice, would it be a diabolical partnership between the two?

She lay in bed and stared at the ceiling and felt completely and utterly *powerless*.

She rolled onto her side and thought about the trip to the Archives. King Callahan's face came to her. The man who had died trying to save her from a dragon attack. The King of Väterlich ...

Her breathing stopped. Her eyebrows clenched. She sat up in bed and threw back the covers.

Perhaps she wasn't powerless after all. She may have been trapped inside the Academy, but there was still something she could do out there in the real world. There was one way she could take a swipe at the witches, and possibly the Vertreiben, from behind the wall. And if her gamble paid off, it could be quite a big swipe indeed.

She climbed out of bed and felt around Maggie's windowsill until she found a quill, an inkpot, and a parchment. Then she crept down the aisle to the latrine, where several candles still burned in their sconces. She sat on the floor with her back against the wall and began to write.

When she'd finished, she crept back down the aisle to the door. She carefully eased it open and stepped out into the night. Her bare feet crunched through the wet snow as she hurried around the back of the barracks to a small storehouse. She gently opened the door and stepped inside.

"Basil!" she said in a loud whisper. "Basil!" She shook him until he snorted and his eyes popped open.

"Evie?" He frowned, pushing himself onto his elbows. "What are you doing?"

"I need you to send this for me." She held up the parchment.

"What? Now? Who are you writing to that's so important you've got to wake me up?"

"Anisette."

"Evie," he said with a sigh. Then he rolled his neck with a crack. "Why in the world are you writing a letter to Anisette in the bloody middle of the night?"

"Because I am the Queen of Väterlich," she said. "And I want her to tear my ancestral home apart."

LEATHERWOLF COMPANY was gathered at the edge of a courtyard behind a castle somewhere in the second ring of campus,
a huge, blocky thing modeled after the fortress at Delsund. The
courtyard, a hundred yards wide in every direction, was bordered by a wall of creeping ivy. The rest looked as though it
had been frozen in time. An empty fountain sat in the middle,
green and black with water stains. Skeletons of trees sprouted
up around it, with overgrown pathways leading to a staircase
and the castle gates. The days had remained cold in the last few
weeks, the air brittle. Brushings of snow lined the branches of
the pines that were scattered across campus.

Six more Leatherwolf girls had boarded coaches home
in that time. Evie had paced through the days, searching her
correspondence each night for a return hawk from Anisette.
The letter she'd had Basil send had given Princess Camilla permission to go to Callahan Manor, of which Evie, as Queen of
Väterlich, was now the rightful owner. Callahan Manor was the
home in which Evie had lived until the dragons had taken her.

And she wanted Camilla and Anisette to search every inch of it for any clues and information about Countess Hardcastle that might be hidden there. She'd hoped they might find something that could give the princesses a new piece of intelligence about the Seven Sisters. But thus far, she hadn't heard a word.

"You three, get in my carriage!" shouted the Fairy Drillsergeant. She pointed at Kelbra, Essendotter, and Basil.

Kelbra and Essendotter dutifully trudged to a battered and beaten carriage and climbed inside. Basil, however, didn't move. "You aren't really going to . . . crash it, are you?"

"Indeed I am," she replied, with no smile to be found. "Or do you think princesses always arrive on time and with perfect hair?"

"Of course not, Fairy Drillsergeant, it's just—"

"Good. In you go."

Basil must have heard the implicit threat, because he took one last look at the rest of the company, then went to the carriage and climbed inside. The door clicked shut behind him.

"Remember, cadets!" shouted the Fairy Drillsergeant. "When there are magic spells flying, you've got to keep moving! Stone still is stone dead!" And with that, she gave three sharp snaps of her wand, and three streams of glowing light shot out from the end. They zipped across the courtyard and bounced off the walls, and soon were zigzagging everywhere. "This is a live fire exercise, cadets!" The light swirled from black to white and back again. The rest of the company screamed and dove to the ground as one of them soared past with a sizzle that sounded like flame hitting water.

"Oh, relax," said the Fairy Drillsergeant, scowling with disgust. "It's only a simulation, it won't kill you. See?" She shot a blast at Cadet Rillia, who fell to the snow with a scream, writhing in pain. "Hold on tight, cadets!" She aimed her wand at the carriage and gave it a flick. The wheels began to turn. The carriage picked up speed, bumbling across the rough ground as the simulated magic spells continued to carom around the courtyard. Evie and Demetra both watched nervously as Rillia slowly began to catch her breath.

The carriage rattled over a tree root, nearly toppling onto its side. Evie gritted her teeth as it raced toward the fountain. With an extraordinary crash, the carriage flipped onto its top and wobbled to a stop. Basil had been thrown cleanly through the window. He sat up, holding his head, and looked around to get his bearings. The other two, meanwhile, managed to get the door open. They crawled out, using the axletree to swing themselves to the ground. Kelbra pointed to Basil, then motioned toward the right of the castle's main entrance. Then she signaled Essendotter to the left. They nodded and ran for cover behind the dead trees. Kelbra dropped to her stomach as one of the spells soared past her head, then scrambled for the cover of a snow-dusted tree. Slowly, the three of them worked their way closer to the castle gates, the spells ricocheting and twisting around them in all directions.

A chill ran up Evie's arms as she thought about the real-world scenario that would produce that many witches' spells.

Kelbra was pinned down behind a dead elm, one of the

spells swirling wildly in front of her. Finally, she stepped out into the open and put her fists on her hips.

"What in blazes . . ." muttered the Fairy Drillsergeant.

The black and white flashes swirled around Kelbra, but she stood with her head high. Slowly, an imperceptible shield began to form in front of her. The magical spells glanced off of it with showers of golden sparks.

"Come on, Kelbra!" shouted Sage. "You can do it!"

But her compassion began to falter. Despite her best efforts, the spells started to slice through the shield until it was gone. One of the bolts slammed into her back, throwing her face-first into the snow.

"Stop! Stop!" shouted the Fairy Drillsergeant. She waved her wand and the whorling magical spells vaporized into the air. "Congratulations, Cadet! You are now dead!"

Kelbra rolled over and wiped the snow and dirt from her face. She was clutching her back and grimacing in pain. "I was trying to use my compassion!"

"Well, that wasn't the mission, was it? The mission was to get inside that castle so you could rescue the king! Has he been rescued? NO! He's just sat there in his throne room window and watched you die!"

"What difference does it make how I do it? This is what a princess is supposed to do!"

"No, a princess is supposed to *complete the mission!*" bellowed the Fairy Drillsergeant. "It's not enough to be courageous and compassionate and kind! You've got to be disciplined, Cadet! You've got to be smart!"

Finally Kelbra stood and brushed off her uniform. Her face was twisted into a mask of anger. "You expect us to be perfect all the time! Well, I'm sorry I'm not perfect, all right?"

"It's not about being perfect. All of you, come here!" The Leatherwolf cadets crossed the courtyard and assembled in front of her. "Listen closely. Perfection plays no part in becoming a princess. Each of you is going to make mistakes in the field. Every princess and every knight who has ever lived has made mistakes in the field. What makes you a true princess is how you handle those mistakes."

Kelbra huffed, but said nothing.

"Cadets, you must be able to perform at a level that's not expected of ordinary people. Your mission is constantly changing, and you've got to have the discipline to recognize what the current mission is. A carriage crash becomes evasion, which then becomes rescue. You've got to be able to assess the situation and adapt to what's around you. Adapt or die."

There was silence beneath the softly falling snow. Nearby, another company cheered for some unseen victory.

"Courage and compassion are your primary weapons, but you can't use a hammer to fix a leak. Assess the mission, and be prepared for change." She snapped her wand, and the carriage began to lift off its top and creak back onto its wheels. "Now, who's next?"

• • •

By the time the morning finally ended, Evie had endured three carriage crashes and been struck by the simulated witch spells twice. The second had hit her squarely in the chest, leaving a lingering sensation of burning skin. It was incredibly uncomfortable, though not as uncomfortable as the giant purple bruise on her leg from the second crash. Still, all the pain faded away when Princess Copperpot handed Evie her usual sack of letters. This time she found a bundle wrapped in a well-worn piece of tanned deerskin mixed in with all the rest. She held her breath as she flipped the folds of the deerskin back. Inside was a large stack of parchments, brittle and aged. And on top of that was a fresh parchment hawk. It was the one she'd been waiting for. It was from Anisette.

Evie, it read. *There's no nice way to tell you this, so I'll just say it plain. By the time me and Camilla got to Callahan Manor, someone else had already been there. Most of it had been burned to the studs. Just about everything was smashed to bits or taken away and there was no evidence for us to collect. We did find one thing, though, and it seems like the sort of thing you'd want straightaway, so here it is. Beneath the rubble and ash, Camilla found a hidden doorway to a secret crawl space beneath the house. There wasn't much there that escaped the fire, but she did find this deerskin bundle. She says it must be enchanted, since it stood up to the fire so well. As for what's inside, well, I'll just leave that to you. Sorry again about your house, Evie. It was a good idea, but it looks like the witches were a step ahead of us this time. Hope all is well there. Lots of love to Maggie and Demetra and Basil.*

Torches had started to go out around the barracks as the girls settled in for the night. Evie set Anisette's note aside and picked up the top parchment on the stack. There must have been forty or fifty of them there, all folded the same, all frayed and torn around the edges. She gently opened it, careful to not break it at the folds. The writing inside was unfamiliar to her. It was done in a heavy hand, the ink strokes thick and swirling.

My dearest Vorabend, the letter began. *What's a sailing ship to do when the winds stop blowing? Or a fish when water becomes sand? Where am I to start? How am I to start? Carrying on without you will be the most difficult thing I've ever done, and I've eaten your mother's cooking.*

Evie laughed, though she still wasn't entirely sure what it was she was reading.

I've no idea how to do any of this without you, the letter continued. *I'm a man broken. Broken and scared. This is not the life for which I'd prepared, my darling. You are the life for which I'd prepared, and now you are gone. It is my fault you are gone, though I know you'd never have forgiven me had I made a different choice. The only comfort I can take from all of this is that even if I can never forgive myself, I know that you've already done so. There is one other comfort, I suppose, and I'd wager that's the one you'd really like to hear about. Not my moaning and carrying on. So let me tell you about this magical little creature you've left me with. This magical little Malora—*

Evie gasped. Her hand went to her mouth. Tears streamed from her eyes. It was her father who had written this letter. And he'd written it to her mother.

Before anyone noticed her tears, Evie folded up the deerskin and carried it back toward the latrine. Her breath was coming fast and short, and she was suddenly feeling quite lightheaded. There were still a few girls coming and going, so she ducked down behind one of the empty bunks that had, until recently, housed one of her company-mates. There, she sat on the floor and started reading again:

. . . This magical little Malora. That's right, my dear, I named her after your mother, just as you'd always wanted. Now you'll forgive me if I never use that bloody name ever again. Ha-ha-ha. This little babe of yours is as soft and sweet and fuzzy as a ripe peach. So that's what I've taken to calling her. My little Peach. Our little Peach. She looks like you, darling Vora, really she does. I can't tell you the comfort that gives me. And it's only in part because it means she isn't a big ugly beast like her father. Ha-ha-ha. I've always known you were meant to be my life's companion. Now it seems this one may turn out to be. But you're in every bit of her. Your face. Your spirit. And so you'll continue to be my life's companion through this lovely little girl.

I'm sorry to write such a dour letter, my dearest, but I know it'll never be sent, so I don't feel too terrible about it. I just want you to know, Vora, wherever you may be beneath these vast, twinkling stars, that I will protect this girl. I will protect her with my life. On that, you have my word. You gave your life and entrusted her to me, and I'll give mine to keep her safe. I love this little Peach with the ferocity of a dragon and the strength of a lion and the tenderness of her very own mother. I love her, my sweet girl, as I have always loved you. Your adoring husband, now and forever, C.

Evie could barely see the words through her tears and trembling hands. She didn't want anyone to hear her. She wanted this moment all to herself, but it was nearly impossible to keep from sobbing. These were her father's words. Her father, whom she could never know, was suddenly alive, and he was speaking about *her* in these letters . . . Evie. More than that, he had found a way to speak *to* her.

She wiped away her tears and peeked over the top of the bunk. Luckily, no one seemed to have noticed her. So she ducked back down, and by the light of the candles in the wall, read another letter:

My dearest Vora. Your little one had her first taste of boar today. I'll never forget the day I gave you your first taste. You spit it across the room and chased me out the door with a frying pan. Well, this little girl couldn't do that even if she wanted to. Ha-ha-ha. I know what you're probably thinking. Callahan, you old fool, she's only got four teeth, what are you doing giving her boar? Well, you wouldn't believe the tiny little morsel I managed to chew off for her. And her eyes when she got it in her mouth! She's got her father's taste for meat, I'm afraid. She must've gummed that piece of boar for half an hour! Ha-ha-ha. I started to think she might learn to talk right then and there just so she could ask for more . . .

Evie set it aside and pulled out another from halfway down the stack:

Beloved Vora, today was a bit of a rough one for me, I'll not lie to you about that. Peach and I went for a ride in the forest. When we came to the spring—you remember that spring, don't you? The one with the smooth stone bottom where we had our first picnic, and you gave me a right tongue-lashing for bringing my sword?—when we got there, she said she wanted to have a swim. "Swim, Dada." That's how she says it. It was a glorious summer day, your favorite kind of day, I well remember. So in we went. We were having a lovely old time splashing about in there. It was her little laugh that got me. I was holding her so her head was above water and she was kicking and having a grand old time. And oh, did she laugh! It was so pure and so innocent and joyful that I just started blubbering, right there in that spring. Can you imagine! Me, a slobbery old fool sopping around in the water like that! I've always done my level best to keep from crying round her. I don't want to worry the poor thing about her big old Dada's tears, but the sound of her laughter went right to my heart. I told her it was just her feet splashing water in my eyes and she believed it, the gullible little sap . . .

Evie smiled through her tears as she took out another letter:

My darling Vora, how often I wonder where you are. The Peach and I spent the better part of the night looking up at the stars. She asked me tonight what's past the stars and I told her she'd find out someday . . .

And another:

Ah, Vora, you would have loved what your little one did last night. She was worried that the dogs would be cold in the night, so she crept out to the kennel with her own little blanket. And that's where I found her this morning, sleeping in a pile of those slobbery beasts. You remember Winston, of course, the gentlest dog known to man. I found Peach this morning sound asleep with her little hand wrapped round his ear . . .

And another, this one from nearer the bottom of the stack:

My dearest Vora, you know by now how difficult it is for me to write you about the Countess, but it's important for me to be honest with you always, and I want you to know your little one is being well looked after. You needn't ever worry that another would replace you in my heart, darling Vora. You are the rest of me, and always will be. You and your daughter, that is. I love the Countess in a very different way. We've both lost someone dear to us, and she can provide Malora with the structure and motherliness that I simply can't. She's also got a little one of her own called Nicolina, a girl with black hair and a cool temperament, but a constant playmate for our daughter. I'm hoping that the two girls will become fast friends as they spend more and more time together. That would be another wonderful thing for our daughter that I can't give her on my own . . .

Evie slammed the letter down. Her heart was racing and her stomach was in knots and she knew she would not be able to sleep that night, or perhaps any night in the near future. She was meeting her father for the first time, and he was proving to be the most caring, the most thoughtful, the most selfless man she ever could have imagined. He'd been raising her, Evie, completely on his own. What had happened to his wife, to Evie's mother? Had she died? Had she been taken somewhere? Had she run off? Whatever the case, it was clear that the King had loved her in ways known only to the poets.

She leaned back and rested her head on the empty mattress behind her. She'd read only parts of some of the letters, but already she felt bone-weary. Tears continued to fall. She'd never imagined it could be possible to feel such profound, blood-level love for someone she had never met, and never would—

Her finger found something on the bottom of the deerskin bundle. She looked underneath and found a parchment stuck there by its wax seal. She peeled it free, and her heart stopped.

The parchment was a darker shade than usual, like the one she'd gotten months earlier. She stared at it for a moment, then slowly, carefully, she lifted it by the corner, as though it were written in poison. It appeared to be a crudely made envelope, two parchment hawks sewn together. With a nervous gulp, she opened the seal. And there she found the same jagged script as before: *Someone inside is more than she seems*, it said. The signature read only, *a friend.* On a separate piece of parchment, there were more words scrawled in that sinister, dried-blood hue . . .

Victory lives inside Pennyroyal Akademie! March, sisters, rise and march!

And just like that, the overwhelming love she'd been feeling was replaced by fear.

The goat nudged a small silver dagger with her snout. The pommel was carved from bone to look like a skeletal hand enveloping the bottom of the blade. "Take a look at this little lovely," said Princess Ziegenbart. "It's quite fearsome, isn't it? But when was the last time you heard of a witch stabbing someone?" There were scattered nervous chuckles. "These are used primarily in the kitchen, preparing cauldrons and potions and the like. So should you encounter a witch with one of these in her hand, I would still recommend paying more attention to her magic than to her blade."

Evie looked over at Maggie, who was chewing the end of her goose-quill pen. Then her eyes went to Demetra, who was pointing at the blade and whispering something to Liv. Her head hurt from the combination of no sleep and a night of intense emotions and tears. And that wasn't even taking the second threat into account. She was overwhelmed. She needed help.

"This next ob*aa-a-a-a-a-agh-agh-agh!*" bleated Princess Ziegenbart. "Ahem, pardon me, this next *object* is of particular fascination. Especially should you decide to join the Cauldron Tippers. When hunting for witches, one must always pay particular attention to mirrors." She used her teeth to pick up a smoky hand mirror inside an elaborately carved wooden frame. She showed it to the cadets, then set it down again. "A witch will use an enchanted mirror to see into the past, the present, or even the future. This is a process called 'scrying,' and I'm sure you've all heard it used in . . ."

"'Snow White,'" said the group.

"'Snow White,' that's correct! Good knowledge, cadets. When the wicked witch asked the magic mirror for help, she was practicing a form of scrying. Pay special attention when mirrors are involved, cadets. They will show you where the enemy is. Witches and their sympathizers love to use them in their dark practices."

Evie's leg was pumping up and down. She was having a hard time sitting still. She needed to talk to someone or she was going to explode. Finally, Ziegenbart finished with the witch paraphernalia and began dividing the class for small-group work.

"Teams of four, please. I'd like you to think through the fairy stories and come up with three other examples of witch artifacts."

Evie shot up off of her straw bale and went straight to Maggie. "You. Come with me."

Maggie looked shocked. She didn't say a word, she just stood and followed. They crossed to Demetra, who was already sitting with Nessa and Liv.

"Sorry, girls, she's working with us today."

"Excuse me?" said Nessa.

Demetra looked up at her in confusion.

"Come on, Demetra."

"Are you serious? She doesn't have to go with you."

Evie glared at Nessa, who wilted beneath it. "Come on, *Demetra*."

Demetra apologized to Nessa and Liv with her eyes, then got up and followed Evie to the back of the room.

Basil was sitting by himself, chewing on a piece of straw. "Oh. Hello." He was surprised to see Maggie and Demetra sitting down with Evie.

"Right," said Evie, "here's our four."

Basil, Maggie, and Demetra exchanged uncomfortable looks.

"Look, I know we've had a rough go of it this year," said Evie, "but right now I don't care about any of that. I just want to figure this out and put it behind us."

"I've got no problem with anyone," said Demetra.

"Nor do I," said Maggie.

Basil sighed and slumped over.

"You," said Evie, wheeling on Demetra. "You've got your new friends and that's fine. That's good. We're happy for you. But it doesn't give you the right to throw us over."

"I—"

"And you," she continued, turning to Maggie. "Yes, Princess Copperpot put you on notice the very first day we were back. That wasn't fair of her, and it threw off your entire year. But you're living your life in fear, and quite frankly, it's annoying."

Maggie's mouth dropped open in offense.

"And then there's you," continued Evie, pointing at Basil.

"Me!" he shouted in surprise. "What did I do?"

"I'm still cross with you for trying to transfer away from us! We're supposed to be stronger than this!"

"Hang on," said Basil, about to be offended.

"Maggie . . ." She took her hand. "Demetra . . ." Then she took her hand. "I need you both."

"I've got no issue with you, Evie," said Demetra. "But I'm tired of her snapping at me all the time. I don't deserve it and I don't like it."

"Well, pardon me for actually caring about my training. Honestly, Demetra, I wouldn't snap at you if it seemed like you actually wanted to be here."

"Who do you think you are?" Demetra stood and took a step toward Maggie. "You've been condescending and judgmental ever since Waldeck!"

Maggie stood and took a step toward Demetra. "How dare you pretend you've even noticed I was here this year!"

"Girls . . ." said Evie. The conversation she'd hoped to start was quickly spiraling out of control. She glanced over at Princess Ziegenbart, but luckily the goat hadn't noticed the commotion.

"You are without a doubt the most ungrateful person I've ever met!" said Maggie. "You have no idea how much you take for granted!"

"Uh, Maggie?" said Basil. "Don't say that."

"Take that back, you jealous hag!" said Demetra, shoving Maggie in the chest.

"No, don't say that either," said Basil.

"Why should I take it back? It's true!" Now she shoved Demetra.

"Stop it, girls!" hissed Evie. Now some of the nearby teams were looking over at the brewing conflict.

"I'm sick of you traipsing around here like you should just be handed a commission!" shouted Maggie. "Sorry if the rest of us get in your way with all of our *hard work!*"

"And I'm sick of you moping about all day because you drove Copperpot into a rage and I didn't! That's not my fault, it's yours!"

Maggie lunged and Demetra ducked. The two grappled

while Basil danced around them, unsure what to do. Evie looked over at Ziegenbart, who, along with the rest of the cadets, had finally noticed the scuffle.

"Let me go!"

"You let me go!"

Evie, panicked, turned to Basil. He stared back in horror.

"Girls!" bleated Ziegenbart. "Girls, what are you—"

"WOLF!" shouted Basil at the top of his lungs.

Princess Ziegenbart's eyes went wide and her legs went stiff, and she fell over onto her side, paralyzed. Cadets screamed in terror and began running out of the classroom. Evie grabbed Maggie and pulled her away while Basil put Demetra in a hold and dragged her to the door. Moments later, when Ziegenbart was able to move her legs again, she stood. Her classroom was empty.

Evie pushed Maggie toward the road behind the screaming remnants of Leatherwolf Company while Basil manhandled Demetra next to them.

"Cadet Basil!" came Ziegenbart's shrill voice from the classroom doorway. "Cadet Basil, get back here this instant!"

He froze, releasing Demetra. Then he raised a finger and pointed it squarely at her. "Sort this out. I don't want to be sent home for nothing." He aimed his finger and his glare at Maggie, then turned and ran back to the classroom to take his punishment.

"Come on," said Evie, shoving Maggie toward a bench beneath a small copse of trees in front of a cathedral.

"She's the one who—"

"Quiet!" Evie's glare was at least as fearsome as Basil's. Maggie and Demetra stopped fighting and sat on the bench. Then she stood over them, hands on her hips, and glowered. "You're acting like fools, the both of you. Last night I was having one of the most incredible moments of my life with my dead father, and the Vertreiben ruined it, and I needed you both but I didn't know if you'd even be there for me and that's not right! I've had it with all this bickering. We need to sort this out so we can get back to the business of being friends."

The close call in the classroom seemed to have taken some of the fight out of both of them. After several tense moments, it was Maggie who spoke first.

"I'm sorry." She didn't sound at all as though she meant it.

"So am I," said Demetra.

"Good. Now, what else do you want to say to each other?"

Maggie looked over at Demetra and her anger seemed to evaporate. "No, really. I'm sorry, Demetra. You know I love you."

Demetra kicked a stone on the ground. "I know."

"I've just been under such pressure this year."

"I know you have, Maggie. You're not used to getting into trouble."

"It's more than that, though. Much more, really." Maggie took a deep breath and blew the air out. "This is the only thing I've ever wanted to do, and . . . and this whole year I've been one tiny little mistake away from losing it."

"I know, Maggie," said Demetra. "It's your dream."

"It's more than my dream. It's my life. One wrong choice and I'd be forced to go back to Sevigny. And then what? What's there for me? The same old stories from the same old people in the same old taverns. I'd shrivel up and die if I didn't have this. I can't live that life, but I'd have to. You . . . you've got this wonderful home waiting for you, and so many friends with similar interests and backgrounds. But I don't. I've got nothing."

Demetra reached over and put her hand on Maggie's.

"You were right, Demetra, I was jealous of you. All the mean thoughts I've had toward you, all the times I snapped, it's because I was so completely jealous. You had us, you had Nessa and Liv, you had your home in the Blackmarsh . . . and I've felt completely alone, just waiting for the ax to fall."

"I'm so sorry, Maggie. I should have realized how you felt. I admit, it's been quite nice having Nessa and Liv to talk to. But it's not because we're these highborn snobs. It's because we're all having a hard time seeing the point of any of it. I'll finish here and then go back to the Blackmarsh. And then what? The Blackmarsh already has a princess, one of the best in all the land, as everyone is forever reminding me. So what does that make me? A just-in-case? A princess only if Camilla falls ill?" She picked a piece of stem off a dead leaf and threw it in the dirt. "I was born to be forgotten."

"Don't be absurd," said Maggie. "Lots of girls have older sisters who are princesses."

"You don't understand. The best outcome for me is to be

married off as some sort of diplomatic tool. At least then I'd be able to breathe. To have my own identity. I don't even exist at home."

"You're not a diplomatic tool, Demetra," said Evie. "There's a whole world out there that needs you."

Demetra peeled off another piece of stem and threw it to the ground. Evie noticed dark spots appearing in the dirt as her tears began to fall.

"I'm sorry, Maggie," she sniffled. "It's not that this place means any less to me. I love it here. This is my home. But for me, it's always been more about the friends and the camaraderie. I don't get to see the future as widely as you do."

Maggie leaned over and hugged Demetra. Now there were tears in her eyes as well. "I'm sorry, too, Demetra."

They both began to sob openly, holding each other tightly. After so much strife and uncertainty, the sight made Evie's stomach flutter. Before she knew it, she was crying, too.

"Oh, thank goodness!" she said, and then she crouched down and embraced both of her friends. The connection that had been missing for months seemed to come flooding back all at once—

"Yeah," came a voice filled with spite and hostility. "Yeah, enjoy your little cry." They turned to find Basil standing near the archway. He had a giant bale of straw lashed to his back and was straining under its weight. "Princess Basil to the rescue."

Ziegenbart ambled onto the road, her bell clanging. "Up you go, Cadet. To the Queen's Tower. Hup-hup."

"But, Princess, I really thought I saw a wolf! Honest!"

"Move, Cadet, before I involve your fairy drillsergeant." Basil tromped up the road toward the center of campus, the huge bale swaying dangerously atop his back. "Everything all right, ladies?"

"Yes, Princess," said Evie with a sniffle that was also half a laugh. "We were just so terrified about that wolf."

"'Someone inside is more than she seems,'" said Maggie as she took a bite of her black pudding. "I think we need to approach this as though everyone is guilty until we can strike them from the list."

"Great plan," said Demetra. "Nessa and Liv can come off."

"Fine. Consider them stricken. But let's start with the staff, shall we?"

Quail stew steamed from the bowls in front of them. Evie tore off a piece of bread and dunked it in. "Rumpledshirt-sleeves. He can come off the list."

"Why?" said Demetra.

"Because the letter says 'she.'"

"Good point. We can knock off all the woodsmen as well, then."

"And it's not Princess Beatrice either," said Maggie. "No chance."

"I didn't think so either," said Evie, "but I still couldn't bring myself to show her the second letter. She's so adamant that the Vertreiben aren't a threat that it makes me a bit suspicious."

"All right," sighed Maggie. "As ludicrous as it is, we'll leave her on for now."

"Well, if we can't rule out the Headmistress, who can we rule out?"

Just then, Basil limped up and plopped down on the bench next to Maggie. "All right, everyone? Enjoying yourselves?"

"Are you only just finishing, Bas?"

"Indeed I am. That old goat made me run to the Queen's Tower thirty times. You're welcome very much."

"Sorry, Basil," said Demetra.

"Yeah, sorry," said Maggie. "If it makes you feel any better, we've worked it all out."

"It does, actually. Pass the bread."

Maggie handed over a seeded loaf. "We were just discussing who on the staff is more than she seems."

"The staff?" he said, stuffing his mouth with bread. "Why are you doing that? Clearly it's Evie."

"What?"

"You know," he said, washing it down with some water. "The Warrior Princess?"

Maggie and Demetra looked over at her. "I mean, I suppose it's possible," said Evie. "But why would someone send me a letter telling me that I'm more than I seem?"

Basil stopped chewing. "Fair point, that."

"Right, back to the staff, then," said Demetra. "What about Princess Hazelbranch? There's not a chance in the world that it's her."

"I agree, Princess Hazelbranch can be safely struck from the list," said Evie.

"Good, that's one gone," said Maggie. "What about Ziegenbart? You've gotten to know her fairly well, Bas. Does she seem like a traitor?"

"Yeah, what do you think, is she a turngoat?" said Demetra with a laugh.

"My heart bleats at your concern," said Basil with a smirk.

The three of them laughed, but Evie didn't. She stared at the steam rising from her stew as memories flashed through her head. Memories from the previous year. Memories that had suddenly become tinged with dread. She glanced over Basil's shoulder to the staff table, where Princess Hazelbranch was chatting happily with Princess Wessin.

She remembered sitting in the latrine of the Ironbone Company barracks the previous year after a fight with Malora, her face bloodied and filthy. Princess Hazelbranch had gently brushed her hair. Evie had looked up and seen her own reflection. Hazelbranch had stared into that mirror as well, then told Evie that mirrors could see what human eyes could not, that mirrors would reveal the truth.

Evie stared at her and heard the words of Princess Ziegenbart from earlier that day: "Pay special attention when mirrors are involved. They will show you where the enemy is."

Evie stared at Princess Hazelbranch and felt her blood run cold . . .

"GET OFF THOSE RACKS and move! The last ten cadets on the
Green in full dress are going home *immediately!*"

Evie lurched out of a dreamless sleep to a nauseated stomach and racing heart. The barracks were dark, but everywhere
there was motion. The Fairy Drillsergeant's words caught up to
her, and she flung herself out of bed. Within seconds, she was
pulling her uniform over her head and lashing the belt.

"You've come too far, cadets! Don't get sent off now!"

Tiny streaks shot through the air. It looked as though every fairy drillsergeant on campus was inside the Leatherwolf
barracks.

"Hurry up, lassies! Time is running out!"

A stream of girls raced for the door. Evie's stomach was in
knots as she pulled on her shoes and ran. Maggie was ahead of
her, but she didn't see Demetra in her quick scan of the heads
and shoulders barreling into the night. She burst through the
pile-up of girls and raced to the middle of Hansel's Green. Other
cadets in dark purple dresses poured out of the Bramblestick

Company barracks. Only now, as she fell in line with the rest of her company, did Evie's brain catch up with her body. It was the middle of the night, not a stitch of daybreak to be seen. The clouds glowed gray above, with white edges, indicating a full moon hiding somewhere up there in the heavens.

"In line! In line *now*!"

"Are you listening? Fall in!"

Evie had never seen so many fairies in one place, and all of them shouting at the tops of their lungs. As she claimed a spot in the formation, she glanced back and saw Demetra racing out onto the grass. *Thank goodness.* And when she realized Basil had made it out even before she had, she knew that her closest friends were safe. For now.

"You're out of time, girls!" came a fairy's voice from inside the barracks.

"On the ground, Leatherwolf! Taste the grass!" bellowed the Fairy Drillsergeant. "I want fifty Court Jesters! Last ten to do it are going home! *Go, go!*"

The entire company dropped to the frosted grass, which crunched beneath them. Court Jesters were one of the Fairy Drillsergeant's more horrid concoctions, a draining mixture of calisthenics that had the cadets bouncing and twisting on the ground like the titular entertainers.

Evie flew through the Court Jesters, her muscles responding much faster than her sleep-addled mind. *What is going on? This can't possibly be real.* She glanced over to see Princess Copperpot and Princess Helgadoon of Bramblestick Company escorting twenty sobbing, devastated cadets across the Green toward a carriage coach waiting near the Academy's main entrance. She fell back to the grass, halfway through her exercises.

"Oh no!" cried Demetra. "No!"

Evie paused and looked back at the cadets who were leaving. There, near the back of the twenty, was Liv. Her heart broke for Demetra. She could only imagine the heartache she'd feel if one of her best friends was discharged.

"I'm so sorry, Demetra," she said. "But you've got to keep moving."

Demetra looked at her, grief in her eyes. Slowly, Evie's words began to sink in. She nodded, then dropped to the ground for a Court Jester. There would be no time for sorrow tonight.

Though the cadets had been doing Court Jesters for over half a year, Evie's arms, legs, and back were already in flames by the time she hit thirty. She'd had a particularly intense sparring session with Remington earlier that day, and her muscles were not happy about this additional work. The girl next to her, a polite, quiet thing named Cadet Dragonflower, collapsed and couldn't push herself back up.

"Come on, push!" said Evie quietly, so all the fairies floating around wouldn't hear.

"I can't," said Dragonflower. Evie saw that her arms were shaking wildly, unable to support any more weight.

"You can! You've done millions of these! You're just scared, that's all. Come on, push!"

The girl screamed as she poured all of her energy into her

arms. But she rose only an inch or two from the ground before they gave out.

"Cadet Dragonflower, you are dismissed!" shouted the Fairy Drillsergeant.

Evie popped to her feet, then fell back to the ground. She wanted to console the poor girl, who was now sobbing face-down in the grass, but she didn't have time. Between Jesters, she noticed some strange things happening in the darkness of this already strange night. There were around fifteen princesses and other staff standing to the side watching. They held parchments clipped to pieces of wood, and were studying the girls closely and making notes. In addition, it seemed that the entire staff of the Infirmary was on hand, except for Princess Wertzheim, and each had a sack full of equipment and potions. One had two large baskets filled with heads of cabbage. Another stood next to a small cart that had been fashioned into a stretcher.

These distractions took her mind from the horrible, scream-ing pain coming from her muscles as she finished her fiftieth and final Court Jester. She stood at attention with trembling legs and waited for her company-mates to finish. *Come on, Maggie. Come on, Demetra. Come on, Basil.* One by one, each of them clambered to their feet. Finally, everyone was standing in for-mation and trying to catch their breath. Or, almost everyone.

"Come on, Cadet Bilberry, one more!" shouted Bramblestick Company's fairy drillsergeant. Bilberry was pushing with ev-erything she had through gritted teeth to finish her final Court

Jester. Finally, she did it, dragging her exhausted body to attention. "Congratulations, Cadet, you finished all fifty Court Jesters. Now get out of here! You're dismissed!"

Bilberry stood for a moment, shocked, and tried to catch her breath. She glanced around at the other Bramblestick girls, but knew there was nothing more to be done. Her fairy drillsergeant floated in place, staring at her intensely, until her shoulders slumped and she began the long, awful walk to the carriage coach.

More fresh recruits for the Vertreiben, thought Evie, and a shiver ran through her.

"Well done, cadets. You've survived your first mission of the night," said Bramblestick Company's fairy drillsergeant, shouting to both second-class companies. She was the same size as Leatherwolf's fairy drillsergeant, but she had short black hair, and her wings seemed to give off a distinctly purple dust as they flapped. "There will be three more missions, and you must complete them all before sunrise. Advance. Escape. And Evade—"

"What is that?" shrieked one of the Bramblestick cadets. Heads turned, and cadets began to gasp. Girls pointed through the darkness toward the southern end of Hansel's Green.

There, along the moon-shimmered hillside, was a line of silhouettes, jet black in front of the glowing gray clouds. The figures' hands were joined, and they were lurching along in a sinister dance. One wore a pointed hat. Another's wild hair could be seen fluttering in the wind. All of the figures wore formless black robes.

"The dance of death unites us all," said Leatherwolf's fairy drillsergeant. "Your mission is to keep from joining that dance until the sun comes up. Welcome to Witches' Night, cadets. Meet your witches."

The figures danced along the hillside toward campus until the shadows swallowed them up. Girls looked at one another in confusion and horror.

"Should you fail to complete any of the three missions, you will be discharged. Should you still be on the course by morning, you will be discharged. Should you be one of the last twenty cadets to complete your missions, you will be discharged. The path to the first class runs directly through Witches' Night."

The cackle of a witch sounded from somewhere in the distance.

"Your first mission is Advance. Make your way through that wood and get to Schummel Tower. There you will be given your second mission. Is that clear?"

"Yes, Fairy Drillsergeant!"

"Good. Then *move out!*"

The ranks dissolved into a mass of panic. Everyone sprinted southward across the Green, straight to where they'd seen the witches. Schummel Tower was on the opposite end of a wide, unused grove that sat between the barracks and the campus proper. In this darkness, with those creatures lurking within, the trees loomed before them like an impenetrable fortress.

"Maggie, wait!" shouted Evie. Maggie, who was several yards ahead, slowed and allowed Evie to catch up. "Where are Basil and Demetra?"

Maggie looked around. "There," she said, pointing to her left.

"Come on!" They ran over to intercept their friends. "We need to work together. The four of us. It's our best chance to make it through."

One by one, they all nodded.

"Good. Let's move out. And be ready for anything." As they crested the hill where the dancing figures had been, they could still see the trail of black through the grass where their robes had wiped away the frost. "I don't know if they're real witches or not, but we've—"

Suddenly, just as they reached the edge of the wood, the silent night was rent with a deafening crackle.

"Down!" screamed Evie, dragging Demetra to the dirt. "Down!"

A swirling black cloud shot through the trees and splattered against a boulder. Within seconds, there was a chorus of sizzling pops coming from all directions. Dark magic flew everywhere. Cadets screamed from the depths of the grove. The voices of the staff shouted over the top of it all.

"Over there! Stretcher near the oak!"

"Nurse! Bitter velvetleaf, three doses!"

"Get off the course, Cadet, you're finished!"

Evie frantically looked for a way off the hill. Everything was so dark, so confusing. The crackling of witches' magic echoed through the trees, mixing with the shouts of cadets and staff. During a momentary lull, something cackled in the darkness.

"Come on," she said. "They must have placed witches near the finish, too." Then, holding her breath, she and the others raced across the grass and took cover behind the stump of a toppled tree. "We've got to go straight up the middle. That way we maintain our options for cover and escape. If we get trapped in these trees, we're dead."

The other three nodded in agreement. Evie peered around the tree trunk and saw several members of staff standing at the edge of the grove. They were talking casually with one another, as though they were evaluating the cadets' dancing technique at the Grand Ball. It was surreal to see them so calm while witches' dark spells were flying all around the woods.

"Right, next blast. Basil and Maggie, there's an oak about fifty yards ahead. Can you make it?"

Basil, looking a bit green, nodded. So did Maggie.

"We'll go for one a little farther up on the right. Climb the ladder. Hand signals only until we're through. Stay low and stay quiet. Remember, witches can't see well in the dark, so don't give them a target."

A swirling stream of black crackled over their heads.

"Go! Now!"

Suddenly, she and Demetra were out in the open, sprinting down a hill through ferns and brush. There were explosions in every direction, and Evie kept expecting the horror of feeling her skin slowly harden to stone. Finally, they reached a sprawling oak and dove behind its trunk.

"All right?"

"All right." Demetra's eyes were filled with fear. "I saw one. Up on a little outcropping. About seventy yards in that direction."

Evie inched forward, her hands scraping against the rough bark of the oak. They were at the bottom of a small ravine, with only one hill to climb until they were through. There, standing beneath a huge, swooping tree, she saw the faint outline of a figure. It was obscured by black haze.

"Well spotted, Demetra." She peered across the ravine to where Maggie and Basil were. Or at least, where she hoped they were. She signaled them with the witch's position, but couldn't tell if they'd seen her or not. "All right, I've told them we'll try to draw the witch's fire so they can get through."

"Draw the witch's fire?" said Demetra. "Which one?"

"You! Cadet Hawthorn! Stay down, you're dismissed!" And another fairy drillsergeant ended another princess cadet's dream. "Nurse! Over here!"

Evie did her best to block it out. Despite the frantic atmosphere in the forest, she was well aware that the witches weren't the only threat. So, too, was the coming sunrise.

When another spell sizzled past, Evie and Demetra swept out from either side of the tree and zigzagged from tree to boulder beneath the witch's position. She could only hope that Maggie and Basil had seen her signals and were advancing behind them. They both made it to another oak tree, where they huddled for cover and tried to catch their breath. After several seconds, with more screams and spells splitting open the night,

Evie peered around the tree trunk. There was Maggie, halfway up the hill, signaling to her.

"Maggie says there's another witch on the far end," she whispered. "But she thinks we can make it through. She wants us to move."

Demetra nodded, and they tore off into the night once again. Spells splattered at their feet with rippling pops. There were screams and shouts and explosions as branches cracked and thudded to the ground. Evie had only one thing on her mind. *Get to that tree.*

She raced up the hillside behind Demetra. Just as they were about to reach the tree where Basil and Maggie waited, she glanced over and saw a witch smiling down with wide yellow eyes and a thorn-sharp smile. She dove, but the dead leaves slipped out beneath her, and she sprawled awkwardly into the undergrowth. Black smoke began to churn in front of the witch's chest.

"No!" screamed Maggie.

Crackity-crackity-crackity! came the spell, which spiraled toward her like a hungry snake. She flinched and waited for the pain to hit her . . .

Then she opened her eyes and looked back to the witch. The spell was there, still coming for her, but something was blocking it. A vaporous barrier. She looked around and found Maggie standing above her. She was facing the witch with a look of determination unlike any Evie had seen before. Her compassion had turned to magic, and her magic had blocked the witch's spell.

Basil reached for Evie, pulling her to safety behind the tree. The ravine they'd just crossed was crawling with activity. Nurses ran through the battlefield, treating cadets who had been hit. Others had twisted ankles or torn flesh. Fairies darted through the trees, shouting at frightened girls. No one would make it through unscathed.

"Go!" shouted Maggie.

Evie, Demetra, and Basil sprang from behind the tree and raced to the top of the hill. Evie glanced back and saw the witch who was pouring her spell out on Maggie.

"Evie, what are you doing?" shouted Basil, but she was already halfway back down the hill. She glared at the witch, using her fear and anger to try to find the courage inside her own heart. Instead, she found a song.

With chaos raging around her, Evie's mind went to a particularly inspiring song that her company liked to sing during free hours. As she stared at the witch on the hill, the lyrics marched through her head like an army of princesses:

Though nighttime be dark and nightmares roam free / When the people stand up, then the people can see / That our courage is stronger than terror may be / And we'll not live to cower, we'll fight to be free.

She could hear their voices, the girls she'd been serving with for nearly two years. She could hear the words echoing through her heart, and she no longer felt alone.

Flares of light sparked across the thicket. She saw the yellow eyes of the witch turn away from Maggie to focus on her. She could feel the witch looking inside of her, disrupting those beautiful voices and their song of victory. Her courage began to falter.

"Run!" screamed Maggie as she raced up the hill. "Go, Evie!"

The yellow eyes hovered coldly in the darkness. There was an earsplitting sound, as though the air itself were fracturing around them. Evie fell to the ground, her courage evaporating into the black of night. The spell exploded next to her. She scrambled through the brush, racing as fast as she could toward her friends. It wasn't until she had reached them, reached the cold night and the big sky on the far side of the grove, that a wave of panic crashed over her.

"It's all right, Evie, we made it," said Maggie, hugging her. "We made it. Thank you."

Evie looked from one of her friends to the next. The sounds of battle were distant now. Behind them.

"We did it?"

"We did it."

"Mission two accomplished," said Basil. "I'm sure the others will be just as easy."

After several moments, Evie's panic subsided and the thoughts ricocheting through her head began to slow. "All right," she said, nodding. "All right. Let's go."

Leaving the shrieks and cackles of the woods behind them, the four friends raced through the crisp night air to the edge of campus, where the Schummel Tower stood. A small collection of cadets in gray and purple uniforms were already racing inside, their faces a mixture of exhilaration and terror.

Evie glanced up at the clouds, ghostly blue and cottony with silver bottoms. Daylight couldn't be far off.

"Get in my tower, cadets!" screamed a fairy drillsergeant with billowing red hair. Her voice was squeakier than the others, but no less intimidating. "Mission three is Escape! Get to the top, recover the enchanted apple from the princess's bedchamber, and get out before you're turned to stone!"

Without hesitation, the cadets ran for the door. It was an open archway of red brick with a portcullis inside. Once they passed beneath those spiked iron teeth, there were two entrances to choose from, one on either side. Half the group ran to the left, half to the right. All around them, more fairies were screaming.

Evie broke for the right. Once she was inside, she looked up and found a spiderweb of staircases stretching up the tower. She paused in the antechamber and turned to her friends.

"She said 'before you're turned to stone.' That means there's a witch in here."

"Got it," said Maggie.

"Let's try this one," said Demetra, pointing to an enclosed spiral staircase on the wall to the right. "She said we're looking for a bedchamber. Those usually face south."

"Good thinking," said Evie.

"But what if the witch is in there?" said Basil.

"We've got to get up somehow," said Evie. "If she's in there, scatter and retreat, all right? Let's look out for one another."

The other three nodded, then ran into the staircase. Round and round they went, choking on the smoke from the rapidly burning torches that lit the way. The staircase was small and the stones were uneven, but they didn't dare slow down. Finally they reached a landing, which emptied into an inner corridor. It followed the wall to the right, and to the left was an open drop back to the bottom of the tower. There was no rail, no balustrade, and the walkway was wide enough for only one person at a time. Similar walkways crisscrossed the inside of the tower, and each had cadets carefully racing across.

"Let's go!" yelled Demetra. As they neared the end of the walkway, Kelbra and Sage emerged from the staircase there.

"Step aside!" yelled Kelbra.

"We can't, there's no room. Just let us pass!" shouted Evie.

"Get out of the way, you imbeciles!" Kelbra pushed past Evie, nearly knocking her off the walkway. She somehow made it past the rest of them, then turned back. "Come on, Sage! Let's go!"

Sage stood aside and let Evie, Maggie, Demetra, and Basil pass, then ran to join Kelbra.

"If you ever make me wait again, I'm going on without you—"

There was a shriek of laughter, followed by the deafening crackle of magic. Evie wheeled to see the sinister grin of a witch in the far staircase just as her dark magic slammed into Kelbra's back.

"AAAAH!"

"Nurse!" called a fairy drillsergeant from the shadows. "First landing!"

Kelbra grimaced. Sage bent down to help, but Kelbra pushed her away, nearly forcing her over the side. "Aah, my back! Why are there bloody witches in a training exercise?"

The shimmering dust of a fairy's wings appeared next to her. "Up you go, Cadet!" It was their own fairy drillsergeant. Kelbra staggered to her feet. Sage held her arm to steady her, but Kelbra shook it off.

"It's not fair to have actual witches in a training exercise," she said through gritted teeth.

"If that were an actual witch, I'd be talking to a statue instead of a former princess cadet."

Evie and her friends watched from the base of the staircase as other cadets streamed past, headed for the top. Kelbra's nostrils flared. She stared at the Fairy Drillsergeant with fury.

"You are dismissed, Cadet Kelbra. See your way down my tower."

"No!" shouted Kelbra. "This isn't fair!"

"Fair or not, you are still dismissed." She turned and began to float away.

"I'm not through with you!" shouted Kelbra. "I want to talk to Beatrice!"

The Fairy Drillsergeant stopped, then turned and floated back until she was only inches in front of Kelbra's face. "By all means, Cadet. Do you know the first step to talking to the

Headmistress?" She somehow managed to float even closer. "Getting out of my tower."

Kelbra's face twisted in rage. Then she stalked past the fairy and went to the far staircase. "You'll regret this. You'll all regret this."

The Fairy Drillsergeant brandished her wand, and Kelbra scurried away down the staircase.

"And you, Cadet Sage? Will you be going up or down?"

Sage scrambled up the tower.

"Come on!" whispered Maggie. "Before she sees us!"

Evie hesitated. She looked into the shadows where the witch had been. There was nothing there.

"I think this is it!" came Demetra's voice from above. "I think we've got the right one!"

After endlessly looping up the staircase, with legs that burned like hearths' fires, they finally emerged into the princess's bedchamber. It resembled Demetra's from the Blackmarsh, though the furnishings were much more modest. There was a four-poster bed with silk hangings, several oak chests, candles in iron sconces, and a dressing table. An earthenware bowl filled with red-skinned apples sat atop it. They each ran across and took one, then hurried back to the staircase. The staccato reverberations from the witch's magic spells echoed up from below.

"She's in there!" said Basil. "We can't go that way!"

"But it's the only staircase," said Demetra.

Evie looked around the room. That staircase did appear to

be the only way back down. But there had to be another. "Our mission is Escape, right? Not Escape by Staircase." She went to one of the windows, covered in oiled parchment, and opened it with an iron rod. There, sixty feet below, a green moat ran around the entirety of the tower base.

Basil peeked out next to her. "That's quite an escape."

A scream echoed up from the staircase, followed by a cackle, and the decision was made for them. Evie stepped onto the windowsill, the cold night air whipping across her face.

"You lot are mad," said a cadet in Bramblestick purple, racing back to the staircase with her apple.

The other three looked at Evie with uncertainty. "Look, I've been in a lot of bogs in my day," she said. "You'll be fine, but don't muck about in there. Get to the surface as quickly as you can. You'll be surprised how thick the water is." She jammed the apple into the pocket of her dress. "Come on! Bravely ventured is half won, right?" She held her breath and leapt out into the air. Her stomach lurched as she plummeted down. Moments later, she splashed into the frigid moat. Her legs slammed into the muddy bottom, sending jolts of pain through her back. Still, she managed to kick off, swimming to the top. The water stank of rot and sulfur. It was as thick as sludge, much more difficult to swim in than water. She ran her hand down her dress and found the bulge of the apple still inside.

There were bubbles and splashes beneath the slime, and she realized it was her friends struggling for air. She saw Basil's hand appear, then slide back under. More bubbles showed where Maggie was. None of them could stay above the surface of the thick liquid. She swam to each of them as her dragon sister had taught her in the bogs near the cave. First Maggie, then Basil, then Demetra. With her soggy uniform dangling from her like a fishing net, she dragged them to the far bank, slopping each of them ashore before climbing out herself.

"Everyone still have their apple?"

They did. Three cadets, sobbing loudly, marched past them, headed for the carriage coach and the long ride home.

"Well done, Evie," said Basil, gasping for breath. "Well done."

"Well done indeed, cadets," came the fiery rasp of the Fairy Drillsergeant. "That would make it all the more tragic for you to go home now, wouldn't it?"

They clambered to their feet, sulfurous water dripping off of them.

"Nice work with the apples," she continued. Then, with a flick of her wand, the apples flew out of their hands and into the moat. "Mission four, pick up a log and get moving." She pointed to the road on the far side of the tower, where cut logs were standing on their ends like begging dogs.

"Yes, Fairy Drillsergeant!" they shouted. Then they ran off and each picked up a log. Struggling under their weight, they trotted down the road to a stone wall, where more evaluators were waiting and watching and scribbling notes. They filtered through an archway and entered an enormous courtyard. A small pile of logs waited just inside the wall. They dropped theirs on the stack.

"Come on, cadets, faster!" barked the red-haired fairy. "Daylight is coming!"

It was still quite dark, and they had trouble finding their footing amidst the rosebushes and creeping vines and decorative stones.

"Over the wall! Move!"

There was a fifteen-foot-high wall inside the courtyard entry, though it was filled with plenty of stones and pocks to climb. Evie scrambled up easily. When she pulled herself to the top, she looked back and saw her friends moving much more deliberately than she had. "Keep it up! You're almost there!"

"Get off my wall, Cadet!" bellowed one of the fairies. *It doesn't matter which one*, thought Evie. *They're like a swarm of horrible screaming wasps.*

She dropped over the wall and froze. It was a courtyard-within-a-courtyard, bordered by overgrown shrubberies, eight feet high or more, and the bones of fruit trees. Giant stones littered the ground, as well as an unused fountain and several trellises covered in the winter skeletons of flowering vines.

And there, not fifty feet in front of her, stood a wolf. It was long and lean, with sharp ears and sharp eyes and sharp teeth and sharp claws. It had its snout in an overturned picnic basket and was devouring whatever had been inside. She carefully stepped to her right, to try to get behind the wolf before it saw her. The creature growled, shaking something in its powerful jaws. If she could just make it to the boulder in front of her without drawing the wolf's attention, she might be able to climb to the top of the shrubbery . . .

Instead, Basil dropped to the ground with a shout. "Augh!"

The wolf wheeled, baring its teeth, its eyes going wide. Maggie fell next, and then Demetra.

"There's a wolf here," said Evie quietly and calmly.

"You don't say," said Basil with a gulp.

The creature stepped forward, lowering its head. Demetra screamed, which caused the wolf to charge with a furious snarl.

"Run!" shouted Evie. She picked up a branch that had fallen from the apple tree next to her and aimed it at the wolf. Its nose scrunched in a ferocious growl as it tried to decide the best way past the branch to its meal. Maggie, Demetra, and Basil crossed the courtyard behind the beast and escaped through an opening in the shrubbery on the far side.

She backed slowly away, waving the branch in front of her like a sword . . .

A sword.

And suddenly the hours she'd spent near the pond that summer, the sparring she'd done with Remington, all came alive in her muscles. She swung with both hands, cracking the wolf in the face. The creature retreated, its eyes flashing with fury. Before it could react to the blow, she charged forward again.

"*Aaaah!*" She attacked. Her first strike missed, but she continued the arc and swung around again. She rained blows on the wolf from every direction. Most didn't connect, but when they did, the creature yelped in pain. She drove the wolf backward across the courtyard, then finally connected with a vicious downward strike to its head, knocking the wolf to its knees. Unfortunately, half of her weapon lay broken on the ground next to it.

The wolf looked up at her, baring its razor teeth. Her eyes flashed to the exit, but she knew she'd never make it at a run. So without even thinking, she leapt onto the wolf and locked her arm around its neck. The creature bucked and snarled, its head darting left and right, jaws snapping, but Evie held tight. She locked her legs around the wolf's middle and let her weight keep the creature down. As she could feel the fight leaving the wolf, she began shifting her weight until finally she was on top of it, and the wolf finally gave in.

Its snarl disappeared, replaced by a gently lolling tongue. Its legs went limp. She slowly released her grip.

"I'm sorry, wolf. Did I hurt you?" she whispered.

The wolf whined and licked her face.

"I'll let you up now." Slowly, carefully, she climbed off. It writhed around until it was upright, lying in the dirt, tongue bobbing with each breath. "I am sorry, wolf. Really."

The wolf whined again, but didn't move. It didn't even watch her as she backed across the courtyard, then disappeared through the shrubbery. *That wasn't princess training,* she thought proudly. *That was growing-up-in-the-forest training.* She emerged into another part of the courtyard, a sculpture garden full of vine-covered arches and water-stained carvings.

"Excellent work with that wolf, Cadet, but you're not there yet!" shouted another fairy from somewhere in the darkness. "Daylight approaches!"

Evie, the cuts and scratches she'd gotten from her battle with the wolf starting to sting loud and red, edged forward into the garden. Considering how Witches' Night had gone so far, she had no idea what to expect next. She could hear the sounds of shouting and witch spells in the distance and thought the nightmare might never end. She hurried through an avenue of rosebushes. When she reached the end, she froze as though she'd been hit with a bucket of icy water.

Standing before her was a beautifully detailed sculpture of a person. It was a girl with a vacant expression on her face, her eyes looking slightly past Evie's head into an unseen distance.

It was Maggie.

For the first time that night, Evie was utterly incapacitated. Her heart broke open as she studied the details in the sculpture's face. The kind eyes and the familiar wide smile with its hint of dimples. Only there was no warmth in it now. It was stone and cold and dead. And it struck right at Evie's heart.

"Eh-heh-heh-heh-heh . . ."

Evie wheeled. Behind her were raised arms, bony and gray, beneath a moth-eaten cloak. A witch's eyes stared at her from the darkness under stringy white hair. "Eh-heh-heh-heh-heh . . ."

Evie's eyes narrowed. Still flush with the adrenaline of her battle with the wolf, she stared straight back into the witch's eyes.

"Go on, Cadet, this is Evasion!" shouted an unseen fairy drillsergeant.

But Evie didn't move. She glared into those dim yellow eyes without a drop of fear in her blood. Within seconds, without even intending it, a swirl of white magic began to light up the night. She glowered at the witch, her nostrils flaring. She could feel the courage coursing through her veins. And in an instant, she pushed it out through her heart and the white swirl blasted across the courtyard and into the witch's chest—

"STOP!" bellowed the fairy. "STOP! NO! NURSE, OVER HERE! YOU! HERE! HERE!"

The light vanished, and Evie was snapped back to the darkness of the sculpture garden. She felt as though she'd just awakened from a dream.

"Hurry! This way!" screamed the fairy. A nurse, the one with the basket of cabbage heads, came hurtling over the flower bushes and raced to the fallen witch. The fairy zipped along next to her.

"Sit her up!" called the nurse. Several others raced in and crowded around as well. She tore off a leaf of a purple cabbage with a shaking hand, then ripped it into small bits. While another nurse eased the witch's mouth open, she gently placed some of the cabbage pieces inside. The witch, groggy and dazed but alive, slowly began to chew.

"More," she croaked.

The nurse tore off another piece, shredded it, and gave it to the witch. She chewed again and swallowed. Slowly, like the rising sun burning through the mist, color began to seep back into her wormlike skin. Her body was changing shape as well, elongating and becoming more human. She took another piece of cabbage and swallowed, gasping as though she'd just had a long drink of water. Then she looked up at Evie. It was Princess Rampion, the woman who had been in charge of the kitchens. She had been transformed into a witch and back again by whatever magic lurked within the cabbage.

"Incredible work, Cadet," she said with a pained smile. "Like a professional princess."

"That's not actually your friend, you lunatic!" The fairy waved her wand, and the statue of Maggie melted into a shapeless hunk of granite. "It's liquid stone! For training!"

Evie blinked her eyes, trying to make sense of all that had just happened. She turned back to Princess Rampion, who was now sitting up on her own. "I'm sorry, Princess! Are you all right?"

"Of course, Cadet. Keep going! You're almost there!"

Evie raced past the liquid stone and through the courtyard exit. She emerged onto a wide road, and her heart began to soar. She'd just found a princess's magic inside her for the second time. She raced through campus under cobalt blue, the first coat of daybreak washing over the night sky. *I haven't finished yet,* she reminded herself. There was a shortcut up ahead, she remembered, an alley that led to a stairway that would put her out behind Pennyroyal Castle. From there, it was only a short sprint back to the barracks.

She rounded the edge of a small castle and disappeared into the alley. It twisted and dove between buildings until finally she emerged into a small hub where several other alleyways intersected. The stairway she wanted was straight ahead, but she didn't take it. Instead she came to a dead stop. There was another stairway to the right, and from the bottom, she heard voices.

"Be quiet! We mustn't talk about this here! It isn't safe!"

Evie's breath caught in her throat. She knew that voice. She'd have known it anywhere. She crept forward, keeping herself tight against the stone, until she reached the head of the stairway. There, at the bottom, was Princess Hazelbranch. Another woman stood with her. She was shorter, in a pale red-sleeved dress with a matching bonnet. By the torchlight from the road beyond where they were huddled, Evie saw that she was crying.

"Did anyone see you come?" demanded Hazelbranch.

"I don't know," whimpered the woman.

"You've got to think. No one must know you're here, or—" Hazelbranch's eyes darted up the stairway as Evie ducked back into the shadows. "Or it could be very, very bad for me, do you understand?"

"Of course I do."

"Good. Come with me. You must stay in the dungeon for now."

"The dungeon!"

"Just your being here threatens everything!" snapped Hazelbranch. "No one must know."

"Of course. You're right," said the woman, wiping the tears from her eyes.

"Come, before we're seen." Evie heard them starting up the stairs. In a panic, she darted behind a rain barrel. Moments later, Hazelbranch and the mysterious woman emerged from the stairway and disappeared down another alley. Once they'd gone, Evie stared after them in the darkness, her mind racing.

It's true. The worst thing imaginable is actually true . . .

In the distance, a bird began to chirp.

"Blast!" She looked up at the sky, then took the stairs three at a time until she reached the bottom. She raced around Pennyroyal Castle, down the hill, and across Hansel's Green. A small collection of people stood in the predawn mist. There were evaluators, fairies, and cadets who had already completed their final mission. As Evie raced across the lawn to join them, she saw the smiling faces of her friends amidst the others. All of them had made it.

"Evie! Thank goodness!" said Maggie, her smile as wide as it had ever been. The four of them exchanged congratulatory hugs, then collapsed to the dew-soaked grass. They had survived Witches' Night.

But Princess Hazelbranch, Evie's most beloved and trusted mentor, was working with the Vertreiben. How could she possibly survive whatever came next?

13

"No, really, your balance and footwork were superb!"

"Thanks, Bas," said Evie, blushing.

"You need to work on your attacks, though. Large movements are slow movements. If you're battling anything with more skill than that wolf, you'll be sliced to bits with counterattacks."

"Basil!" said Maggie.

"What? It's true. And Captain Lamarche would agree with me, by the way." He turned back to Evie. "You do have great form, though. And the way you lunged at that wolf. Utterly fearless. I wanted to stay and watch, but the fairies threatened to send us home."

The four of them were sitting at a table in the Fir-Apple Library, a cozy, fire-warmed place tucked inside one of the small groves of trees at the edge of campus. Mounted animal heads lined the walls, and antler chandeliers hung from the fir-beam ceiling. They were meant to be studying the history of the Cauldron Tippers, but had yet to open their books.

"Can we please forget about the wolf?" said Evie. "We've got to focus on finding this woman. She's the key to everything, I know it."

"You're serious, aren't you?" said Maggie. "You actually believe that Princess *Hazelbranch* is working with the Vertreiben?" She shook her head at the absurdity.

"I saw them." She stared straight into Maggie's eyes, as sober as an undertaker. "I heard her say that if they were seen together, it would ruin everything. Those were Hazelbranch's words."

"I'm with Evie," said Basil. "No one else is having secret meetings with strange women talking about hidden plans. It practically screams 'more than she appears.'"

Evie glanced over at Demetra, who was sitting with her head slumped on her fist. She was absently doodling on her parchment. "All right, Demetra?"

"Yeah. Fine."

Evie reached over and rubbed her shoulder. "I am sorry about Nessa. And Liv. I wish I would've made a better effort to get to know them."

"It's all right. I'm happy the four of us sorted everything out before Witches' Night, though. Otherwise you lot would think I'm only here because my other friends are gone."

They had all seen Liv get eliminated at the very beginning of Witches' Night, but it wasn't until morning broke that they discovered Nessa hadn't made it, either. The entire following day was a strange mix of jubilation and sadness, as so many Leatherwolf and Bramblestick girls were no longer with them.

"Hi, Evie," said a third-class cadet as she walked past.

"Hiya."

"Would you sign my book?"

"Of course."

Basil had to hold in his snickering as Evie scratched her name on the inside of the girl's book.

"Thanks! My mum won't believe it!"

"Don't say a word, Basil," she warned.

"All right, look," said Maggie. "Can't we all agree that Hazelbranch is the kindest princess on campus? The least likely to be working with the enemy?"

"Yes, and my stepmother was able to fool Princess Beatrice for years," said Evie.

"But why? *Why* would Princess Hazelbranch be working with the Vertreiben? Or the witches? What possible motive could she have?"

"That's why Evie's saying we've got to find this other woman," said Basil. "Perhaps she'll give us the motive."

"We've just survived Witches' Night and we're less than two months from the end of the year. Now's not the time to be chasing ghosts and getting ourselves thrown out because we tried to topple one of the most beloved princesses at the Academy!" She opened her book with finality, hoping she'd settled the issue.

"So how do you explain the mysterious woman?" said Basil. "The secret meeting in the dark of night?"

"I can't. But I do know that Princess Hazelbranch isn't a villain, and that's all there is to it."

"What do you propose we do, then, Maggie?" said Demetra.

"We could take the letter to Princess Beatrice."

"There's no point," said Evie. "She'll just say it was sent by someone who wants to have a go at me. She didn't believe the first letter, so why should she believe the second? No. If we're going to figure this out, we've got to find real proof on our own."

"And how do we do that?" said Basil.

"By following Princess Hazelbranch."

The next week went past like a sparrow in flight. There were two major changes after Witches' Night, one welcome and one not at all. The first was that Leatherwolf Company had finally finished its work in the kitchens. Aside from the drastically smaller numbers in its own barracks, the third class had also begun to thin out. Pennyroyal Academy was starting to take on the eerie yet familiar feel that it had toward the end of Evie's first year, with larger numbers of bunks and dining tables starting to go empty. As a result, the staff was able to resume all food preparation. The unwelcome development—the thing that rendered spying on Princess Hazelbranch all but impossible—was that the Fairy Drillsergeant had promised to begin the "real" second-class training after Witches' Night. And she had delivered with a flourish. Everything became more difficult. Much more difficult. The bulk of the year had been primarily for observation, and now the culling had begun in earnest. Each class, each drill, became a proving ground as the staff worked to determine which cadets were truly good enough to continue to the first class. In addition to an increased physical workload, the cadets' courage was being tested on a daily basis, with regular trips to the Haunted Castle of Waiserberg (actually just an empty replica rigged with false witches and simulated spells, but terrifying nonetheless). Even Life at Court, far and away the company's easiest course, took on a more serious edge. Princess Elmstein had actually discharged a cadet for using the word *honored* instead of *revered*. Their grueling schedule made it impossible for Evie and Basil to attend sword-training sessions with the knight cadets, which meant that Evie really only saw Remington during meals.

One night, after a particularly windy day of training where two Leatherwolf girls had lost their dreams of becoming princesses, and one more had ended up in the Infirmary with a broken leg, the cadets trudged into the barracks and collapsed onto their bunks. Moments later Princess Copperpot entered and they had to haul their exhausted bodies back to attention. Evie's arms and back ached as she carried her sack of letters back to her bed. She could barely think as she leafed through them absently.

"Is it possible for one's soul to be sore?"

"Sorry, Evie," said Maggie. "I don't even have the strength to laugh."

Evie glanced down at the sack and saw something that gave her a jolt. There was another dark gray parchment inside, sealed with bloodred wax.

"Maggie!" she hissed. "Look!" She lifted the corner of the parchment.

"Uh, Demetra? Could you help us with something in the latrine?" said Maggie as she shot out of bed.

Demetra, who was writing a letter, looked over in confusion. "Help you? In the latrine? No, thanks."

"Now, please."

Demetra set her parchment on the sill, then put on her slippers and followed them to the latrine. Evie quickly folded the letter under her nightdress before anyone else saw. Once they were all there, Evie produced the letter and tore the wax open.

"What's that—oh," said Demetra, her eyes going wide when she saw the dark parchment.

The three of them crowded around as Evie carefully unfolded it. As with the others, there was a parchment wrapped around another note that was written in blood. The first read, *Your time is up. The only way to save yourselves is to take what they want out of the Academy.* The three of them looked at one another nervously. Then Evie unfolded the blood-streaked parchment inside. It read:

Vertreiben kommen!
We take what is ours and burn the rest!

The three of them stared at the note, but no one spoke. Candles flickered across the stone walls, giving the bloody words an even more sinister edge.

"You're right," said Maggie. "We've got to find that woman."

Cadet Rillia walked in. Evie quickly hid the letters behind her back.

"Hello," she said.

"Hiya," they all replied at once.

She crossed to the washbasin and began to brush her teeth, but in the mirror she saw all three of them standing there looking at her with strange, disquieting smiles. She quickly finished and turned to go. Her toothbrush clanked to the stone. She hurried to grab it and raced out.

"I had a thought," said Maggie, though she was clearly saying it reluctantly. "It may not be a good thought, but it is a thought."

"What is it?"

"Keep in mind, I'm very much opposed to all of this and I wish we could just focus on our training and forget these silly letters—"

"Noted," said Evie.

Maggie took a deep breath and checked the doorway to make sure they were alone. "We could take them to an authority."

Evie and Demetra stared at her blankly. "That's your plan?"

"I'm not talking about Beatrice. I mean a different authority. Lankester."

Evie and Demetra exchanged a look.

"At least we know she'd believe us."

"She's been completely marginalized by Beatrice," said Demetra. "Still, it might be better than doing nothing."

Evie paced near the washbasin, pausing in front of the mirror. She looked at her friends' reflections, then at the reflection of the letter in her own hands. "All right. Tomorrow after lunch?"

"Lights out, ladies!" came the harsh squawk of Princess Copperpot. Maggie's eyes went wide, and she bolted out of the latrine like a rabbit in a kennel.

The barracks were quiet. The night was moonless. Evie was at the precipice between waking and sleep, and with the exhaustion in her bones, she was preparing for a long fall . . .

There was a noise outside, though it wasn't enough to wake her. Her leg twitched. Her eyes rolled back. The noise came again, and although she heard it, her body wanted to stay asleep.

What is that? I need to . . . to . . .

Her mind drifted away. She'd nearly fallen completely asleep this time when the noise came again.

Why doesn't someone shut that bloody frog up . . .

Her eyes popped open.

Frog.

She threw back the blankets as another *ribbit* sounded outside. She went to her window and saw the frog sitting outside on the grass looking in. She glanced around in the darkness. No one else seemed to be moving. Yet.

"Ribbit."

She pushed the window open. "Quiet!" she hissed.

"Ribbit."

With a scowl, Evie pushed herself onto the sill, then climbed through into the brisk night air. She pushed the window until it was almost closed, then went over to the frog.

"Have you lost your mind? What in the world are you doing over here?"

The frog's air sac began to expand with a long, loud *crooooooak*. A moment later, it swept back into a cloak, with Remington underneath. "Just out for an evening hop."

"Come on!" She grabbed his hand and pulled him around the barracks. The trees at the top of the Pit were covered in parchment hawks, hundreds of them, all sent by Evie's admirers. She led him beneath the trees and down into the ravine. "You're going to get us both discharged!"

"So you'll only sneak out when it involves library espionage. I see."

"It wasn't a library!" She led him to a log that the cadets used as a bench during their company sings. "Now, what's going on? Why are you here?"

"Isn't it enough that I missed you?" he said with a smile.

"You could have told me that at breakfast."

"That's true. Though I do have something I thought you'd want to hear straightaway. Well, actually, it might have waited until morning, but I decided I'd rather spend the night looking at you than waiting to look at you."

"Stop trying to charm me." She was happy the night was so dark that he couldn't see her blushing.

"So I finally managed to speak to your friend Forbes. I realized there was never going to be a time when he wasn't hostile, so I forced the issue a bit. Though I'm afraid I didn't get the answer you would have liked."

"What did he say?"

"Bearing in mind that the poor bloke is in the process of losing everything he has to war, he said, and I quote, 'I hope that bloody portrait burns and my father with it.'"

Evie looked down at the ground with a furrowed brow. "That's quite a harsh thing to say."

"Indeed. And from the sounds of things round the barracks, he may just get his wish. No one's seen King Hossenbuhr in weeks. Some of the boys think he might already be dead inside his castle, waiting for the torches to come and finish the job. I'm sorry, Evie. It sounds as though the portrait is going to go up in flames, if it hasn't already."

She sighed.

"Are you all right?"

"Yes. Though I'd be lying if I said I wasn't disappointed."

"I am sorry. Sometimes the Fates have their own ideas about things."

"Well, thank you anyway." She turned to look at him. "And thank you for being there for me as well this year. It's been quite difficult over here, actually. There were times I would have been completely alone if not for you. So . . . thank you for that."

"Of course." He smiled, utterly disarmed by what she'd just said. "It's been good fun bashing you with swords."

They looked into each other's eyes. Neither of them said anything more. Remington leaned toward her, and their lips met. Evie's heart began to race, and all of the pain in her body vanished. After a moment, they broke the kiss. She smiled and looked down at the ground. Her head felt light, and nothing he'd said before about the portrait mattered in the least.

Finally, they decided to head back up to the barracks before someone noticed they were gone. As they stood, he took her hand in his own, lacing each of his fingers through hers. Her insides felt as thin and fluffy as a cloud.

"You know," he said as they strolled up the dirt path toward the barracks, "if you really want a portrait of yourself so badly, I might be able to help."

"Is that so?" she said with a smile.

"Oh, indeed. I've become quite good with finger paints—"

"*Buh-gawk!*" came Lance's squawk from the top of the Pit.

Before she knew what was happening, Remington had thrown her backward into the undergrowth.

"Who's down there?" It was the horrible caw of Princess Copperpot. "I see you, lad! I see you there!"

Evie looked over and saw Remington bounding away through the Pit. Her eyes shot up to the barracks where Copperpot stood, her finger extended toward him like a searchlight. Then, suddenly, he vanished.

"Ah! Aha! Changing forms won't save you, lad! I've seen you! I've seen what you did!"

Evie was in a panic. She raced the other way in a crouch,

trying her best to stay quiet and hidden. If Remington had been seen, then surely Copperpot would check the barracks next to see if anyone was waiting for him. She barreled up the far end of the ravine and flew around the back of the barracks. She scrambled through her window and pulled it shut, then dove beneath her blankets just as the front door creaked open. She pulled them over her head and tried desperately to get her breathing under control.

She stayed like that for what might have been ten minutes, or an hour. Finally, she lowered the blankets and saw that Copperpot had gone. She took a deep breath and let all the air out of her lungs. That had been entirely too close.

"Are you going to eat that?" asked Basil, pointing to the still-steaming bowl of porridge in front of Evie.

"Help yourself." She slid it across to him. She had absolutely no appetite this morning. Her stomach was in knots after what had happened last night. She kept glancing over at Remington, but he was laughing with the other Huntsman boys without a care in the world.

"So," said Demetra, "are we still on for our plan? Today after lunch?"

"Yes," said Maggie. "Though the whole thing make me incredibly nervous."

"Cadet Remington!" bellowed Princess Beatrice, sending the whole Dining Hall to silence. She was standing in the doorway, a look of fury on her face. "You will come here NOW!"

Remington rose and walked toward her, and Evie's heart sank. He glanced over and gave her a smile, but his self-assurance was clearly shaken by Beatrice's tone. The Headmistress turned and marched out into the drizzling morning without a word.

Evie jumped up and ran after them. She looked outside and found Beatrice giving Remington a withering glare. Though he was taller than her, she seemed to loom over him.

"Tell the truth, boy! Now!"

Evie couldn't see his face, though she could imagine the fear in his eyes. He stood tall and straight, then said in a clear voice, "I'm afraid I did, Headmistress."

"And just what were you doing sneaking about after hours?"

"Nothing, really. I couldn't sleep and it was just a bit of fun. I'm sorry, Headmistress, I didn't mean any—"

"Get out," she said, turning away from him.

"But . . . but, Princess, it was only a moment of stupidity. I never meant to—"

"Cadet Remington, you are hereby discharged from Pennyroyal Academy. Now see yourself out."

Evie gasped. Her hand went to her mouth. For once, Remington seemed at a complete loss for words. He stood silent, his shoulders slumped, as the rain began to fall more intensely.

"I'm sorry, Cadet, but you've left me no choice. This is an outrageous violation of the rules. I could have you for the frog bit alone, much less sneaking around campus after hours. There is nothing more I can do for you. You have made your bed, and now you must lie in it."

Panic swirled through Evie's stomach. There must be a way to stop this. As long as he was still there, it wasn't too late—

"I understand," he finally said. "And I'm sorry to have disappointed you, Headmistress." He bowed his head, then began to walk down the road toward Pennyroyal Castle and the black carriage coach that always stood at the ready. Princess Beatrice, without looking back at him, headed off for the shelter of the Dining Hall.

"Please, Headmistress!" shouted Evie, springing out from the doorway. "You can't do this!"

"Oh no? Do you have something to add to this conversation, Cadet? Because there are more than enough seats on that coach."

"No, I—"

"Of course it's my fault," said Remington, running back over to them. "And it's an entirely fair punishment. You are a just and merciful ruler, Princess." He took Evie's hand, tightly, and began to pull her away.

Beatrice's eyes narrowed. She watched with suspicion as Remington pulled Evie down the rain-spattered road. "You have one minute to say your goodbyes or else you may join him, Cadet Eleven. I am in no mood for petty confrontations with children today."

The rain intensified, pounding the cobblestone road that led to the Pennyroyal Castle courtyard. The drops were as cold as a mountain stream. Thunder rumbled, then receded far across the land into the mountains.

"I'm sorry, Remington. This is all my fault. I shouldn't have asked you to talk to Forbes." The rain was so intense that her tears were invisible.

"It would take some incredibly pliable logic to make this your fault. I'm the one who broke both rules she just accused me of breaking, not you." He took her face in his hands and looked at her with eyes so bright that they seemed to shine through the rain. "None of this is your fault, do you understand? I'd do every moment I've spent with you exactly the same. Except the ones where you were shouting at me and accusing me of various things, those I'd leave off."

She laughed through her tears, then buried her face in his chest. She could feel the hard plate of stone beneath his doublet where Countess Hardcastle's spell had struck him the previous year. "Please don't go."

He wrapped her tightly in his arms. "I'm afraid the choice is not mine." He kissed the top of her head. Then his arms loosened, though hers did not.

"Don't let go. Please."

"I've got to, Evie, or she'll throw you out as well. But I want you to remember something, even after I'm gone." She looked up and met his eyes. "Now and always I will keep by you."

Footsteps splashed toward them from the direction of the Dining Hall. "I'm very sorry, lad," said Captain Ramsbottom in his airy voice. "It's time for you to go."

"Of course, Captain." He looked into Evie's eyes once again, and then walked off into the pouring rain.

She stood and watched, her tears coming freely now. By the time he reached the courtyard, the rain was so ferocious that she couldn't even see him anymore. He vanished into the gray and boarded his coach, then rode off into the forest. There was nothing more to say, nothing more to do. Prince Remington, heir to the throne of Brentano in the Western Kingdoms, was no longer a knight cadet at Pennyroyal Academy.

He was supposed to be the crown jewel of the knight companies, she thought as she looked out over the tops of the castles. *The Academy's most celebrated graduate since Rapunzel.*

Leatherwolf Company was gathered on the wall walk of a white brick castle on the eastern half of campus. Under a driving rain, the Fairy Drillsergeant was drilling them on wall climbing. One by one, she had them lower themselves over the battlements, then climb down to a lower balcony. Needless to say, it was far more difficult in the rain than it had been earlier in the year when it was only cold and windy.

Evie, however, was thankful for the rain. It made it much more difficult to talk. And talking was the last thing she wanted to do. So she stood atop the castle, wrapped tightly in her cloak, looking at the misty horizon. *He's out there somewhere.*

The day crept past without a break in the weather. The cadets' fingers and toes were wrinkled and puffy from the rain, bloody and scraped from the stone. After nearly two hours, Leatherwolf was dismissed to change for lunch, though Evie wasn't sure what good that would do. The rain was as violent and angry as it had been all morning, and dry clothes would soon be as wet as everything else.

"I'm really sorry, Evie," said Maggie as they changed for lunch. "That must have been quite a shock."

"Yes. Yes it was."

"Are you all right?"

"Well . . . no. But what can I do about it now? It's over."

They each finished tying their belts, then Maggie and Demetra looked over at Evie. "Are you still up for it?"

"Yes." She took a deep breath to compose herself. "Yes, we're running out of time. We've got to do it now."

Demetra stepped over and put a hand on Evie's shoulder. "He'll be all right, Evie. Some of the courtiers and dignitaries might sniffle behind his back a bit because he didn't graduate, but he'll still end up king of the most powerful kingdom in the west. It won't mean a thing that he wasn't knighted."

Evie gave her a pursed smile. She didn't believe that for a second. "Shall we?"

"You know we're here for you, don't you, Evie?" said Maggie.

"Of course." She smiled a steely smile, willing herself not to cry. She looked at Maggie, then Demetra. "It's happened and it's over and we've got important things to do. So let's just do them."

"You've got the letters?"

Evie touched her dress and felt the parchments in the pocket. "I do."

Maggie took a deep breath. "Then let's go destroy our futures."

. . .

After a mostly silent lunch of stew and sandwiches, Evie, Maggie, Demetra, and Basil remained at the Leatherwolf table. Everyone else cleared up and headed for the barracks and a much-needed hour of dryness and rest, but the four of them sat in silence, their nerves growing tighter and tighter. Finally, the Dining Hall was nearly empty except for some of the staff.

"Is everyone ready?"

One by one, each of them nodded. Then they stood and followed the last few cadets to the door. While they were eating, the rain had slowed, and now it had stopped with only the occasional flurry of drops that quickly faded to cool, dry air. Evie, Maggie, and Demetra stepped outside and waited by the road, just above a large muddy puddle.

Moments later, Basil came out to join them. "She's on her way. And Princess Hazelbranch is still in there tidying up."

"This is it," said Evie. "No turning back."

"No turning back," said Maggie.

Just then, the door opened and Princess Lankester emerged. She was small and silver, with a scowl on her face and an urgency in her step.

"Pardon me, Princess?" said Evie, her voice shaking.

"Yes, what is it?"

"We need to speak to you. It's rather important." Evie nodded to Basil, who slipped back inside to watch for Hazelbranch.

Lankester's mouth curled down into a frown. She stood a

head shorter than any of them, and up close she looked a bit like an overgrown doll playing dress-up. "Well?"

Evie was cowed. She looked to Demetra and Maggie for help.

"Get on with it before this wind cuts me in two."

"We have some information," said Maggie. "It's . . . a bit sensitive."

"This is becoming ever so tedious, girls."

Maggie nodded to Evie. "Show her."

Evie took the letters from the pocket of her dress and handed them to Lankester.

"What's this?"

"Open them," said Evie.

With trembling fingers, Lankester opened the first parchment and began to read. Then, without a word, she opened the other. "How long have you had these?"

"The first one came a few months ago, and that one is from last night."

Lankester carefully folded the parchments, but made no attempt to give them back. "Do you have any idea the trouble you've caused me?"

"We weren't sure that—"

"I have been screaming into the sea that this is a different Vertreiben than it has been in the past. You three have successfully kept from me any real evidence I needed to protect us from them."

"But, Princess, there's more—"

"Beatrice scoffed when I mentioned the Drudenhaus! Dismissed me as a crackpot! To her, I have served as nothing more than a clanging alarm bell with no emergency in sight. I could have used these letters, girls!"

"There's more, Princess, please—"

Basil burst out the door. "She's coming!"

"Princess Lankester, you've got to listen!" said Maggie. "The letter says that someone inside the Academy is more than she seems. We believe that it's referring to Princess Hazelbranch."

"Princess Hazelbranch?" said the incredulous old woman.

"Hurry!" said Basil.

"Evie's seen her sneaking about late at night. She's got someone else in here now. A woman. We think the two of them might be working with the Vertreiben."

Lankester looked from Maggie to Evie, her face contorted in disbelief and anger.

"It's true, Princess," said Evie, her voice filled with urgency. "I heard her tell this woman that it would be bad if she was seen. She's got her hidden away in some dungeon somewhere and no one from the staff knows it, not even Beatrice!"

"Princess Hazelbranch . . ."

"We think she's helping them to orchestrate a raid on the Academy—"

"Here she comes!" hissed Basil.

"Please, Princess Lankester," said Evie. "You've got to help us!"

They all fell silent as the door opened and Princess Hazelbranch emerged. She had a smile on her face and a small platter of food in her hands. Lankester's eyes went from the platter to Hazelbranch's face.

"Well, hello, everyone," said Hazelbranch. "What a lovely after—"

Shing! Her words were sliced off by a sword being unsheathed. Like the strike of a snake, Lankester had a blade pressed to Hazelbranch's throat. The platter clanged to the ground.

"What are you doing?" yelped Evie.

"Princess, stop!" shouted Maggie.

Lankester's eyes bored into Hazelbranch's. "You'll receive full and sincere apologies should they be necessary. Barring that, I've got some questions for you."

"Put the sword down!" called Demetra. "Are you mad?"

"It's all right, girls," said Hazelbranch, though her soothing voice contained a ripple of fear. "It's all right. Is this really necessary, Princess Lankester?"

"I'm not sure," said the old lady. "Why don't we step away from this busy road and find out? Over there, please." She nodded to the side of the Dining Hall, where they would be more concealed.

Hazelbranch stepped very carefully and slowly, the blade hovering just in front of her neck.

"Princess Lankester, please put that away!" said Maggie, but the old woman ignored them all.

Once they were in the shadows between the Dining Hall and a retaining wall, Lankester backed Hazelbranch against the wall. The cadets stood to the side, afraid to come too close.

"What's this about, Princess Lankester?" said Hazelbranch. "I'm certain that whatever the problem is, we can figure it out together."

"This is about deception. Collusion. Treachery."

"I don't understand—"

"Are you harboring someone at the Academy, Princess?"

"Me? What are you—"

Lankester bared her teeth and leaned forward. The point of the sword pressed into Hazelbranch's skin.

"Stop!" called Demetra.

"Who are you hiding?" hissed Lankester. "Answer very carefully."

"You're making a mistake," said Hazelbranch, and for the first time, her calm began to crack. She was panicked.

"Take me to her. Whether you're witch or Vertreiben makes no difference to me. I'm as good with my heart as I am this blade. Either way, you'll be dead before you even think of trying something."

Hazelbranch had gone ashen. She sniffled back tears, then nodded her assent. Lankester's tiny, shriveled face looked as fierce as a lion's. She slid the blade back into its scabbard, which was hidden inside her dress.

Evie looked at her old House Princess and tried to make sense of what was happening. For as shocking as Lankester's actions had been, there was no doubt that Princess Hazelbranch had the look of someone who had been caught.

"March," said Lankester. Hazelbranch wiped her eyes and

began to walk around the Dining Hall and up into campus. Lankester was right behind her, one hand resting on the pommel of her sword. Evie, Maggie, Demetra, and Basil followed behind her. They were huddled close, terrified of what might happen next.

Hazelbranch walked slowly and deliberately through campus, her slippers splashing through the mud puddles that had formed that morning. She entered a small castle in the first ring. It was silent inside, so silent that their nerves coiled even tighter.

"I hope you're not thinking of trying to lose us in here," snarled Lankester. "There's never been a castle built that I couldn't escape."

Without a word, Hazelbranch took a large candle from a sconce and led them through the main hall. They went down a corridor that twisted and turned until it finally ended in a stairway that led down to a lower level.

The dungeon.

"I beg you, Princess Lankester. This is not what you think it is, and for all of our sakes you should—"

"Go," said the old woman. "Now."

Hazelbranch, who looked as though she was going to be sick, started down the stairs. The candle threw jagged shadows off the stone walls. There was a steady drip from somewhere in the darkness. Finally, when they reached the bottom of the staircase, Hazelbranch reached into her dress and removed a key. She opened a thick wooden door, barred with iron spikes, and entered the dungeon. There were several candles lit, but it was still dank and dark, and thick with ghosts. The corridor split in two directions, with cells along each wall. They were sealed with iron bars. Hazelbranch led them to the right. Each cell they passed contained a smattering of straw for a bed and several iron hooks and chains attached to the walls. Finally, when they reached the end of the corridor, they found a cell whose door was open wide. Hazelbranch stopped, her back facing them all.

"Please," said Hazelbranch. Even her voice sounded different now. It was deeper. More brittle.

"Go on," said Lankester.

Hazelbranch didn't move.

"Go on!"

"You can come out," said Hazelbranch softly.

Nothing happened for several seconds. Evie clutched Demetra's arm, her eyes fixed on the open cell door.

"I'm warning you, Hazelbranch," said Lankester. "I will cut down whatever you've got in there if you try anything."

"It's all right," said Hazelbranch. "You can come out now."

Finally, a hand appeared on the stone. The woman Evie had seen with Hazelbranch that night peeked out and looked at them, fear in her eyes.

"Come out of there," said Lankester, unsheathing her sword. "Slowly."

The woman limped into the corridor and stood next to Hazelbranch, who turned to face them.

Lankester stepped forward and raised the sword to the mysterious woman. "Who are you? Vertreiben? Are you Order of the Fang?"

The woman, her breath coming fast, looked up at Princess Hazelbranch. Her eyes were sad. *Regretful*, thought Evie. *They look regretful.*

"Answer me! My patience is scarce!"

"This is my sister," said Princess Hazelbranch. "Well . . . my stepsister, actually. This is Princess Javelle."

"What's she doing here? And why are the two of you sneaking about in the dark of night?"

"I came to warn her," said Javelle. "She's in terrible danger."

"She certainly is. Anyone who threatens Pennyroyal Academy in my presence should consider themselves in terrible danger."

"What?" said Javelle. "She hasn't threatened anything! She's the one *being* threatened!"

"Princess Lankester, if you'd only let me explain," said Hazelbranch.

"Her," said Lankester, pointing the sword at Javelle. "I want to hear it from her."

Javelle looked up at Hazelbranch, who closed her eyes and nodded.

"My sister—my other sister—has always been a bit . . . *disturbed*," said Javelle. "I hadn't spoken to her in nearly fifteen years, but she somehow found me. Tracked me to my village and kidnapped me from my bed at knifepoint. She took me to a horrible place and . . ." Javelle sniffled and looked at the floor as her tears began to fall. "She tortured me. Just as she had when we were younger. It went on for days until finally I couldn't take any more."

"Why? What did she want?"

"Her," said Javelle, looking up at Hazelbranch. "Javotte has been looking for her for years."

"Did you say Javotte?" said Lankester. And for once, the unflappable Vertreiben hunter seemed shaken.

"I'm afraid Javotte is also my stepsister," said Hazelbranch.

"So you admit it!" said Lankester. "Your sister is the leader of the Vertreiben!"

"No, Princess, you don't understand," said Hazelbranch, slowly shaking her head. "Perhaps the only one who wants me dead more than Calivigne is Javotte. She's hated me from the moment we met."

The water continued to drip from somewhere in the shadows. Evie's mind was reeling as she tried to make sense of what she was hearing.

"I'll explain everything, Princess Lankester, just, please . . . take the sword away from my sister."

Lankester's eyes narrowed. Slowly, the blade began to fall. She didn't sheath it. Instead, she held it in front of her with both hands, ready for anything. Except, perhaps, what came next.

"My name isn't Hazelbranch. I'm afraid it was necessary for me to disguise my identity with a sister like Javotte on the loose. You see, many years ago, all three of us attended the Academy.

Javotte, obviously, never graduated. When Javelle and I did, it drove an even deeper wedge between us. It was always my fear that Javotte might end up with the Vertreiben one day. As deranged as she is, she is equally charismatic."

"When I escaped her house of torture, I knew I had to find my sister before she did," said Javelle, looking up at Hazelbranch again. "I had to warn her that Javotte is coming, and she's bringing an army with her."

"Offering no offense, Princess Hazelbranch, or whatever your name is," said Basil, adopting the professorial tone he sometimes did when puzzling through new information. "Why would your sister go to all the trouble of reassembling this secret society and then marching it across the land just to kill you?"

"Well, Basil, it's because of my real name."

"Which is?"

Hazelbranch took a deep breath and shared a meaningful look with Javelle. Then she turned back to the group and smiled. "My name is Cinderella."

No one said a word. The water drip drip dripped down the corridor.

"My stars," said Lankester.

Maggie fainted dead away.

"I CAN'T BELIEVE I didn't see it!" said Maggie, a smile embla-
zoned across her face. "When Cinderella's father went away,
he asked the girls what they'd like him to bring back from his
travels. One wanted beautiful dresses. The other wanted pearls
and jewels. That was Javotte and Javelle! But Cinderella," she
said, raising her finger, "asked him only to bring back the first
branch that brushed his hat on the way home. And it was a
hazel branch!"

"It is rather incredible, isn't it? Cinderella, our old House
Princess," said Demetra.

"It certainly qualifies as 'more than she seems,'" said Basil,
watching Demetra with a nervous grimace. Much to his unease, she had his sword in her hand and was absently slashing
the air. The four of them were in his storehouse taking advantage of the free hour between supper and lights-out. "That's
not quite right, Demetra. If you'll just hand me back the sword,
I'd be happy to show you a proper strike."

"It certainly is incredible," said Evie. She was sitting atop an old grain barrel, deep in thought. "But it's also seriously bloody dangerous."

Maggie continued pacing around the storehouse, telling the story as though she were the only person there. Nothing could disrupt her bliss. "Cinderella took that hazel branch and planted it on her mother's grave . . ."

"Dangerous?" said Demetra, nearly hacking Basil's hand off.

"Javotte tortured her sister just to find out where Cinderella was. And now she knows," said Evie. "She's here."

"Her grief at her mother's death caused her to weep, and her tears watered the branch until it turned into a beautiful tree. There were two white birds who lived in the hazel tree and helped Cinderella with every awful task her stepmother presented her . . ."

"That's got to be why the witches are standing down," said Evie, slamming her fist in her hand. "Lankester was right. They are in league with the Vertreiben, and they're letting them do the dirty work!" She jumped down and began to pace next to Maggie. One paced in ecstasy, one in worry. "If Cinderella is captured, we'll lose the most iconic princess in all the land. We can't let that happen!"

"That blade is awfully sharp, Demetra, and you've really got to apply immense focus to—YOW!" Basil jumped back just as she took another careless swipe, nearly slicing him in two.

"This is fun!" she said. "I can see why you went to that knights' course."

"It's not fun, it's a dangerous weapon!"

"It wouldn't make any difference to the witches who captured her," said Evie, as much to herself as anyone. "As long as Cinderella is dead or in chains, the result is the same. A princess's currency is hope. Hazelbranch herself told me that. If the witches or the Vertreiben or whoever else can capture the greatest princess ever to live, then what hope is there for the rest of us?"

"The birds in the hazel tree knew all along that Cinderella was a true princess. They helped her see it for herself, and that helped her prove it to everyone else . . ."

"If you'll just allow me to show you," said Basil, easing the sword from Demetra's hand.

"So what do we do?" said Demetra. "If their goal is to capture Cinderella, surely they won't care who dies in the process. They even said in their last threat that they'd burn the Academy to the ground."

"Why can't we just wait?" said Basil. "Princess Lankester has gone off to confront Javotte, and you saw how well she handled Hazelbranch. If anyone can handle her stepsister, it's that old bird."

"But what if she can't?" said Evie. "Javotte sounds like a maniac." She thought for a moment. "We've got to get Cinderella out of the Academy. Just as the last letter said."

"Are you mad?" said Demetra. "According to Javelle, there are Vertreiben everywhere! At least here we've got the wall to protect us."

"All it would take is one other person to be working with them. Just one. And the wall might as well not even be there.

Do you trust everyone in here that much?" Evie chewed her fingernail. Her mind was racing. Maggie's mind, meanwhile, was still in the clouds.

"The birds told the prince that the stepsisters weren't the true owners of the slipper, and that Cinderella was. The same birds who wouldn't have been there if there hadn't been a tree, and a tree that wouldn't have been there if there hadn't been a *hazel branch*!" Maggie flopped down on Basil's pallet and let her arms fall straight out. The smile looked as though it might remain on her face forever.

"Maggie, are you quite finished glowing over meeting Cinderella? We could really use your thoughts."

"You're right, Evie," said Demetra. "There are too many people in here to trust them all. At least if Cinderella's out there, she isn't cornered."

"And if she's not actually at the Academy," said Basil, "perhaps she could let the Vertreiben know so they'll leave us alone and go after her out there." He glanced out the window into the darkness. "I'm sorry to break this up, but I think it's just about lights-out. I just heard Lance squawking in the barracks."

"Let him send me home," said Maggie. "I've just met *Cinderella*!"

"We've got to keep calling her Hazelbranch," said Evie. "Can we all agree to that? No matter what happens, no one can know who she really is."

Evie left her torch burning long after the others had been snuffed. She lay on her back and watched the smoke flutter up and disappear into the beams of the ceiling. She was convinced that sneaking Cinderella out was the only way to save her, and possibly to save the Academy itself. But there was one piece of the plan that she just couldn't crack.

How?

Javelle had told them that Vertreiben were lurking everywhere. Strolling past them with Cinderella would be impossible. If only there were a way to frighten them off, even temporarily. To create a path through them where Cinderella could escape. But the Vertreiben weren't afraid of anything. Not even princesses.

She glanced over at Maggie, who was sound asleep with a smile on her face, no doubt dreaming of her meeting with her idol. Evie smiled, too. It was nice to see her friends happy again. It finally felt like it used to when—

An idea hit her like a tree falling on a cottage.

She bolted up in bed. Perhaps there was something that could frighten the Vertreiben . . .

She climbed off her bed and looked underneath. It was chockablock with some of the parchments she'd received. She began pulling them aside in piles until she found some that had been there since earlier in the term. She wrested a small stack free and picked up the parchment on top. A layer of feathery dust fell from the page, and the stripes of black ink with it. The parchment had molted and was now blank. She brushed away the last bits, then grabbed the quill and inkpot off of Maggie's windowsill.

Still on the floor, she began to write. She scribbled frantically and feverishly, then blew the ink until it was dry. Her torch was flickering, having nearly burned down to the nub. That was all right. She was finished.

She hurried to the barracks door and eased it open. The cold night air slithered in just as she slithered out. Standing on the patch of grass just outside the door, she hastily folded her parchment and held it in front of her. She jerked her arm up and let go, but the parchment just floated back to the ground.

"Come on, come on."

She picked it up. The wrist, Basil had said. The wrist was the key. She flicked her wrist and snapped the parchment into the air. It floated back down, but before it touched the ground, wings began to sprout from the top. The letter struggled to stay aloft, halfway between parchment and hawk, but with each flap of the wings it became more and more bird.

She smiled as she watched it flap away into the darkness. But as the bird disappeared, her smile did, too. Cold dread began to creep over her. The letter was gone and there was no getting it back.

What have I just done?

"The end of the year approaches like a horde of moaning witches," said Princess Ziegenbart, leaping atop a straw bale. "I shall begin accepting applications for the various branches of the princess service in one week's time. If you haven't already, finish reading the chapter on the Cursebreakers this evening.

Princess Mansfield will be joining us tomorrow to answer any and all. She is one of the finest Cursebreakers of the last twenty years, so it should be plenty interesting indeed. And remember, she's the one who developed the Waking Sleep."

The cadets were already busy packing up their things, rolling parchments and capping inkpots and heading out into the foggy gray afternoon.

"Well? Shall we pop by Ironbone barracks and see if Princess Hazelbranch has heard from Lankester?" said Demetra.

"I need to speak to Princess Ziegenbart quickly," said Maggie, and she walked to the head of the class and began chatting with the goat.

Evie's heart was racing. The plan she'd put into action the previous night, the plan about which she was now so uncertain, needed one more element. And this was the perfect chance to finish it.

"Go on," she said to Demetra. "I'll wait for Maggie and we'll catch you up in a minute."

Demetra and Basil followed the rest of the class outside. Evie glanced to the front of the room and saw Maggie and Ziegenbart deep in conversation.

"It says on page seventy that some princesses prefer the Western Kingdoms because of the climate, but I'm from Sevigny, so cold weather doesn't particularly bother me. How important is that, really?"

Ziegenbart was only too happy to explain the particulars of life in various climates for the Towersitters. Evie saw her chance. She eased over to the table near the wall where the witch artifacts were housed. They were strewn across it like farm implements in a stable. She made sure she wasn't being watched, then picked up a spindle and the small vial next to it. This was the Waking Sleep potion that Ziegenbart had just mentioned. It would surely be missed when Princess Mansfield turned up tomorrow, but by then it would all be done. Her heart was thumping as she slipped the spindle and the vial up her sleeve and hurried to the door.

Outside, she dropped them into her pocket and waited in the cold for Maggie to finish, which took another fifteen minutes. Finally she came out.

"Oh, sorry, Evie, I didn't realize you were waiting."

"It's all right." They began to walk through the fog toward the Dining Hall.

"I'm quite excited to see Princess Mansfield tomorrow. The Cursebreakers sound fascinating."

"I thought you'd decided on the Towersitters."

"I honestly don't know what I'm doing. I'm all over the shop."

Evie's stomach was in knots. She had things to tell Maggie— immense things that loomed over her like thunderheads—but she couldn't bring herself to do it. They walked all the way to the Dining Hall, and she hadn't said a thing she'd wanted to. Third-class cadets continued to look at Evie with adulation, but she'd stopped noticing long ago. She and Maggie joined Demetra and Basil, who were already finished with their lunch. The

Dining Hall was filled with the aroma of smoked meat and fish. There was also the usual assortment of fresh fruits and small pots of honey yogurt and toasted bread. Evie sat and began nibbling on an apple.

"Spoke to Hazelbranch," said Basil. "No word from Lankester."

Evie twisted in her seat, unable to sit still.

"You look as though you've sat on an anthill, Evie," said Demetra. "Are you all right?"

"Not really!" she said with a nervous smile, her foot tapping the floor.

"What's wrong?" said Maggie.

"I've done something and I probably shouldn't have, but by the time I'd thought it through, it was too late and that's just how it is and I'm sorry but it's done."

"What did you do?" said Maggie, her cheerful expression fading.

"I was trying to think of a way to get Cinderella past the Vertreiben, and it occurred to me that if we could just scare them a bit, they might back off enough for us to sneak her through."

"And?"

"And I thought of something that might work. That might put some fear into them."

The three of them stared at her with grave expressions. "Evie," said Maggie, finally. "What?"

She took a deep breath. "Witches."

Maggie, Demetra, and Basil all looked at one another.

"Witches?" said Basil.

"The Vertreiben aren't afraid of princesses because our skills aren't designed to work against them. But they have to be afraid of witches, because *their* magic works against everyone."

"Evie," said Maggie. "What did you do?"

"As I lay in bed thinking it through, it occurred to me that it's got to be Malora who's been sending me the warnings."

"Evie? What did you do?"

"Hear me out. She's still my sister. Yes, she's a witch, but she sent those letters because she wanted to protect me—"

"Evie! What did you do?"

"I asked Malora to take Cinderella prisoner."

Maggie's head thumped on the table.

"You did what?" said Demetra.

Basil picked his teeth with a bone. "Well . . . wasn't expecting that."

Maggie groaned.

"Have you lost your mind?" said Demetra.

"The only way to safely get Cinderella out of the Academy is if she's with someone the Vertreiben are afraid of. That certainly isn't any of us. But it is a witch. A witch we can trust."

"I don't mind it, actually," said Basil.

"So let me get this straight. You want us to hand over the greatest princess ever to live to *Malora*?" spat Maggie.

"I know it sounds mad, but I'm sure she's the one who's been sending the letters! I know she'll help us!"

"Evie, this was not a good idea," said Demetra.

"Not a good idea? This is a disaster!" said Maggie. "Malora

will tell Calivigne, and soon we'll have witches at our doorstep alongside the Vertreiben!"

"On the other hand," said Basil, "they couldn't possibly expect that a witch would be voluntarily helping the princesses."

"Please tell me you didn't reveal her real identity," said Maggie.

Evie said nothing.

"What happened to 'no one must know'? That was *you* who said that! Oh, Evie, what have you done?"

"I don't know," said Evie. "But I've done it."

They went through the rest of the day's training without really talking to one another. During the Fairy Drillsergeant's drills, during their off-hour, during a lecture on high teas with Princess Elmstein, they all stayed close, though none of them spoke. It was as if they were waiting for Beatrice to come storming down from the Crown Castle to personally chuck them over the wall and watch the witches haul them away.

The worst of it was at supper. They sat at their normal places at the Leatherwolf table, which had a clear view of Princess Hazelbranch's throne. She gave them compassionate glances throughout the meal, as if to thank them for helping keep her secret. And each time Evie's eyes met hers, she felt just a little bit queasier inside.

As night fell once more and Princess Copperpot arrived with the mail, Evie found herself wishing desperately for word from Princess Lankester. If she had somehow managed to thwart

Javotte, then Evie's plan to work with Malora wouldn't be necessary. Yes, Hazelbranch's true identity would be exposed. But that would still be a far better outcome than a bloody confrontation with the Vertreiben.

Lance strutted down the aisle. Everything was silent except for his soft clucking and the *thunk thunk* of Copperpot's wooden leg on the stone. As usual, she carried a small burlap sack.

"As we are closing in on the end of our time together," said Copperpot, "I feel I must acknowledge something that, to my mind, is rather extraordinary." She slowly hobbled down the aisle, glancing sideways at each cadet she passed. "Each year, there is one cadet who puts an intolerably bad taste in my mouth on the first day of term. This year was, as expected, true to form."

Evie could see Maggie starting to sway next to her. She decided to risk a scolding from Copperpot to look over. Maggie's skin had gone gray, and she seemed as though she might collapse. "Are you all right?" She didn't answer.

"I have never once, in all my years at Pennyroyal Academy, seen that cadet survive the year. And this year is no exception."

"Please, Princess Copperpot!" wailed Maggie. "Please don't send me home! I'll do whatever—"

"Yet."

The barracks were silent except for Maggie's sniffling.

"You have not finished the year *yet*, Cadet," said Copperpot, stopping in front of Maggie. "But I see no reason why you shouldn't. Lance has been particularly impressed with your engagement and attention to detail over the course of the year. As have I. You are quite an impressive young lady, Cadet Magdalena. For the first time in my career, I am starting to think I may have misjudged someone."

Maggie stared up at her, bewildered. "What?"

"I am simply offering you a mea culpa in front of your comrades. And a word of encouragement. Barring some sort of collapse with your final exams, I see no reason why you shouldn't be here next year as a first-class princess cadet."

Maggie blinked. "What?"

"The rest of you, when tomorrow comes, you must be more a princess than today."

"Yes, Princess!"

Evie grunted as Copperpot thrust the sack into her stomach. "Your letters, Cadet."

"Thank you, Princess," said Evie, rubbing her middle.

Copperpot and Lance ambled back down the aisle and disappeared into their quarters. Evie began leafing through her letters. As the rest of the company got ready for bed, Maggie remained standing at the end of her bunk.

"All right, Maggie?" said Evie.

Maggie didn't speak. Her shoulders bobbed, just a little. She was crying. Demetra walked over to her and put her hands on her arms.

"I'm proud of you, too, Maggie. Everything she said and more is true. You're going to be an excellent princess when this is all over."

Maggie collapsed into her arms. Demetra held her tight as a year's worth of fear and frustration came rushing out.

"You're all right," said Demetra. "You're still here."

Evie smiled and left them to it. They had all kept swimming and found one another once again. With her heart warmed, Evie glanced down at the pile of letters in her hands. Her blood ran cold.

"Girls," she said. "Malora's written back."

The owls called to one another in the dark forest beneath the hilltop Academy. A pack of wolves began howling in the distance, a chorus of voices that existed only to warn others to be afraid. Evie, Maggie, and Demetra stepped out from the barracks and hurried around to Basil's storehouse. They let themselves inside and woke him with a rough shake.

"You lot are lucky I don't sleep with my blade," he said, rubbing his eyes.

Evie lit a candle, then another, until the storehouse glowed in the night. "Malora's sent a bird."

"Has she?"

Evie sat on a stump the woodcutters used to split logs and picked the crude wax seal away from the parchment with her fingernail. Then she unfolded it and began to read:

"I'm quite impressed you worked it out, sister. I never intended to write you at all, but when I saw what the Vertreiben were up to, I figured you at least deserved some sort of warning. I'd heard the rumblings that

306

someone inside was not who they seemed, but I'd no idea it was Princess Hazelbranch, and even less idea who she really was. I told you when last we spoke that I would never lift a finger to help you again, but I think this situation calls for a reevaluation of that policy. I've no love for the princesses, nor the Vertreiben, nor the witches, but for some strange reason Cinderella does still mean something to me. I suppose I was indoctrinated deeply enough as a child that she will always be something of a hero to me. In short, I've no interest in seeing her captured. By anyone."

"Fantastic!" said Basil.

Evie continued: "I know it must've been awfully difficult for you to write me, but it's good that you did. The Vertreiben are already in the Dortchen Wild, and there is very little time left. As luck would have it, I, too, am in the Dortchen Wild. If you'd like to see Cinderella make it out of there alive, bring her to me tonight. I'll ensure she gets to safety."

"Tonight?" said Maggie. "This is madness! Cinderella's going to kill us when she hears what we've done!"

"Is that all it says?" asked Demetra.

Evie read on: "I've written detailed instructions on how to find me, so when you turn this back into a bird, it'll lead you to my location. Hurry. They're coming. And it won't be days. It'll be hours."

The four of them sat in silence. The muted *hoot-hoo-hoot* of an owl sounded from the trees.

"We've got to tell Princess Beatrice," said Maggie as she stood. "This has gone too far."

"No, Maggie," said Demetra. "This is our best chance."

"So now you agree with this as well?"

"I don't believe Princess Cinderella is safe here," she said. "They're coming, Maggie. We've got to do something."

"I can't believe what I'm hearing!" Maggie looked from Evie to Basil to Demetra. "What happens if Javotte finds Malora with Cinderella? Or worse, if Calivigne does?"

"Nothing happens," said Evie. "Malora's a hero for capturing Princess *Hazelbranch*."

"How would they not know that Malora's betrayed them?"

"Because of this," said Evie. She reached into the pocket of her nightdress and took out the spindle and vial she'd stolen from Ziegenbart's classroom.

Maggie looked at them for a moment, piecing together what Evie had in mind. "You're going to put Cinderella to sleep? Am I the only one with any sense round here?"

"She has to be a *prisoner*, Maggie, that's how no one will know Malora's betrayed them. Just until they're through the forest. Then Malora will give her the Waking Kiss and Cinderella will be safe."

Maggie shook her head and looked from one of them to the next. "So that's it, then? You're off to hand over the most important princess we've got to a *witch* and I'm supposed to go along with it."

"Well . . ." Evie looked from Demetra to Basil. "Yes."

"I won't do it. I'm going to Beatrice before you get us all killed." She charged toward the door.

"Maggie, no!" cried Demetra.

They all jumped up to stop her. She writhed out of Demetra's grip, struggling like a fly in a web, then knocked Basil to the floor, causing a pot of gardening supplies to crash over.

"Jab her, Evie!" Basil said.

"What?"

"Jab her!"

Maggie pulled open the door. In a panic, Evie grabbed her wrist, raised the spindle, and jabbed her finger.

"Aah!" Maggie clutched her hand and fell to her knees. She looked up at Evie, her face full of reproach. Then her eyes rolled back in her head and she was asleep.

They all stepped over and looked down at her. She was peaceful. Dead asleep.

"She's going to be furious when she wakes up," said Basil. "Glad I wasn't the one who did it."

"You made me do it!" said Evie.

"Well done," said Demetra. "Just when we're all getting along so well, you go and put her in an eternal slumber."

"I ought to open the gates and whistle a wolf call," said the Fairy Drillsergeant, chewing on a small piece of fairyweed. "This is without a doubt the most ill-conceived, foolhardy plan I've ever heard."

"And yet it's something we must do," said Cinderella. They were huddled in her quarters at the front of the Ironbone Company barracks, only a single candle providing any light. "Fairy Godmother," she continued, "you remember Javotte. She used to torture the mice for her own amusement. She killed the birds because she could. She took the fire poker to the horse whenever—"

"Hang on," said Basil. "*You're* her fairy godmother?"

"Of course I remember Javotte," said the Fairy Drillsergeant, ignoring him.

"Well, now imagine Javotte with an army behind her."

The Fairy Drillsergeant threw her fairyweed to the floor and floated back and forth, pacing through the air. "This is madness! Ever since I was assigned to you, I've dedicated my life to keeping you out of the witches' hands. And now you want to walk right into them?"

Cinderella held out a finger, on which the Fairy Drillsergeant landed. They looked at each other. Evie could see the depth of their relationship in that one, brief moment. "I've no choice, Fairy Godmother. I do believe Evie is right about Malora. I saw many awful things in her last year, but I also saw the capacity for goodness. I've never seen that in a witch before." She reached up with her other hand and flicked her fingertip, gently wiping a tear from the Fairy Drillsergeant's cheek. "Come on, Mum, we've made it through some tight spots before, haven't we?"

"None tighter than this, I daresay." As if realizing the cadets were still there, she sniffled away her tears and growled at them. "Get out of here, will you? Let the adults talk."

Evie, Demetra, and Basil went out into the night and waited. The moon had not yet risen, leaving the earth as black as the sky.

"Maggie's never going to speak to me again," said Evie.

"If this works, she will," said Demetra.

The door opened, just a crack, and the Fairy Drillsergeant flew out. "She wants me to stay here." Her voice was gentler than any of them had ever heard it. "She says Malora is bound to be on edge and seeing me would only make things worse, which is probably quite true. She won't even let me send you three home, which is what I'd like to do more than anything." She was looking off into the distance, in the general direction of the flickering torchlight that marked the campus roads. "She's just writing a letter now. I'm to deliver it to Princess Beatrice tomorrow, once you've gone." The three cadets stood in the dark, motionless and wordless. "I'm trusting you with her. That woman is more than just a princess to me, do you understand?"

"Yes, Fairy Drillsergeant," they said quietly. The night was still. They could hear the soft chime of the dust falling from her wings. Another owl hooted, *hoot-hoo-hoot*.

"An animal can sense a person's kindness better than any fairy or human can. The same is true for cruelty. That's why the princesses in all those stories are surrounded by animals. They know our hearts." For the first time in nearly two years, the Fairy Drillsergeant's voice sounded like that of an ordinary fairy. It was soft and tender. Evie looked over at her, unable to reconcile it with the screaming rage she was used to.

"I'll never forget the day those mice came to our tree. Their bodies were covered in scars. Big chunks of fur missing. But they weren't there for themselves. They'd come because the girl who was doing that to them was doing the same things to her own stepsister. They told our village elders that this stepsister was the most kindhearted person they'd ever met. They couldn't bear to see the torment she'd been put through. I was assigned to investigate. I was skeptical at first. I'd seen enough humans to know that their suffering was usually self-inflicted. But I'd been given an assignment, so off I went with the mice. And what I found . . ." She shook her head and chuckled softly. "It changed my life.

"I watched that girl for days before I spoke to her. What the mice said was true. She didn't have a cruel bone in her body. And yet she was forced to live with three of the cruelest people I'd ever come across. It was as though they lived only to torment her. To humiliate her. Belittle her." Evie saw the fairy's jaw harden at the memories. "I wanted to fly in and burn the place down, with the stepmother and stepsisters inside. Adults are supposed to *protect* children, to keep them safe and let them be innocent and free before they're turned loose into this horrible world . . ." She trailed off. Though it was dark, Evie could hear the emotion in her voice. "Javelle turned herself round, obviously. And it was due in no small part to Cinderella's kindness. But the stepmother and that other one, *Javotte*. They're humanity's worst . . ."

She glanced over her shoulder at the barracks and saw that the door was still closed.

"You remember the story of Cinderella at the ball? That happened as much because of my pettiness as her kindness.

She was so excited about it. She hadn't been to one since her mother passed. And the stepmother and stepsisters snatched it from her just before she was meant to go. That drove me right over the edge. Of course I gave her the gown and the carriage and all the rest because of her kindness. Certainly that's true. But really I just wanted to see the looks on the faces of those filthy hags when she walked into that ballroom. It was petty and mean-spirited, and it was the single most exquisite moment of my life.

"As for Cinderella, she met her true love at that ball. Such a good chap, the prince. He had a heart as kind as hers until that giant got him. It would have been awfully easy for the two of them to ride away in a bridal carriage and live happily ever after, but they didn't. He helped form a party to drive the giants back into the mountains, while she set her own happiness aside and enlisted at the Academy to train to battle witches. And she trained harder than anyone who's ever stepped foot on this campus. She even brought her horrible stepsisters here, and Javelle blossomed into a very respectable Princess of the Shield in her own right. It wasn't until much later that Cinderella and the prince finally married." She paused and glanced at the dim candlelit window at the front of the barracks. "You know, I was never a particularly good fairy before I met her. I liked to use my magic to play tricks on people. They were nothing but big, dumb animals to me. But Cinderella infected me with her compassion. I like to see the goodness in people. I really do. But I *love* to see the greatness in them. That's what being a fairy drillsergeant allows me to do. And Cinderella taught me that."

The door opened and the princess emerged, a folded parchment in her hands. She handed it to the Fairy Drillsergeant, who used her wand to hold it in the air. "Remember, don't deliver it until morning."

The Fairy Drillsergeant fluttered over and gave Cinderella a tender kiss on the forehead. "I'll find you when the year is out. Until then, be safe, child."

"I will, Fairy Godmother. All will be well."

And with that, she flew off into the darkness. Cinderella turned to her three cadets. "Shall we?"

With shaking fingers, Evie held up Malora's letter. She flicked her wrist and tossed the parchment. It snapped into a hawk, much more smoothly than the last time she'd tried it. The hawk circled above, then began flying north. The four of them hurried across the field toward the edge of the meadow that led down to the wall and the enchanted forest beyond. Evie's sister awaited them there, that much was known. But would they find Cinderella's sister first?

DRIED LEAVES RATTLED across the ground, swept along by a breeze so cold that it passed right through the cloaks they wore over their uniforms. Evie wished they could move a bit faster, but the terrain was so steep and the ground so pitted, it was difficult enough just keeping their eyes on the bird. The ferns shuddered in the wind, waving wildly as though warning them to turn back.

This is discipline, she reminded herself. *Control your fear and move forward. You're trained for this.* She kept her right hand on the hilt of her sword. Basil had his as well, but Demetra and Cinderella carried only their courage.

She scanned the ground before her. Her eyes had adjusted to the darkness as best they could, but with no moon in the sky and a thick tangle of winter branches overhead, the forest had become even more treacherous than usual. Dead leaves and dead needles, and tree trunks like the iron bars of a dungeon cell sprouting up all around them. Vertreiben and witches out there in the darkness.

Something was coming alive in the night, though she couldn't decide if it was the enchanted trees or just her imagination. They swayed in the wind, boughs groaning and leaves whispering. *If we don't find Malora soon, we'll have more trouble than witches and failed princesses.*

None of them spoke as they worked their way farther and farther into the dark forest. The parchment hawk waited on a branch for them to come into view, then flew ahead into the darkness to wait for them again. Cinderella, with her vast years of experience, led the party. She was the only one capable of tracking the bird.

Evie brought up the rear. The only thing she needed to follow was the dim outline of Demetra's shoulders. Her head ached from the intensity with which she stared into the shadows. She was convinced Javotte herself would appear at any moment, then the rest of the Vertreiben and the witches and Calivigne and even a wolf or two for good measure.

She tried to ignore the sounds of the forest popping and rattling and swishing with every gust of wind. She thought back to that day on the tower at the end of the previous year, to the ruins of Pinewall, when Malora had first learned that she wasn't a highborn princess, but a witch. She had still helped Evie save Remington, even after discovering that her entire life had been a lie. She had gone against her own mother, Countess Hardcastle, one of the Seven Sisters. And in doing so, she had given Evie the courage to fight.

She'll do it again, she tried convincing herself. *All Malora needs to see is that she is still my sister.*

Finally, two hours after they'd left the Academy, and one hour after the fog had begun to creep in like a wolf tracking its prey, Cinderella stopped. The hawk screamed from the darkness. *"Fie-yaah! Fie-yaah!"*

"We're here," whispered Cinderella.

Basil turned around and looked at Evie. She gave him a nod, though she felt far less confident than she must have looked.

They threaded their way through the trees to the top of a hill, where Cinderella paused once again. She was peering into the mist that had settled in the lower parts of the forest. Evie did the same, but could barely make out anything in the gloom.

"There." Cinderella pointed into the distance. Evie looked, but could see nothing aside from endless trees and wafting mist. "Come."

She started off down the hill. Evie hesitated. The bird was sitting on a branch looking at her. It dared not go any farther into the woods.

Cinderella was moving quickly now. They raced through the undergrowth, dodging the lazy swipes of the sprawling oaks at the bottom of the valley. Evie's feet splashed through icy puddles. Her slippers were sodden, as was the bottom of her dress. Finally they reached the far side of the basin and started up the hill. Evie's eyes darted around, searching every shadow, every pocket of hanging mist, every snapping branch. They were not alone. She could feel it.

Once they reached the top of the hill, Cinderella stopped, her eyes boring through the darkness. "It's just there," she said. "Now listen, all of you. Once Malora and I have gone, I want you to get back to the Academy as quickly as you can. Don't dawdle. I've written the way back on this hawk. Do you understand?" She handed a parchment to Demetra, who put it in her pocket.

"Yes, Princess," they said.

"Good." She nodded to herself, as though running through a list in her head. "Good." The densely packed firs growing atop this hill were covered in hair-like branches, which gave them the appearance of tall, thin monsters. Cinderella stepped into them. Her cadets followed.

After a minute's walk, the trees thinned. There was a clearing ahead. And Evie's dread turned to panic.

A structure rose up from the fog. Or, rather, the ruins of a structure. As they drew nearer, Evie could see the remains of an outer wall of stone lined with wooden posts. Most of it had fallen away, leaving only the earthen ramparts, but here and there patches remained. An iron gate lay twisted and rusty on the ground. Inside, the hulking mass of an ancient series of buildings loomed. What had once been a triple tower had been reduced to one. The remaining tower was topped with a diamond-shaped spire. The other two were only broken stone and moss and memories. Beyond the towers was the main bulk of the structure. It was high and thick, with small windows and no doors. Ivy clutched at the walls, some of which were blanketed in thick, green moss. The final piece of the structure stood behind. It resembled a giant's chimney, a tall stone rectangle covered in black char, as though centuries of rain and snow and wind had been unable to erase whatever horrors might have happened inside.

"What is this?" asked Demetra.

"This is the Drudenhaus," said Cinderella. Then she stepped forward and walked through the opening where the gates had once stood. The others followed, afraid to fall too far behind her.

"Oh my," she said, stopping abruptly. "Oh no . . ."

Demetra gasped. Evie walked up next to her and found a statue made of granite flecked with black and silver. It was a woman, small and frail and dressed in a princess's gown. It was Princess Lankester. She had been turned to stone.

"What a shame," said Cinderella. "What a cold, gray shame."

Evie studied Lankester's face. Terror coursed through her veins at the sight of such a fearless princess trapped in a cold, helpless eternity.

"Be afraid," said Cinderella, looking each of them in the eyes. "Be afraid, but do what needs doing."

"Yes, Princess," they said softly.

Leaving the lifeless statue of Princess Lankester behind, the four of them headed for the triple tower, which had once served as the Drudenhaus's main entrance. A quick look at the other two structures led Evie to conclude that it was not just the main entrance, but the only entrance. *The only exit as well.*

They climbed the three eroded and water-pocked stairs to the doors, which had long ago rotted away. Hideous stone beasts leered down at them from above, black-furred creatures with looping tongues and curved horns. Some had long fingers and toes with birdlike claws. Others had the bent hooves of goats. Several held hooked staffs. Thankfully, much of the cornice had fallen away with the other two towers, and the beasts had fallen with it.

They entered. Evie was surprised to find that it felt a bit like stepping inside a cave. There was a great hole where the other towers had once stood, giving the impression that, despite being inside the Drudenhaus, they were still mostly outside. The floor was overgrown with weeds and ferns. In spots, it was completely crumbled and gone. Evie looked up into the hollow shell of the remaining tower. Instead of finding a bell, she saw only dangling chains and a crumbled staircase.

"This way," whispered Cinderella. "Malora's got to be here somewhere."

She passed through the towers toward a small, square cutout in the wall. This had once been the entrance to the main structure of the Drudenhaus, but the wooden doors had disintegrated, leaving only the rusted iron bands and spikes that had once held them.

Be afraid, she said, thought Evie. *I'm afraid enough for all of us.*

Cinderella passed through first, followed by Basil and Demetra. Evie went last. It was like walking into a tomb. There was no happiness inside these walls, and may never have been. As large as the structure had seemed on the outside, it was quite claustrophobic inside. The ceiling was low, the stone bricks only a few feet above Cinderella's head. Suddenly, there was a *chink* and a candle sparked to life.

"A princess is always prepared," said Cinderella with a smile.

The room itself was a vast empty space, with a staircase leading to an upper floor and a pile of rubble where another had once been. Each wall was lined with doorways. Each doorway had once been a cell.

They stepped carefully through the debris-strewn prison. Evie didn't want to look inside the cells, but found she couldn't help herself. Each contained a small window, though many had crumbled away, leaving jagged holes in their place. Inside one cell, Evie saw iron rings that had been screwed into the walls. There were rusted chains piled on the floor, along with other iron implements, and all of them had once been sharp.

"Look!" whispered Basil. Evie and Demetra joined him and Cinderella at one of the cell doors. He was pointing to words that had been etched so deeply into the stone that they had survived years and years of rain and weather. "'Innocent have I come into prison, innocent have I been tortured, innocent must I die.' Cheery place, this."

"Come on," said Demetra. "Let's check upstairs—"

"Welcome," came a voice. Evie yelped. The faint outline of her sister stood in the doorway between the towers and the prison. She was just far enough away that the candlelight couldn't reach her, though the dim yellow orbs of her eyes shone through the blackness. "So? How do you like it? This is where your people used to keep witches. Torture them. Burn them alive."

She stepped down into the prison and moved slowly from cell door to cell door. "I assume that princess out there was one of yours. I didn't mean to do that to her, but she surprised me. And as we all know, once you've been turned to stone . . ."

She was close enough now that the candle lit up her face. It was hard to believe that that voice—Malora's voice—was coming from that . . . thing. She wasn't at all recognizable as the girl Evie had known. Her hair was white and stringy, her eyes as dark as twin moons on a cloudy night. Her nose had grown longer and sloped toward the ground, as though it were melting from her face, the end of it having already fallen away. Deep wrinkles made her skin look like rotting meat, though she was only as old as Evie. And the smile on her face, little dagger teeth behind cracked lips, caused Evie to take a step back.

"Well, *Cinderella*," she said with a sneer. "It will be my sincerest pleasure to be your captor."

"Where are you going to take her?" said Evie.

"Somewhere safe," said Malora with annoyance. "Oh, stop being so suspicious. I have no intention of letting anyone else get hold of her. Did you bring the spindle?"

"Yes, and the antidote." Evie's hands fumbled inside her dress until she found the objects. She held up the spindle and the small purple vial.

"Well, then, shall we stand round here gaping at one another or shall we get on with it?"

"You've got to call me Hazelbranch," said Cinderella. "No one must know."

Malora's scowling mouth stretched into a grin. "But of course. This way, *Hazelbranch*."

Malora rejoined the shadows as she disappeared back into the towers. Cinderella looked at her cadets, trying to project calm. She gave them a nod, then followed Malora through the prison doors.

"Keep your eyes and ears opened," said Evie softly. "Something doesn't feel right."

They followed Cinderella through the ruins of the towers and back out into the night. The fog had grown even thicker in the short time they'd been inside. Malora stood next to a simple wooden cart joined to a horse. It was piled high with tatty furs and blankets. She was still grinning that awful grin.

"Right," said Cinderella, giving her candle to Demetra. "Let's have it."

Evie reached into her dress and took out the spindle and vial. Cinderella tossed the vial to Malora, then held the spindle in front of her. She raised a finger.

"Wait," said Demetra. "I want to know why she's doing this."

Malora's grin vanished. "Shouldn't you be off somewhere weeping behind your sister's skirts?"

Demetra didn't respond.

"You don't belong at Pennyroyal Academy, Demetra," continued Malora, and for a moment she was less a witch and more an angry girl with a grudge. "You're frivolous and foolish and you'd make a terrible princess."

"Now, girls," said Cinderella. "Let's not—"

"Why am I doing this? As if I owe you an explanation." Her yellow eyes were trained directly on Demetra the entire time she spoke, spittle flying out from between her sharp teeth. "Princesses lock up witches and torture them and burn them. Witches steal children and kill them and eat them. And on and on and round and round. I have no love for any of you. The only thing I want is to watch you all scramble like insects beneath a lifted stone."

Evie cringed. To Malora, a princess and a witch were the same thing, two different evils, two different groups that had betrayed her.

Malora stepped forward, her eyes going so wide that they looked like they might pop out of her head, her lips stretching into a manic sneer. "Now, would you like to sing a song and braid each other's hair or can we go?"

"Calm down, Malora, please," said Cinderella. "I'm doing it now."

She climbed into the cart and held up the spindle.

"Malora," said Evie. "Promise me you'll take care of her. I'm trusting you. As my sister."

Malora slowly turned her head toward Evie. The crunch of

her grinding teeth echoed across the courtyard. "You have my word, sister."

"All right," said Cinderella. She tapped her finger down on the point of the spindle. She looked at Evie with a grimace, then fell dead asleep onto the pile of furs.

In an instant, everything had changed, and all of them could feel it. Where there had been five of them there were now four, and the most powerful was gone. Malora pulled some of the furs free and draped them over the top of Cinderella's sleeping body. Evie, Demetra, and Basil could only stand and watch.

"What's that?" said Basil.

Sure enough, there was a noise from somewhere deep in the forest. It wasn't the crackle of branches or the rustle of leaves. It was the rumble of hooves. And it was growing steadily louder.

"Who is that?" demanded Evie. "Who's coming?"

Malora shrugged and gave her a smile. "Who could it be?"

The hoofbeats had come to a stop somewhere on the far side of the Drudenhaus, and everything had gone silent once again.

"Be careful," whispered Evie. They turned their backs to Malora, who was climbing into the seat of her cart, and faced the Drudenhaus. Basil slowly unsheathed his sword.

Evie stared into the fog to her right, around the entrance towers, while Basil and Demetra watched the length of the prison that was still visible to the left.

"I suppose I'll be off now," said Malora with a soft cackle.

"Evie . . ." said Demetra.

Evie's eyes flashed left. A figure stepped slowly out from the fog. She was dressed all in black. Two more appeared to the right, around the towers. Then another from the left. And another. Each wore a wolf's fang around her neck. More began to filter out from the trees like apparitions. Six. Ten. Twenty of them.

The Vertreiben.

"Where are you, witch?" called a woman's voice from the fog.

"In prison."

Evie turned to look at her sister. In that awful grin, she could see everything, every betrayal. "How could you? You gave me your word!"

"Well, here's another word," she said, her smile growing even wider. "Oops."

"Ah, here we are!" came the woman's voice again. It was loud and full of life, bordering on manic. A figure pushed through the rest of them and stepped out of the fog. Evie recognized her instantly from the Registry of Peerage. The missing eye, gashed and pecked by birds. The sunken cheeks that made her face look like a skull. The frizzled black hair wisping around her head in the wind.

"Sister, allow me to present Princess Javotte," said Malora.

Javotte trained her eye on Evie, and it was just as frightening as the glare of a witch. She looked like a madwoman. "The only sister I care about is my own. Where is Cinderella?"

"She's just there," said Malora, nodding to the back of the cart.

Javotte clutched her hands together dramatically, like an

actress putting on a performance. She traipsed across the courtyard to the cart. Evie moved to block her, but Malora shook her head. Javotte gently lifted the furs and saw her step-sister asleep underneath.

"Oh, how wonderful! How wonderful and lovely! You don't know how long I've been waiting for this moment. It took me years to track down Javelle, and then another fortnight to break her. But break her I did! And now I'll break this one as well! Break her into a million tiny pieces!"

"No," said Evie, with a flare of anger. "That's not going to happen."

Javotte looked at Evie with a beatific smile. "No?"

Evie said nothing, but her fingers found their way to the grip of her sword.

"This creature," said Javotte, pointing to the back of the cart with that same delighted smile, "ruined my life. She stole my prince." Now she took a step toward Evie. Then another. And in an instant her smile was gone, replaced by fury. "It was *her* birds that did *this* to me at their bloody wedding!" She pointed at her horrifically scarred right eye. "A wedding that by all rights should have been mine!"

"Well," cackled Malora. "Sound familiar? How is old Remington?"

"Everywhere I went, it was the wonderful Princess Cinder-ella!" Javotte hopped onto a stone and twirled her hand with a flourish. "The greatest princess ever to live!" She laughed so loudly that it sounded like a flock of ravens squawking. All around them in the fog, the Vertreiben echoed the laughter. She leapt off the stone and landed in front of Evie, her eye wide and her chest heaving. "Every time one of those miserable fools fell in love with her, they fell in hate with me! *Her* fame, *her* popularity cannot exist without a villain to demonize. She climbed to the top by kicking me to the bottom!" Her voice was growing louder and louder, her anger more ferocious. "She's a fraud and a wretch, and she deserves everything I'm going to give her!"

She began to dance and skip through the courtyard, a spoiled little girl in a woman's mangled body. "My sister is going to die! My sister is going to die!" she sang.

"About that," said Malora, the reins in her hands. "I've decided to change the plan. I think I'd like to keep Cinderella after all."

Javotte's smile slowly sizzled away. "No," she said, shaking her head. With a fearsome *shing!* a silver blade came free from its scabbard. "No. We had an agreement!"

Malora laughed. "Why do all of you people trust witches?"

Javotte took a step forward. She held her blade high above her head, the tip pointed down like she was wielding some sort of spear. "Give me my sister, *witch*." Behind her, there was a chorus of metallic shrieks as the Vertreiben's swords emerged into the night.

"I'm not going to do that," said Malora. "You see, my mother created me with the intention of turning me into the most powerful witch ever to live. With Cinderella in my possession, I finally am."

"You should have kept your word," said Javotte, slowly stepping forward.

Malora ignored her. "Don't be upset. I wouldn't leave you empty-handed. As a token of my appreciation, I've brought something for you. Though I will be keeping your sister, you are welcome to have mine instead. She should be every bit as valuable to you. She is, after all, the famous Warrior Princess."

Voices sounded from all directions . . .

"The Warrior Princess!"

"That's even better than Cinderella!"

"Leave her, Javotte, let's take the Warrior Princess instead!"

"Quiet!" shrieked Javotte, her furious skull-like face aimed squarely at Malora. "No plan is changing! I will take Cinderella and that is all there is to it!" The Vertreiben began to object. She wheeled, her sword held high. "The next one of you who questions me will spend the rest of her life, which should last about ten more seconds, in this disgusting prison!" Her followers went silent. Her nostrils flaring, she turned back to Malora. "Give. Me. My. Sister."

Malora chuckled and shook her head dismissively. "I'm afraid not."

"Step forward, Vertreiben! Let us take what is ours!"

The night itself seemed to close in around them as dozens of black dresses emerged from the fog.

"Look!" said Basil, pointing at the road down into the forest. It was filled with women in black dresses. More appeared on top of the wall enclosing the courtyard.

For the first time, Evie saw her sister's confident expression fade. "What is this?"

"You yourself said I shouldn't trust witches," said Javotte, still creeping forward. "Well, I don't."

Malora's eyes flicked from one princess to the next. There was genuine fear in them.

"Malora!" came a voice from the wall. She peered into the darkness as one of the Vertreiben hopped down into the courtyard. She was shorter than the rest, and younger, too. "Malora, it's me."

"Kelbra?" Now her look of fear turned to one of profound disappointment. "Kelbra, what are you doing here?"

Kelbra's smile fell. "My sister brought me." She pointed to the woman behind her atop the wall.

"You're meant to be at the Academy, not out here with these simpletons. You're meant to become a princess."

"As are you." A look of disgust came over Kelbra's face as she studied her old friend. Disgust and betrayal. "So it's true. You really are a witch."

"Yes, but you're not a Vertreiben—"

"Shut up, witch." She shook her head as tears began to fall. "How could I have been such a fool? I *defended* you!"

"Kelbra, none of it was my fault. I had no idea that I was a witch until—"

"Why don't we all stop talking?" said Javotte, the point of her blade quavering in the air. "And some of us can start dying instead."

Everyone stood in silence for a moment, the tension thicker than the fog. Evie's eyes went from Kelbra to Malora to Javotte to the horde of Vertreiben blocking any path into the forest. They were trapped.

"Inside!" she shouted.

And then everyone began to move at once.

16

THE MIST HAD GROWN thicker, creeping up the hillsides and slinking through the trees. The eroded stones scattered across the courtyard gave the Drudenhaus the appearance of a cemetery, and the black-clad Vertreiben were its restless spirits.

They swarmed from the forest, and they swarmed from the sides of the prison. Basil's sword flashed like lightning in the night as loud clashes rang out. Evie drew hers as well, the red blade smoldering like an ember as it swirled through the air and met the swords of the Vertreiben.

"Inside!" she shouted again. "Get her inside!"

A waft of black materialized in front of Malora's chest, sweeping around Cinderella's body and lifting her in the air. She followed Demetra back into the Drudenhaus.

"Put her down!" shrieked Javotte, her blade sparking against Basil's.

"Let's go, Bas! There are too many!" Evie swung her sword at each blade coming toward her, without a moment to think. She could only react, knocking them away one after another, as she retreated to the entrance. With a huge arcing slash, she knocked one woman's sword clean out of her hands. It spun across the stones with a rattle.

"Your movements are still too big, Evie," said Basil as he ran after her. "You need to tighten your attacks!"

"Yeah," said Evie, incredulous. "I'll work on that."

"Surround them!" shrieked Javotte. "No one escapes!"

As Evie hurtled through the doorway, she glanced back over her shoulder. It looked like an army of shadows pouring after her. She followed Basil through the darkness toward the main chamber, but the Vertreiben were climbing over the broken walls as well. She ran as fast as she could, but she wasn't going to make it. Three of them dropped from the crumbling tower wall and ran straight for her.

Suddenly, there was a scream, and a silver blade swished past Evie's face, knocking away a sword that was just about to strike her. Evie fell to the floor and looked up. It was Kelbra. She was fighting off two Vertreiben.

Evie scrambled to her feet and bolted for the doorway. "Come on, Kelbra!"

"Betrayal!" screamed Javotte, her voice echoing up the tower. "Betrayal!"

Evie took Kelbra's hand and pulled her through the prison. More Vertreiben were climbing through the walls where the windows had broken away. "This way!" She could see Demetra huddled at the top of the lone staircase. As the Vertreiben teemed through the prison, they bounded toward the top floor.

"Now!" screamed Demetra as Evie and Kelbra reached the top of the staircase. A large iron door, the rusted bars of a prison cell, slammed down over the opening. Malora had used her magic to drop it there. The Vertreiben had already filled the staircase and were struggling to move the heavy door above them. It would only be a matter of minutes before they were through. Javotte's one eye peered up at them from beneath the bars.

"Climb the walls!" she screamed. "They're on the second floor!"

Basil raced into one of the cells and peered out the window. "Here they come!" he shouted. "They're everywhere!"

"What do we do?" said Evie. She looked over at Cinderella. "Give her the antidote! Wake her up! She'll know what to do!"

"It doesn't work like that," said Demetra. "Ziegenbart says it takes at least a day to wake up completely."

"AAAAH!" screamed Javotte, pressing against the bars with everything she had. The door scraped against the stone. Inch by inch, it was moving. Soon they'd be through.

"S-s-s-secret passage!" said Kelbra, terror in her voice. "Remember? Dungeons have secret passages in case of revolts. Prisons must as well!"

"Demetra! Basil! Look for a secret passage!" shouted Evie. She raced to the back wall and began feeling the stones, looking for the telltale smoothness that the Fairy Drillsergeant had trained them to seek.

"Here! Here!" shouted Demetra. She gripped a stone with

both hands and pulled down on it like a switch. The stone slid free, and a gap opened in the wall.

"Come on!" said Evie. "Malora, let's go!"

Malora's spell once again enveloped Cinderella and carried her down the narrow staircase into the darkness. Demetra and Basil followed. There was another thump and scrape, and another. One of the Vertreiben was almost through.

"Kelbra, let's go!"

Kelbra drew her sword. "Go on. Get her out of here."

"What are you doing? Come on!"

"I've made too many mistakes this year. I won't make another. I'm sorry, Evie. It seems I was wrong about you. And her."

The first Vertreiben squeezed through the narrow gap between the stone and the bars. Kelbra kicked her in the chest, knocking her back down the stairs. Another followed immediately behind. As Evie ducked into the secret passageway, she heard swords clashing behind her.

The staircase got narrower toward the bottom, then evened out into a long hallway that curved to the right. She ran after her friends just as they emerged from another hidden doorway into a tall, thin chamber stained with black. She and Demetra slammed the door shut. Demetra picked up a sharp stone and jammed it beneath the trigger on the wall so it couldn't open.

They were in the third and final part of the Drudenhaus. A rusted gate hung between them and the main prison. Basil checked the latch, which seemed secure, but they were still just as trapped as they had been before.

They heard shouts behind the secret door in the wall, but Demetra's stone held fast. Moments later, Javotte slammed into the iron bars at the room's entrance, heaving like a rabid dog. Other Vertreiben filled in the space behind her until all Evie could see were murderous smiles and blackness.

"Give her to me, Malora! Give her to me and I'll kill you quickly!" screamed Javotte.

Evie turned to Malora, who looked less like the most powerful witch in all the land and more like a terrified girl. But for now, the only thing that mattered was Javotte and her army.

"Do something! Use your magic!"

"I can't," said Malora. "There are too many of them."

Evie scanned the room for a way out. Fifteen feet above, the windows had crumbled away, leaving jagged holes in the wall, but aside from that the structure was the most intact of any in the Drudenhaus. The walls were striped with black. There had been a fire in this chamber. Fire and smoke, and great quantities of both. The crumbling remains of a staircase led up from where they were to the windows. There was enough of the stone left to provide a perch right at the window level. A giant brick-and-mortar oven covered the far wall, nearest the secret passageway. There were rusted metal implements—chains and blades and hooks and saws—everywhere.

"They'll be in here soon," said Demetra as the Vertreiben threw their bodies against the bars. "What do we do?"

"I'd kill for a pot of bear urine right now," said Basil. Demetra gave him an exasperated look. "You know, to disguise ourselves—"

"Bas, can you watch those windows?" asked Evie.

"Of course," he said. He began climbing the ruins of the staircase just as the first black dress appeared in the window. He charged the rest of the way and swung his sword. The Vertreiben in the window managed to bring hers up to block, but the blow was enough to knock her back to the ground.

Evie bounced her blade in her hand, eyes on the doorway. The pounding of stone on iron thundered through the Drudenhaus. "Break it down!" screamed Javotte. "Bring me my sister! You can keep the Warrior Princess for yourselves, Vertreiben, but *bring me my sister!*"

Evie glared over her shoulder at Malora, who huddled next to Demetra. Cinderella lay helpless beneath them.

"Aaaah!" shouted Basil from above. There was a flurry of clashing metal as he managed to hold off two more Vertreiben. "They're coming by the dozens!"

BANG! BANG! BANG!

Demetra raced to the bars and began using a stone to smash the Vertreiben's fingers as they tried to break the gate down. Evie, meanwhile, continued bouncing her sword in her hand. Her mind was racing, flying through ideas as quick as a dragon. Basil was fighting them off admirably, but with each one he knocked out of a window, two more appeared in the next. Demetra was beating them away from the bars as best she could, but they'd be through in moments.

"Do something, Malora!" shouted Evie, but her sister was frozen in place.

I need warriors, not cowards. I need dragons, not witches. I need ...

Her palm wrapped around the hilt with such force that the whole blade shook. Basil was shouting for help at the top of the stairs, but she couldn't hear him. Javotte and her army were battering the iron bars, but she couldn't hear that either. The only thing she could hear was her mother's voice.

I believe you are a dragon, daughter. And there is only one place any of us can truly be a dragon ...

With her free hand, she clutched the dragon scale dangling against her chest. It was dried and weathered, only a hint of what it had once been, but there was still strength alive inside of it. And in the only place that mattered, Evie knew her mother was right. She was a dragon.

She wheeled and charged toward Malora. She gripped her sister's shoulders as tightly as she could, though the sting of ice shot through her palms. "Malora! Listen to me: you've got to watch the doorway! Malora!" She shook her violently and stared straight into her cold, yellow eyes. "Sister. I need you to watch the doorway. Use whatever magic you've got to keep them out. Can you do that?"

Malora looked back at her with a blank expression. Her face was like death, her once-perfect skin riddled with veins and tendons. Her cheeks and nose were wasting away. Her eyes were perfect circles of yellow, with black hollows beneath. And her hair was stringy, pulled back from her face as though it didn't want to be near her either.

And yet, somehow, Evie could feel her sister looking inside of her. She knew the sensation from her previous encounters with witches. It was a horrible, invasive, terrifying feeling, but Evie let her do it. She could tell from the expression on Malora's face that it was working. She was finding her way back from her own private horror and into the Drudenhaus as she drew strength from Evie. Slowly, she began to nod.

"Good. Get over there and do whatever you have to, do you understand?" Malora nodded again.

Basil was shouting as he slashed again and again and again at the swords of the Vertreiben trying to breach the holes above the staircase. He moved like a swordsman with decades of experience, always seconds ahead of the next enemy to appear. Even with his remarkable blade work, the Vertreiben were threatening to overrun his position.

"I can't hold them! Someone help!"

Evie shoved Malora to the door, then turned to Demetra, thrusting her sword into her hands. "The mission has changed, Demetra, and it's time to adapt. I've been training with a sword, but this mission calls for a dragon."

"Where are you going?"

"If this works, I won't be of any use after. So it'll be up to you to get Cinderella out of here, all right?"

"Evie, please. What are you doing?"

Evie hurtled across the room to the oven, kicking the metal implements out of her path. Then she crouched down and stepped inside. It was claustrophobic, darker than a witch's spell, and even after all these years of disuse it choked her with the stench of fire. She pushed herself in, shimmying all the way to the back until she found the opening to the chimney. She peered up, but could see only a faint patch at the top that was slightly less dark than the smoke chamber that led to it. She took a deep breath and her lungs seized up from the stink of ash and smoke. Then she reached into the chimney and began to climb. There were plenty of footholds and handholds amidst the roughly assembled stone. The problem for Evie was that there wasn't much room to use them. The chamber was so tight that her back and knees scraped against the walls every time she pulled herself higher. She looked up. Perhaps it was her imagination playing tricks on her, but it seemed as though the chimney was getting narrower as she climbed.

She kept going, wincing with each scrape of the stone. She could feel her dress tearing. The clash of steel and bang of stone echoed up from below. The shouts of the Vertreiben outside the Drudenhaus rained down the chimney from above. And still she climbed.

She neared the top, but the smoke chamber was so narrow that she couldn't lift a leg and couldn't lower her arms. She had to pull with her fingers until her toes found a new stone, then push with her feet until her hands did the same. Finally, inch by inch, her fingers reached the open sky. Then she worked her hands free, and then her arms. Grimacing at the pain, she shimmied higher and higher until her chest was free and she was able to lower her shoulders. The top half of her was out, but her hips were stuck. *I'll not die trapped in a chimney*, she thought. Then, with an effort worthy of a dragon, she pushed herself free.

She was sitting atop the crumbled chimney with nothing else around. She could see through a hole in the ceiling that the Vertreiben had not yet managed to break through the gate. She could also see the black dresses hoisting each other up the side of the wall to get inside. Basil's shouts poured out of the windows, as did the clashing sounds of his sword. From Evie's vantage point, she could see the entire sweep of the forest, which had been almost entirely swallowed up by fog. There were Vertreiben swarming everywhere. She was thirty feet in the air and the only ways down were to climb or to jump. She suspected she'd have to do a combination of the two.

"Hey!" she screamed as loudly as she could. "I'm the one you want! Up here!"

Down below, the princesses in black began to stop their assault on the Drudenhaus. Some of them looked around for the source of the voice. One saw her and pointed, and soon there was a wave of them looking up at her.

"It's me, the famous Warrior Princess! And while you're at home feeling sorry for yourselves, I'm still at Pennyroyal Academy becoming a princess! How do you like that?"

She could see their faces turning to fury at her words. As

they surrounded the base of the chimney, she realized she had to move. Using the instincts she'd learned from her family, she climbed down the chimney almost as quickly as an ordinary human might fall. The Vertreiben were racing toward her from all directions, so she pushed off from the stone and jumped over their heads. She landed in the dirt with a thud, then hopped to her feet and sprinted into the woods. She didn't dare look back, but she could tell from the shouts behind her that a significant number of Vertreiben were giving chase. *I only hope it's enough of them.*

She ran as fast as she could without losing them. She wanted to be chased, to lure them away. Once she judged they were far enough out, she began a wide arc through the trees until finally she was running straight back toward the jagged silhouette of the Drudenhaus.

"Over here, false princesses!" she screamed.

From the corner of her eye, she could see them descending on her in a wave of black. Like the Piper of Hamelin, she was leading them right where she wanted. Up ahead, a massive oak tree sprawled through the fog. Its limbs were starting to twist and groan as it sensed an intruder.

I believe you are a dragon, daughter . . .

As she raced toward the tree, the swarm of black dresses behind her, Evie could feel something burning in her stomach. She winced from the pain, but kept her thoughts focused on her mother.

There's only one place any of us can truly be a dragon . . .

Something was bubbling inside of her. She could feel it scalding her from the inside out. She let her emotions run wild through her heart. Grief at how she'd treated her family. Anger at Javotte and the Vertreiben. Fear for her friends trapped inside the Drudenhaus. Love for her father, the man she'd recently met in letters. But above all else, the emotion that swirled the strongest inside of her was pride. She was a dragon, and ever would be.

Unbidden, the roiling fire inside of her flooded up through her chest and throat and mouth. An invisible heat poured out of her, still not enough to produce the liquid flame that her family could, but enough to cause ripples in the air and char the oak tree black. She glanced back at the Vertreiben, coming from multiple directions now, then turned to another branch and let another surge of dragon fire come up from her belly. The tree swung its boughs wildly, angrily, as its lower branches turned to smokewood.

Evie doubled over in pain, the worst pain she'd ever felt in her life. She coughed and coughed, though each spasm sent a new sword blade of agony down her throat and through her lungs. With tears streaming from her eyes, she glanced at the Vertreiben, who were nearly on her now. The first to arrive slowed, blades drawn, smiles on their faces. Their wolf's fangs glinted through the fog.

"Take her alive," said one. "We need her alive."

Evie lurched to her feet, clutching her throat.

"She's trying to make smokewood," said Kelbra's sister with

a chuckle. "My sister told me about you. Just because you were raised by dragons doesn't mean you are one."

"That's not what I believe," said Evie. Her voice was a horrific rumble sending screams of pain through her body. She coughed again, flecks of blood splatting against the leaves. With a crack as loud as thunder, the oak swung at her. She dropped flat on her stomach, and the branches crashed into each other just above her head.

Fire exploded into the sky, showering the ground in bright orange flames. The dead leaves beneath the oak quickly caught, and within moments there were fires burning everywhere.

Evie lay on her side, blood streaming out of her mouth from somewhere inside. She could barely breathe from the smoke and pain coursing through her body. Her vision filled with new brightness as the fires joined together and quickly became an inferno. The oak swung its branches wildly as the fire attacked its trunk.

In the black gaps between flames, she could see the Vertreiben trying to scatter. The tree had become a fire monster, its enchanted limbs throwing flames everywhere. As they all ran away and left her to be swallowed up by the fire she'd just created, one dark silhouette ran toward her . . .

It was Demetra.

"Evie!" The flames crackled and roared around them. Evie could barely keep her eyes open. Suddenly, she felt herself being dragged through the leaves. "Come on, Evie, stand up!"

Demetra jerked her to her feet, which was the only part

of her body that didn't hurt. And with her friend's help, Evie somehow managed to stagger out of the flames. There were only tiny windows of unburnt ground left now as the flames spread rapidly through years of dead leaves. A massive oak limb swatted the ground next to them. It had missed its mark, but in doing so, it had scattered even more kindling across the forest.

Evie tottered forward, but it all felt like a dream to her. She wasn't in control of her body. It was moving on its own. She couldn't even feel the pain anymore. All she could see was the furious red all around her, and Demetra's face, and then nothing at all.

17

"THAT'S IT, EVIE," said the dragon, her voice as dry and hollow as the last log in a fire. "I'm so proud of you, my darling."

Her face appeared out of the fuzzy gray, as wide as a carriage. Her scales were a soft yellow-green, her teeth as long and sharp as swords. But it was her eyes that sent a rush of peace through Evie's body. Her mother's eyes hadn't looked so serene, so joyous, so *proud*, in as long as Evie could remember.

Another face appeared next to her mother's. It was smaller, the scales a more vibrant green. It was the face of her sister.

And then, from the fog of the dream, a third face. It was old and battle scarred, the scales nearly white.

"Father," she cried. "Oh, Father, I've missed you."

"And I you."

She looked from one dragon to the next, to the faces that had raised her and made her into the human she now was. "When I was trapped with no way out, it was you who led me through."

"We're family, Evie," he said in a voice she hadn't realized she'd been so desperate to hear. "We will always be inside of you, just as you will always be inside of us. We are together, even when we're apart. Even after we die."

Evie felt the most peculiar sensation then. It was a peace so total, so deep, that nothing would ever be able to hurt her again. Even when she was alone, her mother, her sister, her father . . . all would be with her . . .

"I've just given her a dose," said a ghostly voice.

"Evie?" said another. The faces of the dragons began to blur, slowly fading back into the gray. "Evie!"

Her eyes fluttered open. The gray was gone, but she had to blink to clear away the fuzziness. She could feel tears running down her temples and into her hair. She must have been lying on her back. There was a field of white above her. As she continued to blink, it started to come into focus. The glass ceiling of the Infirmary.

The Infirmary at Pennyroyal Academy.

"Thank goodness you're all right!"

Evie turned her head, only slightly, and saw a poof of red hair above her. She tried to say Maggie's name, but nothing came out. Instead, searing pain shot through her body from just above her stomach all the way through her throat.

"No no no, you mustn't speak!" said Maggie.

Another face appeared in the right side of her vision. It was Princess Wertzheim. She had a long metal object and was using it to prod around inside Evie's mouth. Evie was so weak, she couldn't protest. Wertzheim disappeared. Evie could hear her issuing orders to other nurses, so she turned her eyes back to Maggie.

"You're in the Infirmary. You've had terrible burns all through your throat." Maggie leaned in closer until her face was fully in focus. Her eyes were soft, filled with compassion. "But you did it, Evie. Your idiotic plan actually worked. Cinderella made it out. Malora used your fire as a distraction and sneaked her away. She's safe now. She sent a hawk to the Fairy Drillsergeant, though it doesn't say where she is. But the important thing is, she's safe."

Images began to flood back into Evie's mind. Fire and the witch prison and the princesses in black, each of them stepping closer and closer with sharp blades in hand . . .

She felt a surge of panic, but she still couldn't speak. She also didn't have enough strength to sit up.

"Be still, be still," said Maggie, gently holding her shoulders down. "You've been through a horrific experience, but you're safe now. We all are."

"Go fetch Princess Beatrice," Wertzheim said to one of the other nurses. "Tell her Cadet Evie is awake."

Evie looked back to Maggie. *What about Demetra? What about Basil? What happened to Javotte and the Vertreiben?* She couldn't speak. Fresh tears ran down her temples and disappeared in her hair. Why couldn't she speak?

"Come quick!" said Maggie, waving at someone to Evie's right. "She's awake!"

Evie turned her head and, like an answered wish, the smiling faces of Demetra and Basil appeared.

"There she is!" said Basil. "The lady of the hour! Or is it the lizard of the hour?"

Demetra slapped his arm.

"Jah—" croaked Evie. Through the screaming pain, her voice sounded like one jagged stone scraping against another. "Ja-votte."

"Evie, please don't speak," said Maggie. "You've only just stopped bleeding."

"You don't have to worry about Javotte anymore," said Demetra. "She's gone. Go on, Basil, tell her what happened."

Basil scratched the top of his head nervously. "I . . . took care of her. We had a bit of a smash-up with our swords, and . . . well, I suppose I got the best of it."

"He's an absolutely brilliant swordsman, Evie. I've never seen anything like it."

"That's what comes from having twenty-one brothers, I suppose."

"Don't be so modest, Bas. If it weren't for him, Javotte would have killed us all in there."

"You were quite the warrior yourself," he said. "Demetra fought through a whole group of them to get to you, Evie."

"Kel . . . Kelbra."

Their smiles faded. They exchanged looks, as though none of them wanted to say anything.

"Kelbra's gone," said Demetra. "I'm sorry, Evie."

She nodded. She'd expected that, yet it still broke her heart to hear.

"Oh no," said Maggie softly, her eyes looking past Demetra and Basil to the door, where there came the loud clacking of heels on stone.

"Make way, make way." Demetra and Basil stepped back, replaced by the humorless scowl of the Headmistress General. She grabbed Evie's cheeks in her wrinkled hand and peered into her open mouth. "Hmm."

"She'll need a battery of potions, Headmistress," said Wertzheim. "I've never seen burns like these before. But—"

"Cadet Eleven, you have done a remarkable thing," said the Headmistress, who looked angry enough to strangle a cat. Evie's forehead wrinkled in confusion. "You have broken a entire volume of rules, but I have received a note from Princess Hazelbranch explaining why. The rules that govern this Academy, the rules that govern all princesses, are some of the most sacred things in the world to me. But even I know they must be broken in extreme circumstances. And this circumstance with the Vertreiben was nothing if not extreme. I was wrong about them. But thanks to you, my mistake was not nearly as costly as it might have been." She looked at Maggie, her eyes as sharp as Javotte's sword. Then her eyes snapped over to Demetra. Then Basil. And finally back down to Evie. "You will still need to take your final exams, except for you, Cadet Eleven, but I've decided to advance you all to the first class anyway. Submit your applications for your service branches to Princess Ziegenbart as quickly as you can. And rest that throat of yours. I shall see you in the fall."

She turned on her heel, several other princesses and advisers following behind, and walked out the door.

"What just happened?" said Maggie.

"I think we made first class," said Demetra.

"We did?"

"We did!"

Maggie grabbed Evie's arm and began to jump up and down. Evie smiled, tears running down her temples.

"Did—" croaked Evie. "Did it."

"We certainly did," said Basil.

"Cadets, if you please, this one desperately needs rest," said Wertzheim.

"Of course, Princess," said Maggie.

Wertzheim walked off, leaving the four of them alone. Evie looked up at Demetra and Basil. "Thank—" She began coughing again, but no amount of pain would keep her from what she needed to say. "Thank you."

"Thank *you*, Evie, really," said Demetra. "The whole thing was incredibly brave. Mad, but brave."

"You know, it's possible we just averted the worst crisis in princess history," said Basil. "I wonder if Lieutenant Volf will think we warrant a chapter somewhere."

Demetra slapped his arm again. "Let's go, Bas," she said. "I think you left your humility outside. Bye, Evie. We'll come back after supper and fill out our applications together, all right?"

As they began to walk off, Basil said, "What? I'm only stating the facts . . ." And the two of them argued all the way to the door.

Evie turned back to Maggie and her heart broke open. Her friend was smiling down at her, as sunshiny as ever, but Evie was overwhelmed with remorse. All she could see in her mind was the look of betrayal on Maggie's face as her finger bled from the spindle and her eyes rolled back in her head.

"Mag—" Evie tried to swallow, but there was nothing there to swallow. Her voice sounded like carriage wheels on gravel.

"Please, Evie, it hurts *me* to see you speak, I can't imagine how—"

"Mag-gie. I . . . I'm . . ." She tried to swallow again, building up the strength to fight through the pain in her chest. "I'm sorry."

The smile on Maggie's face transformed into something altogether different. It was still a smile, but a deeper, more truthful one. "You've no need to apologize, Evie. I was too scared to see what you saw." Tears began to pool in her eyes. She took Evie's hand in her own, cupping it with the other. "After my mother, Cinderella is the most important woman in my life. She's all I've ever wanted to be. And you saved her. I owe you a tremendous debt of gratitude."

Evie squeezed Maggie's hand. "I'm. Sorry."

Maggie's smile faded. She looked deeply into Evie's eyes. "I forgive you, Evie."

And now it was Evie's turn to smile.

"Cadet, I do apologize, but I've simply got to get this serum into her," said Wertzheim.

"Of course," said Maggie. She pointed to the chair next to the bed, where the deerskin bundle containing Callahan's letters sat. "I've brought you some reading material in case you get bored. Goodbye, first-class princess cadet. I'll see you this evening. And when we've finished our applications, we're going to write a letter to Remington." She raised her eyebrows with a cheeky grin. Evie squeezed her hand once more, and then she was gone.

Evie glanced around as Princess Wertzheim busied herself around her bed. The Infirmary was just as it had been the previous year when she'd first arrived for her memory treatments. There were statues scattered around the floor. Some were in beds of their own. Animals roamed here and there. A donkey lay curled on a pile of straw next to her.

And there she was. A dragon.

"I've got a special treatment for you, my dear," said Wertzheim. She turned and held up a small jar full of a clear liquid, as thick as honey. "We've had a lot of experience with burns, as you can imagine. The knights keep us quite busy with that sort of thing. Now, I've never treated burns in a throat before, but . . ." She pulled some of the liquid into a syringe, then carefully squeezed it into the back of Evie's mouth. There was a quick, almost unbearable burning sensation as it touched the tender skin inside her throat, but within moments it was gone. And what it left behind was beautiful, cooling relief. "If you apply this three times a day for the next week, your throat should be back to normal before the carriages leave for home." She put the lid back on the jar and set it on a small wooden table next to Evie's bed. "There is one thing I must tell you, Cadet. I'm afraid with a burn as bad as yours there is bound to be some adjustment. So even once your throat has recovered, it may feel a bit strange when you talk or breathe or even eat. There won't be anything wrong with you. It's just something you'll have to learn to live with." She patted Evie's hand. "Just a bit of scar tissue is all."

Princess Wertzheim walked away. A soft, small sound came from Evie's throat. It was laughter. Her sister had told her before she'd left the cave that she would need to develop some scar tissue before she could be a proper dragon. Well, in a very roundabout way, she had done it after all.

She rested her head on the goose-down pillow, thinking back to everything that had happened. But with all the turmoil and danger she'd dealt with that year, her mind kept returning to her father's letters. He had thought, after losing his wife, that Evie would become his life's companion. But Countess Hardcastle and the witches had tragically shortened that life. Now it was he who would be her life's companion. She had his letters, his words, and she would carry them inside her until her dying breath.

She could feel others inside her as well as she lay in her recovery bed. In her darkest hour, in the moment when she was trapped with no way out, it had been her mother who had emerged to save her. Her dragon mother. The mother who had raised her, who had tended her wounds and dried her eyes. And there was more. Although she had tried to betray Evie, it was her sister who had ultimately saved the day by spiriting Cinderella to safety. Her witch sister.

Human father. Dragon mother. Witch sister. It was all family. Perhaps Evie wasn't made up of pieces of them all, like stones in a basket. Perhaps, instead, they were more like watercolors, each swirled together to form one image. To form Evie.

Her eyes slid to the side, to where King Callahan's letters sat. All she wanted to do was read them over and over again until she'd memorized them. But that would have to wait. Because the only thing she could do at that moment was to rest and to heal. Soon enough it would be time to board a coach, then to go and find Boy and give him a good hug and a brush, and then ride back to the cave to be with her family. *I am different from them*, she thought. *And I always will be. But we are the same as well.*

And if that meant another summer of listening to her sister call her "girl," well, that would be just fine with her.

Acknowledgments

I'M TEMPTED to just say, "See previous book," since so many of the people to whom I owe thanks are the same. But there are two in particular who were integral to the writing of this book.

The first is Jennifer Besser, my editor, without whom this book would quite literally not exist. She saw around corners that I couldn't and realized there was a book where I hadn't seen one. She is patient and intelligent, and I owe her a debt of gratitude.

The second is Arianne Lewin, my other editor, a woman of great ideas and great speed. I told her it felt like we were Olympic Ping-Pong players, volleying the manuscript back and forth at a ridiculous pace, yet somehow each time it came my way, it was filled with fresh insight and artistry. I owe her, too, a debt of gratitude.

Thanks as well to all of the following: To my agents, Alexandra Machinist, Sally Willcox, Michelle Weiner, JP Evans, and Jon Cassir. To my lawyers, Kimberly Jaime and Debby Klein. To my producers, Reese Witherspoon and Bruna Papandrea.

To Ian Wasseluk for drawing another stellar medieval map. To Antonio Caparo for his superb cover art. To all the copy editors, art directors, marketing people, assistants, and everyone else at Penguin Young Readers who have helped put the whole package together. What a fantastic team.

I would also like to thank all the readers who have continued on to their second year at the Academy, and to the teachers, librarians, parents, friends, and fairy drillsergeants who brought those readers in the first time around.

And an extra special thanks to my wife and daughters, who graciously allow me to be the Basil at the princess table.

EVIE'S GREATEST BATTLE
IS JUST GETTING STARTED.

TURN THE PAGE FOR A SNEAK PEEK INTO
THE THRILLING CONCLUSION TO THE
PENNYROYAL ACADEMY SERIES!

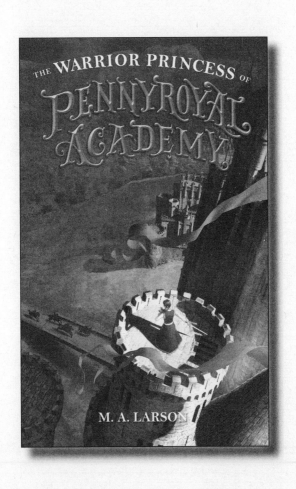

Forbes, Evie, Demetra, and Basil traversed the ridge of the cliff while thunder echoed across the valley to their right. The kingdom's wall loomed larger and larger as they got closer. Its surface was smooth sandstone bricks inlaid with small colored stones that had created the golden shimmering effect. It looked dense, thick enough perhaps to repel a giant. They tracked the base of the wall to the gatehouse, which stood facing away from the cliff. The portcullis was wide open. The gatehouse spire was flanked by two bartizans sprouting elegantly from either side. An ornamental carving stretched across the stone above the gates. It read: HERE MAY ONE LIVE FREELY.

"Let me do the talking, will you?" said Forbes as they approached. "It's bad enough to turn up in this state; we don't need to embarrass ourselves with our behavior as well." Basil rolled his eyes as Forbes disappeared inside.

There's something odd about how casual it all seems, thought Evie. Even in the best of times, what kingdom would leave its gates open to the outside world like this? They passed beneath the teeth of the raised portcullis and walked inside. A handful of people milled about the roads as though this day was no different from any other. Men in linen breeches and puffy tunics bowed graciously to women in sleeved dresses. It wasn't as frantic as Marburg had been when she had first entered that kingdom to enlist, but it was alive nonetheless. Evie and Demetra exchanged confused looks as they continued inside. It was a remarkably clean and orderly kingdom, though spotted with puddles, and no one seemed at all concerned about the possibility of witches strolling in through the raised defenses. The packed dirt roads didn't have any of the wheel ruts that even Pennyroyal Academy's did. They were perfectly smooth, well-tended and even. Shrubs had been meticulously trimmed into small balls of green, lining the roads at regular intervals. Flowers sprouted everywhere.

"This is stunning," said Basil. "Mum would kill for these groundskeepers."

They followed what appeared to be the main road as it curved around the glimmering golden castle. Everyone they passed gave them a nod and a smile. Evie glanced back at one point and noticed that a man and woman were still watching them. Their smiles had gone.

"No one mention the siege," she hissed.

"Good day, madam," said Basil, smiling at one of the locals. "What a lovely kingdom you have here."

She nodded back without a word.

Evie looked up at the lone tower rising above. It stretched three times as high into the air as the spires atop the castle. And there were no windows on this side of it either.

She felt someone looking at her and turned back to see a small group watching them. They were whispering amongst each other. "We should go back," she said. "I don't like this at all."

"Of course you don't," said Forbes. "It was my idea."

"To be accurate, it was my idea first," said Basil.

Forbes tromped on without a word. The road curved around to the castle's main staircase. It swept up in a beautiful arc that led to the open doors. Standing there was a fat man in a deep purple velvet robe with a sparkling crown atop his head. It matched the glorious castle behind him. Beneath the robe, he wore crisp white breeches and a billowing scarlet tunic. His hair was a bob of white that curled around his ears. He offered them a charming smile. A small retinue of guardsmen and members of court stood behind him.

"Hello!" he called with a hearty chuckle. "Welcome to the golden kingdom of Stromberg!"

"Thank you very much indeed, Your Majesty," said Forbes.

"All travelers have a home in Stromberg, weary and otherwise!"

Forbes stepped forward and knelt, his head bowed in deference. "I am Sir Forbes, knight cadet of the first class at Pennyroyal Academy. It is an honor to be welcomed into your charming kingdom." Evie had to admit, for as little as he knew about relating to other people, Forbes certainly knew how to speak to royalty.

"I should think the honor would be mine!" said the King. "A knight cadet in my home!"

Forbes hissed over his shoulder at the others: "On your knees!"

Evie, Basil, and Demetra dipped to one knee.

"This is Evie, that's Demetra, and that's Basil. They're princess—" He stopped himself, coughing with embarrassment. "They're also from the Academy."

"It is an honor and a delight to have four esteemed cadets in our midst." Then, to the people standing behind him, "This is the future of our great land!" They all mumbled their agreement. "Come, I never interrogate my guests without something steaming in their bellies." He gave them a hearty laugh. "Join me at my table!"

Forbes rose. The others followed his lead. "You are too kind, Your Majesty. It would be our pleasure."

"Well then, it looks like pleasure all around!"

Several of the King's group scurried inside, presumably to begin preparations for lunch. Forbes turned back to the others and muttered, "Do as I do. And try not to offend anyone. This could be a very pleasurable experience if you'd all stop being so paranoid."

"Why didn't you tell him who I am?" said Basil. "I'm a princess cadet and proud of it."

Forbes shook his head disdainfully and turned up the stairs.

"Forget it, Bas," said Evie. "Let's just find out about Rumplestoatsnout and get out of here."

Once they passed through the castle doors, they found that the grand entrance was dimly lit. Torches flamed throughout, but there were no windows. Instead, both walls opened into various corridors and chambers via large arches carved into the stone. Suits of armor occupied small alcoves between these archways, each posed and polished. Some were missing parts. Others were covered in chinks and dents from long-ago battles. A crimson carpet of crushed velvet covered the stone floor from end to end. A wide staircase at the back of the hall led to a landing, which flared off in both directions to the higher levels of the castle.

"I must say, Your Majesty, Goblin's Glade doesn't seem nearly so menacing as we'd been led to believe," said Forbes.

The King's laughter bellowed down the hallway. "We do have quite the reputation, though most of it is utter nonsense. The oldest enchanted forest in all the land? Certainly. The most haunted?" He laughed again. "Say, lad, something's just come to me. You say your name is Forbes, is that it?"

"Indeed, Sire."

The King abruptly stopped and grabbed both of Forbes's shoulders, giving him an affectionate shake. "You're King Hossenbuhr's boy!"

"That's right, S—"

The King pulled him into a bear hug with a hearty laugh that echoed off the stone walls. "I know your father well! He's allowed me to hunt his land many times over the years. Such a gracious host. How is he?"

He's a miserable, murderous monster, thought Evie. She kept walking in silence.

"He's well, Your Majesty. Quite well."

"Wonderful! Wonderful!"

Evie kept her eye on the guardsmen standing in the corners. None of them seemed to notice the small group passing between them. They kept their eyes forward, their spears straight. The advisers trailing behind offered polite smiles, but none of them spoke.

"Well? What do you think of my armor?" asked the King proudly. "As a Pennyroyal boy, I assume you must have some appreciation for fine workmanship." He took Forbes by the elbow and stopped in front of a massive suit of steel-plate armor. It looked large enough to fit even someone as large as Commander Muldenhammer. The armor had been cleaned like all the rest, but there was no disguising the black scorch.

"A Spitzbergen, if I'm not mistaken," said Forbes.

The King erupted in laughter. "A Spitzbergen indeed!" He turned to his group with more joyous chortling. "The lad knows his armorers!"

With an arm around Forbes's shoulders, the King used his free hand to point out the finer features of the suit. "Notice the deep overlay of the plate here. Very difficult to get a sword through that. And there . . . the knight who wore this armor took down three full-sized drakes before he was done in. See the markings?"

"The black stain of bravery," said Forbes, inspecting the char along the armor's left side.

A sharp ache shot through Evie's throat. She would have loved nothing more than to open her mouth and roast these two alive where they stood. Basil must have sensed it, because he grabbed hold of her arm and held it tightly.

"Indeed, indeed. Spitzbergen no longer works in this design. It's quite a rare piece, I daresay." He turned to Forbes and pointed a fatherly finger at him. "And you've a rare eye, my boy. Come, let us dine."

The King led Forbes farther down the hall. Evie, Demetra, and Basil followed with the rest of the group.

"Your Majesty," said Evie suddenly. "Perhaps we could just tell you about our mission and be on our way? We'd hate to be a bother." She could see Forbes wince.

The King turned back with a look of confusion. Evie blushed. She had stepped over some unseen line, broken some unknown rule. "Bother? Have my gates closed without my knowledge?"

"No, Your Majesty—"

"Well then? Let's eat."

He led Forbes left through one of the archways. Several of the advisers looked at Evie warily as they followed the King inside. Basil shrugged at her, then went through as well.

"That smells so good," said Demetra. She and Evie entered and walked down an open staircase into a cavernous dining room that was every bit as stately as the entrance hall. A long table of stained pine ran from end to end with chairs carved from the same wood. It was covered in candles spiked atop iron holders. Tall, thin windows lined the far wall, each inlaid with a frame of red stained glass surrounding clear glass. Banners hung from the beams of the ceiling alongside dangling chandeliers made up of arrangements of various antlers and horns. An immense hearth sat unused on the end of one wall, with doorways to the serving rooms and kitchens off the other end. The King ushered Forbes to a seat next to the head throne. Basil sat next to him. Evie and Demetra followed, while the members of court took seats opposite them. The bulk of the table went unused. Servants entered with trays and cutlery and drinks and hot cloths, and within moments came the food they'd been smelling.

"Eat, please," said the King. "You are my guests, and you are always welcome in Stromberg."

"I must say," said Forbes, "it is nice to be amongst adults again."

Evie had to bite her lip to keep from splashing him with boiling soup. Basil, meanwhile, missed the insult and helped himself to a steaming turkey leg, shoving it into his mouth with glee.

"You are a very gracious host, Your Majesty," said Forbes. "Even if my companions are not the most gracious of guests."

Basil stopped chewing, his mouth packed with turkey. His eyes went to the King. "Yuh, 'anks, Sire," he mumbled.

"What's food for, if not for eating?" said the King, helping himself. "All of you, tuck in!"

Though her unease refused to leave her, Evie could not deny her hunger. She saw from the corner of her eye that Basil was consuming everything within arm's reach, and that Demetra had already finished several poached eggs, so she decided to join in. Beetroot and mutton and turnip soup. Roasted cauliflower and baked lung pie and grilled breast of eagle. It was a feast that never seemed to end. And, apparently, a feast only for five. The King's advisers took just enough as to not be rude and ate a fraction of it.

There was a sudden pattering on the windows as the storm arrived in force. Within seconds, the glass was streaked and everything outside became a gray blur. The steady rain made the dining hall feel cozier, somehow, and the low rumble of thunder across the valley only added to it.

"If there's one thing I've learned in my time in this world, it's that there's no conversation that cannot be improved with gravy," said the King, dumping the lumpy brown sauce over his entire plate.

"I thought I smelled lunch." A woman entered. She was tall and thin, draped in a frock that stretched to the floor. It was the same purple as the King's robes, spotted with shimmering jewels. An overlong silk wrap trailed off both of her shoulders, dragging along the floor behind her.

"Ah!" said the King, mouth full of meat. "The Queen arrives!"

Forbes pushed back his chair to rise, but the Queen extended a slim hand to stop him. She came down the short flight of stairs and took a seat at the end of the advisers. They looked uncomfortable, as though unsure whether to vacate their chairs to her or not. But she seemed utterly at ease sitting where she was.

"My darling, these four travelers are visiting us from Pennyroyal Academy," said the King. "This is Sir Forbes. He's King Hossenbuhr's boy, you remember Hossenbuhr, don't you? And . . . I'm terribly sorry, but I seem to have forgotten your names."

"It doesn't matter," said Basil, wiping lamb grease off his mouth with his sleeves.

"I'm Cadet Evie, this is Cadet Demetra, and this is Cadet Basil."

The Queen dipped her elegant head. She didn't look away from Evie, even as the King resumed talking. Thunder cracked, making the Queen flinch.

"Right, now that we're all properly gorging ourselves, what's this about a mission?" said the King, slurping gravy off his fingers.

Evie felt the Queen looking at her. She glanced over and saw a look of pity on the woman's face. Sympathy and sorrow. Evie quickly broke the glance and turned her attention back to the King.

"We've set out on a rather dubious mission, I'm afraid," said Forbes.

"How so, lad?"

"Well . . . you see . . . how shall I put this . . . there's been a bit of trouble back at—"

"We're looking for Rumplestoatsnout," said Evie.

The room went silent. Now all the advisers were gaping at her as well.

"I say," said the King. He snorted in disbelief. "Many of the legends of Goblin's Glade are untrue, but any story of that creature is perhaps underexaggerated. Why on earth would you want to find . . . him?"

"It's a personal matter," said Evie. "One of his brothers is an instructor at the Academy."

"You're joking," said the King, his mouth hanging open. "They let one of those brothers teach the good guys?"

"He's one of the best we've got," said Demetra.

"I've been trying to run those hooligans out of the Glade since I took the throne. Four have gone and never come back, but the two that are still here are the worst of the worst." He dropped his elbow on the table with a clatter and pointed at Forbes with excitement. "My men are closing in on Rumplestiltskin, though. Hawk came this morning with the word."

"So you know where he is?" said Forbes. "Perhaps you could help us find the brother?"

"My boy, if I knew that, he wouldn't be in the Glade anymore.

I run a tight ship here. I keep my forests clean. Wild, but clean."

"What about the Gray Man?" said Basil, swallowing his bread.

"Bloody hell, are you looking for him as well? These are dangerous outlaws, children!" Silence fell over the dining hall like a laundered sheet whipped across a bed. The King slowly sat back in his throne. "I'm sorry. I shouldn't have called you children. That was rude of me. You're cadets from the Academy and you're here on official business." He picked up a cauliflower spear and popped it in his mouth. "Last we heard, Rumplestoatsnout was somewhere in the Wood of the Night. There's a ravine at the far end of the valley, beneath the Dagger. It's so deep that the sun can't reach it; that's why they call it the Wood of the Night. I won't send my men near it anymore, except on very rare occasions."

"W-why?" said Basil. "What's wrong with it?"

"The thing that's wrong with it is exactly what you claim to be seeking. The Wood of the Night is the home of the Gray Man. If you'd like, you can find all your monsters at once."

Basil gulped loudly. Then he took another bite off his turkey leg.

"Listen, chil—er, cadets. Far be it from me to advise you to disobey your orders, but this seems like an awful risk just to reunite two trolls. Especially with this storm. Why not go back to the Academy and tell them you couldn't find him? Might save your own lives in the process."

We can't go back, thought Evie. *There will be nothing left to go back to.*

"That's not possible, Your Majesty," said Demetra. "We need to find Rumplestoatsnout."

"Well," sighed the King, throwing up his hands. "I tried to help you." Another sheet of rain slammed against the windows. "At least stay the night. We do get some tremendous storms in the valley. And your villains will still be there tomorrow."

"Thank you very much indeed, Sire," said Forbes. Another crack of thunder sounded just outside the castle.

"Then it's settled. I'll have a man take you to the Wood of the Night at daybreak."

We've already spent one night in Malora's carriage. And now another here. Who knows how many we have left?

As lightning flashed and thunder rumbled, the conversation turned to other royals that Forbes and the King had in common. Pudding came, then tea, then more pudding, then cold meat and cheese. Basil piled it all dutifully into his mouth. Evie sat quietly as Forbes told the King stories of his first year of training. The King, for his part, couldn't get enough. The Queen, however, kept shifting her eyes between Evie and Demetra in a way that both found deeply unsettling.

BEFORE SHE EVEN HAD A NAME,
EVIE'S ADVENTURES BEGAN IN
PENNYROYAL ACADEMY.

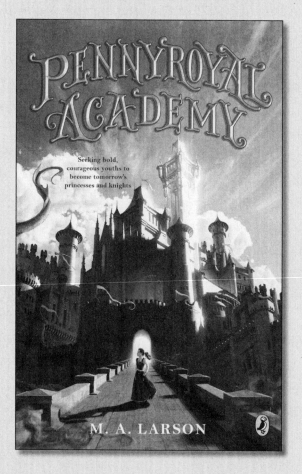

"A breathtakingly exciting novel."
—*The New York Times*